HE WAS FEELING THE TOUCH OF ANOTHER MIND ...

Not one of his companions, either.

Very near.

Swift and silent, the attacker pulled Cabe from his saddle. He had a glimpse of reptilian features and then was locked in a life-or-death struggle. His mind, dulled by constant exposure to the Ice Dragon's numbing spell, could not ready a proper defense. He was forced to go hand against hand with his adversary.

"Bedlammmm!" The drake hissed. His voice was chillingly familiar, and the young mage decided then that death was fast approaching.

The Dragonrealm Series:
Firedrake
Ice Dragon

Published by
POPULAR LIBRARY

THE DRAGONREALM
ICE DRAGON

RICHARD A. KNAAK

POPULAR LIBRARY

An Imprint of Warner Books, Inc.

A Warner Communications Company

POPULAR LIBRARY EDITION

Popular Library®, the fanciful P design, and Questar® are registered
trademarks of Warner Books, Inc.

Cover illustration by Larry Elmore

Popular Library books are published by
Warner Books, Inc.
666 Fifth Avenue
New York, N.Y. 10103

 A Warner Communications Company

Printed in the United States of America

First Printing: December, 1989

10 9 8 7 6 5 4 3 2 1

I

The bone-numbing winds of the great Northern Wastes tore at the cloaks of the two riders, seeking to remove their only real protection. One rider paid the wind no mind though it often threatened to thrust him from the back of his steed. The other rider, his form, like that of his companion, hidden by the enveloping cloak, would glance from time to time at the first one as if seeking some response. After a moment or two, he would return his gaze to the endless white world before them—and specifically to the jagged, treacherous range of ice-encrusted peaks near the horizon.

He urged his steed forward, knowing that the other would follow if he could convince his own. His urging however only succeeded in gaining a slight increase in speed; the mounts had suffered greatly and were, in fact, the last of six that he had started out with.

The slow movements of the steeds angered him, but he knew his choices had been limited. The mounts he would have desired would have been dead long before, the cold of the Northern Wastes having an even more pronounced effect on those creatures than the horses he and the other rode.

Already he felt sick of the cold, sick of the snow and ice—but what choice did he have? The others were fighting among themselves or, worse yet, were dead or turned traitor, which was the same thing in his eyes. He let loose a hiss of anger, disturbing both horses. It took him several moments to calm them down. His companion made no move despite the jumpiness of his own steed. There was no need to. His legs had been tied to his horse by the other rider.

It was a necessity.

They rode on, and as they moved closer and closer toward the mountains, the one rider's anger turned to uncertainty. Who was to say that he would gain aid here? This land was ruled by the most traditional of his kind and that tradition conflicted with his own desires, namely the rule of his own and other races by himself. Under the laws governing birth for his kind, he was ineligible. As his father's warlord and the ruling duke of the clan, he should have been satisfied. He was not, however, knowing as he did that his command of the power was greater, far greater, than many of his father's brethren.

But for a few birth markings . . .

The snowbank before him rose, and continued to rise.

It towered over him and his companion, blotting out the landscape before them.

The snowbank grew eyes, pale, ice-blue eyes—and tremendous claws designed for digging through frozen earth and easily tearing through soft flesh.

The first of the guardians of the one he sought.

He had now two choices, it seemed. Either kill the guardian or be killed, and neither was particularly wise.

The horses began turning and bucking. Only the rider's skill kept his own animal from throwing him and only the rope fastened from his own animal to the other kept him from losing his companion. The other rider teetered back and forth like some toy, but his hands were also tied to his mount's saddle, preventing him from falling too far.

The lead rider raised his hand and made a fist. He could not, of course, allow either of them to die, which meant he had to halt the guardian. He began to mutter under his breath, knowing that it would require a strong spell to turn, much less destroy, this creature.

"Halt."

The sorcerer paused, checking but not canceling his magical assault. He peered through the snowstorm the guardian had caused in rising and finally noticed the figure to his front right. The mage blinked.

It walked stiffly toward him, one hand holding a staff which he was sure controlled the great snow beast. A blue gem pulsated on the top of the staff. The figure holding the staff was not human.

"You are in the domain of the Ice Dragon." Its voice was emotionless and reminiscent of the whirling wind. There was something about it, something that made it difficult to see until it was practically on top of the sorcerer. "Only one thing prevents your death . . . and that is that you are one of the master's kin, are you not, drake?"

The lead rider reached up and pulled back his hood. As he did so, he revealed the dragonhelm that should have been noticeable, hood or no hood. The magical cloak which had hidden it allowed him to travel through the lands of men, but that function was no longer necessary here.

"You know who I am, servant. You know your master will see me."

"That is up to the Ice Dragon."

The firedrake hissed. "Tell him it is Duke Toma who awaits!"

The declaration did not impress the odd-looking servant. Toma studied it with narrowed eyes—narrowed eyes that widened when he saw the thing's true nature. His estimation of the Ice Dragon's powers grew and the nagging fear of the Dragon King, which he had kept safely locked in the back of his mind, poured over his mental barriers.

Necromancer!

The servant turned. It was a thing of ice, a caricature of a man made all the more horrible because its binding structure, its skeleton, was a figure frozen within its core. The corpse, whether man or drake or elf or some other creature of similar form, was impossible to identify and moved within the ice man like a twisted puppet. Leg moved with leg, arm with arm, head with head. It was as if someone was wearing an all-encompassing suit—save that, in this case, the suit was wearing the someone. Toma wondered about what had occurred here in the months since his escape from the battle between the human mages, the cursed Bedlams.

Thinking of the Bedlams, Azran and Cabe, reinforced the drake's resolve. He knew that Cabe had won and that the Dragon Kings were in disarray. Black was secluded in his domain, Lochivar, and the Gray Mists, which covered that land, were so thin that there had been talk of confronting this one particular King at last.

The servant raised its staff toward the behemoth, which had remained silent and unmoving since its initial rise. The tip of the staff was pointed at where Toma estimated the huge creature's head might be.

The leviathan began to sink back into the snow and ice. The two drakes' horses, only barely under control, now panicked. Duke Toma had to raise his hand and draw a pattern in the air. The horses calmed.

Turning back to the two visitors, the servant indicated Toma's companion. "And him? He also wishes to visit my lord?"

"He wishes nothing," said Toma, pulling the other horse over to him. He then reached up and took hold of his companion's hood, and pulled it back so the face and color of the other drake could be easily studied. "He has no mind with which to wish for even the smallest of favors. Yet, he is your lord's master, your lord's liege, King of Kings, and he will be treated and cared for until he has recovered. It is your master's duty!"

Nearly identical to Toma in form save in height and color, the Gold Dragon stared forward mindlessly. A bit of drool flowed from the left corner of his mouth and his forked tongue darted in and out at random. He would not, or perhaps could not, return to his dragon form, and so Toma had also remained in his semi-human warrior form. They were two scale-armored knights with helms topped by intricate dragon faces, their true faces. Within the helm itself, bloodred eyes stared out. Though harder by far than any normal mail armor, what they wore was not clothing but their own skins. Long ago, their ancestors could have assumed some other form, but continual contact with humans and the realization of the advantages of a humanoid form had made this second shape something learned from the time of birth. It had become as natural to them as breathing.

The Ice Dragon's servant bowed its head briefly in the direction of the Kings of Kings, acknowledging or mocking the mindless monarch's sovereignty. Toma hissed loudly.

"Well? May we go on, or are we to make camp here and wait for spring?" Spring had not come to the Northern Wastes since before the rule of the Dragon Kings. Now, the land was buried under a perpetual coat of snow and ice.

The creature stepped aside and pointed the staff at the mountains toward which the drakes had been riding. "My lord knows of your presence. He is coming to meet you." This, at last, seemed to impress the servant. "He has not come to the surface since returning from the last Council of Kings."

The surface?

The chilling wind picked up, going from a constant annoyance to a howling, storming, chaotic whirlwind before Toma could even pull the hood back over his father's head. The temperature, already distressingly uncomfortable for a firedrake, became truly numbing, almost threatening to lower both riders' temperatures below a safe minimum. Visibility dropped to nothing, so that all that Toma could see was snow. He only knew his father's horse remained near thanks to the rope.

Something *very* large came to rest before them. Toma reinforced the restraining spell he had laid on the horses.

"Myyyy greetingsss to you, Duke Toma, hatchling of my brother, my king. My home issss open to you and our majesty."

The wind died down, though not to the level it had been previously. Visibility improved to where the firedrake could see his host. Yet another surprise met his eyes.

The Ice Dragon loomed tall, wings spread, maw open wide. He was huge, greater in length than even Gold. This was not the Ice Dragon who had last visited the King of Kings just prior to the chaos. This was a creature in every way more frightening than either of his bizarre servants. Thin to the point of emaciation, so much so that each rib was apparent, the Ice Dragon might have been some ghoulish thing risen from the dead. Even the eyes, which never seemed to settle on dead white or icy blue, were those of something that measured life by other standards. Its head itself was long and lean and from its maw clouds of cold air erupted regularly.

A transformation had been wrought on the Lord of the Northern Wastes in the months that had passed since that last visit. This was not the Dragon King Toma had expected and almost definitely not one that he wanted, either.

It was too late to turn back and the firedrake could not have even if he had wanted to. This creature was his best hope of restoring his father and, therefore, Toma's own dream of rule from behind the throne. The question now, however, was how similar his goals and those of the Ice Dragon actually were anymore.

The frost-covered leviathan spread its ice-encrusted wings and smiled as only a dragon can smile at his tiny relations. There seemed no real emotion behind that smile, though. Nothing.

"I've been expecting you," the Ice Dragon said at last.

II

To his horror-stricken eyes, the blade seemed twice the length of a full-grown man. From the handle, two horns, much like those of a ram, curled outward, giving the sword an evil appearance. The weapon was called the horned blade, a creation of the mad warlock Azran Bedlam, and it was evil. Cabe knew that all too well, for not only had he wielded the demonic sword himself, but he was also Azran's son.

"Your blood is mine," hissed the figure now wielding Azran's toy. He stalked without difficulty toward the young mage who, in his panic, could not seem to find his footing. Cabe stumbled away from the huge, armored figure, trying to recall a spell, trying to find a way out of the lifeless stretch of baked mud called the Barren Lands. How long he had been running, he could not say. It did not matter. In the end, his foe had stayed with him.

His pursuer laughed mockingly, blazing scarlet orbs the only portion of his visage not buried in the murky depths within the dragonhelm. A false helm at that, for the face within was less the visage of his pursuer than the intricate dragonhead crest was.

Even now, the glittering eyes set in that reptilian visage watched with growing anticipation.

This was a drake, one of the creatures that ruled the lands known collectively and singly as the Dragonrealm. More so, this was one of those chief among those who ruled—and who now chose to give the human his personal attention. There were only a dozen like him and only one of the others would this one call lord.

Cabe was alone and at the mercy of a Dragon King.

Something caught him by the foot and he went crashing down onto the centuries-old, stone-hard earth. He was blinded momentarily as his face swung toward the relentless sun. When his eyes cleared moments later, he saw what had brought him down.

A hand. A huge, clawed hand that had emerged from the ground itself. Even now, it refused to relinquish its grip.

Cabe struggled and struggled and only after several seconds did he remember the greater threat. Only when the one shadow for miles draped over him did he recall and then it was almost too late.

"Your blood is mine," the Dragon King repeated with a satisfied hiss. He was as pale a brown as the dried earth below him and this made no sense to Cabe.

The demon sword came rushing down—only to miss by inches as the young sorcerer succeeded in rolling aside despite the hand gripping his ankle.

His new point of view found him face to face with a long snout and narrow, savage eyes. A creature reminscent of an armadillo—but no armadillo grew this large. The thing hooted once and then rose from beneath the ground, revealing a form taller and wider than any human and huge, clawed hands identical to the one holding Cabe by the ankle.

"Shall I let them rend you limb from limb?" The Dragon King asked sweetly. "Or would you prefer the kiss of this blade, Cabe Bedlam?"

Cabe tried to recall a spell, but, again, he failed. Something had severed his ties to his power. He was helpless and unarmed. But how?

In his mind, there suddenly came an image—an image of hate and fear. An image of his father, Azran. He was as Cabe had seen him last, handsome with a groomed beard and his hair exactly half silver, as if he had dyed one side of his head. The silver was the mark of a human mage and Cabe had such a mark in his own hair, a vast streak that seemed ready to devour the dark color of the rest of his hair.

"You would not be mine, my son; therefore, you will be theirs." Azran smiled benevolently for no other reason than that he was very, very insane.

As if on command, the Quel who had risen from the earth took hold of his wrists. Cabe struggled, but the tremendous strength of the creature was too much.

He heard the rasping breath of the Dragon King and for the second time the sun was blocked by the armored form. The drake lord spat at him, the sword already positioned for a deathstroke. "With your death, I bring life back to my clanssss!"

Cabe shook his head in disbelief. He knew which of the Dragon Kings stood above him now—one that should not have been able. "You're dead!"

The Brown Dragon, lord of the Barren Lands, laughed—and plunged the horned blade into Cabe's chest. . . .

"Yaaah!"

With a start, Cabe woke from the dream, only to stare straight into the inhuman eyes of another drake, which resulted in a second shout. The drake ducked down and scurried out of sight as fast as its four legs could carry it.

Light burst forth from everywhere, bathing the room in brilliance. He caught a glimpse of a green, leathery tail disappearing through a half-open doorway. A hand gripped his shoulder. He only barely succeeded in stifling yet a third shout.

Gwen leaned over, her hair a long, fire-red tangle, save for a great streak of silver. Even though it was dark, her emerald eyes captured his attention as she sought to calm him. He briefly wondered how she always managed to stay so perfect. It was not all due to her magic, which, in its own way, was greater than his and certainly better honed.

"It was one of the hatchlings, Cabe. It's all right. The poor thing must've gotten loose. Probably nibbled through the grate."

She moved toward his front side and he saw that she had conjured up a robe of forest green. Lady of the Amber, she was called, because of her imprisonment within that substance generations before by Cabe's father, but she might well have been called the Green Lady or the Lady of the Forest, such was her love for nature and the color which represented it best.

With a quick gesture, she made the door shut. This time, it would take more than a curious young dragon's bumping to open it.

"No." He shook his head, as much to clear it as to correct her misconceptions concerning his screams. This was not the Barren Lands, he kept telling himself. This was a room in the palace of the Gryphon who ruled Penacles, the city of knowledge in the southeastern portion of the Dragonrealm. He and Gwen, friends and allies of the inhuman ruler, were here as the monarch's guests.

"That's not what I yelled about—not the first time, anyway. I—" How could he describe what he had dreamt of? Did he dare? Gwen, too, had suffered at the hands of Azran and the Dragon Kings, yet, the sort of dreams he had been having of late—dreams in which he had been helpless, bereft of his own abilities—might very well mark him as insane as his father. Would she understand?

The Dragon Kings. He thought of the one in the dream and shuddered anew. The reptilian creatures were now trying to reclaim their once-mighty power from the human vermin. Though their power had been absolute once, there had always been few of the intelligent drakes and, therefore, they had allowed, perhaps even trained, the first humans in the duties of trade and farming. From that point on, there had been no stopping the growth of the younger race. Only after it was too late did the Dragon Kings realize that they might have trained their own successors—and the drakes had no intention of surrendering control without a fight. Were it not for the fact that they lacked numbers and even needed the humans, the reptilian lords would have started a full genocidal war long ago. The only thing that had held the humans back was the incredible, savage power of the drakes that more than made up for there being so few.

Gwen looked at him, the picture of concern and patience. Cabe chose to downplay the dream. It was something he must deal with alone. Instead, forcing his voice to a semblance of annoyance, he said, "I'd like to find something that will keep those lesser drakes penned up long enough for us to arrive at the Manor. They'll escape one time too often during the journey and it's important we don't lose even one."

"Another dream?" The concern in her voice was as evident as that on her face. She had had no trouble seeing through his poor attempt at deception and refused to be sidetracked by anything else.

Cabe grimaced and ran a hand through his hair where the silver which marked both him and his love as magic-users vied for dominance with the darker strands. Of late, the streak in Cabe's hair seemed to have taken on a life of its own; it was difficult to say what pattern his hair color might take each day. Sometimes it was nearly completely silver, sometimes it tended toward the dominance of his original hair color. As entertaining and amusing as the sight might seem to some, it definitely worried the young magic-user. The shifting had begun soon after he and Gwen had married two months before. She could not explain it and he could draw no knowledge from the memories of the archmage Nathan, his grandfather, who had bequeathed to him, at birth, much of his own soul and power.

"Another dream. This one was a bard's epic. There were the Brown Dragon, my father Azran, and one of those Quel things. The only one missing was Shade."

"Shade?" She arched an eyebrow, something she did quite beautifully, so Cabe thought. "That could be it. That damned no-faced warlock might have escaped from wherever the Gryphon said Darkhorse had taken him."

"I don't think so. Darkhorse was a powerful demon and if anyone could keep Shade trapped in the Void, it's him."

"You have too much faith in the monster."

He sighed, not wanting to be drawn into the same useless argument they always had concerning the two. Both Darkhorse and Shade were unique, tragic figures to Cabe. Darkhorse was a shadowy steed, part of the Void itself. Shade was a sorcerer who had been too greedy far back in history; he had attempted to harness both the "good" and "bad" aspects of the powers, two contrary pieces of nature, but instead had become a pawn between the two forces, an immortal who served good during one lifetime and who worked hideous evil in the next. Each incarnation sought to break the curse. For that, Shade had attempted to use Cabe as a conduit in a great spell, and only Darkhorse had saved Cabe, but apparently at the cost of his own freedom. What was sad was that Shade and the demon had been the closest of friends during the former's more pleasant lives.

"It's not Shade," Cabe finally decided, "and before you suggest it, I doubt this is Toma's style, either. I think this has to do with what I am—a warlock, mage, whatever. This is still all too new to me, that's all. Sometimes my fears return. Do you know what it's like to be as confident as—as Nathan, the Dragon Master, was—and then suddenly revert to my untrained self in the midst of doing something?"

There. He had said it. His self-doubts were returning and, with their return, the confidence he had gained from being the legacy of Nathan Bedlam was retreating rapidly. Cabe yearned for the days when he had simply been an innkeeper's assistant, before the Brown Dragon had sought him out as a sacrifice to return the Barren Lands to the lush fields they had once been.

Gwen leaned forward and kissed him lightly. "I do know what it's like. I have them myself. I saw them when Nathan learned of the death of his elder son by his younger son, Azran. I experienced them through my training and all through the Turning War over a hundred years ago, up to the day that pig Azran ensnared me in my amber prison near the end of that war. I still feel them now. When you stop having doubts about your prowess, you usually make a fatal mistake. Take my word for it, husband."

Men and women were shouting and Cabe realized they had been shouting for some time. It was not the shouting of men in battle or people under attack, but rather the curses of those seeking to herd a frightened minor drake back into its holding pen.

"Do we really have to do this?" The thought of what they would be attempting come the next day was almost as frightening as the nightmares.

Gwen gave him a look which brooked no argument. "The Gryphon made an oath with the Green Dragon and we're the best ones to see that it holds. When we're sure that Duke Toma and the remaining Dragon Kings can be kept at a safe distance, then we can move them elsewhere. Right now, the Manor is the best place for the Gold Dragon's hatchlings. Besides, I think the Gryphon has other worries to deal with besides the Dragon Kings.''

The shouting died down, indicating that the wayward drake was once again under the control of its keepers. Cabe wondered how the other drakes were holding out. Among the young there were seven major drakes, the species from which the Dragon Kings had come. These were intelligent dragons, the true enemy as far as many were concerned. Wyverns, lesser drakes, and such were merely animals, albeit deadly.

He was not fond of the drakes, but neither could he abandon them. The Green Dragon, Master of the Dagora Forest and the sole Dragon King thus far to make peace with humanity, wanted them raised as human as possible. The Gryphon, Lord of Penacles, had agreed in part, but only if, in addition, the hatchlings received equal training from their own kind—a request which both astonished and pleased the reptilian monarch. The Gryphon, who seemed to have little or no background of his own, as far as Cabe knew, was determined that the drakes learn about their own heritage as well as that of mankind. It was a grand experiment, but one that *had* to succeed if the lands were ever to be at peace.

It fell to Cabe and Gwen to care for them for the time being. As much as the powers of the two were welcomed by the Gryphon in his struggle to raise a people that was not his own, he knew how important this long-term project was and who was best suited for the potential dangers. As long as Toma lived, the hatchlings stood the chance of falling into his hands and being subverted to his cause. The two mages would not be babysitting. If the Gold Dragon was dead or died later on, Toma's only hope was to plant a new puppet on the Dragon Emperor's throne. . . .

There were three such potential puppets.

''Cabe?''

''Hmmm?'' He had not realized he had been ignoring her.

''If nothing else, consider this a trial for the real thing.''

Puzzled, he studied her face. She was smiling devilishly. ''Trial for what?''

''Silly.'' She settled down next to him. ''For when we have children of our own.''

Gwen laughed quietly at the look on his face. For all he appeared physically older than she, thanks to the properties of her amber prison, there were many things he was still naive about.

It was one of the things she liked best about him. One of the things that set him apart from her first love, Nathan Bedlam. The enchantress put a finger on his lips in order to still any further comment. "No more talk. Go back to sleep. You'll have plenty of time to think about it once the caravan is on its way."

He smiled and abruptly reached up. Taking her head in his hands, he guided her mouth to his. Even as they kissed, she dismissed the light.

Penacles was perhaps the greatest human city in the Dragon-realm, even though its rulers had never been human themselves. From time immemorial, those drake lords who had chosen purple as their mark had ruled in a steady succession. There had always been a Purple Dragon, and so it had been believed that there would always be one. The Dragon Masters and the inhuman mercenary called the Gryphon had succeeded in at least changing that, and it was now the Gryphon who ruled here in the place known as the City of Knowledge. Through his efforts, Penacles rose to new heights, but, because of that success, he was diligently watched by the brooding, angry Dragon Kings. They had still not recovered from the Turning War with the human sorcerers—but watch they did. Waiting. Waiting until Duke Toma rekindled hostilities between the two races for his own ends. Now, even the previously untouchable merchants, they who dealt with both drake and man, were not safe.

It was only one of his many concerns. The Gryphon, accompanied by the guards General Toos, his second, had demanded always be with him, strode majestically toward where Cabe and Gwen were supervising the last bit of packing. Watching the two was frighteningly like watching the witch and her first love, Nathan Bedlam. The lad (anyone below the Gryphon's two hundred odd years of age could be considered a lad) was so much like his grandfather that the lionbird was often tempted to call him by the elder's name. What truly prevented him from doing so was the fear that Cabe would respond. Something of Nathan literally lived within his grandson, and though he could not describe it the Gryphon knew it was there.

Heads turned in the courtyard. The Gryphon was a startling figure in himself, for he was as his name implied. Clad in loose garments designed not to impede his astonishing reflexes, he almost looked human from the neck down, if one ignored the white, clawed hands so much more like talons or the boots that did not totally hide the fact that his feet and legs were more like those of a lion. The swiftness of his movements came not just from his years as a mercenary but also because, like the savage creature whose name and appearance he bore, he was a predator at heart. Every action was a challenge to those around who might dare to oppose him.

It was the head, however, that grasped all attention. Rather than a mouth, he had a great, sharp beak easily capable of tearing flesh, and instead of a normal head of hair, he had a mane like a lion that ended in feathers like that of a majestic eagle. And his *eyes*. They were neither the eyes of a bird of prey nor the eyes of a human being, but something in between. Something that made even the strongest of soldiers turn away in fear if the Gryphon so desired it.

Cabe and Gwen turned just before he reached them, either due to some power to sense his coming or a chance glance at the awed faces around them. The lionbird was pleased that the two mages showed no such awe. He had enough followers and all too few friends as it was. Waving the guards back, he joined the two.

"I see you have just about everything ready," said the Gryphon, studying the long caravan.

Cabe, looking worn despite what the Gryphon would have assumed was a good night's slumber, grimaced. "We would have been done long before now. Lord Gryphon."

"I have told you time and again—you two need never call me lord. We are friends, I hope." He cocked his head slightly to the side in a manner reminiscent of his avian aspect.

Gwen, a radiant contrast to her husband, smiled. Even the fierce visage of the Gryphon softened at that sight. "Of course we are your friends, Gryphon. We owe you too much for what you've done."

"*You* owe *me*? You two seem to have forgotten all the work you've done here and now you are even taking those hatchlings off my hands. I owe *you*. I doubt if I will ever be able to repay you properly."

"This is silly," Cabe finally decided. "If we're all such good friends, then nobody owes anybody."

"Much better." Even as the lionbird nodded, an unwelcome thought squirmed its way into his mind. *They may be lying. They may be anxious to be away from the monstrosity that rules over their fellow humans*.

"Is something wrong?" Cabe put a hand on the Gryphon's shoulder. The monarch forced himself not to brush it away.

"Nothing. Exhaustion, I suppose." What sort of foolish thoughts had those been, he wondered. There was no reason he should think of such things. He knew these two too well. They were honest about their emotions.

"You should rest more, Gryphon. Even *you* need sleep."

"A king's work is never done."

"It is when he tumbles over from lack of rest."

The Gryphon chuckled. "I won't hold you any longer. The sun is already fairly high in the heavens and I know you want to get started." He glanced toward the caravan. "How are your charges doing today?"

Gwen indicated the cart that was a little behind their horses. In it were several reptilian figures coiled about one another in slumber. Other than by color, it was impossible to tell where one creature ended and another began. Behind that cart was another one likewise packed. "Last night's escapades wore them out. They should sleep for at least part of the journey today."

"If I ever let you begin." The Gryphon reached out and took the Lady of the Amber's hand. His features contorted, then blurred. When they rematerialized, they were human. By most human standards, the Gryphon's new face would have been considered quite handsome. His features were, appropriately, hawk-like, the kind that young maidens dreamed their heroes had. He kissed the back of Gwen's hand.

"Should I be jealous?" Cabe asked innocently.

The enchantress laughed lightly, a sound like tiny bells—at least to the two males near her. "If you aren't, maybe I should find a reason you should be."

"This is where I definitely part company with you," the Gryphon said. He stepped away and his features returned to their normal state. Gwen smiled toward him and then had Cabe help her mount her horse. Cabe then mounted his own steed and took the reins from a well-trained page who had been waiting quietly all this time.

Farewells were said by those in the caravan to friends and relatives standing nearby. Cabe finally looked at Gwen, who nodded. Raising his arm, the young mage signaled to the rest of the travellers and then urged his steed forward. The Gryphon waved once and then stood silently watching.

It will fail, he realized. *The experiment will fail. The hatchlings should be back with the drakes. With their own kind.*

The Gryphon swore. That was *not* the way it was going to be! This experiment *must* succeed! It had every chance of succeeding—didn't it? He felt the uncertainty grow. Oddly, it was not restricted to this one thing. If his judgment concerning the young drakes was incorrect, then so might his judgment concerning any number of things.

He shivered, belatedly realizing it was not from his thoughts. It *was* cold! Bone-numbing, mind-chilling cold.

As quickly as it had come, the intense cold vanished.

"Milord!" A page, little more than a dozen years in age, perhaps, rushed over to the Gryphon. "General Toos is looking for you! He . . . he makes it all sound so urgent, your majesty!"

"It will wait a few minutes longer." He would wait until the caravan was out of sight. The lionbird was astonished at how hard it was to part company with those two. Being both ruler and an outsider, even after all this time, he savored the few close companions he had—and with the Dragonrealm in such turmoil of late, there was always the chance he might not see them again.

When the caravan was out of sight, the Gryphon still stood staring, and only when he heard the messenger fidgeting next to him did he recall that one of his oldest companions, perhaps the one who knew him best, had urgent news for him.

He sighed and turned to the page. The boy was, of course, in awe of the being before him. Most likely his first time delivering a message to one so important as well.

"All right, lad," he said in his friendliest voice, his worries forcibly pushed to one corner of his mind. "Show me where Toos is so that I can reprimand him for the hundredth time on proper chain of command. After all, *he's* supposed to come to me, not the other way around."

The page smiled and, if only for a moment, the Gryphon's worries seemed pointless.

III

By horse, the center of the Dagora Forest, where the Manor was located, was several days journey to the northwest of Penacles, and with a party of more than thirty—the Gryphon had insisted on supplying Cabe and Gwen with all sorts of servants—the time tripled. Wagons had to maneuver around obstacles, people kept losing things, and there were even children to consider. (If the young of the Emperor Dragon were to be raised among humans, they had to be made to understand human children as well, and if the barriers could be broken between the young, there was hope.)

From their carts, the drake hatchlings watched with guarded expressions. Occasionally, one could tell when the hatchlings grew curious because their eyes would widen to literally twice their normal size. Excitement was the easiest emotion to read. Those of the intelligent drake race, looking like bizarre, two-legged lizards, jumped up and down in copy of the human young they had observed, while the young lesser drakes, pure animal, swayed frantically from side to side, hissing all the while.

As they were doing now.

The forest was suddenly alive with men. Masked men.

They all wore baggy traveling outfits and Cabe suspected that beneath those outfits was armor. It was obvious that this had been planned in advance. The caravan was more than a day's journey past the borders of Penacles' lands, and there was nothing in sight now but more and more trees.

"The fools!" Gwen hissed. "The Green Dragon will never tolerate this assault in his own domain!"

"He may not find out about it. We're far from where you said he makes his home."

She looked Cabe squarely in the eye. "The master of the Dagora Forest knows everything that happens anywhere in his domain."

The apparent leader of the band urged his horse a little closer to the group, seemingly unconcerned about his safety, even with two mages present. He was a tall man and probably a veteran of many a fight, judging by his stance and the way his eyes took in everything. There was little else that could be said about him since much was covered to preserve his identity.

"We only want the damn lizards! Give them to us and the rest of you can go on your way!"

Cabe tensed, having recognized something in the tone of the man's voice. He was fairly certain that the spokesman was from Mito Pica.

"Well?" The spokesman was growing impatient.

Gwen spoke up. "The hatchlings are under our protection and will not be turned over to the likes of you! Depart before it is too late!"

A few of the marauders chuckled, which did nothing to ease the disturbing feelings Cabe was experiencing.

"Sorcerers' spells won't touch us, witch, not with these." He lifted a medallion out of his clothing. From such a long distance, Cabe could make out very little other than that it appeared to be quite worn. Gwen let out a slight gasp.

"Those things are the work of the Seekers," she whispered. "I've seen one or two, battered and broken, but if they have more. . . ." She did not have to complete the thought. The Seekers, avian predecessors to the drakes, had left behind more than one secret which hinted of a power once far, far greater than the Dragon Kings at their finest.

"So you see," began the hooded figure once more, "we don't have to be nice. We've no quarrel with you unless you give us trouble. That'd be bad, considering we have you surrounded and outnumbered."

"Are those things really that effective?" Cabe muttered.

The Lady of the Amber nodded sourly. "Try casting something and the spell will go haywire some way. I don't know about prepared spells, but I think it works for those as well."

"There's only one way to find out. . . ."

The marauders were stirring. The leader shifted in his saddle. "You've had all the time you need to discuss it. We'll take them by force if need be. . . ."

"Touch them and not one of you will live to sssee the morrow. Your bonesss will be picked clean by the birds of the foresssst."

Marauders and caravan alike jumped at the commanding voice. The spokesman looked this way and that before seeing the single figure riding atop a fierce-looking lesser drake. The riding beast hissed hungrily, disturbing all the horses in the area.

"You are not wanted in or near my forest," hissed the Green Dragon. Like his brethren, his humanoid form resembled an armored knight wearing an immense and elaborate dragonhelm. He was covered by glittering green scale armor (which was really his own skin). Gleaming red eyes stared out at the assembled examples of humanity.

It was evident that this was one of the last beings the leader had expected to see. Nevertheless, when he spoke, there was only a hint of uneasiness in his voice. "These are not your lands. You have no control over this region."

"I share a common border with the lord of Penacles and I am his ally. I protect hisss side when necessary and I would expect no lessss from him. As for you, the east or the north is where you should be, human. Fight Silver or the remnants of Red's clans. Challenge the Storm Dragon, but do not presume to hunt in or near my domain. I will not permit it. Tell your benefactor King Melicard that."

"Melicard?" Cabe whispered to Gwen.

"A rumor, nothing more. They say he supplies them. He hates the drakes as much as they do. Remember, it was Toma's nestbrother, that sadistic Kyrg, who drove Melicard's father, Rennek, mad."

Cabe nodded slowly, recalling the incident. "Rennek thought he was going to end up as part of Kyrg's dinner."

The hooded spokesman started laughing. One could almost picture the sneer hidden by his mask. "There's nothing you can do against us. These things have put a damper on your powers. I know how to use these. You can't even shapeshift to your dragon form."

The Green Dragon was not put out by this news. He reached slowly into a saddle pouch and pulled something out. "Would you care, gelding, to match your bits of bird magic to mine?"

The Master of the Dagora Forest held up something in one clawed hand and muttered sounds akin to the constant call of some raven.

There was a yelp from the marauder leader and a second later the man was working desperately to take the medallion from around his neck and cast it away. It was a waste of time, though. The medallion crumbled as all watched, until all that remained was the chain. The hooded figure quickly removed the chain and tossed it as far away as he could.

"I have not kept control of this domain for so long without reasssson. Did you think my brethren approve of the freedom the people of my landsss have? Those concessionsss were hard fought—and I ussse the last word literally." The Green Dragon returned the item to the saddle bag. "Depart now and we will forget this incident happened. You serve a purpose to me, but only to a point. Rest assured, I have other tricksss, if it comes down to it."

The intruders looked to their leader, who in turn looked from the Dragon King to the two mages to the cart where the hatchlings watched with agitated interest. Finally, he turned back to the Green Dragon. "If they leave your lands, we will seek them out."

"Your war isss with the Council, not hatchlingsss." The Green Dragon took a breath. When he spoke again, his words were measured and the hiss inherent to his kind was all but unnoticeable. "Now go, or do you wish to test your trinkets against a full-grown dragon again? Be assured that I have eyes watching you even now. They will continue to watch to make certain that you do indeed depart and never return unless invited—which I doubt you would ever be."

The spokesman hesitated, then finally nodded in defeat, and signaled to his men to retreat. Reluctantly, the marauders departed, the leader last. He seemed to spend most of his time studying the two magic-users, as if they were traitors to their own kind. When the last of his men had disappeared into the forest, he followed.

The Master of the Dagora Forest hissed, but this time it was in satisfaction. "Fools grow rampant these days. The only reason they made it this far into the border lands at all is because I was forced to reprimand one of my own for plotting to take the hatch-lings from you just before you reached the Manor."

"Your own clans?" Gwen's surprise was evident.

"Drakes will be drakes, as humans will be humans. I have dealt with that one as I have dealt with this one. I suggest you and yours follow close behind me for the rest of your journey. We will save time if I lead you through the secret ways of the forest."

"Milord . . ."

"Yes, Cabe Bedlam?" The emphasis on the last name struck hard. The Green Dragon still remembered Nathan and the Dragon Masters, the group of mages who had fought the Kings in the Turning War and reduced the power of the drakes to its present state despite losing in the end.

"That disk . . ."

"This?" A clawed hand brought forth the item in question. "I have had many an occasion to gather and study the artifacts of our predecessors. The Lady Gwendolyn is not the first to stake claim to the Manor. That place has housed many since it was abandoned in the waning days of the Seekers. I believe the lower levels may even predate them."

"They planned well—perhaps too well. The dampers like those marauders wear are excellent creations, but, like all Seeker magic, those were created with a countermeasure already in mind. That, I believe, is what led to their downfall. They planned too well and someone took advantage of that."

The Green Dragon nudged his lesser drake toward the front of the group. As he passed them by, Gwen whispered into Cabe's ear. "You will find that the Seekers are a pet project of his. It was the original reason he dealt civilly with Nathan. They both wanted to know how such a powerful race could fall so rapidly."

"Like the Quel?"

She nodded. "These lands have seen many races rule. Each has had its cycle and it appears the time for humans is close at hand. Nathan didn't want us falling as the others had and the

Green Dragon wanted to preserve as much of his people's ways as possible. For the sake of both races, they shelved their differences."

It was not what Cabe would have expected from the stories he had heard, but it rang true in his memories, which were partly Nathan's as well. There was some knowledge of the Seekers back in there, he realized, but it was like trying to find one's way through a thick fog. He could not dredge out anything specific from the past.

The hatchlings were growing extremely agitated. The presence of the Green Dragon was something new to them, having spent all of their short lives either under the watchful wings of the great dams who guarded the hatcheries or under the untrusting eyes of the humans. They had never seen a male adult of their kind so close, but they knew kin when they saw it.

One of the royal hatchlings, the one Cabe reckoned as eldest, stood confidently on its hind legs. His face seemed punched in, less like a beast and more like a man. The tail had shrunken as well.

He's learning, the young mage realized. He's starting to shift from dragon form to manshape. All he needed was an example to get him started.

With one to lead them, the others would soon follow suit. First the other two royal hatchlings, then their unmarked brethren—who would be the dukes or soldiers of their species—and finally the single female (Gwen had assured him it was indeed female; he had not wanted to find out close up). That the female would take longer was no fault of her own. Female drakes had a different metabolism and, while she would take much longer, her human form would be near perfect, perhaps more than perfect, Cabe remembered, having almost fallen prey to three such enchantresses who had once taken up residence in the very place they were now heading.

He did not look forward to the future where the drakes were concerned. He knew that the Dragon Kings, while silent now, had not yet given up.

Cabe guided his horse as near as he could to the drake lord. "Why didn't you destroy the raiders while you had the chance? They may choose to ignore your warning."

The Green Dragon's eyes narrowed to two tiny pinpoints of red. "With as many as there were, there was too much of a chance for something to happen to the hatchlings. A lucky shot by an archer might have struck down the heir to the dragon throne. I chose the best way to avoid all of that. If they try again, *then* they will forfeit their lives. Not this time, though."

Satisfied, Cabe slowed his horse until he was even with Gwen. The rest of the caravan slowly trudged forward again. Despite the Dragon King's words concerning eyes that watched over them, more than one person could not help glancing around from time to time. Regardless of their renewed vigilance, however, no one, not even the Green Dragon, who prided himself on his skill, noticed the single figure perched high in the trees. No wyvern this, but an avian creature who watched all with arrogance and something else.

The Green Dragon had been correct when he had said the Seekers designed with countermeasures already in mind. The watcher wore one such measure now and kept it quite well hidden from the mages and drakes below.

The observer waited until the caravan was lost from sight before finally moving. Then, silently and swiftly, the Seeker spread its wings and rose into the heavens, its destination to the northeast.

Alone in his chambers, the Gryphon sat quietly, his mind on a number of scattered items of interest. Like someone putting together a puzzle, he manuevered the pieces around, trying to see if there were any relation between them. It was the way in which he ruled this city. He had learned more through this process than a hundred meetings with the various ministers that protocol demanded he pretend to listen to. He doubted any of them would be able to help him with even one of the problems he now considered.

A servant brought him a goblet of fine red wine. The Gryphon's face twisted and contorted as he formed a human visage in order to drink without spilling it all over his person. The wine was excellent, as usual, and he nodded to the servant, a half-seen shadow that immediately thereafter melted into the walls. Such servants unnerved many who lived in the palace, but the Gryphon refused to do anything about them, for he needed them in more ways than one. They were not only servants, but his eyes and ears as well. Merely with their presence, they made him feel as if he were not the only unique creature in all of Penacles.

His keen hearing detected the sound of someone walking purposefully and he turned toward the doorway. Two huge, metallic figures stood next to the doorway, one on each side. Rough conceptions of men. The Gryphon waited expectantly.

Suddenly one of the figures opened its eyes, revealing nothing but an iron-gray blankness where the pupils should have been.

"General Toos requests admittance," it grumbled.

"Let him enter." The golems made very effective doormen, since nothing short of the most powerful magic would stop them if they believed he was in danger.

The doors swung open of their own accord and a tall, thin, foxlike man stepped into the chamber. Most noticeable in his hair was the silver streak, a surprising thing since most people believed the general to be unable to perform magic. He was, however, noted for shrewd hunches and last-minute miracles. Though human—he also claimed a bit of elfin blood, but that was debatable—Toos was by far the Gryphon's oldest companion. More than that, he was a close friend.

"Milord." The man bowed in one smooth, sleek action. Age had done nothing to slow him. He was already far older than most humans ever got—almost *twice* as old, the Gryphon realized with a start.

"Sit, please, Toos, and forget formalities." It was always this way. The general was of the sort who always followed protocol even when dealing with those he had known for years.

Toos took the proffered seat, somehow managing to sit without wrinkling his dress uniform. It amazed the Gryphon that his comrade should go around so unprotected—even Penacles had its assassins. Yet, though there had been attempts, Toos had survived most without a scratch.

The old soldier pulled a parchment from his belt and reluctantly handed it over to his lord.

"More concerning . . . what you showed me?"

"No. I suggest you read the report first."

The Gryphon unfolded it and studied the contents. A report from one of his spies who passed as a fisherman in the coastal city of Irillian by the Sea, the main human habitation in that region and a city that was controlled by the aquatic Blue Dragon. It was not the location that the Gryphon would have expected news to come from.

He started reading the portion he knew Toos had wanted him to see and ignored everything else. Two figures wearing the distinctive black armor and wolfhelms of eastern continent raiders had been spotted traveling out to the caverns which served as the above-ground entrance to the palace of Irillian's true master. One matched the description the Gryphon had given his spies of a raider named D'Shay.

D'Shay.

A name, but one the Gryphon felt he should know, and remember. An aristocratic raider from across the Eastern Seas.

D'Shay was a wolf in human form, though not in the literal sense. Still, the Lord of Penacles would have felt safer with a pack of ravished wolves than alone with the raider. With wolves he at least understood what he was up against.

His uncertainty returned. D'Shay in contact with the Blue Dragon. The Lord of Penacles did not care for the potential that such an alliance might offer. The Master of Irillian had raiders of his own and they were a constant problem even to some of his fellow Dragon Kings, yet nothing had been done because they were too swift, too skilled. Dragon Kings did not wage true war with other Dragon Kings; that was a stated fact, though there had been rumors to the contrary occasionally.

He had not realized that he had uttered D'Shay's name out loud until Toos spoke up. "Please reconsider this, milord. We cannot afford any new campaigns at the moment. There is no telling when the Black Dragon will recover completely. Now would be an excellent time to rid ourselves of him. His fanatics are weak and the Gray Mists are merely a wisp right now. Lochivar is visible for miles inward."

Shaking his furred head, the Gryphon rejected the suggestion. "We can't afford such an action. Despite the weakness of both the Gray Mists and the Black Dragon, the Lochivarites and those that the raiders brought over will indeed fight. That's all they know any more. The Mists only enforce Black's will even more. Most of those people have grown only knowing servitude to him. If he says fight, they will.''

"But D'Shay is . . . Gryphon, I know what's forming in your mind, dammit! Don't even consider it!''

They stared at one another and it was finally Toos who turned away. The Gryphon stared down any further comment before reminding his second-in-command, "D'Shay represents a threat we know nothing about. The wolf raiders want to set up some permanent base in the Dragonrealm, either because they are expanding their hunting grounds or because they are losing whatever war they fight across the seas. It may even be that D'Shay is simply after me. He knows something about me, and I would like to know what it is. One of the puzzles I've been mulling over of late.'' The lionbird patted the report. "This gave me the extra piece I needed. Lochivar is too volatile at present for them to consider as a port, but Irillian is perfect. I should have realized it sooner.''

Toos looked at him darkly. When his lord spoke like this, it meant he was about to do what most rulers would imagine unthinkable. "Who will lead while you are away? We are not speaking of some local journey. We are speaking of the realm of the Blue Dragon. Other than the Master of the Dagora Forest, he holds the greatest respect of his human subjects. You will not find so many allies there. You could be gone for months or—yes, I'll say it, dammit—forever! Dead!''

The Gryphon was unmoved by the emotion. The idea of journeying to Irillian in order to seek out the wolf raider D'Shay was becoming more and more of a priority. Carefully, so that his growing obsession did not show, he asked a question of his own. "Who leads when I am away?''

Another unseen servant brought forth sweets, but the general irritably waved away both bowl and creature. "Damn you, I'm a soldier, an ex-mercenary. Arguing with politicians is your specialty—and what do I care about the price of wheat as long as my men and their horses get fed? You've ruled here so long that no one can imagine any other as lord! Only those like me still remember that there ever was a Purple Dragon!''

"Are you through?" The Gryphon's face had reverted to that of a bird of prey, but his voice indicated amusement.

"Yes," sighed Toos.

"You'll take over—as usual?"

"Yes—dammit. You could have at least mentioned our other problem to the sorcerers while they were here. Then, I wouldn't be so worried."

"The frost incident appears to be isolated. No one else has reported any animals found frozen solid or fields of ice-encrusted oat. I've already contacted those with the resources to investigate more thoroughly. If I'm not here, they will find you."

A crafty look crept over the human's face. "Why not send these—hell, they're elves—to Irillian?"

"Because there are no elves in that region, save the seagoing kind, and they, like the people there, are loyal to the Blue Dragon." The Gryphon rose with the ease of a cat. "Why do you always persist in this show of reluctance?"

"Because old habits die hard and I always have this feeling you're going to stick me with this king business and run off permanently."

"It would serve you right, you old ogre."

The general chuckled, then recalled what he had shown the lionbird the day before. "I still wish the Bedlams were here. They might know something. That mule was as solid as a chunk of iron, Gryphon! What could freeze a creature so?"

The Gryphon found that he no longer cared about mules, fields, and sorcerers. Now that he had decided to depart the city, he was anxious to get away as soon as possible. It was not like him to be so uncaring about such puzzles, but perhaps that was because he had never before been offered such a chance to capture the wolf raider D'Shay. At the very least, the information D'Shay could give him concerning the wolf raiders themselves would surely be more valuable. The ice was probably the error of some fledgling sorcerer or witch. Perhaps even some sort of insane joke by sprites. Yes, that made some sense, he decided. Now, there was no reason to hesitate.

Turning to his aide, the Gryphon outlined his thoughts. General Toos did not seem taken with the ideas, but he soon gave in. The lionbird knew that Toos would understand as time went on.

"Now that that's settled," he continued. "there is no more reason for me to hesitate. Toos, I have full faith in you and your men, but this is something I have to do myself. D'Shay once claimed a connection to me; I want to find out what that connection is or whether he spouted it purely in jest."

"I could stop you no more now than when you led our company in battle, though, now that you are king, I would have hoped for different." The general looked highly displeased with the situation, but knew better. "How soon will you be departing?"

"Before tomorrow morning. Have someone saddle a horse for me."

"*Before morning*? You—" The soldier broke off at the look on his monarch's face. "Aye, dammit, as you say."

The Gryphon dismissed his oldest companion with a gesture. Toos sputtered, but said nothing. It did not matter to the Gryphon, anyway. The complaints of Toos or the ministers did not concern him. Only his journey to Irillian did. That—and the man called D'Shay.

He felt a brief pounding in his head and started to question its cause, but the pounding ceased and, with it, his curiosity concerning it. All that mattered, he reminded himself again, was Irillian and D'Shay. Nothing else.

IV

Toma entered the frozen hall of the Ice Dragon with great trepidation. From the first, he had come to loathe this cold, dead citadel and its even more gruesome inhabitants. This was not the Dragon King he had expected. The Ice Dragon who ruled here was nearly as dead as his kingdom—but far more powerful than any of the other Kings. Something was afoot and Toma doubted he would care for the answer when he found it.

He shivered, and not just from the cold.

The Ice Dragon lay across the remains of some ancient structure. It was a thin, cadaverous creature but still larger than any of his kin. A gigantic corpse, the firedrake thought. I am dealing with a gigantic corpse.

At first, there was no acknowledgment of his presence. A lone drake warrior stood nearby. Had Toma not seen the chest rise and fall, albeit slowly and shallowly, he would have thought the drake a frozen ghoul much like the unliving thing that had first met him. The guard ignored him, instead staring straight ahead at something that, to Toma at least, was not there.

Slowly, as if rising from some grave, the Ice Dragon stirred. Massive frost-covered wings spread with a crackling sound that the firedrake realized was the breaking of thick layers of ice that had formed on the leviathan while he slept. The eyes opened, revealing a chill blue hue much like the skin color of a human long frozen. It reminded Toma all too much of some of the Dragon King's servants. It was also wrong. When last he had visited the Dragon King in this hall, only the day before, those eyes had been white as the eternal snow outside.

The Ice Dragon studied him with a total lack of interest. "There is something you wished of me, Duke Toma?"

They were not speaking as equals, that was something the bone-white dragon had established soon after their first meeting. The Ice Dragon was one of the Kings; Toma was merely a drake whose duty was to serve.

"My father, your *emperor*," Toma began purposefully. His only authority existed when it concerned the King of Kings. The Ice Dragon seemed oddly unused to warm life these days and the few of his clans that Toma had seen were of a similar attitude. It was as if they had completely forgotten what life was.

"Yesss?" A trace of impatience escaped the Dragon King. Toma was pleased, as it meant at least some of the old Ice Dragon still remained. Where there was emotion, there was life.

"I've yet to ssssee any aid for him. He hasss ssslept—" Toma cursed inwardly. He was becoming unsettled. "—he has slept as you suggested, but there has been no change. I lack the knowledge and skill for what ails him, though I think a little more warmth could certainly not hurt. You, though, are a Dragon King. I came here because of your power and experience; you must know something that will aid in his recovery!''

The Ice Dragon jerked his head up and, for a brief moment, Toma thought the leviathan had remembered something that would help. Much to the firedrake's disappointment, it was immediately apparent that his host was now concerned with something totally unconnected to the present situation.

"The sssstupid creaturessss!" hissed the Dragon King. His eyes were alive with rage. "Not now!"

Suddenly, the chamber became the center of a massive snow-storm. Toma cried out in surprise, then pulled his cape about him in a feeble attempt to protect himself from the elements. Snow blew about wildly. There was thunder and lightning. The wind whipped things around so much that the firedrake could not see. He could only hear the howling of the wind and, above it, the angry voice of his benefactor as that one roared his frustration out on some unfortunate.

As spontaneously as the storm had erupted, it ceased. He realized with surprise that it had lasted for barely a minute.

Brushing the frost and snow from his face, Toma gazed up at the Lord of the Northern Wastes. There was a momentary glow about the Ice Dragon so short that the firedrake would have missed it had he blinked. He did notice how more energetic his host became after the glow faded.

The massive head swung back to face him and Toma could not help stepping back a few feet. He still had not reverted to his dragon form and had no desire to even now. It was too difficult to keep from losing body warmth when he was in his birth form, and if the Ice Dragon truly wanted him dead. . . .

"Someone invades my domain—with sorcery yet," the great dragon suddenly told him. "My children will deal with them. It will give them a taste to savor."

He could feel the chilling breath of his host and frost gathered on his brow. The Ice Dragon looked beyond the chamber and then at the firedrake. The incident of the moment before had already seemingly been forgotten.

"You may rest assured, Duke Toma, that my loyalty is to the throne. Everything I do here is in his name, for what he represented. My emperor will be cared for. You will see. Now, I must rest more. . . ."

"If I may . . ." Toma began.

The Ice Dragon eyes narrowed to slits. "Is there something more you wanted?"

The firedrake stared into the cold, dead eyes of his host and shook his head. He knew well enough the signs of danger. Now was not the time to pursue *any* subject. The Ice Dragon, satisfied, laid his head back down upon the ruins. For the first time, Toma looked at them closely. The rubble had once been a temple, he decided. A temple which still housed something, for there was a pit or hole within and it was over this that the ghostly leviathan rested.

The Dragon King watched him with one baleful eye, then closed it. Toma whirled and departed the chamber, realizing that his earlier fears of something going on had been all too correct. In fact, he suspected that he had greatly underestimated how wrong things were. His whole trip here had been a waste of time and now quite possibly threatened his existence as well.

The trouble was, he doubted very much that the Ice Dragon was about to let him leave the Northern Wastes alive.

Somehow, some way, the lord of the Dagora Forest led them along a hidden path that took half their travel time off. The Manor crept up on them and then seemed to spring into existence full-grown. Cabe stared at the edifice and wondered how it had grown so large. His memories of this place were only months old and, while his visit had been short and hectic, he was certain that he would have noticed all of this.

The Manor was a magnificent blending of nature and construction. Much of it had been built within a great tree, yet just as much had been constructed by artisans of great skill and care. It rose several stories high. In many places it was difficult to see where exactly the two portions mixed. The latest of more than a thousand generations of vines enshrouded some portions, but most looked as if someone had been living here just yesterday.

The grounds were equally as fascinating as the Manor. Here, instead of clearing the land, the creators had sculpted the sur-

rounding regions so that what they built actually benefited from
the hills and plant life. If the Seekers had built this, which Gwen
believed, then it revealed a side of the avians that no one else had
ever seen before.

From his right, where Gwen sat on her own steed, he heard a
tiny, muffled gasp. The memories she was experiencing were not
ones that Cabe cared to dwell on, for he knew too well who many
of them revolved around. It did not matter that she loved him and
loved him greatly; Nathan was her first love and a tragic one at
that. She had gone from Nathan to Cabe with hardly any gap in
between, at first drawn by the similarities, then ensnared by the
differences.

Still, Cabe could not help feeling some jealousy.

The Green Dragon reined his drake to a stop and dismounted.
The party came to a halt behind him and waited. It was clear that
the Dragon King was in the midst of something. A few of the
humans muttered uneasily, but Cabe waved them quiet.

Raising his hand and forming a fist, the Green Dragon called
out something that neither Cabe nor Gwen could hear. A moment
later, the forests around them were filled with drakes of the humanoid kind. Cabe, fearing that the Dragon King had lied all
along about his part of the oath, readied himself for a swift but
bloody conflict.

Surprisingly, it was Gwen who held him back. He turned his
head and looked at her in amazement, thinking, ever so briefly,
that she was another of the King's pawns. Hurriedly, she corrected
his misconceptions.

"I'm sorry, Cabe, we thought it best to wait until we arrived
here."

"We?"

"The Gryphon, the Green Dragon, and myself."

He suddenly felt surrounded by enemies—all because his name
was Bedlam.

"It is not like that!" She added quickly, evidently able to read
his mind. "It was decided that we should have an equal number
of drake servants. This way, both races will learn."

"Drakes?"

The two parties eyed one another uneasily. The humans muttered to one another, not caring for the thought of sleeping in a

den of dragons. The drakes, on the other hand, knew that the lord and lady of the Manor were human mages of great power and that their own lord was turning their well-being over to the grandson of the greatest of the Dragon Masters, which was akin to being turned over to their worst nightmare.

"Cabe?"

He finally nodded. The two reluctant groups began to merge as Gwen dismounted and commenced supervising the unpacking and organizing. The tension was so strong one could almost see it, but no one wanted to anger the magic-users or the Dragon King. Cabe dismounted his own animal and began to walk off into the forest. Trying somehow to come to grips with everything. He had gotten used to the hatchlings—somewhat—but an entire clan?

Somehow, the Green Dragon was suddenly standing in front of him. Cabe had not even noticed when the Dragon King had dismounted, much less how he came to be here.

"I feel, despite the differences between our races, that I understand some of your fears. That is why I place the responsibility for any actions by any of my clan members on my own shoulders, Bedlam. Whatever happens, I will share the punishment. I want you to know that."

Cabe nodded slowly, not comforted in the least. The Green Dragon proffered a scaled, four-digited claw/hand. The human mage stared at it for some time before finally taking it. The Dragon King's grip was strong and hard and Cabe thanked whatever deity was watching over his fingers.

"Lady Gwendolyn will not need you for the moment, I think. Please walk with me. I would like to discuss some things with you, yes?"

He tried to read the burning eyes within the dragonhelm, but they were as enigmatic as everything else concerning this firedrake. Cabe turned to look briefly for Gwen, but she was nowhere to be seen.

"The servants know what to do and both sides will keep as much apart as possible for now, so there is no worry. Your mate is altering the spells that surround the Manor. The original protective spell was decaying. When she is finished, only those with the permission of the Lord and Lady will be able to pass." When Cabe did not apparently plan to ask one question in particular, the

Master of the Dagora Forest added, "Even I will require permission. Your home will be secure."

The boundaries were to be closed to the Dragon King? It made sense, as the spell could not possibly differentiate between one King or another and both Silver and the Storm Dragon were close neighbors. So was the Crystal Dragon, but no one knew what his intentions were.

"Pleassse, Bedlam. That is not why I came to speak to you. If we may walk and enjoy the forest."

He followed the drake lord as the latter began to walk the boundaries of the Manor's grounds. Cabe could not tell where the borders were, but his inhuman companion seemed to know when not to step too far to the left or when to turn.

"There are," the Green Dragon began abruptly, "bad feelings between the drakes and those who bear the name Bedlam. That is understating the fact, actually. There are those in my own clans who have dared almost to defy me completely because there is a Bedlam now living in the midst of my kingdom."

It was always comforting to know that the forest was filled with friends, Cabe thought wryly.

"I had discussions on more than one occasion with the Dragon Master Nathan, you know. I suspect I have been tainted by humanity far more than any of my brethren. Even my speech patterns have degenerated."

The Dragon King paused and turned his head toward Cabe. The fierce dragon visage atop the helm seemed ready to make a meal out of the human, but the words of its owner belied that image. "I have learned to welcome what the others call the human threat. We were never numerous, never imaginative in the ways of your kind. Our rule is one of stagnation; I suspect that nothing would have prevented our fall soon."

Such bald truths from what was supposed to be a hereditary enemy made Cabe stumble as he tried to follow every word and, therefore, paid little attention to the path before him. The drake seemed not to notice.

"You fight among yourselves, you lie, you destroy, you run, and you steal. Despite that, you have become our superiors. You also create, look beyond the future, refuse to give in to impossible odds, and pick yourselves up when you've been defeated. We can only touch upon these qualities at present. That's why I requested that the hatchlings be raised as human as possible. To give my race a second hope. To give both races a place in these lands."

There was nothing Cabe could say that would have felt sufficient at that moment. The two continued to walk, gradually moving farther away from the boundaries of the Manor. In his days at the inn, he would have never been able to imagine himself walking side by side with one of the horrifying Dragon Kings.

He froze. The drake looked at him.

"Is something—"

"Gwen!" Cabe whirled and started running, not caring whether the Green Dragon followed or not. She was in danger. Briefly, her mind had touched his. What sort of danger threatened her, he could not say. Cabe had only felt her panic, nothing more.

He leaped over a small rise and felt a tingle through his body. It lasted barely a moment and he surmised that it must have been the barrier. From behind him, he heard an angry shout. The Green Dragon called out his name. Despite the urgency he felt, Cabe stopped and turned quickly.

The drake lord was standing behind the rise, his hands pushing against the air. Apparently, Gwen had already altered the protective spell and now the Dragon King had no way of entering the Manor grounds without help. Cabe recalled how he had once let in the demonic Darkhorse.

"Enter freely, friend!" The words were not the same he had used that last time, but the meaning was clear enough. He saw the drake stumble forward. Satisfied, he turned and began to run again. The Dragon King would either catch up or meet him there—wherever there was.

Cabe ran, passing by startled drakes and humans. He was on the right path, he realized. Gwen had once told him how close relationships between magic-users sometimes formed a link. It was not always a steady one, but there would be times when one felt the need of the other—as he had this time.

He was beyond the immediate grounds of the Manor before he realized it. The barrier had to be near. Where—

She lay crumpled in a heap on the outer edge of what Cabe would have called the garden, close, it dawned on him, to the place where her amber prison had once stood. She was alone and facedown next to a long overgrown row of bushes. Rushing over to her, Cabe gently turned her onto her back. From memory, he reached out with his mind to what he perceived as a spectrum and manipulated one of the soft, reddish bands. His spell washed over Gwen. A sigh of relief escaped his lips when he was able to determine that, at least physically, she was unharmed.

"There isss nothing here."

Cabe shook. His thoughts buried in concern, he had not heard the Green Dragon approach. "She seems unhurt, but . . ."

". . . we will know when she wakes," the drake finished. "Which she appears to be doing now."

Gwen was indeed stirring. She shivered and slowly opened her eyes. When her gaze found Cabe, the relief in her eyes was nearly overwhelming.

"I was afraid . . ." The enchantress paused as if unsure of what she had been afraid of.

"What happened?"

"The spell. I completed it, didn't I?" Suddenly, she was very much frightened again.

"Yes." Cabe could not help glancing around. Had something slipped inside beforehand?

"Nothing lurks within that I can discern," the Green Dragon added. "I have been searching since Cabe first felt your danger."

"What was it, then, Gwen?"

She blinked. "The ground is untouched. The—thing—is not here. Nor is the Seeker."

"What thing? What Seeker?"

"There is that," the drake suggested. They followed his gaze to a statue poised near the top of the Manor. It was a Seeker in mid-flight. There were other such statues scattered around the Manor and the grounds. As with this one, they were amazingly lifelike.

Gwen frowned. "No, it couldn't have been that—I think. That would still not explain the abomination that I saw."

"What did it look like?" Cabe asked softly.

She shivered. "Huge. All white fur and great claws like some digging creature. I swear, it tore up the area!"

Cabe and the Green Dragon studied the area, but saw nothing. The young mage looked up at the drake lord.

"It isss possible," the reptilian monarch began. "That, in re-working the ancient spells, you unleashed some old Seeker magic, perhaps something meant to frighten away outsiders."

The enchantress did not seem convinced. "They were fighting one another! It was as if I felt the avian's thoughts—even its death! It did—did succeed in killing that thing, though."

The drake gave a very convincing copy of a human shrug. "I can think of no other reason. No one else ssseems to have noticed it."

"Am I going mad? Is that what you're saying?"

"By no means. I believe my theory isss—is sound. Not perfect, perhaps, but sound."

Gwen looked off into the distance. "I was so certain it was real. . . ."

A few drakes and humans had gathered behind them. Curiousity—and possibly uncertainty—had drawn them together as nothing else had so far. Cabe looked at them and frowned. This was not the way to start out.

"It's all right," he shouted. "Exhaustion, nothing more. Back to the unpacking."

The servants slowly dispersed, but Cabe knew that they were not completely satisfied. What could he have said?

Gwen struggled to rise and both Cabe and the Dragon King aided her. She was still staring off into the distance. "I'd swear that—that at one point the Seeker actually saved my life. Not for altruistic reasons—but because it was a necessity, I think. I re-member falling, being grabbed—and then blanking out."

"Forget that for now," Cabe suggested. "You need rest. Later, we can discuss it again."

"I suppose so."

The Green Dragon put a gauntleted hand on her arm. "For you, Firerose, I will send word to my servants to investigate the area. Though Seekers are cunning, there is a good chance they will discover if one has been nearby."

She shook her head. "It's not necessary."

"I think it isss."

Gwen smiled and then started to sag in Cabe's arms. Both he and the Dragon King were forced to assist her to the Manor. She made no protest.

Had they spent even a few more moments studying the area around the spot the Lady of the Amber had fallen, it was likely they would have found nothing. It was also possible that, if they had looked a little closer at the bushes, they might have seen the two feathers that Gwen's weight had buried deeper in the branches of those bushes. Feathers from a very large bird—or possibly something else.

V

Irillian By the Sea was a city that thrived on fishing. War or not, the plentiful bounty its fishermen brought back was bought by all those neighboring regions too far from the Eastern Seas to do their own fishing.

While scores of boats moved outward seeking the first catch of the day, only one boat was headed in the opposite direction, to shore. Its path was one avoided by the fishermen, for that path led to the Aquias Maw, the vast caverns, partially submerged, which were the entrance to the undersea world of the one the human Marshal of Irillian called master.

The Blue Dragon.

In the weak light of predawn, it was barely possible to make out the three figures in the boat. One was the boatman, a figure shrouded in a soaking cloak woven from plant life taken from the seas. The passengers knew that he or she or it was not human and had probably never been, and did not really care. The boatman performed its function without complaint and that was as it should be. There was no reason to think about the being further. Both men had observed stranger things in the spans of their lifetimes.

The two passengers were like leaves on the same branch. Both were clad in furred armor, black as a moonless night, and upon their heads they wore tight-fitting helms with broad noseguards and a stylized wolfhead. A tail of fur ran from the back of the wolfhead down past the bottom of the helm and another hand's length further. Both were veteran fighters, yet both had airs about them as only ones who were born to lead can have. One was slightly shorter than the other and clean-shaven. The other, his apparent superior, sported a small, well-trimmed beard, a goatee.

The boatman brought the craft ashore by itself, displaying amazing agility and strength yet never revealing any portion of its person, including hands or feet. The two wolf raiders disembarked and watched silently as the boatman set out once more.

D'Shay raised his helm and wiped the mist of the seas from his face. "We have been sighted, D'Laque."

His companion followed suit while asking, "How long ago, Lord D'Shay?"

"At least a week, maybe two."

"Could he be here already, then?" D'Laque began to eye the beach.

"It's possible, but I think not. The animal is too good a hunter and too mistrustful of his prey to move like that. No, I think he's near, but not quite here yet. Scouting, perhaps."

D'Laque eyed his superior. "You make it sound as if this is some sort of game between you two. He is secondary; a permanent place for our ships is what we need most. The Pack Leaders are growing impatient, even D'Zayne, who, of all of them, should mirror your desires."

D'Shay was unmoved by the thought. "We shall accomplish that mission, my friend, but think how well we shall be received if we bring the Gryphon's head back with us. The news of his survival did not please the Pack Leaders. D'Morogue's . . . dismissal . . . is proof of that. He was supposed to assure our success, if you remember."

The other wolf raider swallowed hard. No one liked to think about what little the Runners had left of the hapless D'Morogue. Raiders in command who failed Pack Leaders in something of such importance never rose in rank and usually ended up as part of the Runners' feast. D'Morogue's name had been stricken from the Pack Commanders' ranks, the caste designation R' replacing his former caste designation D', and he had been tossed, bound and gagged, into the lairs of the toothy Runners.

Eyeing D'Shay as the other replaced his helm, D'Laque could not help wonder why that one had not risen to Pack Commander. Certainly, his unofficial authority was known to all. No Pack Commander moved if D'Shay spoke out against it, and no Pack Leader approved new front strategies unless he was assured that D'Shay would have no major objections. Here, across the seas, was a man whom even the assembled Pack Leaders respected— yet he was not one of them, despite his superiority.

"Was there something you wanted, D'Laque?" asked the aristocratic raider. He had not so much as glanced anywhere near his companion.

"No," D'Laque quickly shook his head. "Nothing, D'Shay."

"So. I thought you might be having second thoughts about joining me. I know how much you fear Senior Keeper D'Rak." D'Shay turned away from the seas and faced Irillian. The city was still buried in the shadows of predawn, but signs of life could already be heard. "Soon, we shall have a treasure trove with which to present the Pack Leaders. New ships, new lands, riches, allies, and the last great stumbling block in our war with the Dream Lands served on a platter. At last."

D'Laque hid the frown that crept up onto his face. He had the distinct feeling he was in the dark about certain decisions and was not going to find out about them until it was too late to do anything about it. He suspected that D'Shay *needed* to capture the Gryphon, or else lose valuable influence. It would be just what D'Rak would want.

It would also leave D'Laque defenseless against the master he had secretly betrayed.

Night-clad raiders and wolfhelms. They now haunted the Gryphon's dreams, haunted his every thought. The closer he got to his destination, the worse it became. There was no way he could have turned back now. This was his chance to capture and question the wolf raider D'Shay. It was not the first time he had undertaken such a mission; there had been several during his years as a mercenary. This was different in one way, though. He knew that this time he was obsessed. He even knew the fallacy of such a feeling. Obsession generally led to death and often it was the death of the one obsessed. His head pounded briefly and, for a moment, he questioned this obsession and its sudden growth. Then, the pounding went away and his determination to continue on returned. He forgot his confusion.

The Gryphon shook his head and then studied the map of Irillian's—or rather the Blue Dragon's—lands once more. Some places were just too damn far away, he decided.

He looked up. The landscape around him was chaotic. While there were fields and trees that grew as if undisturbed for generations, there were also the occasional enigmatic craters, as if something had once happened here.

To reach Irillian by land, one had to pass through the uncharted domain of the Storm Dragon. The Gryphon's fur and feathers ruffled. The Storm Dragon was one of those Kings who revealed little about his full strength. The lionbird had never encountered him during the Turning War or the years after even though he and the leviathan were neighbors. The extent of his knowledge was a passing glimmer of Wenslis, the human city on the western edge of these lands and the nearest major human settlement to Irillian, which was not saying much. Wenslis was as far from the seaport as it was from Penacles, but, while it would have been an excellent place to stop, it would have taken him several days out of the quickest and shortest path.

I hope you're not expecting me for dinner, D'Shay, the Gryphon thought wryly. *I'm going to be late.* If the charts that he had succeeded in wresting from the libraries were correct, the trip got no better. Supposedly, this land had many swamps, and the worst of those was in his path and large enough that it was pointless to try and go around it.

Lochivar had looked bad, but much of that was due to the mind-numbing Mists. These lands were soaked the deeper one wandered.

This is the kingdom of the Storm Dragon.

As if the last thought had been a cue, the skies began clouding up with unbelievable speed. The winds began to howl. He quickly rolled up the charts, returned them to their case and packed the horse. This was not the place to be caught out in a storm, not by these trees. There was an overhang off to the right, perhaps an hour's journey. He'd be high and dry if he could make it there before the first rains fell.

His steed, having long ago learned to trust its rider, allowed him to choose its path and pace. The Gryphon envied such trust, hoping against hope that he could return that trust by not leading it into some hidden gap or straight into the den of some hungry minor drake.

It was almost as dark as night, now, with both moons being hidden. The horse's hooves sloshed in the increasingly wet grass and the Gryphon knew he was coming to the outskirts of the swamp sooner than his charts had indicated. He prayed it would not be too rough going before they made it to the overhang—providing he had not read the charts wrong about its location.

The sky rumbled.

Small, half-unseen creatures flittered, darted, and loped around him. Where had all these blasted things come from? Even despite his predatory background, he had had the worst time attempting to catch food. It was as if the oncoming storm was drawing them from the earth itself.

Or something was chasing them, he realized all too belatedly as the huge, ugly head rose from the swampy fields.

The horse sought frantically for dry, speed-slowing earth, but found only slick grass and mud. The Gryphon was nearly flung from the saddle as his mount spun in nearly a complete circle.

The minor drake turned its weak gaze toward the commotion. This was an older one, the Gryphon determined. A younger drake would have been on his tail already, jaws wide, claws fully extended. The elderly dragon, though, was only just realizing that the huge thing before him was the food he sought. Much bigger and better-smelling than the tiny marsh creatures it was normally forced to eat.

The heavens were split asunder as the first bolts came home to the earth. Its prey was momentarily forgotten as the minor drake looked upward and shivered. By the brief but brilliant light, the Gryphon could see that the thing was a mottled, unhealthy green. It was very old and probably dying, but evidently it was going to live long enough to give him trouble.

He'd wanted to avoid using any magic for fear that would draw the Storm Dragon or one of his underlings to him, but now was no longer the time to worry about that. Old or not, the dragon was a threat he could not avoid. At the very least, he would probably lose his horse if he attempted to go around it. Old and infirm though it might be, the thing only needed one sweep of its claws to decorate the landscape with bits of horse and rider.

The beast put a massive paw down in the direction of the two, then nearly fell forward when that paw sank deep into the mud. The dragon roared in annoyance and began the task of pulling the leg back out, the action accompanied by a loud slurping noise as the mud fought until the very end.

The Gryphon's eyes brightened. He raised both hands, keeping his balance by locking his legs against the horse's sides.

The spell was a simple one that might easily escape notice. Essentially, he was allowing the absorbtion of water by the soil to speed up. At least, that was what he was hoping he was doing. Generations of experience did not necessarily make a mage a master of the natural elements. All it meant was he knew how to manipulate the powers to create the end result he desired.

And this time it worked. The minor drake put its massive paw down on what it knew to be safer ground, only to have it sink even further than it had at the other spot. The beast howled with rage and the Gryphon was barely able to keep his horse from bolting into some of the muck itself.

The creature struggled in vain to release the one leg, working its remaining three into the mud as it pulled the fourth. Now, it was completely trapped. It hissed and glared balefully at the Gryphon, as if realizing that he was the cause of its misfortunes. When it opened its maw, he raised a fist in sorcerous defense against its flame, but nothing came out. The dragon was too old, too spent. Had it been younger, it might have freed itself or managed a flame stream long and intense enough to do the lionbird some damage, but such was not the case. Slowly, cautiously, the Gryphon began to urge his horse around the right of the thrashing obstacle.

The rain was starting to come down. The Gryphon shook his mane in disgust. He hated dampness and he hated rain even more. There was a place for cleanliness, but this was not it. Silently mouthing a curse at the Storm Dragon, he eyed the distant over-hang. The old drake ceased thrashing, either worn out or finally realizing it was better off for the moment if it made no move. The mud was already up to the bottom of its body.

As the rain continued to come down in an ever-increasing fury and the ground threatened to suck horse and rider beneath it, the Gryphon once more began to think obsessively about the problems. Obviously, he thought morosely, it wasn't something to keep you warm and dry at night.

The overhang did not seem any closer. If this were any indication, the Gryphon suspected he was in for a very long, very slow, and very *wet* journey.

Much to his misfortune, his suspicions proved all too correct.

More than a few days had passed and, at last, the border between the domain of the Storm Dragon and his aquatic brother was only another day's journey away. To the Gryphon, however, it seemed more like a hundred days. The rain had let up only once in the days it had taken to cross this land and that meant that it had taken even longer to make that crossing. Both the lionbird and his mount were sick of water and mud. It was a wonder anything could grow before it drowned, the Gryphon thought. What sort of life must the inhabitants of Wenslis have?

The weather was not his only problem, however. Twice, dragons had flown overheard, obviously on patrol and perhaps on the lookout for him in particular. He knew that the Dragon Kings had their eyes and ears in his domain. He had not expected his departure to be kept a secret. He *had* hoped to be nearer to the outskirts of Irillian when that happened, though.

Ahead of him lay more soggy fields of marsh grass and one more swamp. Up until now, he had been lucky. Both patrols had missed him, but now he faced the watchful eyes of the Blue Dragon's servants as well. If he was *extremely* lucky, he thought sourly, maybe a patrol from each would spot him and the two would kill one another in the fight over who should claim the prize. He knew how much each of the Kings desired his death and the prestige that such a kill would bring both patrol and King.

He sighed, knowing that nothing would be accomplished until he moved on.

The horse trod carefully on the half-sunken path, knowing from the past few days that even the safest-looking piece of ground was treacherous at times. The Gryphon knew the odds were that he would lose his horse at some point on this journey, most likely in Irillian if he made it that far, but he was determined to do his best to see that, if it came to that, the animal might be "accidently" found by someone who would care for it. He realized that it was a foolish, romantic notion, but it had always been his nature to reward those who had proven themselves, be they men or whatever. A good hawk or steed was sometimes more valuable, more worthy, than a hundred soldiers.

It was clouding up again. The clouds seemed almost alive, so perfectly did they gather over his head. He contemplated the possibility that he was being stalked, but decided it was his paranoia. The rain began to fall again. The horse snorted in disgust, as did the Gryphon.

The sky thundered. There were flashes of lightning. The Gryphon had become accustomed to both. Neither had, as yet, swayed even in the least from his goal.

The bolt struck not more than twenty yards from him. The shock threw his horse off the path and into the boggy field. The animal cried out in alarm, but its rider had troubles of his own as one foot was caught in the stirrup and the Gryphon nearly ended up having his leg crushed. Only his inhuman reflexes allowed him to pull himself free in time.

The horse landed on its side with a loud splash and the Gryphon was enveloped by a muddy wave.

Another bolt struck, this time a little closer.

He *was* being stalked.

They were there now, flitting in and out of the cloud cover. There were at least two, maybe more; it was difficult to say since only two were visible at any one time. He did not recall much about the clans of the Storm Dragon, save that they were very protective of their lands and they were capable of producing something very much akin to an actual lightning bolt.

Why wait until now? Or had they just discovered him? Somehow, he did not think so. He was being set up for something.

His horse was struggling unsuccessfully to rise, but the mud was proving too slippery to support it. The Gryphon started toward it, then glanced up quickly when he heard a sound he recognized all too well.

One of the dragons was diving toward him, maw open in a frightening display of teeth.

The speed with which it dove was shocking. The distance between it and the earth shrank rapidly. The Lord of Penacles was forced to leap away from his steed and land once more in the marsh. He knew that nothing would save him now. There was no time to utilize a spell, no time even to pull out the tiny whistles that he kept around his neck for such life-and-death situations. He could only hope that somehow the dragon would miss. A near-miss was not sufficient; the claws of the dragon would probably take most of his backside with it.

There were shrieks from both the dragon and the horse and then waves of rank water were washing over everything, including the lionbird. Several seconds rolled by and when the Gryphon still felt nothing, he cautiously rolled over. His eyes widened as he realized that his luck had changed considerably.

The dragon had struck, but against the horse, not the rider. The gallant mount hung limply from the claws of the dragon as the latter made for the cloud cover. From the angle, the Gryphon knew the animal was dead already.

It was still raining, but not half as badly as it had prior to the attack. The Gryphon stood there, water up to his knees, and pondered what had just occurred. The dragons had stolen his mount, but had left him unharmed. Very strange. It was almost as if he was meant to continue on, but not without knowing that the Storm Dragon had *allowed* him to pass.

Curious.

He located the path and stood there, almost defying the dragons to return. They did not. He was going to be allowed to continue. Out of one fire and into another. The Gryphon succeeded in locating one saddlebag, but that was it. He now had no rations and only a few essential items. The idea that someone was trying to manipulate him increased. Still, if they wanted him to move on, they certainly could have planned better than this.

By all rights, it would have been more intelligent to turn back. He was expected and that could only mean trouble. Everything within screamed for him to return to Penacles . . . yet, he found he could not. Each time the thought of going home entered his mind, the image of D'Shay in Irillian reared its head again and crushed all other ideas. Sighing, he slung the bag over one shoulder and stared in the direction of the port city. If he was lucky, he might reach the seaport by the end of his lifetime. The Storm Dragon's domain was swampy; the Blue Dragon's domain was dotted with countless lakes, ponds, rivers, and any other body of water one could think of. Even with a horse it would have been difficult going. On foot, it was going to be nearly impossible to make good time; most of the journey would involve going around places rather than across them.

The Blue Dragon had little reason to fear attack along his western borders. No matter how one looked, the land itself was a natural defense. Armies would become mired down. Only the skies seemed open and free, but the Gryphon suspected that they too were defended. Irillian's master was nothing if not thorough.

Briefly, the Gryphon thought of the tiny, inconsequential wing stubs on his back and what they might have accomplished if they had been full-grown. Only a few knew they were there. Useless for flight, he saw them only as another flaw and therefore kept them hidden. It was at times like this that he truly wished he had all the attributes of the creature he so resembled. Flight out of the question, the lionbird contemplated daring a teleport, but, since he had no way of knowing what lay ahead, the risks tended to outweigh the gains. He might very well end up at the bottom of a lake or in the middle of a bog—or worse.

The Gryphon adjusted the pack on his shoulder and started walking.

VI

Despite the incidents of the first day, life at the Manor went on fairly smoothly. True, the drakes and humans there did live an uneasy peace, but that was all that could be hoped for. It was not surprising that, for the most part, the two races remained separate whenever possible. Cabe was just happy no one had tried to kill anyone yet.

There was no news concerning the vision Gwen had suffered through. The Green Dragon's eyes in the forest reported little unusual. There were almost no traces of Seeker activity, but both Cabe and Gwen knew that meant nothing; the avians were a secretive race and quite adept at covering their trails.

However, one bit of news passed along by the monarch of the Dagora Forest interested Cabe. Here and there, portions of the forest had been found dead or dying. The apparent cause was the extreme cold—yet winter was still far away and would only barely affect the Green Dragon's domain when it finally did arrive.

Cabe stood in the garden, his eyes on the forest, though he did not actually see it. His mind was elsewhere. Becoming a mage, he had once decided, made one paranoid. Perhaps he was overly anxious, but he could not get the freak incidents of frost out of his mind. They nagged at his memories, both the ones from his own life and those passed on to him by his grandfather, and he was fairly certain now that there was a connection between that and another brief incident not so long ago. A chill wind it had been then, one both he and Gwen had felt in the very palace of the Gryphon. The chill had not just been physical; it had struck at their very souls.

Oddly, that made him think of his dreams. He could not say why, but he felt there was a connection with them as well.

He smiled ruefully. The thought was too wild. Cabe forced the idea away and began strolling about the grounds in the hopes of clearing his mind of such irritating puzzles.

He saw a few drakes and humans working to clear what a lifetime's worth of unimpeded plant growth and general disuse had wrought on the Manor grounds. The drakes seemed fairly calm, despite the fact that their powers were fairly nonexistent within the confines of the protective spell, something new to them. They could not even shift to their dragon forms unless they departed the area. Even then, the spell would probably prevent them from returning unless they became humanoid again. The complexities of the spell amazed him at times and he was quite thankful for them, especially when arguments flared between the two groups.

The Manor was almost livable now. The garden, the spot where Gwen's amber prison had stood, was nearly cleared. It was the one place in the Manor where drake and human associated freely at all. There was a peacefulness to the garden that Cabe had not noticed on his prior visitation, most likely because he had been assaulted by drakes, pelted by magically flung chunks of crystal, and dropped on by Seekers. It was hard to believe that it was the same garden.

It had not originally been the Green Dragon's news that had brought him here so early, but yet another nightmare, this one a futile flight from his ever-present father over countless mountains and through hundreds of deep, damp caverns. Each time, Azran was waiting for him. Each time, Azran slashed at him with one of his demon swords. The Horned Blade, which Cabe had even carried for a while, had been bad enough. The enigmatic thing that his father had called the Nameless . . . Cabe did not even want to think of that weapon. In the end, it had proven to be his father's master. That was the way with demon swords. That was why only madmen like Azran Bedlam created them.

Cabe touched his head. He knew without looking that most of his hair was silver. It generally was after particularly strong nightmares. Again, he found himself with a connection between two events, but with no cause. Cabe scowled. It was bad enough that the nightmares had started again after having abandoned him right after the start of the journey here. It was almost as if they had tracked him down like bloodhounds.

The young mage sat down on a bench and stared up into the heavens. Again, he thought about how simple his life had been before the Dragon Kings had sought him out.

There was a sudden hiss of indrawn breath. No human was capable of making a sound like that. Cabe leaped from his seat, hands ready to cast a defensive spell—any defensive spell.

A drake stood crouched before him, preparing to be struck down by the powerful sorcerer for entering his presence.

"Who—" Cabe took a deep breath and started over. "Who are you? Why are you sneaking about?"

"Milord," the drake hissed. "I am only one who ssserves you.

I did not sssneak up on you. I did not even sssee you until I almossst fell over you.''

The mage studied him. From head to toe he looked no different from any other humanoid drake. Cabe quickly corrected himself. There was a difference, all right, one that he realized he had seen on most of the other male drakes who now served him.

''Your crest,'' he said, indicating the dragon's unadorned helm. ''Where is it?''

Though it was dark, he was certain the drake looked at him in curiosity. ''I am permitted no crest. I am a sssservitor.''

''Servitor?''

''We perform the duties unfit for the drake lords.''

So, Cabe realized, yet another caste. First and foremost were the Dragon Kings and the royal dams. Then came the ones such as Toma or Kyrg, who belonged to drake aristocracy by virtue of having been born in a royal clutch. These made up the soldiers, the warriors.

No one had ever told him of servitors, and the memories he had inherited from Nathan only hinted that his grandfather had known of such things.

The drake was waiting, no doubt a bit annoyed at the human's curiosity, Cabe assumed. ''What're you doing out here?''

''I will depart if my presssence disturbs you, milord.'' The servitor began to turn away.

Cabe surprised himself by putting a hand on the drake's shoulder to halt him. When the creature whirled, Cabe fully expected to lose that hand and therefore jerked it back quickly.

The drake merely looked at him questioningly. ''Was there something else, milord?''

''I didn't say you had to leave. I only asked why you were out here.''

The other looked uncomfortable. ''It is easier to think here.''

Cabe nodded. ''About what?''

''What is to be expected of us? Only the royal drakes have had any true contact with your kind, milord. You are—forgive me— odd, weak creatures that we are superior to—so it is said, milord.'' The last, Cabe noticed with some wry amusement, was added swiftly when the drake realized he was insulting his new master.

''What's your—do you have a name?''

Now it was the drake who was insulted. "Of course! I am no minor drake. I am Ssarekai Disama-il T—"

Cabe held up a hand to quiet him. "How long are full drake names?"

He thought he saw what might have been a smile, though on a drake that might have a different meaning. "The sun will have risen before I am finished. All clan members deserving honor are incorporated into the name."

Considering how long the Dragon Kings had ruled, Cabe suspected the drake was not joking about the length of time it would take to repeat his name. Another tiny fact he had never known about his new servants. "Ssarekai is what I shall call you."

"Sssatisfactory, milord. That isss how I am called by my own kind."

"What is your function?"

"I train and care for those minor drakes utilized for riding— though"—the drake hesitated—"horsesss have been of interessst to me of late."

Cabe grimaced, misunderstanding at first. "You are not to touch the horses. They're not meant for food."

"They are sssaid to be somewhat coarssse, milord, but I meant asss—as riding animals. A swift horse has great advantage over a riding drake, milord."

An idea was beginning to form in Cabe's head. One that might warm relations between the two groups and ease his own worries. "Have you approached the human who trains the horses?"

The drake shook his head.

Smiling more to himself and feeling at least a little brilliant for once, Cabe said, "See me in the afternoon. We'll go together. I want you two to meet."

Ssarekai shuddered. "Mussst I, milord?"

"Yes." Cabe hoped it sounded blunt enough.

"As you wish. If I may be excusssed, milord, I have duties to perform. The day ssseems suddenly busy."

"Then go."

Cabe watched him depart, pleased with himself for a change. Perhaps he was finally coming around to this. Perhaps the nightmares would finally stop if he came to grips with his own abilities.

He made a mental note to remember his appointment with the

drake. He also made a note to request that the staff as a whole cease calling him "milord" so much. It smelled of hypocrisy.

Something moved near the garden gateway. At first, Cabe thought that Ssarekai had returned, but then he saw that the figure was too small and not quite right for a drake.

An elf? There was more than one type—some tall as men, some short like dwarves—and the Dagora woods was home to a great many.

"Who is it? Who's there?"

There was a slight intake of breath and then the figure was darting through the shrubbery. Cabe swore and followed. He remembered Gwen's fear that whatever she had seen might have gotten in before she was able to complete the spell. If something had indeed gotten in then everyone might be in danger.

He caught a glimpse of the figure again. A child? The glimmers of sunlight were now peeking through the trees. It could not be a child; the shape was distorted, too narrow and hunched over oddly.

There were still two Dragon Kings whose borders touched those of the Green Dragon. One of their minions, perhaps . . .

He was close to the edge of the spell when the tiny intruder suddenly veered back in his direction. Momentum kept Cabe going and suddenly he was tumbling over the figure.

There was a whining hiss, a jumble of limbs as the two of them became tangled together, and then Cabe's world spun madly. He spouted a stream of phrases enriched by his years at the inn.

When the world had at last stopped rolling, Cabe was staring upward, and into the face of —a drake?

It squirmed in his arms, but his grip, despite his astonishment, held fast. It was a drake—and it was not. The face was pushed in and more human than any other male. The dragonhelm was missing; there was no false helm at all. The head was like an incomplete and ugly doll, a doll that hissed and whined its fear.

One of the hatchlings. The eldest. A royal hatchling, but shifting like no drake he had ever seen. It was more like the females of its species, so much better was it at mimicking the human appearance than its adults.

"You," he finally managed to say, "are going to be a problem."

"Prrroblemmmm," it hissed back at him.

He almost lost his grip then and there. He knew from the Green Dragon that drakes grew rapidly and had to learn certain essentials before those few years were over with. Shifting was the most important of those essentials. Speech was another, and one he had forgotten.

A four-digited hand swatted his face and he forgot for a moment that it was a firedrake he held. The hatchling was losing its fear. Cabe knew he was considered clan leader by the young—at least as far as they understood the term. He was in charge, despite his alien appearance.

The young drake swatted him again and this time he recalled that it was not a human child he held, for one of the hatchling's claws scratched a line across his cheek.

"That's all the playing for now," he muttered. Cabe rolled over and, clasping the squirming drake to his chest—at the expense of his robe—stood. . . .

And noticed the irregular mound beyond the trees.

"Hold still," he absently mumbled to the hatchling. Cabe moved toward the mound and felt a tingle. He had passed the barrier. His grip on the young drake tightened, which only made it squirm more.

This, he thought ruefully, is not going to be a good day.

The mound, unidentifiable beyond that for the moment, stretched far beyond the boundaries of the spell. Any other time, Cabe would have not noticed it or would have thought it a part of the landscape. Close up, though, he could see that something —something huge—was buried here. Cabe continued to stand there, the hatchling still squirming—and occasionally mumbling something that sounded like "porrrbllmmm"—and debated whether he should go and get help or not.

"Cabe?"

Gwen's voice, soft but still commanding, came from the direction of the garden. "Cabe, where are you?"

That settled it for him. He tucked the annoyed drake under his arm and made his way back to the Manor. The way seemed slower, trickier than before, but that was probably due to the fact that he had been too busy chasing "the evil minion" under his arm to notice.

Gwen, clad in an emerald hunting outfit, was waiting for him in the garden and she was not alone. There was another female with her as well, one with the incomparable look of beauty that a few years of maturity can bring and dressed in a shimmering gown. Cabe was sure he would have recalled such a woman in the party and then realized why he could not. This was a drake. He swallowed uncomfortably.

"Looking for this?" he asked casually and held up the yawning hatchling. Let them think he had risen with this in mind.

The drake let out a gasp of relief and took the hatchling, which instantly clasped itself to her. Gwen smiled in relief and some pride, making Cabe feel more like the schoolboy who had pleased his favorite teacher than a master mage.

The female drake was eyeing him in another way. If there was one thing they loved more than wrapping males around their fingers, it was power. Cabe represented an opportunity to gain both. He ignored her as much as was politely possible.

Fortunately, Gwen was speaking. "The dams stepped away only briefly to check on some of the other young. He was gone in that instant." She looked with interest at the hatchling's humanoid form. "Now I see how. Remarkable."

"More than remarkable. Look at the face."

Both women did and Cabe was pleased to see the knowing look vanish, albeit briefly, from the dam's face.

"Have you ever seen that before?" he asked her.

She used his question to give him a look which had nothing to do with the present situation but rather hinted at other possibilities. When Cabe's face remained frozen she finally replied, "Never, milord. I've heard it once in a while. Only old stories. They say Duke Toma did something similar to that, but I know of no one else."

"Toma. It figures he would be special."

Gwen nodded. "We're going to have to watch this one closer. All of us. This is a royal hatchling with amazing potential if its shapeshifting is already better than an adult's."

No male drake could assume more than one shape other than its true dragon form and that shape was always of an armored warrior, possibly because it had been the one first chosen by earlier Dragon Kings. The females could become several women of human appearance, but they would always retain certain physical features, making them look like sisters of their former forms. That was the extent of shapeshifting save for one such as Toma. Toma, it had been discovered, was capable of not only assuming his warrior form, but he had on more than one occasion copied the form of one Dragon King or another and had secretly joined in council meetings. Toma confessed to not being able to retain such a form permanently; still, it was far more than even the Dragon Kings were capable of.

The two women were beginning to turn back to the Manor when Cabe remembered the mound. He allowed the dam to depart with her charge, but asked Gwen to stay. When they were alone, he led her back toward where he remembered seeing the thing.

"What is it?"

"I think—it's only a hunch—I think I found something you should see."

She glanced around them. "If we go much further, we'll be out of the protection of the spell, Cabe. What is it you have to show me?"

"I really don't know." He did know, however, that something about the mound disturbed him.

Gwen followed silently. It took longer to reach the mound than it should have, for Cabe was suddenly having trouble remembering exactly where he had last seen it. That should not have been possible. Then he happened to look down and saw the spot where the plant life had been crushed by the combination of his body and that of the hatchling. He looked out into the woods and, after some scanning, finally noticed the mound again. That he still had only barely noticed it unnerved him even further.

"There." He pointed toward it and, unmindful of the barrier, walked through. Gwen, after some initial hesitation, followed after, swearing to herself that, love or not, she was going to take Cabe to task if this proved to be nothing.

As they moved nearer, Cabe felt the ghost of a chill that even touched his soul. It made him pause momentarily, but curiosity proved stronger in the end. Gwen, too, paused, but for another reason. The mound was striking at some memories of her own. Terrible, recent memories.

"Cabe." Her voice was tinged with growing apprehension.

He looked at her, worried.

"Stand back." As he obeyed, she raised her hands and gestured. Earth began to fly away from the mound, as if invisible diggers were at work.

Cabe frowned. Gwen waited nervously, biting her lip as the first traces of—something—were uncovered. She immediately cut off the spell and, to Cabe's surprise, rushed over to examine the find. Gwen moved near it, but did not touch it. He could not blame her. There was a feeling so unreal about the thing that he almost wanted to shrink away from it.

After a few moments, she rose. The expression on her face frightened him.

"What is it?"

She did not answer at first, merely stood there shaking her head, both frightened and repulsed by what lay beneath the soil.

"Gwen?"

"It's my vision, Cabe," the enchantress finally whispered. "It—it's that abomination from my vision. I know it is!"

When she then collapsed, he was so surprised he only barely succeeded in catching her before she would have struck the ground. He stared over her prostrate body at the deathly white form that his wife's spell had partially uncovered.

He shivered again.

VII

Cabe tore his gaze away from the mound and looked down at Gwen. Her eyes fluttered open and she met his gaze. The fear was still there, but she was trying to cope with it.

"Help me up, Cabe. I—I have to stand."

He aided her to her feet. The moment she had her balance, she pulled away from him and stumbled back toward the object of her fright. Gwen paused an arm's length from it and stared. Cabe remained where he was, but readied himself should she faint again.

Gwen continued to stare at the mound, her eyes wide and red and one hand covering her mouth. She began whispering. "It's real! It's real!"

Cabe stepped up behind her, trying to soothe her as he, too, studied the mound. "Whatever it is, it's dead. There's nothing to fear. Nothing at all."

It would have helped if he could have felt that way. Regardless of the absence of life, the creature continued to fill him with an uneasy fear. He knew what that fear was now. It was the feeling that the abomination would suck him dry of everything he was. An irrational fear, yes, but a powerful one.

"No dream," the sorceress muttered to herself. "No dream after all."

"Dream?" Cabe recalled suddenly the entire vision that Gwen had described. The attack by the digging creature and the rescue by the Seeker. This was the thing from that dream? He shuddered, thankful that most of it was still buried beneath the ground. How long had it been roaming around the Manor? Had it actually been within the boundaries of the old spell? Why had it been so difficult to find?

There were shouts from behind them. One of the servants had evidently seen the Lady of the Amber collapse and now several figures, both drake and human, stumbled uneasily toward the two mages. Cabe made them halt out of sight of the creature. He wanted as few as possible to know about this. He spotted the drake known as Ssarekai and summoned him.

Ssarekai eyed the unmoving mound with great trepidation as he hurried over to Cabe. "Milord, what is—"

Cabe cut him off. "You can handle riding drakes well, I suppose—or would you be faster in your true form?"

"Riding drakes are riding drakes because they are swifter than personal flight, milord. We lack the stamina for long, sustained flights and tire quickly. Patrols are fine, but—"

"Then take one of them and hurry to your lord. Tell him for me that we have something requiring his attention. Describe it if need be."

"Milord, the forest—" Ssarekai sighed and shut his mouth as he noticed Cabe preparing to cut him off again.

"Will the news move faster than you can ride—and as accurately? How many will know about this by the time it reaches him?"

The drake shook his head, but he understood. "I will depart immediately."

"Thank you." As Ssarakei departed, Cabe gazed at the others and grimaced. He was getting too excited over what might not be anything. All he had so far was a dead creature and Gwen's too-real dream.

The others waited expectantly, murmuring among themselves on what might possibly be the cause of the lady's collapse. Some thought to question Ssarekai, and Cabe realized he had not exactly ordered the drake to remain silent. Ssarekai apparently took such a command for granted, for he ignored all questions and continued running.

"A Seeker."

"What?" Cabe spun around, expecting to see the avian leaping at him from atop some tree. There was nothing to see, though, only Gwen kneeling near the great corpse, studying it without touching it.

"A Seeker." Gwen's voice was low. Even distressed as she was, she did not want to spread further panic among the others. "There was a Seeker in my—vision. I wonder what happened to it? Why did it save me?"

A point that Cabe had not even considered. If the mound creature was real, why not the Seeker? And why had it rescued Gwen and fought the monstrosity that now lay before them?

"It had to be real, Cabe. There had to be a Seeker here." She stood up, her eyes never leaving the corpse, her body never touching it.

"What makes you say that?"

"The vision. It must have been an involuntary transmission from the Seeker. Distorted, since it neither sees nor thinks as we do. You remember."

He did remember. He remembered the Seeker who had come to him while he had been a prisoner of his father. The Seekers had served Azran, but they hated him more than any other human and this one had tried to convince Cabe to strike out against Azran if it freed him. Cabe, barely understanding his powers at that point, had refused. Not once had the Seeker spoken; it had touched his head with its hands and revealed its thoughts through emotions and images. Images of Azran murdered a thousand hideous ways. Cabe had never mentioned that to Gwen. It was what had made him refuse, aside from the obvious fact that he lacked the confidence if not the skill.

"I'm still certain the Seeker died killing this thing, Cabe. I think that's what made me black out in the end."

"Why you? Why would it speak to you?"

She still had not looked away from the creature. Her arms were wrapped about her, as if she were freezing. "I was trained to feel the land, Cabe, even better than those that live their lives here. I feel things you don't. I suspect the Seeker was projecting randomly, possibly to any of its ilk that might be near. Perhaps the "rescue" was never real. It may have actually been only how I perceived the Seeker's thoughts. I do know that its actions saved me, intentionally or not. I—I'm guessing all of this."

Cabe nodded. The noises of the gathering were growing stronger and closer and he turned back to the assembled group. "Go back to whatever you were doing. You and you." He pointed at a human he knew to be a soldier and one of the drakes who wore a crest. "This area is forbidden to everyone until the Master of Dagora arrives. See to it."

What sort of mind was he developing, he wondered belatedly, that even during this chaos he was still striving to improve relations between his people and the drakes? Choosing one human and one drake to guard an area he could have thrown a spell around smelled more of foolishness than anything else, but he stuck to the idea. Use the potential for danger to draw them together, something had whispered from the back of his mind.

Advice from Nathan?

Something else was nagging at him. Something about the creature. He had not really come in contact with it yet, but, unlike Gwen, the desire was starting to grow within him. He felt he should know something about it. Touching it, though . . .

It would take the Green Dragon some time to return here. Even at top speed tomorrow was the soonest. He might have asked

Gwen to question the inhabitants of the Dagora Forest, but he suspected they knew little save perhaps the path the creature had taken. That no one had sought to warn them before led credence to that. This creature had been a mole, a digger, and probably had passed unseen for the most part.

"We should destroy it," he heard Gwen say.

"Not until the Green Dragon has a chance to see it."

She eyed it with disgust. "I suppose so, but it disturbs me. I —I still feel like it wants to drain me."

Drain her. That was the feeling Cabe had had. This was not an ordinary creature. This was something that had been perverted by some power. This creature was an abomination to nature, to life itself.

Was this Toma's doing?

Cabe shook his head. A possibility, but no more. There were other threats than that one drake. Far too many other threats.

If I could touch it, I would know.

His hand was nearly upon it before he had realized what was happening. With a start, he jerked it back. Gwen, who had turned away, looked back and gasped.

"Cabe! Don't touch it!"

For a brief time, the old Cabe returned, unsure and unwilling to commit himself to such a potentially dangerous task. Then his face hardened, resembling another more and more, a face that Gwen knew well, for she had once loved that person as much as she now loved his grandson.

He muttered something under his breath and the sorceress felt the tug on the powers. The tug became a wrenching, threatening to cut her off from them. Whatever spell was being cast, its potential was far more than any she had ever cast.

The palm of his hand touched the snow-white fur of the creature.

To Cabe it was as if someone had opened up a book to the past and he was watching a story unfold. He was in the Barren Lands, but they were lush, much like they were today. This was long ago, though.

This was the Turning War and he was Nathan Bedlam.

There were others with him. Yalak, who disliked what was about to occur, but had abstained in the voting. Tall Tyr, cloaked like a priest; he heartily approved this measure. Somber Salicia, a tiny woman of tremendous power. Basil, the true warrior of the group. It was up to him to keep the enemy away if they should come before the spell was cast.

There were others, too, but they lurked beneath the ground. Horrible things, twisted from what they had originally been. A spell that Nathan and his companions would never forget; their greatest shame and sin.

The picture vanished, to be replaced by one of the Barren Lands more as Cabe had known them. What remained of life was shrivelling fast. Somehow, Cabe/Nathan knew that some of the clans of the Brown Dragon had yet survived; the Dragon Masters had been too human to make full use of the ancient spell. Yet, even as much as they had called forth might be too much, for now the hunger was turning outward, seeking new lands, and the horrible thing was that Cabe/Nathan, as the focus of the spell, hungered with them.

They were a tired and tattered band now. Salicia was dead, torn apart by the hunger as she sought to halt it on her own. Cabe/Nathan felt the revulsion within him as he realized that he had grown stronger with her death, with the . . . the . . .

The revelation refused to come.

Then, the Dragon Masters were combining their might, seeking to turn the flow back upon the creatures that they had twisted. Only with the cessation of hunger could they hope to destroy them all. Yalak had tears in his eyes; he had foreseen all but the death of Salicia—that hurt him the most. Basil was supporting Tyr, ever the faithful companion.

Cabe/Nathan stood with his back before them, haggard, guilt-ridden. If he had known what it was he had unleashed, he would have never suggested it. Better that the spell remain locked forever in the darkest recesses of his subconscious. Better that they lose the war with the Dragon Kings than ever let loose the hunger again.

The mounds of earth were moving toward them, some as great as the dust-covered hills of this region. The Dragon Masters prepared themselves.

Great digging claws broke through the surface and a mountain of white death rose.

Cabe shook violently as that which had been Nathan wrenched

him from the horrors of the far past to the terrors of the present. These new memories, however, were drawn from a creature only remotely intelligent, though far older than the ones unleashed by the Masters. The memories were fragmented pictures, much like the communications of the Seekers—not a surprise, considering that the first of this monstrosity's kind had probably been brought forth by the avians themselves. A last-ditch effort to defeat some foe—but the Seekers came to realize that the abominations they were about to unleash were far more of a threat. Better to bury them within the cold, frozen earth and hope there would never be a need. Better to let the lands become the domains of . . . the Draka? The Seekers would wait centuries, if need be.

More disjointed images appeared before Cabe. Long periods of sleep, of darkness, of a tiny, gnawing hunger. Awakening in the cold, hearing the rasping voice of the new master. Knowing joyfully that soon there would be a chance to appease the hunger—if they could appease the hunger of their master first.

A few had been given freedom. They had only to obey the cold ones, the dead ones of the master.

Disobedience! The hunger had been too strong and there was life to the south—but the One They Served had known and punished most of those who had disobeyed! It was not yet time, He had cried angrily at them! Better to flee to the horrid warmth than face the punishment inflicted by that one. There was life there. Life to feed the hunger . . .

Cabe fell back as if lightning had coursed through his form.

Gwen was at his side before he realized it. Her hands passed over his body, seeking any damage. He knew he was unharmed . . . merely drained, exhausted. As if the memory of the creature alone had been enough to pull his life from his body. It had not been Cabe's choice to break contact; he had become engrossed in the images.

It had been Nathan who had broken the link. Almost too late. It had been that part of Cabe which was also a part of his grandfather that had realized that the beast was a conduit and, even dead, it retained some of that facility.

Given a little more time, it would have drained him of everything—all for the one it still sought to serve in death.

Death, cold, and magic of the highest, most dangerous caliber. The images explained much to him. This creature, Cabe knew, had been unleashed by the Ice Dragon to feed a greater spell—but what?

Then, he recalled the frost again.

Toma woke to find a somber, bone-white figure standing near his chamber. One of the few of Ice's clan that he had seen. Like his lord, the warrior was as thin as a cadaver long dead. The eyes, bright ice blue, were those of a fanatic, a reflection of the Ice Dragon himself. Toma would find no allies with his cousins here. They seemed little more than extensions of their lord.

"What is it? What do you want?" Toma bared his teeth to show that he had no fear, only disdain for this poor excuse for a drake. The warrior ignored the look. Outsiders were to be tolerated as long as the Ice Dragon desired that. Other than that, they were nothing. Even Toma knew that.

"My lord wishes to speak with you." The drake's voice was flat, dead. The ice servants had more life in them.

This was not what Toma had sought. These were not allies, but threats to his existence and that of his parent. Time and time again, the Ice Dragon had made promises concerning the Gold Dragon, promises which Toma saw now were actually twisted threats. What the Lord of the Northern Wastes saw as aid was just the opposite of what the firedrake had sought.

Madness! I am surrounded by a sickness, he realized. *A sickness more dangerous than a hundred Dragon Masters.*

He looked to his parent, but there was no change. The Gold Dragon lay still, his humanoid form stretched across a furred couch with more furs wrapped around the body itself.

Toma rose silently and followed the other drake. He was led along the same corridors he had traversed countless times before and knew now as well as his own mind. He was forbidden to travel them alone now and that was another change that disturbed him. Whatever the Ice Dragon sought to accomplish, it was coming to a head. Already it might be too late for Toma to escape—if escape was what he should do. It was possible that there still might be some way of twisting his host's plans to his own needs. Toma had not become a power behind his father's throne for nothing. What he lacked in a few silly markings he more than made up for in all else.

At last, the two entered the central chamber. For once, the great leviathan was not perched atop the ruins. Toma now saw what had been hidden. There were the remains of the building—a temple, yes—and there was a hole. A vast hole. Far more vast than Toma had imagined. The entire temple must have covered that hole.

He felt a chill run through him the longer he stared at the hole. It was the chill which ran through the soul and so he quickly turned his eyes away, only to find his gaze ensnared by that of his host.

"You have been wondering for some time about that, haven't you?" There was no curiosity in that voice, no emotion whatsoever. The Ice Dragon might very well have been asking Toma if he was enjoying the weather.

Here was another change. The Ice Dragon had transformed to his humanoid form, looking like a drake warrior left frozen in the ice for centuries. The dragon crest had taken on a haunting quality and Toma could not make out any of the features within the false helm. Ice clung to the white drake's form, so much that he looked almost like one of the unliving servants.

Toma finally found his voice. "Yes, I admit to some curiosity. I admit to being curious about a number of things, though by this time I no longer expect to get answers concerning them."

The Ice Dragon chuckled dryly, but the brief display of emotion only served to put Toma more on his guard. His host was playing at life for the firedrake's sake. The master of the bitter Northern Wastes had no more a sense of humor than the snow itself did.

"Spoken like the Toma I know. Still, I can answer some of your questions now, for the time has come for the Final Winter."

"The what?"

"The Final Winter—the answer to the human problem. The cold that will sweep them from the Dragonrealm forever."

Glancing around, Toma noticed suddenly that his guide had been joined by five other drakes, all of whom were positioned strategically near their master's guest. Toma was no fool; he knew his odds of surviving a battle. Best to continue playing the part of audience.

"I admit my ignorance, milord. Tell me of your Final Winter."

It was a mistake. He had asked the very thing that the Ice Dragon had wanted him to ask. He had not played the fool after all. He had *been* a fool.

"I will do better than that, Toma. I will show you."

Strong, cold claws gripped him. He thought to shift to his true form, to take the battle to them, but something held him back. Something prevented him from changing his form.

He was trapped.

"Rest easy, nephew. My warriors only hold you in the extreme possibility that you might lose courage before you look down. I want you to see what it is that I have discovered. I want you to see what I have wrought for the glory of the Dragonrealm!"

Insanity! Toma's mind cried out. He did not want to go near that pit. He did not want to see what was down there, but he seemed to have no strength. The Ice Dragon's warriors dragged him forward much the same way Azran had toted him around after defeating him in the Tyber Mountains. There, Toma had only felt anger and shame at his defeat. Here, he now felt fear for what the humans called the soul.

The steps of the temple were nearly as ruined as the building itself. Bits crumbled as the drakes moved upward. Toma found himself counting each stone step, as if he were heading to his own execution—which was a possibility. Yet, the Ice Dragon had no reason to lie to him. Perhaps, his host merely wanted him to see what lay at the bottom of the pit. The thought did not soothe the firedrake; he had no desire to see the contents of the hole. Not when each step nearer made the chill more numbing.

At last, they stood at the top. His "companions" appeared ready to go no further and Toma almost sighed in relief. That was before four of the undead servants stepped from—somewhere. Within each was some unfortunate creature, at least one a drake not of these clans. The macabre puppets came and replaced the drakes as his guardians and once more the procession moved toward the pit. Toma did not even struggle, despite a voice within that shouted for some resistance. Belatedly, he knew he was under some powerful spell of his host, more powerful than he had imagined the Ice Dragon to be anymore.

They stood at the edge of the pit and it was then that the Ice

Dragon spoke. "Lean over, Duke Toma. The hole is deep and only by being directly over can you see my surprise. Rest assured, my servants will prevent you from falling in."

Had he a choice, Toma would have refused. As it was, two of the unliving creatures bent him forward until the upper half of his body was stretched out over the hole. The firedrake's eyes were sealed tightly shut.

When he was not thrown in immediately, he dared to open his eyes a crack. From a crack, they widened, then shut quickly again. One glimpse was all he needed. One glimpse, even from this height, was more than he wanted.

Toma knew things were far worse than even this portended, for then the Ice Dragon was speaking again and his words were nearly as chilling as what the firedrake felt from the thing below.

"She is my queen, hatchling of my brother! She is the future of the furred vermin that have risen to defy our rule! A very short future and a very definitive one! Through her and the children, I will bring a winter down upon the Dragonrealm such as no being has ever seen! A *final* winter! One that shall *forever* cover this land!"

As Toma was dragged back from the pit, he noted with nervousness that, for once, the Ice Dragon spoke with true emotion.

VIII

It was nearly noon the next day when he finally trudged over what he knew to be the border between the lands of the two Dragon Kings. There was no sudden change, no marker that proclaimed the sovereignty of one drake over another; it was merely something the Gryphon felt—which meant that there were forces in play here that went beyond the five obvious senses. Subtle ones, he realized, but strung across the land like a great web.

Even before his journey here had barely begun, they knew he was coming—or rather that someone had invaded the lands of Irillian. The Gryphon could only marvel at the spell that draped across this land; it was far more than he would have ever expected. This was a spell of such potency that he suspected it was not part of Dragon King lore. Rather, it was older, perhaps something from the Seekers, perhaps something from one of the races that had come before them, such as the Quel.

Whatever the case, his mission appeared hopeless. D'Shay was no doubt laughing at him even now. Yet, he *had* to continue on. He could not say why he was so determined and, when he tried to think about it, the headache returned again. It did not vanish until he put the question from his mind.

"The bird stands in puzzlement; does the bird think to wait for a dragon, perhaps?"

The words were spoken in a tone reminiscent of a drake's hiss but they were accompanied by the sound of water being spewed, as if the speaker had swallowed some liquid beforehand. The Gryphon scanned the area, but all he saw were the damp fields of high grass, several ponds of varying sizes, and a few marsh trees.

"The bird is blind; does the bird need a hand to guide him, perhaps?"

Something tugged at his right hand and the Gryphon jumped away, landing in a combat position with his daggerlike claws extended. His eyes narrowed as he saw the thing slink out of the water of the deepest of the ponds.

It was and it was not a drake. More like an amphibian, a salamander possibly. The Gryphon cursed himself for missing the obvious. The Blue Dragon was a creature of the seas; it should not be surprising that his servants included all sorts of water creatures.

This was it, then. He waited for others to join the first. They would no doubt seek to overwhelm him with their numbers, for the first creature stood no higher than his shoulders and was sleek but not well-muscled. Like drakes, it was scaled and of a greenish tinge.

No others joined it. The creature waited expectantly, its long snout pointed at the Gryphon, sniffing his scent possibly.

"The bird jumps around like an anxious chick seeking food; does the bird think to attack, perhaps?"

Its sentences were almost nonsensical and seemed to flow with a rhythm. It stood in what was almost a squatting position.

The creature sighed and blinked its very large eyes. "The bird is mute as well; does it plan to stand here until the dragons come for it, perhaps?"

"Dragons?"

"The bird speaks; does it plan to speak anymore, perhaps?"

The Gryphon lowered his hands but did not sheathe his talons. "What are you? Are you one of the Blue Dragon's servants or not?"

A long, forked tongue darted out of the water creature's mouth, and caught a passing insect. "The bird is mistaken, obviously; does it not know about the Sheekas, perhaps?"

"Sheekas?" The lionbird puzzled over the unfamiliar title. Possibly . . . "Not—Seekers?"

It grunted. "The wet fowl says 'Seekers'; does it not know their proper name, perhaps?"

The Gryphon bristled. The odd speech patterns of the creature were beginning to tell on his nerves. "Are they the same? Nod yes or no, please."

It nodded.

"You serve them?"

"The bird does not know that all Draka once served the Sheekas; does it think all betrayed the masters, perhaps?"

This was becoming unnerving. The Seekers—or Sheekas—were becoming unusually active. Perhaps their long enslavement by Azran had stirred them to greater action than in the past. Perhaps they were no longer satisfied with watching the world that had once been theirs.

"Are you here to help me?"

The creature nodded.

"At the Seekers' request?"

"The wet one—"

"Yes or no will do."

The amphibian nodded again. Through a pattern of questions,

the Gryphon pieced together a story of sorts. The Draka, as the thing was called, had been created to serve the Seekers or Sheekas—obviously the name had been corrupted at some point in the dim past. There were even fewer Draka than Seekers now and most remained hidden unless summoned, but the avians had sent this one to await the Gryphon's coming. The Seekers knew about the warning spell that laced across the land; it was indeed one of theirs.

Much of what the servant spoke of made little or no sense to the lionbird, but he did come to understand that the Draka would lead him along the safest path until they neared Irillian. It refused to say what bothered the Seekers so much that they had decided to deal with an outsider.

"What about the warning spell? They'll know where we are at all times."

"Bird thinks Draka stupid; does bird think Sheekas not prepared for own spell, perhaps?"

The squatting creature held out one webbed hand, revealing a symbol etched into its palm. "Loyal Draka will never be seen by the hatchlings of nest vermin."

It was said as bluntly as was probably possible for the amphibian, and it was filled with hints of past events the Gryphon would have liked to discuss.

"The bird is silent again; does that mean we can move on, perhaps?" It was quite obviously annoyed at wasting so much time.

The Gryphon opened his beak and then shut it tight. If the Seekers were coming to his aid, he would not turn such a powerful alliance down. He knew, though, that it was temporary at best, for the Seekers would always have their own interests at heart first and the Gryphon suspected said interests did not coincide with those of the humans.

With something resembling a cross between walking and hopping, the Draka led the way. The ground was soft and moist and stable footing was at a premium. The Gryphon hoped that his mysterious guide was correct and that he was now invisible to the all-seeing spell that the Blue Dragon had shrouded his domain with.

He almost hoped D'Shay had been there to see his quarry vanish.

It was a minor but very satisfying thought and he held onto it for much of the journey.

In the first hour of their journey, they passed several streams, two or three lakes, a marsh, and, at last, a raging river. The Draka was very specific about the path they took, so much as to chide the Gryphon for stepping too close to one of the lakes. The lionbird would have asked what the danger was, but then the lake had started bubbling and the Draka had ordered the Gryphon to keep his beak shut tight. After a few seconds, the bubbling ceased. The amphibian signaled for him to follow once again.

The river was more of a problem. It was obvious that the Draka normally would have swum across it and, despite his aversion to any task that forced him into a body of water larger than a pond, the Gryphon could have done the same. Still, the Draka seemed to think that it was a bad idea.

Too many Regga was the answer that he finally got out of the amphibian. The Draka did not bother to explain what Regga were save that they had almost met one back at the lake.

The Gryphon's guide located a tiny body of water and proceeded to wipe water over its skin in order to keep it from drying out. It stared at the river and then at the lionbird.

"Regga watch the lands; do they watch the misty paths, perhaps?" it mumbled to itself.

"What are the—?"

He received a hiss in response. The Draka glared at him with its huge, round eyes and motioned for complete silence again.

"Misty paths," it mumbled again after several seconds of thought. In the Gryphon's eyes, the creature seemed confused, as if it had made a decision it was not certain about. As if—

His own head started to pound. This time, the Gryphon tried to hold onto the feeling, despite the annoyance of it. There was something not right about the way he had been acting. In all his years as both soldier and ruler, he had never made so many abrupt decisions.

The Draka chose that moment to seek his attention and all of his thoughts vanished as he remembered how urgently he had to get to Irillian. The pounding ceased.

"No talk from bird; does bird think that possible, perhaps?"

The Gryphon nodded. Not completely satisfied, the Draka none-

theless began to lead his charge once more—but away from the
river. The Gryphon hesitated. He might not know the land the
way this creature did, but he did know they had to cross this river
if they wanted to get to Irillian. The lionbird almost opened his
mouth to speak, but finally decided to let the amphibian have its
way for the time being. It could not be so stupid as to believe he
did not know which way to go; therefore, it had an alternate route
in mind. Something about "misty paths" . . .

They were almost out of sight of the river when the Draka came
to a dead halt before a tiny pond. Tiny frogs and crabs moved
about the area and water bugs skittered on the pond floor. It could
not have been more than two feet at its deepest point. Though the
Gryphon could see no reason to stop here, his guide seemed very
satisfied with what it saw. It began drawing patterns on the surface
of the pond.

Just when he was about to finally say something, the Gryphon
froze and stared. The bottom of the pond was shimmering as if it
really was not there. He blinked and it was *not* there. Instead, he
saw a stairway that led down so deep that he could not see the
end of it. It was old and made of crude stone blocks left unadorned,
but it was a stairway nonetheless.

"The path is open; does the bird wish to take it, or wait for
the Regga or some other servant of the blue one, perhaps?"

The Gryphon's mane bristled. "Down there? I don't breathe
water too well, friend."

"The Draka is not stupid; can the bird say the same, perhaps?"

In other words, the lionbird thought, *the stairway will protect
you, idiot*. Where was his mind?

His guide glanced toward the river. The Gryphon followed his
gaze and saw that the surface of the river was frothing.

"Regga!" the amphibian hissed, forgetting his usual singsong
speeches. He pushed his charge toward the stairway. The Gryphon
did not argue, but he could not help moving with some trepidation.
It still *looked* like it was covered by water. His first step did nothing
to help the situation. His boot came down on the first step with a
splat of water. The Draka urged him on. The river, meanwhile,
frothed even greater, as if something were seeking to manifest
itself.

Taking a deep breath, the Gryphon ran down the steps.

Water closed about his head and he briefly felt a dampness. He almost panicked, but then the water was gone and he found himself a dozen steps down a walled stairwell. Looking up, the former mercenary saw nothing but ceiling. The stairs seemed to lead down directly from it. He could see no opening. Turning his attention to the lower steps, he saw that they ended about twenty feet lower at what was probably a hallway.

"The stairs move nowhere; does the bird think they will do the walking for him, perhaps?"

He almost stumbled down the entire flight. The Draka stood on the higher steps, grinning its malevolent-looking smile. It practically sat on the steps, so wide was its stance.

"Where are we? The name only, if you please."

The amphibian snorted, but it merely said, "The misty paths."

"A portal of some sort?"

This time, the Draka only grunted. It waved him on and started waddling down after him. The Gryphon followed the stairway to the bottom and then paused. A single hallway met his gaze. While it was not gloomy—or, as he had figured, completely dark—it was still not very inviting. Menacing was the word he would have chosen.

He could see how this path had gotten its name. Less than five feet down, the entire corridor faded into a white mist so thick that he wondered whether he would have to chop his way through it. What was worse was that it seemed to beckon to him, to be inviting him to enter.

Behind him, he heard the Draka snort in derision—and then moist hands were pushing him forward. The mist enveloped him.

The walls, the ceiling, everything was gone. The Gryphon wondered briefly how he was supposed to find his way through this fog. Then, he saw a vague figure in the mists ahead of him. It beckoned to him, slowly at first and then impatiently when he did not move. The Draka, he realized. It had gotten ahead of him and was trying to lead him. He followed after the creature, but, despite his best efforts, he could not catch up to it. He thought about calling out, but was not certain that would not attract some denizen of this region that he would regret meeting.

Always his guide succeeded in staying just ahead of him. The Gryphon never saw more than a vague arm or backside. If he ever

completely lost sight of the Draka, the lionbird doubted that he
would ever find his way back.

How long he wandered, it was impossible to say with any
certainty. Two or three hours—maybe. The Gryphon hoped they
were at least far beyond the river. Whatever the Regga were or
was, it or they seemed to be well respected by the Draka. Respected
enough to be avoided.

The path was unearthly silent. The Gryphon could not even
hear his footfalls. He even tried slamming one boot on the ground,
but all he achieved was a muted thud that no one who was not
standing right next to him would have heard. The silence and lack
of sights made him turn to his thoughts.

His desire to reach Irillian had dwindled to little more than a
shadow of itself. The Gryphon began contemplating all the dangers
of entering a city directly controlled by a Dragon King. Irillian
by the Sea was one of the most loyal human cities in existence.
He could really not blame them. The Blue Dragon had always
treated his subjects fairly and he could not be condemned for the
ways of his brethren. The Dragon Kings did only what they themselves chose to do; the only other being who had any say over
them was their emperor—and no one, save Toma, perhaps, knew
whether he still lived or not.

The more he thought about it, the more he wondered about his
sudden decision. When the throbbing that had previously prevented him from continuing such a line of thought failed to do so
this time, it finally dawned on him what had happened.

Like a fish on a line, he had been played with and led to the
net—and the claws that held that net undoubtedly belonged to the
master of Irillian.

He would have tried to turn back then, but it came to him that
his guide had vanished while his mind had wandered. The Gryphon
took a step forward and tripped. He put his hands up to stop his
fall and met resistance. Stone, but not a wall. The mist began to
dissipate.

His eyes focused on another stairway, this time leading upward.
The Gryphon's first thought was that he had somehow turned
around in the mists. He looked around for the Draka and discovered
the creature just exiting the misty path.

"How did you get behind me?"

"The Draka has always been behind you; does—''

The Gryphon cut him off. "You were in *front* of me. You led me here!''

"The Draka has always been behind the bird; does the bird not know of the mist dwellers?''

"Mist dwellers?''

Snorting, the amphibian lumbered past the Gryphon and up the stairs. He turned back to his charge just long enough to say, "Follow.''

Evidently, the Draka was not going to elaborate on the mist dwellers. The Gryphon came to the conclusion that it was probably best he did not learn more. There were probably dangers on the path that he would not have wanted to know about.

He stopped momentarily when the Draka vanished from the steps, then realized that this was the same way that both of them had entered. Bracing himself, he continued up, trying to ignore the ceiling that he appeared about to walk into head first. The ceiling—and the stairway—vanished just as the top of his head was about touch stone. The Gryphon now found himself standing near a dark, damp tunnel.

It stank, too.

The Draka waited impatiently while he got his bearings. "Where are we?''

"Destination,'' the creature mumbled. It cared for the stench as little as the lionbird did. Talking meant having to breathe more.

"Destination?'' Had he a nose to wrinkle, the Gryphon would have. Where would—

The tunnel was part of a *sewer system*. A vast sewer system. The Gryphon turned his gaze upward. A huge wall encompassed nearly all of his view. It ran on as far as he could see. A city, then. He sniffed and recognized at least part of the source of the stench. Rotting fish. More than that. A smell he recalled from the past with disgust. The smell of the sea.

"Irillian!"

The Draka nodded slowly. "Destination,'' it muttered again.

"Where is he?''

D'Shay was furious, almost insanely so, and D'Laque knew

better than to answer him now, at least with the unhelpful and unnecessary answer he had to give him. The Gryphon had simply disappeared. The crystal which monitored the spell lying across all Irillian and her surrounding lands was blank where the lionbird was concerned. The few things it did reveal were the occasional border crossings of drake patrols from the domain of the Storm King. These were tolerated by the lord of Irillian so long as they lasted no more than a few minutes.

"He is not to be found," rumbled a voice akin to a wave breaking on the rocks.

D'Laque winced and prayed that his superior would not say something to offend their host. D'Shay's mouth, however, was clamped tight as he sought control over his emotions. He was not quite so far gone that he was willing to snap at what was most definitely a potential ally.

"Is there, perhaps, something wrong with the spell? Does it no longer cover the land?" Both questions were asked with the greatest politeness and only D'Laque read the sneer behind them.

May the Ravager guard us if he loses his reserve, the wolf raider thought.

The Dragon King raised his massive head, water still dripping from his muzzle. The Blue Dragon was at home in the Eastern Seas and it was there that he conducted the business of ruling both the land and the waters of Irillian. He was sleeker than his brethren, more like a serpent than a dragon. His paws were webbed so that he could swim and he was longer than any other Dragon King, though that length did not make him the largest in terms of mass. His eyes seemed to have no color save whatever was reflected to them by the water. It was disconcerting to D'Laque, who understood that some of the other Dragon Kings had features which made those of the Blue Dragon look rather ordinary and commonplace—which he most certainly was not.

"The spell is perfect; I cast it myself."

"Then, where is he?"

The dragon eyed him coldly. "There are other powers than those of the Kings. They may, for a time, be an annoyance. He will be found."

"He must be."

D'Laque flinched. The Blue Dragon leaned forward so that his head was no more than an arm's length from the two men. The smaller raider took a step back, overwhelmed by the size. The room was suddenly filled with the smells of the seas.

"The Gryphon's capture is of as much importance to me as it is to you, manling. He owes for the death of at least one of my royal brethren."

Reality had at last reached D'Shay. He nodded quickly and then added a bow. "Forgive me, milord. There are certain— passions—which I normally keep in check, but have of late found difficult to do. I apologize if I have appeared impertinent."

No one believed the apology, least of all the Dragon King, but it was accepted by the drake with a tip of his head, bringing his snout to within a foot of his "guests".

The Blue Dragon pulled back and closed his eyes as if in con- templation. Both wolf raiders were familiar with this routine by now, as they had observed it countless times. It was the Dragon King's way of organizing his thoughts, of deciding which matters were of the utmost importance. On the surface, it seemed trivial. Yet, the Blue Dragon ruled most securely of all the Kings, save one.

It was that one which concerned the dragon now. "There is no news from the Wastes. Your agent and my guides have ceased to be."

D'Shay looked at D'Laque, who cleared his throat and replied, "If D'Karin is dead, we would have known."

"Hmm?" The dragon seemed to find this mildly humorous. "Ah yes, your little tokens. Paltry pieces of power when compared to the glories of my kind."

This time, it was D'Laque who almost lost control. D'Laque was a trained keeper and carried a Ravager's Tooth, which marked every wolf raider under his Pack Leader's command. Anyone marked by a fragment—a scratch was all that was necessary pro- viding there was blood—was attuned to it. Pack Leaders used it to keep in contact with their spies and their staffs. One only had to think of the person. The keepers, made highly attuned by con- tinual marking, were guardians. If something happened to the fragment, the keeper reacted as if someone had stolen part of his very soul. Needless to say, D'Laque and his kind were very sen- sitive about their duties.

D'Shay put a hand on his companion's arm. "Explain to our host why we cannot verify what he says."

The other raider nodded gruffly. "D'Karin's death would leave a shadow of his soul within the Tooth. It is that part that each of us owes the Ravager and at death we willingly give it up. When I think of D'Karin, there is only blankness; he is invisible to us, yes, but I have neither seen nor felt that bit of his soul pass within."

The Blue Dragon looked on with mild interest now. "I should like to see this—tooth—sometime. Perhaps it is like a Demon's Cup, a spell for ensnaring the souls of one's enemies."

"It is nothing of the sort!" shouted D'Laque. The sudden look of anger on the Dragon King's massive visage sent a shiver through him that broke the rage. "It is from the Ravager."

Having no interest in what he considered the worship of a lump of rock, the dragon returned to his original thoughts. "Whether your man is dead or not, he, like the Gryphon, is hidden from our eyes. I like it not. I am sealing the north shores of my domain from all. I am sending an emissary of my own to my brother. The time for games is far past. With the chaos created by the emergence of this new Bedlam, there has been too much trickery, too much treachery. If the Northern Wastes are now a threat to the security of my kingdom, I must deal with that threat first—and I cannot afford to become your back door at the same time."

"What?" shouted both men. D'Laque turned to his superior. D'Shay stroked his finely clipped beard. "We have an agreement."

The dragon laughed mockingly. "So far, I have only seen and heard of your wants. I have seen nothing profitable. Brother Black dealt with you. See how his lands fare now. I cannot afford to waste my time if my chilling brother has become a danger."

"The Gryphon—" D'Shay began.

The eyes of their host burned through them. The two raiders fell silent. The Blue Dragon studied them, especially D'Shay, for some time before speaking again. When he did, it was with a knowing smile.

"Let me offer you a . . . deal. Bring me the Gryphon, manling, and I will reconsider your request. Yessss . . . My emissary to the Northern Wastes must bring a gift to my brother. What better to open the gates than a prize like the lionbird?"

D'Shay almost turned down the second chance, but he thought better of it. There was one that he had to answer to if he failed —and the death of the Gryphon, regardless of who was responsible, would please that one greatly. "Very well, milord. I will give you the Gryphon. We know he is coming here; the only question is when and where in the city. You'll have his head before long."

The Blue Dragon chuckled again, for D'Shay's true desires were evident. The drake drove in another nail. "No, raider. Not just his head. I want the whole body, alive and breathing. More or less unharmed, in fact."

The aristocratic visage of the wolf raider darkened considerably.

"That is my offer," the Dragon King continued. "Take it or leave it."

After a moment, D'Shay finally nodded curtly. Without another word, he turned and stalked from the cavern. D'Laque quickly bowed and followed.

The Blue Dragon watched them depart, a savage reptilian smile that D'Shay would have questioned spreading across his visage.

IX

As he stared at the quite sturdy walls of the city, walls which appeared to stand taller than two full-grown dragons and which were remarkably smooth—climbing was out of the question—the Gryphon thought seriously about turning around and demanding that the Draka lead him back to Penacles.

Irillian by the Sea had always had walls; he knew that long ago. He had never known that they were so incredibly high or that the smoothness of the sides could only be compared to a well-formed pearl. The comparison was more apt than he knew. The Blue

Dragon did, after all, have the resources of the Eastern Seas to draw upon.

"The bird goggles at the walls of the city; does the bird really intend the folly of scaling the walls, perhaps?"

Even in the darkness, the Gryphon could tell the squatting amphibian was smiling as best as his jaws permitted. It ruffled his feathers, but he held his peace. The Draka had, after all, performed the function he had promised. The Gryphon was safely at the edge of the city. Not only that, but, thanks to the paths that the creature still refused to explain, he had covered in mere hours what should have taken days.

"You have another way?"

"The bird must be a fish; does he dare be a fish, perhaps?"

"A fish?"

The Draka indicated the grate behind them. With his webbed hands, he removed much of the rotted plant growth on it. "The bird is strong; does the bird have a stomach to match, perhaps?"

It was not necessary to ask what the thing meant, for removing the generations of rotted plant life released an even more foul stench than the Gryphon would have thought possible.

"This *is* part of the sewage system, I gather."

The Draka nodded, chuckling throatily at the other's predicament. "The Draka goes no further; does the bird think he can find his own way, perhaps?"

Coward! thought the Gryphon wryly. The stench was almost enough to keep him from moving on. Years and years of decaying garbage, much of it fish, had given the sewage system a unique, powerful scent. Yet, he had no choice. He had to go on.

"Draka." The creature gazed up at him. "Why are the Seekers willing to help me? Why did the Storm Dragon allow me to pass through his lands? He knew I was there."

Shaking its head as a parent might do when asked inane questions by a small child, the Draka replied patiently, "The Storm Dragon does what the Storm Dragon desires; does the bird think such arrogant creatures obey the Sheekas, perhaps?"

Much as it tore at him, the Gryphon had no time to question the creature about the exact relationship between drakes and the Draka.

His guide raised a webbed hand as if indicating a major point.

"Manlings differ on many things of import; does the bird think the Sheekas are any different?"

Meaning that not all Seekers were in favor of this assistance and that the lionbird should be moving on. The Gryphon nodded understanding and, taking a last deep breath, stepped into the sewage tunnel. The tunnel was a hand's width higher than him and about half his height in width. Brackish water rose over his ankles.

Behind him, the grate closed. He turned to see the Draka replacing the dead foliage with great care. The Gryphon cocked his head and chuckled. How infuriated the Blue Dragon would have been had he only known his vast defenses could be penetrated at any time by a creature such as the Draka—which was not to put the amphibian's abilities down. He could certainly not deny it himself.

He expected some last word from the Draka, but perhaps that was an expectation originating from his years in human company, for his guide merely shuffled off, perhaps to return to its home. If the Gryphon survived, which he never took for granted, he planned to see what the libraries beneath Penacles might have to say about the Draka—and how they might relate to the Dragon Kings.

He wondered if once Dragon Kings had served the Seekers? Small wonder, then, that the ruling drakes often inhabited former dwellings of the avians.

The odors of the sewage system began demanding his attention and he suddenly realized that it might be hours before he was out of here. The thought sent both fur and feather up in disgust and the lionbird set out without further hesitation, less concerned with locating D'Shay specifically as he was with finding a good, safe place to depart this underworld. Preferably the sooner the better.

His passage was preceded and followed by numerous ripples as he sloshed his way down the tunnel. As if the odor was not bad enough, he now had trouble remembering the last time he had been, if not dry, at least minimally damp.

He was several minutes into the depths of the system when it dawned on him that he was no longer protected by the spell carried by the Draka. His thoughts turned to treachery, to carelessness, and then puzzlement. If it had been a trap, it was certainly an intricate and confusing one. There would be no reason for such a charade. They could have had him long before now.

The Gryphon continued on, but there was always the nagging doubt in his mind, strengthened by the idea that he truly could not say he understood the workings of the Seeker mind. For all he knew, such a convoluted trap was normal for them. They were certainly unpredictable.

An odd ripple in the water told him suddenly that he was not alone in the sewers.

It slithered down a side tunnel, but in the very dim light that slipped through the occasional vent, he made out what could only be its hind quarters and tail. The tail was incredibly long and probably thicker than his arm. Unless the creature was mostly tail—and the short glimpse of the back legs did not back up that assumption—the lionbird's temporary companion was about twice as large as he. He hoped it was a plant-eater or, at the very least, something satisfied with rats and other tiny scavengers that made their homes down here. Whatever the case, it soon became evident that the thing was not headed back his way. The Gryphon gave a sigh of relief, but kept a sharper look out just in case his visitor had a mate or family.

The terrible odor seemed to lessen as time went on, though it might have been that he had just become more used to it. Light was rare at best; more than once he stumbled, but fortunately never so that he fell face-first into the muck. At one point, the object over which he had stumbled proved to be a corpse of something—human, drake, or whatever—but the Gryphon had no intention of discovering its true identity. It was possible that what had killed this creature, and made off with most of the lower half of the body as well, was still near.

The Draka had not given him any directions, and the Gryphon had assumed that meant he was to find a safe exit as soon as possible. He had passed two already, but both of those had been rusted shut and to open them would have required much more noise than he was willing to make. The third door proved in better condition, but he was forced to ignore that one because feet kept rambling across topside.

After what he estimated to be a little over two hours, he found a functional, deserted exit. Peering through a vent, the Gryphon assured himself of that before climbing back to the surface. After getting this far, he had no intention of turning back and spending even more time in the sewer. The memories he had already were more than enough.

There was a slight sea breeze which irritated his system. The sea always reminded him of that day so long ago, a past memory too deep to forget. His battered figure on the beach, the mind never fully recovering. Fortunate it was that he had not drifted to the shores of Irillian. The Gryphon's tale would have ended before it had begun.

He found himself in a street not far from the seashore itself. A few figures moved slowly in the distance. The Gryphon shrank against a wall when he recognized them for what they were. Guards. A patrol, perhaps.

This was insane, he knew. Insane, but highly invigorating. The chase always was, regardless of the obstacles. It was one of the things he missed as ruler. It was one of the reasons he sometimes contemplated leaving Penacles to Toos.

At first, he was tempted to go back into the sewers and see if they could bring him nearer to where the maps had said the Marshal's residence was. If anyone knew where D'Shay might be staying, it would be the Dragon King's human aide. The Gryphon doubted he would have too much trouble getting inside. Security was more slack in this city than in his own.

In order to move about on the surface, he would have to risk shapeshifting. It was a chancy thing; even inherent form-change, such as he or the drakes were capable of doing, disturbed the lines and fields of power—or the spectrum, if one believed in that theory of magic. There was a chance that the Blue Dragon would be observant enough to catch it. Still, it *would* be easier than trying to skulk about the city or, worse yet, returning to the sewer for a second engagement with the aroma of city life.

The Gryphon moved around a corner and *changed*.

It was over in less than a minute. He peeked back around the corner, but the guards were no longer in sight. Drawing his cloak about him, he stepped out into the open. How much time he had until dawn he could not accurately say, but he knew he had more than enough to make it to safety, if necessary. As far gone as he had been during his "obsession," he had remembered to check the maps for places of safety, places that sentries and such assumed were too obvious to check thoroughly.

For the first few minutes he passed only a few people, late-night revellers and those who made their money in the night—how was debatable. A few were cloaked like him. This was not, he decided, one of the better districts of Irillian, which was probably to his advantage.

One patrol passed by, but far enough away that they did not even notice him. His worst moment actually came when a rather seedy creature he assumed to be a female stumbled up and offered to show him tricks that would have required amazing flexibility on both their parts. His first refusal fell on deaf ears and only when he gave her a coin did she leave. Much to his surprise, he discovered that the commotion had disturbed no one. This district was apparently seedier than he had first imagined.

His decision to locate the Marshal's home for the information he needed vanished as he turned the next corner. It was a credit to the Gryphon's years as both king and mercenary that he did not stop in his tracks and stare open-mouthed. The six wolf raiders stumbling out of the tavern would have spotted him in a second.

Stumbling was perhaps the wrong word. It was true that they were definitely inebriated, but they were not so drunk that their guards were completely down. Their uniforms were still in good order and they studied their surroundings with clear eyes. One of them mumbled something about there being no hurry; the ship was not going out until dawn. The other, an apparent officer, reprimanded the first.

"The serpent's fur's up," the officer reminded his companions, unmindful of the fanciful image he had created. "He's decided we should have the ship out of port by sunrise."

"What about the Fox?" From the way one of the other raiders asked, the Gryphon took the last word for a name, not merely an animal.

"That shifty one'll be staying here, along with the keeper. There's something up, and I think it'll make the difference between us staying here and having to go back and face the Pack Master with nothing but empty holds."

There was an almost simultaneous shiver from the six. None of them was eager to face their superiors.

Little more was said than that. Talk of the one called the Fox and the danger of returning home emptyhanded to their superiors had dampened the spirits of the group. Now they were all eager to return to the ship and make preparations. If they made a good showing for Irillian's master, it might help in their efforts to secure a port here. The Gryphon debated on continuing on his present course or following the six black figures. He finally chose the latter.

Wolf raiders permanently based in Irillian. The thought did not settle well with the lionbird. He knew who the Fox was without even guessing; D'Shay would be the one in charge here, just as he had been when dealing in Lochivar with the Black Dragon.

There was something about the raiders' mood, though, that hinted of a change in circumstances. Now and then they talked of home as if things were not going as expected. The enemy, whom they did not name other than by colorful metaphors, was still holding its own, and there was talk that this port here was actually an emergency measure should the tide really turn against the Aramites—which was what the wolf raiders called themselves.

Aramites? The name struck a chord far back in the deep recesses of the Gryphon's memories. He knew them, knew of them, but, whatever he knew, it would not as yet come to him. He cursed silently and continued to shadow the six figures.

They were heading toward the docks. The lionbird slowed, knowing he could observe them from a longer distance and thereby lessen the chance that they might discover he was following them.

Behind him, a boot scraped against stone.

The Gryphon did not whirl, did not give any indication that he had heard anything. Instead, he moved on after the Aramites, but more slowly than before. When they turned a corner, he waited a count of twenty and followed suit.

The wolf raiders were already some distance ahead. The Gryphon gazed around and smiled.

Only a minute or two later, a dark figure stepped quietly around the corner—and paused. The wolf raiders were long hidden by the night, but the one following them should have been visible. Immediately, the figure looked upward, but, if he had expected to see his quarry clinging to one of the walls, he was disappointed.

One hand opened and suddenly there was a knife in it. The figure pressed against one wall and took a step forward.

A longer, much sharper blade than the one he carried flashed before his eyes and then came to rest against his jugular vein.

The Gryphon reached from behind his prisoner and took the other's knife. "You were," he whispered, "looking for me, I assume. I know you are not a common mugger, so it may be that you work for our six friends. Anything to say?"

"Urk."

"Not too loudly. I have sharper tools than this little blade at your throat." He relaxed the touch of the knife just a bit.

"Know—knowledge is a danger—dangerous thing."

"Eh?" The Gryphon whirled his prisoner around. "Where did you hear that?"

The man, who looked and smelled like a fisherman, clamped his mouth shut.

Understanding dawned. The Gryphon nodded. "But only if misused. That's what you are waiting for, isn't it? Has to be. Toos made that up."

"No names, you fool!" the man hissed. "Didn't they teach you that?"

"You're right." The Gryphon studied the man closely. This was one of his spies, apparently. His nose, now that he had one, wrinkled at the smell of fish. Evidently, spying meant you did not have to bathe too often—if at all. "Why were you following me?"

"I wasn't, idiot. I was following them. Orders. I saw you and knew that no sane mugger would go after six of those hounds. You had to be like me. How'd you get around me? Who set you on them?" It was obvious that the man's opinion of the Gryphon was getting worse and worse. The lionbird was tempted to tell him who he was, but thought better of it.

"My secrets," the Gryphon said with a thin smile. With his agility, even as a human, it had proved no problem to climb up one side of the building and climb back down another—behind his shadow.

"Is it a secret why you're on my mission?"

"I have my own mission—which is to find the one called D'Shay. They were my guide."

That made the fisherman's eyes widen. "I wouldn't wish that for anything—but you're wrong, my quick friend, about that one. No one's seen him for days, except maybe the Lord and Master of this city."

"I—" The Gryphon froze. It occurred to him that he might find information concerning his adversary down on the beach.

Down on the beach? He shook his head. Where had that thought come from?

A familiar pounding filled his head. The grubby fisherman/spy took hold of his arm. "You okay?"

Not this time, the Gryphon thought madly. *Not this time*! He had been found much sooner than he had expected! Perhaps his earlier transformation *had* been noticed.

"Eye of the hurricane!" the other whispered in shock. "You're—you're changing into something!"

The lionbird glanced down at his hand as he tried to fight off the mental thrust. He was losing his human form and, in the eyes of his compatriot, that meant that the powers-that-be in Irillian had discovered him.

Go to the beach of your own free will, then, something boomed in his head. *You will be unharmed. You have come this far. Will you back out now?*

"Get out!" rasped the Gryphon. His nameless associate took this to mean him and darted off. Under other circumstances, the Gryphon would have been disappointed in the man, but now it was better that he had departed.

Come to the beach. The beach facing the sea caverns.

His mind was suddenly his own again. He stared at his hands and felt his face. The transformation was now complete. He was once more the creature that had, during his first encounter in the Dragonrealm, caused an entire village to run off in fear and panic.

I'm coming, he thought at his would-be master, *and my mind will stay mine or else.*

He received no acknowledgement.

The shoreline was not difficult to find nor was that particular beach, but it was getting too close to daylight as far as the Gryphon was concerned.

A boat might prove necessary, the Gryphon determined with a shudder. Over the years, he had grown more or less accustomed to rivers and lakes, but the sea still unnerved him. He could now suddenly recall the taste of salt in his mouth; the horror of fighting for each breath as all the water in the world seemed to be forcing its way into his lungs.

These were not memories he was familiar with. These were memories he had blotted out over the years. Now the vivid terror of those memories came back as well. The feathers and hair on his body rose in shivers.

He was afraid. Afraid that this time the Eastern Seas would take him for good. Afraid that this was what D'Shay had planned for all this time, though that was likely not to be the case. Had his mental adversary chosen to strike again at that moment, he could not be certain that he would have had the necessary concentration to fight back successfully.

The night was slipping away. Come the dawn, he would be trapped. There was nowhere to hide unless he returned to the sewers, and he doubted there was time to reach them. Long before the first rays of light struck the rippling water, the fishermen would begin their day. It was the best time to catch in this region. There was some saying about that, but the Gryphon forced such trivial thoughts from his mind and wondered impatiently if he had walked into the dragon's jaws of his own free will after all.

He gazed at the boats that dotted the shoreline, large black lumps in the dark that might have been an invasion of giant slumbering turtles, and then turned his gaze once more to the moonlit water. *Well*? he projected.

As if in answer a tiny black dot appeared on the sea, between the jagged caverns out in the distance and the beach he now crouched on. It was a boat, he knew, but who was in it he could not say. A single figure, that was all he could make out.

The boat grew only a bit in size, becoming large enough to hold perhaps six or seven people. It had one lone sail, which was open and full despite the wind blowing in the wrong direction. The boatman was still a mystery.

When it became apparent that the boat would go no further, the figure climbed out and began to pull it in by hand, which spoke volumes of its strength. All the while, it gazed—at least, the Gryphon thought it gazed—at him. At last, he was able to see that the being was wrapped from head to foot in what resembled a shroud. Even the hands and feet were not visible. No simple fisherman this. Likely not even human.

The Gryphon rose. "Are you the one who has tried to lead me around like a puppet?"

The formless boatman shook his head and indicated for the lionbird to board. He did so without hesitation, knowing it was foolish to attempt anything else—and was this not what he had wanted all along?

When he was aboard, the boatman, seemingly unhindered by the added weight, shoved the vessel back out to sea. The Gryphon sat down and stared out in the general direction of his destination. Effortlessly, the shrouded figure maneuvered the boat around. Once more, the sail was full of wind, though the single passenger could feel nothing.

"How long will it take?" he asked the boatman.

The being did not respond, intent now on the sailing of the boat. He turned his attention to the sea caverns, where the vessel was indeed headed. The Blue Dragon had gone through a lot of trouble to bring him here and, judging by the tone of the last attempt, that meant that he needed the Gryphon. Desperately.

Why?

The thought of what would disturb one such as the Blue Dragon was almost as unnerving as the thought of entering the citadel of the Dragon King himself.

X

The Green Dragon arrived without warning. No one, not even those of his own clan knew it until he called forth from the outskirts of the protective spell. Ssarekai was with him, the drake looking as important as he could in such august company. They were not alone. By the crests, a good six of the royal drakes of the Clan Green were there. Cabe identified only one of rank duke but quickly realized someone had to be in charge when the lord was away. The others served as commanders.

He glanced around at the hastily assembling throng. "You wished to see me concerning something of great import. Coincidently, I wish to see you for the same reason."

Not encouraging first words, Cabe thought.

As the minor drakes lumbered in, the inhabitants noticed for the first time the bundle on the back of one. It was man-sized and there was no question as to what was wrapped within. Cabe and Gwen stared at one another and then back at the bundle. Definitely not encouraging, Cabe repeated to himself.

The Green Dragon dismounted and handed the reins of his beast to Ssarekai, who bowed as low as possible, which was difficult considering he had not yet dismounted himself. The drake lord made directly for the two magic-users and his walk indicated that he was disturbed. Greatly disturbed.

"Well," he said upon reaching them. "Shall you begin or shall I?"

"What—who is that?" Gwen finally blurted out.

"I do not know." From his tone, that bothered the drake at least as much as the corpse's presence—wherever that had been. "If I may be permitted to include one more member in our party?"

Cabe nodded.

Snapping his fingers, the Green Dragon summoned forth an individual that no one had managed to notice before now. A tall, narrow fellow who reminded Cabe of the man who had pretended to be his father for so many years, Nathan's friend and with elf blood to boot. His true name had been Hadeen something, so Gwen had said. This was Hadeen again, only more so. The blood was pure in this one.

"This is Haiden, one of my—eyes in the north."

The similarity in names startled Cabe, but he suspected there was no further relationship between this elf and Hadeen save the blood of that older race.

Haiden bowed, he, like Hadeen, a definite contrast to the tinier, more annoying sprites that Cabe had encountered in the past. Cabe understood that the taller elves were very sensitive about maintaining the distinction between the two types. Like many humans, they found their smaller cousins troublesome.

"Lady of the Amber, Cabe Bedlam." He looked up at both of them—admiringly at Gwen and in slight awe of Cabe, not only because he was Nathan Bedlam's grandson, but because his hair today was nearly all silver. It had remained that way since contact with the creature. Both sorcerers assumed there was a connection.

"It was Haiden's people who I sent to scout the rim of my brother's domain."

"The Northern Wastes?" Cabe blurted out. The Northern Wastes and their monarch were the kind of places he had heard about in fright stories as a child. No one save the Dragon Kings really had any traffic with the denizens of that numbing place.

"Yes, the Northern Wastes." The drake lord eyed Cabe with unease. "It was there that they found this."

Two drakes carried the bundle to the little group. One of them began to untie it until Gwen raised her hand. A number of servants had gathered, as they had when Cabe had discovered the creature. She looked from her husband to the Dragon King.

The Green Dragon gazed down at the bundle and then at the assembled group of humans and drakes. He turned his attention back to the lord and lady of the place. "It is your decision. In my opinion, they should be made aware of this. The unfortunate within is only one of many."

Cabe nodded agreement and Gwen indicated for the drake to continue.

They almost regretted that decision. The corpse was perfectly preserved—and the look on the man's face, what remained of it —revealed that he had not died easily. Haiden, who surely must have seen the body several times, turned away after a few moments. Many of those assembled stepped away and an uneasy murmur grew. The Green Dragon and Cabe both stared at it with the greatest intensity. Gwen found herself looking away and then forcing herself to look back again, only to repeat herself twice.

She finally dared put a hand near it. "It's cold. Colder than . . . than *death*."

Cabe understood what she meant immediately, though not because of her emphasis. He understood because, as with the creature, he was seeing another time, another place, and things similar to the dead monstrosity.

There had also been corpses such as this in the memories of his grandfather. He had not understood them at the time, but Cabe knew now that they had suffered the same fate as the drake clans of the Barren Lands.

"Don't touch it," Cabe finally muttered.

Though she had no intention of doing such a thing, Gwen still asked, "Why?"

"You wouldn't like it. It—it's like the absence of all life force. As if everything including the soul had been yanked out and replaced by—nothing. Absolutely nothing."

Gwen pulled her hand away for fear she might accidently brush the body with her fingertips. "What happened to him? Who was he?"

"A wolf raider. Look at the crest on his helm." Cabe recalled a conversation he had had with the Gryphon after the final encounter with Azran. The story of the lionbird's encounter with the Black Dragon and the dark wolf raiders and how the Gryphon had felt a connection with the plunderers from across the Eastern Seas. He explained the tale to the others.

The Green Dragon was the most interested. "I've heard a tale or two about such."

"What he was isn't important for now," Cabe remarked as he bent near the corpse. Unknown to him, his manner and look resembled Nathan Bedlam more and more. "It's what happened to him that is."

"He was, as I mentioned, in the Northern Wastes. Haiden?"

"Milord." The elf bowed. "He was one of at least three riders. We found no physical trace of the others save some tracks before the attack and some scattered objects near this one. Whatever killed them was fairly thorough about cleaning up afterward—to a point. For some reason, they missed this one. Possibly because he had been thrown some distance."

"What?" Gwen forced herself to look at the body again. The wolf raider had not been a tiny man. "How—how far?"

Haiden grimaced, remembering the elves' estimates. "Far enough. We think at least one of the . . . the attackers . . . must have been taller than the trees."

Cabe did not raise his eyes from the corpse. "How so?"

"When one of us went to the top, to get a view of the surroundings in case there were more, he found traces of fur. As he came back down, he noticed that there were traces all the way down that he just hadn't noticed."

"What color was the fur?"

"White. Deathly white, like some undead creature."

Gwen turned pale as Cabe stood. She glanced back in the direction of where the large mound creature lay. "Then, it's the same thing!"

He wanted to say "You don't know that," but he knew she was correct. He knew it with far greater conviction than she did.

"Those three were not the only victims," the elf reluctantly added.

The mages stared wide-eyed at him.

Haiden looked at his master, who nodded slowly. He took a deep breath, forced himself to glance once more at the sorry remains of the wolf raider, and began. "The northernmost lands are all in the midst of winter."

"We're not even out of summer yet," Gwen protested.

"Be that as it may, Lady, in the domain where the clans of the Iron Dragon still cling to life, the hill dwarves have burrowed deeper into the depths of the earth. The drakes themselves have moved southeastward to join their brethren in Esedi, where the clans of Bronze still hold sway. Many there are who did not survive the trip and some simply . . . died, such as this one."

"The confusion is made greater by the fact that neither has a king anymore," the Green Dragon added. The Dragon Kings of those two regions had attempted the unthinkable—open revolt against the emperor. Nearly the entire army, including the traitorous rulers, had died at the claws of the Gold Dragon.

"What of the humans?" Cabe asked quickly. In the scheme of things, it was almost always the humans who were overlooked by the other races, possibly due to jealousy in some cases.

Haiden shrugged. "There are humans on the coast of Iron's domain, off of the Seas of Andromacus." Such was the name for the western seas. Andromacus was the demon who supposedly had instigated the gods into creating the world, for reasons no one knew. The seas had been so named because they were far more turbulent than those on the eastern side. "I cannot say what has happened to them or any in the northeast. My brothers and sisters do say that the cold had reached past Talak and is fighting its way into the Hell Plains and the lands of Irillian. They also say that something follows it, something they could not get close enough to discern at the time."

"Of Talak I have no pity," the master of the Dagora Forest commented. "Let the human king Melicard freeze with the rest; but, the Hell Plains? Haiden, you made no mention of this before."

The elf looked chagrined. "Forgive me, lord. I—I fear the lack of sleep is finally catching up to me."

"How long has it been?"

"I have not slept since we discovered this one." He pointed at the icy corpse. "I forced two faithful steeds to death to bring this to you as soon as I could. I am ashamed."

The drake shook his head, "You are loyal, Haiden. When we are through here, you mussst rest. I fear I will need you again before long."

Haiden looked relieved.

The Green Dragon's eyes burned crimson. "The creature. The mound of fur. Yes, I want to see your catch now." To the drake who had untied the horrid bundle, he added, "Wrap that up again. No one comes near it unless I say so. There still may be something to learn from it, and it really is not necessary for it to lie revealed, disturbing everyone further. Haiden, you will accompany usss."

"Milord." It was difficult to tell whether the pallor of the elf's face was all natural, or due to exhaustion or distaste at what he had been seen of late.

Gwen was already turning. She was not eager to return to the abomination's corpse, but she wanted the drake lord to see for himself, so that hopefully he would recognize it and know what to do. Cabe and the Dragon King followed closely behind, the former caught up in ancient memories of another, the latter silent and brooding. Haiden remained respectfully in the rear.

"You know," the Dragon King hissed, "that the frost which my domain hasss sssuffered isss only the beginning. I believe thessse little—sssspatterings—are the first sssigns that the magic isss extending even farther to the sssouth."

"I tried to contact my brother to the north. He hasss not resss-ponded. I am—a traitor in hisss eyesss."

Cabe knew it was best to say nothing about that.

The latest pairing of drake and human stood guard near the spot, their differences losing substance what with the boredom of guard duty and curiosity about what exactly it was that they were guard-ing. The drake heard them first and quickly assumed a position of attentiveness. The man, who had been in the midst of saying something, followed suit a moment later.

Cabe set them at ease. The Green Dragon stepped past Gwen and over to the hole she had created. He caught his first glimpse of the beast and came up just short of the huge form. He squatted and hesitantly held out a clawed hand toward the thing.

"Don't!" The cry was Cabe's; he assumed that the Dragon King meant to touch the monstrosity. The drake lord looked at him and held up his hand to indicate he was planning no such thing.

The mages joined him. "Thisss—this was once a harmless digging beast, I think. Their kind is—was—fairly common some time back, but they've become rare now."

Gwen could not believe what she was hearing. "That thing was harmless?"

"Not as it was just before it died, by no meàns. This is, as you said, a 'thing.' An abomination of the highest order. Someone has perverted its nature. Just being near it, I can feel it attempting to leech out my—this is old, old magic. Seeker magic at the very least, I'd say. Amazing how much of that is around of late. One would almost think the birds were on the rise again." The drake lord's tone indicated he thought it more than just a possibility.

"It was horrible," Cabe muttered without realizing it.

"Hmm?" The Green Dragon looked up at him.

The young sorcerer blinked. "I'm sorry. Nothing."

The drake rose and glared at him. "The Barren Lands. You are remembering the Barren Lands."

"I—"

"You told me what occured with you and Nathan Bedlam, Cabe. I know you recall things that had happened to him. Things like the Turning War and the Barren Lands."

"They didn't understand what it was they had released!"

The Dragon King seemed to tower over Cabe. The armored figure was obviously fighting with various emotions. At last, the drake let out a very human sigh. "Many things happened in the Turning War that both human and drake feel shame about. I apologize, especially considering what I believe is happening up in the Northern Wastes."

Cabe nodded. "The Ice Dragon knows the spell, the same spell that my grandfather used. That's what I think."

Gwen, who had lived in that time, put a hand to her lips. "Rheena!"

"Woodland goddesses will be of little use to us now," commented the Dragon King dryly, "and I fear, Cabe, that my brother to the north knows more than the Dragon Masters did."

"How so?"

"What Nathan Bedlam discovered was only a fragment of the whole spell. That may have been why they were able to stop it as late as they did. My knowledge of our predecessors—most especially the Seekers—is greater than that of most who study them. I may say that without prejudice. Nathan knew much and knew that this was not the entire spell, but what did exist served the purpose he needed it for."

Cabe's eyes widened. "You sound as if you knew about it in advance."

The Dragon King looked down. "I did. I hoped he would not use it, but I knew that he had little other choice at the time. They were losing. Brown's clans were fierce, every drake a fighter until death. Even sorcery can be hard-pressed against such fanaticism. When I discovered that Nathan Bedlam had gone ahead and used the spell, I was revolted—as much by my inactivity as I was by his use and the fact that we Dragon Kings had forced him into it. There had been possibilities of peace, but the Council had rejected them. We did not deal with humans; we ruled."

"What about the Ice Dragon? How does he enter into this?"

"You know of the Northern Wastes." The drake lord glanced at both of them, assuring himself that they did indeed know before continuing on. "What you probably do not realize is that, of all the Seeker ruins—and they left many, being a once vast race—

it is the ruins within the mountains of the Wastes that are the oldest. The region of the Northern Wastes, you see, is the true home of the avians."

Gwen's eyes scanned the trees, as if she thought the Seekers might be listening. The avians always disturbed her. "They lived in that cold land?"

The Green Dragon chuckled, but there was no humor in his voice. "You've seen what the Barren Lands became. That was with only a fragment. Once, so I believe, the Northern Wastes had been more lush, more lively than even this forest. Until the Seekers created the ssspell."

"That was when the Wastes began to spread."

Neither of the mages could say anything. The images in their minds were too overwhelming, too horrible for mere words.

"The worst yet," the Dragon King continued—and there was a touch of fear in his voice as well—"is that the Northern Wastes are the results of an incomplete spell themselves. I know nothing of the circumstances, but it appears that the Seekers chose whatever befell them over what the end results of their experiment would be. They brought the process to a halt, but too late for so many."

"And now the Ice Dragon may have the complete spell."

Cabe turned his gaze northward, though this far south he did not expect to see the edge of the Dagora Forest, much less the Tyber Mountains and the Northern Wastes far beyond. Talak was in there somewhere, too.

"The Ice Dragon knew nothing about the spell before Nathan discovered it," he suddenly stated flatly.

Gwen and the firedrake looked at him and then the Dragon King nodded slowly. "That is as it seems."

"Then I—we—he—was responsible for this."

"It would have been discovered eventually."

"Perhaps. Perhaps not. As it stands, the responsibility is still my family's."

Gwen was the first to understand the look in his eyes, for it was identical to that of the first man she had loved. It was a look filled with a determination. Determination to step into the jaws of the Ice Dragon himself if that was what it took to set things right. She knew what he meant to do.

"Cabe, that would be foolhardy! We need to know more!"

"We don't have time. I know that. What little I recall shouts that in my face. The Ice Dragon is ready!"

Now, the Dragon King understood as well what Cabe planned. Unlike Gwen, however, what the sorcerer intended seemed necessary to him. "Haiden will guide you. I will see to that."

"I only need him to lead me to the edge. I will take it from there."

The elf frowned, but held back from saying anything.

"I'm going with you!" Gwen added suddenly. She raised a hand when Cabe began to protest. "There are others who can watch the hatchlings, and I hope that my lord drake will see to the safety of the people here. The memories you inherited from Nathan are incomplete; I may be able to help. Besides," she added with a grim smile, "no one is separating us again if I can help it!"

The Green Dragon nodded. "Do not argue, Bedlam. While you are away, I will spread the word to human and drake rulers alike—even Talak, if need be. This is something that goes beyond our differences. It seems to me that Brother Ice is intending to create one kingdom, one Dragonrealm, where he and his frosty clans will be the only rulers. The Dragon Kings will not stand for that."

"So that's it then," added Cabe, pretending to be more confident that he actually felt. Despite everything, there was still within him the young inn worker, the one who would have preferred to turn away from such danger and let others handle it. Cabe knew that was beyond him now. He was the one who had to handle things. There was really no one else.

"Tomorrow we set off for the Northern Wastes—and the Ice Dragon."

Toma completed the spell and waited.

The wall before him crackled a little, as if someone had poured warm water on its icy surface, but nothing more.

I still have my power, he thought coldly, *but it has been rendered ineffective here. I am a prisoner of madness.*

He had been separated from his father. The Ice Dragon would not say what had happened, but Toma suspected that either he or his parent was going to be a part of this depravity before long. Perhaps both.

"Duke Toma."

The firedrake turned to find one of his northern cousins, a torch in one hand, awaiting him at the entrance of his new "room." After witnessing what lurked at the bottom of the pit, Toma had tried to convince them that their lord was mad and would bring about their own destruction. They seemed not to care a bit. They were as emotionless as their master.

He could still see it. A vast . . . mass . . . of white fur that never ceased moving. It had no claws, no eyes, no sharp fangs —not even any legs. Yet, it frightened him as nothing else had. Just to stand near it was to endanger his life, Toma realized. The thing could feel his presence, sense the life within him. That was what it wanted. His life. It wanted to suck it out and discard the husk like the leftover shell of an egg.

Even in here, far away, he could feel it stirring.

The other drake was still standing there. Duke Toma finally looked at him again and asked, "What is it now?"

"Your presence is required in the royal chamber." Three more of the icy drakes, one with a torch, materialized behind the first. Toma was being given no choice in the matter.

"Very well." If only his magic would work! This was madness! An eternal winter would be the death of these drakes as well, did they not see that?

With two guards before him and two behind him, there was little he could do. The frost-covered halls glistened as the torches brought light to the depths of the ice caverns. Each step echoed forever and ever. Toma realized that in all this time he had still not seen either a female drake or any young. For that matter there were only a handful of minor drakes, and those creatures generally bred to great numbers unless strictly controlled.

He suddenly wondered just how they had been "controlled."

Like a corpse on display, the Ice Dragon was once again draped over the pit, eyes closed. Unlike Toma, he seemed to draw strength from the leviathan below, the thing that the Dragon King insisted on calling his "queen."

The dragon raised his head as the five stepped forward. To each side, an ice servant stood like a marble statue.

"Aaaahh, Toma. So good of you to come so quickly."

"I just couldn't stay away," the drake retorted angrily.

One of the icedrakes reached for him, but the Dragon King shook his head. "Leave him. Despite his outspoken manner, he is as dedicated to the race as any of us. Is that not so, nephew?"

My madness can in no way compare with yours! Toma wanted to shout, but thought better of it. Instead, he bowed slightly and replied, "The reign of the Dragon Kings has always been utmost in my mind, milord."

"I thought as much. That is why I hope you will forgive me as time goes on. I know that eventually you will see that what I do is the right decision—the only decision—where our race is concerned. This foul system of cycle after cycle—one race overwhelming the previous only to be eventually overwhelmed by successors of their own—must cease. Humanity will never rule the Dragonrealms; they will not survive another year!"

The Ice Dragon's eyes glistened, the most life Toma had seen yet in the behemoth. He turned to one of the unliving servants and nodded. It and its counterpart made their way to the small group of drakes and Toma was certain it was now his turn to be fed to—whatever that thing was. He quietly cursed all those he felt responsible for his presence here: Cabe Bedlam, the Lady of the Amber, Azran Bedlam, the Gryphon, the cowardly Dragon Kings—everyone but himself. He even found himself blaming his father.

It was a shock then, when, instead of taking him to the pit, the servants instead merely held him by the arms. They needn't have bothered with that measure. Toma knew that without his sorcery he was helpless here. He could not even shift to his true shape.

Things grew even more puzzling when the four icedrakes marched forward and up the crumbling steps of the ruined Seeker structure. As they neared the top, the Ice Dragon crawled off the pit and over to one side. The drakes did not turn to watch; they continued to march until they were at the edge of the hole.

Toma shook his head. This could not be happening! They wouldn't!

"For the glory of the race," the Ice Dragon whispered, though his words carried through the entire chamber.

One by one, the four drakes stepped off the edge of the pit and vanished into the depths. There were not even any screams, Toma noted with great unease. It was as if . . . this was what they'd wanted.

The Ice Dragon was addressing him. "There is loyalty, Toma. There is the faith that will mean the end for our would-be successors. The last four have given themselves over so that my power can grow."

"The last . . . four?" The firedrake's eyes were wide crimson suns and his mouth gaped open, revealing long, sharp teeth designed for tearing and a forked tongue that darted nervously to and fro. "All of your clans—dams, warriors, and hatchlings—all of them?"

"The last of the minor drakes went no more than an hour before. These were my most trusted warriors, these four. They were to be last so that they could witness the culmination of my researches, researches begun in the days of the Turning War."

Hands of the coldest ice gripped Toma harder, though he had made no move.

"I have decided that it is time to release all of my children, my selves, out into the realms, nephew. They will draw the life from the land and make me stronger. Already my spell spreads across the northern countries and even touches as far south as the forest lands of cursed Green. With all my children loose, I will bring forth a winter like none has ever witnessed before. . . ."

". . . and that none shall live to witness ever again."

None . . .

Toma hissed nervously. None. Not even the clans of the Ice Dragon—which no longer existed. This was not a mad plan of conquest. This was death for everything. Everything. If the Dragon Kings could not rule, the Ice Dragon was saying, then no one would.

He had to escape, had to find help. All of his dreams were dying and he would soon be joining them, he knew, unless he found allies of power—like Cabe Bedlam.

All he had to do first was escape from the chilly depths of the Dragon King's caverns.

The Ice Dragon chose that moment to rise to his full height. The servants forced Toma's head back, so that he was forced to watch the drake lord's face, which was the picture of death itself, so lifeless did it appear.

The Ice Dragon hissed something that, even with his booming voice, was unintelligible to Toma.

The thing in the pit began to stir. Toma briefly felt the touch of the leeching force, but something—his host, he realized belatedly—turned its attention elsewhere.

Toma screamed as thousands of hungry minds cried out at the shock of being full wakened and freed. The two unliving servants strengthened their grip on him—a good thing, for he nearly lost consciousness.

It's too late, he thought through a battered mind, *it's too late*.

XI

The Gryphon had been promised things, but all he had received so far was food, wine, and countless glares from the drakes that served the Blue Dragon. He was not even in the main caverns; the boatman had deposited him in what could only be termed a waiting area.

Waiting for what? he wondered idly.

Left to his own musings, he turned his attention to other things. The Draka may have lied or perhaps been lied to. Maybe the amphibian had indeed believed it was serving its masters or maybe its true master was a Dragon King. The speculation was pointless, but it kept creeping into the lionbird's mind. It had seemed to believe what it said.

The Storm Dragon, on the other claw, *was* indeed a part of this. That much the Gryphon knew. The other dragon had toyed with him, revealed to him that he could have had the Gryphon at any time yet had let him pass. The lionbird doubted, however, that the two drakes were working that close. None of the Dragon Kings really trusted one another or else some of them would have answered Silver's call for unity. The Storm Dragon had also always been one of the most independent.

His surroundings were extravagent, albeit a bit bizarre. A cavern decorated with items that had been scavenged from the seas, by the looks of them. Treasures that would have otherwise vanished from the sight of all, ancient statues, magnificent coral displays, even tapestries of such superb quality that the lionbird almost had the feeling the merpeople depicted were about to leap out at him. For his comfort, chairs and cushions had been provided.

It had almost been sunrise when the boat reached the rocky formations that were the above-water portion of the caverns. The Gryphon had expected the boatman to drop him off on one of the jagged shoals, but, as they rounded the caverns, he saw that there was a tiny beach on one side, with a cave that was not the product of nature lying about ten yards in from the shore. The boatman brought the vessel ashore, once again displaying remarkable strength but not one bit of his form.

At that point, two drakes had ushered the Gryphon into this place. They were sleeker than their cousins and possibly taller, with a hint of blue in their skin color. His needs would be taken care of, one of them had finally said with slight disdain, while he waited for the summons of the lord. He had waited almost an entire day so far.

He heard someone approach but, after all this time, he had no intention of standing up unless he had to. There had been too many disappointments already.

They were drake warriors. The nearest one carried a wicked barbed spear that was pointed directly toward the Gryphon. "You will come with us."

"Your lord wishes to see me at last, I gather."

"He has found time for you, yesss. Please ssstand ssso that we may assure ourselves of your good will."

They had searched him earlier, but he relented in the name of time, which he knew was running out. He had been stripped of his weapons and his few surviving supplies already; they had examined but had not taken the chains around his neck, thinking them perhaps religious ornaments or signs of vanity. The lionbird refrained from showing any pleasure, as they had left him his most powerful weapon if it came to fighting. Even the Blue Dragon's sorcery was not enough to fully contain the power within the charms. One such charm had devastated the first major assault by the drakes during the brief siege of Penacles.

When the guards were satisfied that he had not succeeded in hiding some weapon from the first search, he was led deeper into the caverns to a staircase which spiraled downward, ending somewhere in the blackness of the earth. The view reminded him uncomfortably of the misty paths the Draka had unveiled. The Gryphon looked at the drakes expectantly. One produced an unlit torch and offered it to him. He tried to start a fire, but nothing happened. His powers, as he suspected, were being suppressed. The Dragon King was taking no chances. The lesson over, one of the guards took the torch and lit it with an odd flint apparatus. Whatever the Blue Dragon was using to suppress the lionbird's powers evidently affected a general area and not him specifically.

The torch was almost shoved back into his face. The blue pallor of the drakes was more evident now, as was the fact that their armor was smoother, less scaled than their landbound cousins. Other than that, they were similar to any other drake.

"Down. All the way."

That surprised him. "Alone?"

One of the drakes grinned evilly. The Gryphon, who had faced Dragon Kings, was not impressed. Like many drakes, this one had teeth that were sharp, but more human than predatory. Its tongue, which darted out once, was only slightly forked.

The scholar within him was taking too much control, apparently, because the guard with the spear poked him in the side with the blunt end. "Frightened or not, you will go down now if we have to throw you!"

The Gryphon glared at them and began to descend, his scholar's mind making one last note concerning the well-trained speech patterns. There was more interaction between drake and human in Irillian than in most of the other areas of the Dragonrealm, and therefore the drakes spoke with either little or no hiss, save when terribly excited.

Down and down he went and the stairway continued to spiral

with no end in sight. Wryly, he wondered whether this was some mind-numbing test on the part of his host, a test to see if the Gryphon, or any other visitor for that matter, could be worn down in advance. Certainly a tired foe was preferable to one ready for any trick.

To his surprise, the bottom of the stairway materialized only a few minutes later. The Gryphon refused to give the Blue Dragon a sigh of relief, though he knew the drake could probably sense his emotional condition with whatever it was he had used on him.

"Halt."

Two more drakes, identical in every way to the two above, blocked his path with the same spears as the one above had held. The Gryphon stood there, torch in hand, and waited.

"Let him enter." The voice was booming, and sounded as if the speaker had not quite finished swallowing a long drink of water.

The guards pulled back their spears, one of them holding out his free hand for the Gryphon's torch. There would be no need of it here, for something in the walls ahead glowed. The Gryphon relinquished the torch and stepped forward to meet the Blue Dragon.

There were those who thought the master of Irillian might be the basis for the Dragon of the Depths, the closest thing to a ruling god for the drakes. That was foolishness, of course; the other Dragon Kings would certainly not have worshiped one of their own brethren, and the legend of the Dragon of the Depths, said by some to be the progenitor of all drakes, would have been far older than the Dragon Kings. However much they might deny it, the drake lords were mortal in the end.

"Welcome, Lord Gryphon. Thank you for coming so . . . willingly," the great dragon bellowed politely.

The polite tone was what worried the lionbird most now. There was no reason for the Dragon King to be civil with him. "Greetings, Lord of Irillian by the Sea and her surrounding domain. I should like to discuss my rather *extreme* willingness with you at some point in the conversation—once, that is, we have dealt with the matters you wished to discuss."

The Blue Dragon gave him a toothy smile. It was not quite as bad as facing the Black Dragon, but not much better. He was surprised by the more serpentine form of the Dragon King, but not very much so. It made sense, considering his domain.

"The Aramite called D'Shay will be sorry he missed you," the drake lord added.

"Where is he, then?" The Gryphon expected the aristocratic raider to step from the shadows at any moment, but the only things he saw were the dragon and glowing walls. Walls that had been carved out by someone.

"Out in Irillian's countryside, I imagine, searching desperately for you and trying to think of some excuse to murder you while still satisfying my demands—which were to keep you alive for the moment."

The Gryphon was perplexed, but calmly answered, "I'm supposed to be grateful to you, I guess."

"Yessss . . ." The Blue Dragon slipped momentarily into a more drakish mode of speech. "Ssssimpleton! The one called D'Shay thinks too highly of himself."

"Many are like that."

The dragon eyed him, pondering whether he should feel insulted or not. At last, he decided to ignore the remark. "Your pasts have intermingled more than once, I understand. I could say more, but then I would lose one of my bargaining chips." The Dragon King closed his eyes and seemed so concentrate.

"Bargaining chips?" The Gryphon finally said, in order to fill the void of silence, "Bargaining for what?"

The eyes opened and they seemed to have no color of their own, for they matched the blue-green glow of the walls perfectly.

"First I shall prove my honesty by explaining what has brought you here. Please, have a seat." With his head, the leviathan indicated a chair that had not been there a moment before.

The Gryphon shook his head. "I prefer to stand for now."

"The poised hunter. Excellent. You will need to be sharp."

"You were explaining . . ."

The dragon nodded. "I have been planning for weeks. My plan was aided by the sudden appearance of the Aramites, who no longer felt secure with their deal with brother Black. Lochivar. As *you* well know, he is not very stable at the moment."

The lionbird inclined his head momentarily. The Black Dragon's problems stemmed partly from a throat wound that the Gryphon himself had delivered with one of Azran's demon blades.

"To continue . . ." The Blue Dragon stretched his wings, which seemed more appropriate for swimming swiftly through the water than for flying. "I had detected something amiss in the Northern Wastes. Brother Ice refuses contact, and every spy, including an arrogant raider sent by D'Shay to negotiate with him, has disappeared. I know a little more than the Aramites suspect and I know that whatever Ice plans, it will be the death of us all."

The dragon paused, as if awaiting a response from the Gryphon. The lionbird finally shrugged. "You say we face a threat from the master of the Northern Wastes. Nothing else. I suspect you are correct in that assumption, but I could do with a little more background if you truly desire my aid, which is what I gather."

"You gather correctly. I know a little and what little I know frightens me. My powers are strong and I am aided by a number of artifacts left behind by the Seekers and, before them, the Quel: the spell which covers like a sheet my domain, and a crystal which allows me to see anything that has disturbed the spell and also can reach out and touch the minds of others. In the latter case, it can either draw knowledge from you or emphasize some emotion that I choose; in your instance, your desire to capture D'Shay and find out what he truly knows about your past. It was wearying and I cannot do it for very long, especially with a mind as strong as yours. Still, once you set out, you worked partially under the assumption that you were in your right mind and that made my own task easier."

"What of the Draka?"

The Blue Dragon grimaced; a disturbing sight, as it appeared as if he had just eaten something or someone that disagreed with him. "The Draka thinks it obeyed its masters—and perhaps it did, since once I felt the touch of a Seeker's mind, only to have it pull away with a sense of satisfaction. Who knows? I, too, may be being manipulated. I found the creature useful when I discovered that he had a way of getting you here without the wolf raiders knowing. Tell me—what are the misty paths like?"

Waving the question aside, the Gryphon asked, "What about D'Shay? What purpose was there in including him?"

"That should be obvious. D'Shay was bait. You certainly wouldn't have come here if he had been in Lochivar. You almost certainly would not have come here if I had asked you. At the same time, his presence gave me a bargaining chip to use against my brethren, Black and Storm. Storm wanted your head, but not if it meant allowing the raiders to establish a permanent base, which I would never have allowed anyway—not that he needed to know that. Black needs the Aramites' prisoners for his armies and if I give them a port here, the raiders will not bother to deal with him again. In return for my 'promise' to turn them away, Black would neither hinder you nor attempt some foolish assault on Penacles—which might have worked, much to our detriment."

The Gryphon nodded, a conclusion forming. "It sounds, then, as if it's actually the libraries you want."

"I hope you do not feel offended." The Dragon King gave his "guest" a brief, toothy, smile. "In the end, yes. The libraries are the oldest artifacts in the Dragonrealms. They actually predate the Seekers and the Quel and two other races I know. I often suspect that when the final day comes, the only thing remaining will be the libraries."

"Then it's a truce you want."

"Yesss, a truce. A temporary one, for now."

Cocking his head to one side, the Gryphon eyed the dragon. "If you'd have offered anything more I wouldn't have even considered it."

"I can still give you D'Shay, if you like. I have no use for him and I have no desire to see a wave of wolfhelms marching across the countryside."

"Now, you're pressing your credibility." They had slipped into an exchange between two heads of state rather than two mortal enemies. The Gryphon had great respect for the Blue Dragon's capabilities, even his leadership, for the people of Irillian were probably nearly as satisfied with the rule of the dragon as those who lived within the domain of the Green Dragon or the Gryphon. Certainly, it would have been difficult to convince them at this time that overthrowing the drake was to their benefit, especially since their city would then become a battlefield.

"Let me offer this, then," the lord of Irillian replied. "I shall deport the raiders from my domain. Whether you pursue them from there is up to you.''

He would go that far, the lionbird knew. No one but the Black Dragon had any interest in the foreigners, and Black was only interested in replenishing his armies of zombie-like fanatics, slaves to the Gray Mists.

''My abilities are at your command, Lord Gryphon. I don't know what Ice plans, but my loyalty is first and foremost to my domain, despite what you might have heard.''

The Gryphon considered. The libraries could indeed be of assistance and, if what the Blue Dragon said was true, time was of the essence. With the last thought came a sudden disturbing notion. His eyes narrowed as he looked up at the leviathan. ''How do I know you are not attempting to influence me now?''

The dragon laughed wholeheartedly. ''You are as distrusting as they say . . . which is probably why you still rule. Wait.''

Rising to near his full height, the Blue Dragon made his way to the center of the chamber, forcing his guest to back up considerably. The dragon closed his eyes.

The chamber became terribly warm. The Gryphon's eyes widened, for he saw that the Dragon King was literally melting away before his eyes . . . yet, the flesh which flowed from the drake lord seemed to dwindle to nothing before it touched the floor. The massive wings folded, then shriveled, shrinking to nothing. The tail pulled into the dragon's body and the legs and foreclaws straightened and shrank, the claws becoming sharply nailed hands. The chest sank in, then readjusted itself, taking on the aspect of an armored human chest.

Most disturbing of all was the face. The neck shrank to nothing as the Blue Dragon's features slid *upward* from his face, leaving in their place a hollow depression which gradually formed a face-concealing helm. Two reflective eyes stared out and a humanish mouth formed, from which sharp teeth could be seen. The dragon visage, shrunken to less than a tenth of its size, continued to slide upward until it was now almost at the top of the pseudo-helm. In a moment the skin of the figure adjusted itself, looking for all the world like the finest scale armor.

The now-humanoid Dragon King studied his temporary ally with some curiosity. ''You have never seen us shift form before?''

"Not this close. Not in this much detail. Battle doesn't allow the time to study."

"How true, how sad." There was no mockery in the drake's tone. "If you will now follow me, I will give you the proof of your free will in this matter."

The Blue Dragon led him behind the space where earlier his dragon form had lain. There was a passage there that the Gryphon had not been able to see before. Like the chamber they had just departed, the walls glowed. It gave them both a rather sickly pallor, he noticed for the first time.

"What make the walls give off such light?"

The drake stopped, reached out, and rubbed a finger against the wall. Some of the glow came off on his hand. He showed it to his guest. "A sea moss, from the dark depths. The light is part of its living process, though I cannot say exactly what purpose it serves. I only know that if the glow is gone, the moss is dead. I have used my power to adapt it for this use. As long as it serves my purposes, I am satisfied. This"—he held up the finger covered with moss— "is only the least of the treasures of the seas. The beauty of the land is nothing compared with the beauty beneath the waves."

With that said, the drake gently wiped his finger off and continued on. He had his back turned completely to the Gryphon, as if offering such trust as proof of his good intentions. The lionbird reminded himself that even if he should succeed in slaying the Dragon King, he would still have to fight his way out and swim to shore, not something which appealed to him. So far, he trusted the drake.

They entered a second chamber, this one larger than the first, and the Gryphon heard the sound of waves breaking against the rocks. The reason became evident immediately, for apparently the far end of the chamber was part of the sea itself. The chamber was actually an underwater grotto.

The walls were lined with books, artifacts, and equipment of all sorts. This was where the Blue Dragon actually maintained control of his domain. Here was where he worked his spells and watched over Irillian.

A large crystal sitting in the middle of a wooden tripod caught his notice and it was to this the drake lord led him. The crystal seemed to glow brighter as they approached.

"What I call home is all that remains of Old Irillian."

"Old Irillian?" As far as the Gryphon knew, Irillian was one of the oldest cities in the Dragonrealms. He knew nothing of a predecessor.

"Before the Seekers, before the Quel, this city was the finest in all the land. But it fell victim to a quake of monstrous proportions, so great that vast areas of the city sank near intact. The inhabitants were much like the Draka, so some survived and made use of the area. They were still essentially land creatures, though, so they began work on the present Irillian. After they vanished, the Quel came along and ignored the city. They used these caverns, dug many of the tunnels. After them, the Seekers came. Most of the artifacts here are theirs, some belonged to the Quel. After the Seekers died out, the first drakes discovered these caverns. Much preferable to the city, which they left for the first manlings."

The Blue Dragon dropped a hand lightly on the crystal. "This is what I used, my—Lord Gryphon. This is the power that bound you to my will for a while." He stepped away from it. "Take it. Use it. I give you leave."

If the Dragon King assumed that such an offer would make the Gryphon trust him completely, he was sorely mistaken. The lord of Penacles had already learned how dangerous overtrust could be. He strode forward with determination, one eye always on his host, and carefully touched the crystal with his right hand.

It was cool to his touch. He felt doorways opening within him. He sought out Penacles and saw it through his mind. Toos. He wanted to see Toos. The general was arguing with two advisors, men who kept trying to bring up a needless tax which the Gryphon knew would go more to lining their pockets than aiding the city. Toos rose and pointed at the door, his voice calm but authoritive. Defeated, the two stumbled out.

Good old Toos, he thought. *I was never able to make them bow so low. You should be leader.*

He returned his attention to a more immediate subject. The Blue Dragon would be waiting. He could not play with this all day. One test should be sufficient.

He focused his mind on the drake and concentrated.

The Dragon King began to pace. Then the pacing turned into

a nervous pounding of his fist against the wall. At last, the drake lord was quivering, shaking so badly that he could hardly stand.

The Gryphon let him remain that way and then released control.

His reptilian ally was breathing heavily and the lionbird found he was as well. The Dragon King glared at him momentarily, then calmed.

Several guards came rushing in, all evidently intent on spreading the Gryphon's bodily parts throughout the caverns. The Dragon King ordered them out immediately. Such was his command of his subjects that they departed without protest. The drake focused his attention on the lionbird.

"You—you did not have to do that! I—I thought . . ."

There was no sympathy. "You thought I would be so noble as not to make use of your toy. You led me around by the beak for days, made me forget my duties, built up an obsession that might have killed me!" Had the Dragon King thought it a simple test of control? "Now, you've felt its touch! Now, you know something of what I've been through so you could play games."

"Now, we know where we stand."

Blue nodded, his breathing nearly normal at last. "Are you then prepared to accept this truce?"

"Of course."

"Only as a temporary measure, you understand?"

"What do you think?" The Gryphon asked wryly.

XII

Sleep did not come easy at the Manor that night. Cabe found himself staring at the ceiling more often than not and knew from the sounds beside him that Gwen was faring little better. He said nothing to her, however, and pretended to sleep. If his play-acting gave her a moment's more rest, then it was worth it. To increase her worries by knowing how much he was worried was pointless.

Poring through what books he had been able to gather over the last few months gave him no more insight into what he faced. Some of the books had supposedly been written by one or two of the Dragon Masters themselves. Yalak, in particular, seemed to think it important to put what he knew down in script. After puzzling through the man's handwriting for three hours, Cabe had come to the conclusion that the ancient mage had been in bad need of a scribe, and finally gave up. Besides, most of what the mage had written down seemed more concerned with obscure predictions and how to interpret them. The unfortunate thing was that most of what Yalak wrote needed interpreting as well.

Why must magic be so mysterious and muddled, he wondered. Why can't it be straightforward and tidy?

It was all up to him, apparently. Most of those who could have told him something had died during or immediately after the Turning War.

He rose before dawn, having at last given up for the night, only to discover her waiting for him. As he had done, she was staring at the ceiling. When she noticed his movements, she turned to look at him.

"Morning," he said lamely. It would have seemed rather odd if he had added "good" before that. Neither of them was looking forward to the journey.

By the time they had dressed and breakfasted—their appetites were unsurprisingly light—their mounts were saddled and packed. Ssarekai and his human equivalent, Derek Ironshoe, were waiting. The two appeared almost companionable to Cabe—as companionable as people can be at such an early hour. It served to brighten his day a little, at least. Gwen, seeing him smile, was able to smile as well. Things were not totally dark.

No one else was up, though that would not last long. Cabe and Gwen intended to be gone before then rather than become part of a scene. Gwen had already left instructions for the coming and going of the Manor's staff, and the Green Dragon had promised to watch over them. The mages took the reins from the two servants and mounted. Cabe gave Ssarekai a nod, which made the drake smile slightly—not a pretty sight—and turned his horse. Gwen followed on her own mount.

That the lands were threatened by something horrible seemed more like a rumor to the two as they rode. The sun was shining, birds were singing, and the forest overall seemed teeming with healthy life. Cabe recalled how dull his own life had seemed just prior to the day the Brown Dragon had come seeking him out. Appearances could indeed be deceiving.

Though these woods belonged to the Green Dragon, that by no means meant that the two were careless in their riding. Things such as basilisks made no distinction between those under the Dragon King's protection and those not. Such creatures were always too hungry to care, since they had to catch their prey just at the right moment. Basilisks, for example, ate the stone figures which were their victims, somehow deriving nourishment from them, but only during the first half hour or so. After that, the only use for the petrified corpse was as a statue in a garden. Cabe had yet to understand the purpose of a basilisk.

Only ten minutes into their journey, the horses came to an abrupt halt. All the encouragement in the world would not make them continue, and Cabe's first thought was that they had run across yet another of the furred abominations of the north, only this time it was still alive.

Such was not the case. From beyond the path, a figure emerged, tall, silent, and clad in green, the favorite color of elves.

"Haiden!" Both mages relaxed, canceling their spells quickly. Haiden, who had been smiling at the way his skill had surprised the two, suddenly realized that he had stood a good chance of being changed into something unsavory. The look that crossed his face made the other two laugh.

"You shouldn't do things like that. Not around magic-users," Gwen chided him.

"I'll remember that," Haiden swore. "I wouldn't want to wake up crawling on my belly, looking for mice."

"Oh, I'd never turn you into a snake. . . . Something else, perhaps, but not a snake."

"How comforting."

Cabe scanned the forest. "Are you alone or do we have more surprises?"

"I'm alone save for one companion." The elf was carrying a long bow; he put that aside for a moment and reached behind the trees. He led out a sleek, pale horse. There was a look to it that no ordinary horse could have duplicated. This animal had been raised by elves to be ridden by elves. It was as different from their own mounts as they were from the elf.

"It's not necessary for you to come with us," Cabe commented.

Haiden stroked his horse. "There are things elves can do that you might find handy. I need to ride north, regardless. I still have companions up there. They decided to stay behind, lord, in case there was anything else to report. They'll meet us at the edge of the Wastes."

There was no sense in arguing. Cabe finally agreed to let the elf join them.

"Which path would you recommend?" Gwen wanted to know.

Haiden smiled, this time with a touch of grimness. "We have the wonderful choice of crossing the Hell Plains lengthwise or passing through the domains of Bronze and Silver, the latter of whom is still very active."

The Hell Plains was a volcanic region southeast of the Tyber Mountains that had once been the home of both the Red Dragon and Azran. Both were long dead now, though some of the Red clans still lived. It was not an easy path, for it meant traveling within sight of Wenslis, the edge of the Storm Dragon's kingdom. There was also the possibility of running into the marauders who had assaulted them on their way to the Manor, or even the scattered remnants of the Red Dragon's people, out for vengeance of their own. One also had to be prepared for the abrupt eruption of a volcano or two.

Going the other way meant the certainty of facing all of the Silver Dragon's minions, not to mention survivors of three other clans, including those belonging to clan Gold.

Cabe sighed. Either way, it was going to be a long, hard trip. "We go through the Hell Plains."

Haiden nodded. "I thought you'd see that. I cannot say I'm pleased with either route, but those were the best—unless you would care to climb the Tyber Mountains. . . ." He grinned at their expressions. "I didn't think so."

Something which had nagged Cabe in the back of his mind

finally came to the surface. "Haiden, has your lord mentioned anything about the other Dragon Kings? Surely, they cannot condone something like this. What the Ice Dragon is doing *must* affect them as well."

The elf looped the bow about his neck and shoulder as he replied, "The Lord Green has said nothing about them. I do know he is disturbed by their inactivity—at least what we assume is their inactivity. None of the remaining Dragon Kings trust one another anymore, at least not since Iron and Bronze sought to betray their emperor, and they certainly do not trust my liege, who turned from them and made peace with the Gryphon."

"No, I suppose not." There was nothing more that Cabe could add to what Haiden had said. They were on their own, unless they had allies they knew nothing about.

"Well . . ." Haiden grinned, and his face again reminded Cabe of the half-elf Hadeen, the one he had assumed for years to be his father—*was* his father as far as he was still concerned. Azran had been his father only biologically. "We might as well be on our way. Can't keep the lizards waiting, can we?"

Their ride was uneventful for the greater part of the day, the only nerve-wracking moments coming when waves of cold seemed to pass through the region. No one had to say out loud what the cold was; they knew now. It did not keep them from clutching themselves tight, useless as that was. The cold was within them as well.

"It's stronger," Gwen said after the final time. "It's pressing south."

Cabe nodded. "It's begun."

Haiden, the least informed of the trio, glanced at Cabe anxiously. "Are we too late, then?"

"No, not yet. Soon, though."

They pressed on harder.

Evening saw them near the northeasternmost edge of the forest. There was a slightly sulfurous odor in the air and the trees and bushes were thinner here, as if the soil was tainted. Haiden sniffed the air with disdain and finally announced, "We'll be entering the Hell Plains some time in the morning."

The Dragonrealm was such a hodgepodge of different lands that some believed they had been designed that way. Certainly, each Dragon King had done his best to shape his kingdom to his liking, but even they did not possess the power needed for such extensive changes. Some blamed past races; others thought it the work of some god. No one knew and it was likely no one would ever know. The Dragonrealm was what it was, and questioning its origin did nothing to change that fact—which meant that the trio had to cross the volcanic region whether they desired it or not.

Sleep came easier this night, if only because they were so exhausted. Haiden offered to keep guard, but Gwen arranged a protective spell which she assured him would be more effective. Besides, they all needed a full night's sleep.

That soon proved impossible. They were unable to sleep for more than two hours before some great eruption threatened to burst their eardrums or some tremor shook them like helpless infants. Worse, it was obvious that there would be no letup.

At one point, Cabe used words he was sure must date back to his grandfather—although he himself might have learned them in the inn—and asked sourly, "Do we have to sleep in this domain for the next few days?"

Spells proved ineffective—unless they wanted to totally isolate themselves from their environment. Cabe suggested it, but Gwen pointed out that such spells would drain them considerably, forcing them to travel slower—meaning more days spent in the Hell Plains.

Haiden brightened at one point. "Can either of you teleport?"

"Both of us can," Gwen replied.

"Why don't we teleport ahead? We'd save days."

Cabe hated to burst his enthusiasm. Gwen had explained it often enough for him to know it by heart. "Neither of us knows this area well enough. If we teleport in the Hell Plains, we might end up above a crater. If we attempt to teleport as far as the Wastes, we run the risk of coming face to face with the Ice Dragon's horrors. Or even if we don't, we would be too exhausted if something came across us soon after we arrived. We can't afford being less than one hundred percent when we enter the Wastes."

Gwen nodded in agreement, pushed thick hair from her face, and added, "We can't even afford to do short hops. They'd have to be so short that we would tire ourselves out quickly. There is also the outside possibility that we might teleport into something, such as a tree or a mountain. It *has* happened.''

Haiden quickly dropped the subject.

They were silent after that, hoping that they might get more sleep before the next eruption or tremor.

Very early the next morning, they spotted the Hell Plains. The name was a bit of a misnomer, for there was nothing really flat about the region. To be sure, some areas were stable—especially near the caves of the drakes—but for the most part, the Hell Plains was an area of hills and ridges, most of them including live or recently active volcanoes. As Haiden put it, this was a land where the Dragonrealm's sorrows were given true form. Here, the earth was revealing its pain.

The horses protested, but eventually the trio entered the land. The last trees had vanished long before and the grass here was thinly spread. The Barren Lands had looked more hospitable than this, Cabe decided. He then recalled that the soil in this region was actually richer than anywhere else, for the eruptions often brought up a variety of minerals and nutrients to replenish those lost. It was in the stable areas that the plant life flourished, encouraged by the drake clans who fed on the wildlife there. Oddly, it was in the Hell Plains that the drakes came closest to being called farmers, though no one could ever have doubted their savagery. The trio had been fortunate. What little remained of the Red clans lived mostly to the north, and it was possible that they might travel through the Hell Plains without ever confronting a single drake.

It was very hot and, as the day passed slowly, Cabe contemplated removing his shirt. Haiden shook his head as the sorcerer suggested it. ''You would not like the touch of a cinder on your back, and I think your magical abilities would be worn to nothing if you attempted to protect yourself so during the entire journey.''

''Besides,'' Gwen added with a smile, ''I don't think it fair that I'd have to keep my blouse on.''

''In the forest, the nymphs run without any sort of covering,'' Haiden commented.

''If my wife does likewise, my first act will be to remove any prying eyes from the area—permanently.''

Haiden smiled at the friendly rebuke, then frowned as he spotted something far off to the northeast. "We appear to have caught the notice of the drakes after all."

The other two followed his gaze and saw them. A large body of riders. Humans, it turned out, not drakes. It also turned out that the other riders had not noticed them, for they continued on their way, their path roughly parallel to that of the trio, but headed south instead of north.

"Who would be out this way?" Cabe wondered out loud.

"Could they be from Wenslis? Maybe Talak?" Gwen suggested.

Haiden shook his head. "If they come from Talak, then they are taking a strange route. Much easier to have gone directly south. No one in their right minds would traverse the Hell Plains willingly. Wenslis might be a possibility, but they have little traffic with either Zuu or Penacles. Mito Pica and Irillian got most of their trade."

"Mito Pica . . ." Cabe muttered to himself.

"What about it?"

"Nothing—except they might be heading home—sort of. It's possible that those are some of the marauders."

"The self-styled drakeslayers?" Haiden took hold of his bow with his left hand.

"The same. It makes some sense. Mito Pica was their home, and its also a good reminder of why they fight. I'm surprised no one thought of that before."

"Maybe no one wants to think about that," Gwen suggested, a dark look on her face. "Toma destroyed their home simply because you had lived there. I think even some of the Dragon Kings were angered at that. After all, Mito Pica was not in Gold's domain. Emperor he might have been, but invading another drake lord's domain was still a bad move."

Cabe nodded. "But that wouldn't keep them from attacking the ruins now. Any Dragon King would know that the only ones remaining in the city now are either scavengers or the renegades. Either one the drakes could do without. Still, it was only a guess. I could very well be wrong."

Haiden encouraged his horse to move on. "We'd better keep going, lord and lady. No sense testing our luck too greatly. They still might see us. You were the ones who told me you had to conserve yourselves as much as possible.''

The two mages followed him, with Cabe temporarily taking up the rear. The riders still disturbed him, but there was nothing he could do. The thought that they might be on their way back to the Manor entered his mind, but after the last encounter that seemed a foolish notion. The leader of the marauders was no fool; Cabe had seen that. The man knew when he was beaten. At the very most, he might travel around the perimeter of the Dagora Forest. With the Green Dragon watching for him, to do any more would be to invite disaster.

By late afternoon, the riders were a distant memory. There was still too much land to cover and too little time to do it to be concerned about dangers that might exist only in his own mind. Cabe forgot about the riders, especially when they came across the first of the skeletons.

He had heard of something similar to this, but that was far to the southwest, in the lands once belonging to the Brown Dragon. It was there that Cabe had once almost been sacrificed, only to have his own latent powers put an end to the Dragon King. The Gryphon had told him later about the end results of that action, for the Brown Dragon had received his desire in death—almost. The Barren Lands became lush once more, but with a deadly twist. The plant life that grew there was inimical to the clans of that drake. A twisted perversion of the spell that he had sought. The plant life sought out the drakes, making no distinction between drake lord and the lowest of the wyverns, so long as they were of Brown's blood. Only a handful that had fled to the lands of Bronze and Crystal still survived—so rumor said of late.

This was also a slaughter, they saw. The first skeletons, picked clean by the various scavengers of the region, led to others which led to others and so on as far as they could see.

They reached a stable rise, rode up, and looked down upon one of the few true plains regions in this domain.

''Rheena!'' Gwen gasped. ''It's a sea of death!''

Cabe nodded sadly. He knew what they were near, though it was hidden by two active craters of recent origin. Without spells to protect it, this area would eventually become unstable. Some day, the citadel which these drakes and creatures had fought over would be torn apart by the violence of the earth.

They would have to find another path around here. The scattered remains of leviathan after leviathan literally covered the landscape. Skulls gazed up mockingly at the sky. Some creatures had apparently fallen in struggle together with their foes, unless the movements of this volatile land had flung their skeletons into one pile somehow. The bones of the drakes mixed freely with the dead of the defenders and it was impossible to believe that any creature had survived this massacre.

One had—for a while—and it was his abandoned citadel which stood nearby. Cabe did not want to see it, but he felt that it might be wise to stop there, if only to let the horses rest in shade before they continued. Perhaps there would even be some book or clue that would be of aid to them, for the master of this place had been one of the most powerful mages alive.

Azran.

Toma struggled at the ice that held him prisoner against the wall. He was furious. Furious at himself, furious at being herded from one thing to another like some mindless minor drake, furious at the Ice Dragon—who would rob him of the throne that was justly his. . . . He could not put into words most of the things which angered him. He did know which angered him most, however.

He was powerless. He could not shapeshift and could not cast a spell sufficient enough to light a twig on fire. That was what was needed now. Warm, cleansing flame. To free him and destroy this overgrown icicle. To wreak vengeance on the lord of the Northern Wastes.

The drake shook his head. Anger was getting him nowhere, despite how easy it was to give in to it. He needed to escape, to regain some measure of power. Allies would be necessary, too. Silver would join him if it was known that his emperor was prisoner here. Blue might also aid him. The others were questionable. Storm did what Storm desired, whether that coincided with his brethren or not. Black was a misfit, a failure. The Crystal Dragon . . . Toma knew nothing. Crystal had come to the early councils, said little, and departed each time without any farewell. Crystal was an enigma that Toma could not trust, although that had not stopped him from utilizing the Dragon King's form so that he could spy on the council and see that his words were heard by those who otherwise would have spurned him.

Silver and Blue, then. They could be allies. He had the glimmerings of a plan; now he needed to escape. Toma hissed in frustration. That was the problem he had started with. His logic was going in circles, most likely because his brain was half-frozen.

There was a noise akin to fluttering, but Toma paid it no mind. Like many of the Dragon Kings, Ice had servants that hid in the shadows—un-things that flew and chittered or crawled and hissed—and none of them was of any interest to him.

Toma stared at the single torch that hung from the wall across from him. His "host" had claimed it was so that the firedrake would not have to wait in darkness. Toma suspected it was some little quirk, some remaining bit of emotion in the Ice Dragon, and that the torch was there as some sort of torture. Only a few moments with that flame would have been sufficient to free him, but the torch was out of range.

I am going to be sacrificed to some abomination so that a demented drake lord can fulfill his deathwish! Toma thought madly. He had yet to speak out loud to himself, but he knew that time was coming soon—provided the unliving servants did not come for him first.

Something fluttered again and this time a shadow passed him. Toma blinked and stared. Before him stood a Seeker where none could possibly have been a moment earlier. It was gazing at him with arrogant eyes, as if deciding if he was worth the bother. Then the avian reached for the torch, removed it, and brought it toward the drake's head.

Toma had visions of himself being burned alive, for even firedrakes have only a limited tolerance to open flame. Instead, the Seeker pulled the torch back and reached up with its free claw. It put the claw across Toma's face.

There were images then, of Toma fleeing the citadel, seeking aid to the south. Toma almost shouted agreement before it dawned on him that whatever he thought was open to the Seeker's mind.

Seemingly satisfied, the creature brought the torch near the drake's right wrist. The ice sizzled and Toma struggled to break free before his wrist did the same. Time dragged horribly slow, each second an invitation to discovery. At last, Toma wrenched his right arm free. While he fought the ice manacle on his left wrist, the Seeker freed his ankles.

When it was done, the avian handed him the torch and pointed to one of the walls. Toma saw nothing. Impatient, the Seeker pointed up. The firedrake saw it finally, a hole near the ceiling, the secret method by which the bird creature had evidently infiltrated the Ice Dragon's home. Toma was to use this hole as his escape route.

When he turned back to the Seeker, he found himself alone. The torch was back in its normal location. Toma cursed quietly, almost expecting to wake and find himself still fastened to the wall. He shrugged finally. If this were a dream, at least he would escape his captors in one way. Perhaps they would find him here later, as mindless as his parent.

Thoughts of his father and liege made Toma hesitate, before he realized that neither of them would be free if he attempted to take Gold with him. It would be better to return with aid. The Ice Dragon was not yet ready to sacrifice his own emperor; the timing apparently had to be just right. His "host" was, after all, still a traditionalist.

That settled, Toma made his way up the wall, his clawed hands turning to ice as he dug deeply. He wished his savior had thought about taking him with it; that would have been much simpler. The Seeker's thought process was as frustrating as the race itself.

He reached the hole and pulled himself through. He did not doubt that the servants would be coming for him soon, and now a new worry entered his mind as he realized how easy it would be for them to follow him through the tunnel.

Having pulled himself all the way in, he twisted round to see if there was any way of blocking the entrance—only to find that there was no entrance anymore. A solid sheet of ice left no trace of his passage and undoubtedly no indication from the outside that this tunnel existed.

There was no turning back now. Toma grunted and began pulling himself forward, his mind awash with many thoughts: how a race as resourceful as the Seekers could have ever fallen; in what way might he regain his own powers; and what the odds were of slipping past the roving packs of Ice's soul-seeking abominations.

Most of all, he wanted to know how long he was going to have to pull himself solely by his arms, a process which, he knew, would have the muscles in his arms screaming before long.

XIII

The Blue Dragon chose to act on the Aramite situation quickly. Before long, he had most of the wolf raiders on their way to their vessels. It was a fairly smooth operation; the raiders seemed to be prepared to move at a moment's notice and therefore there was little time for them to organize and stow away. Finding D'Shay and his companion was a bit more difficult, but in the end they were led by a guard of some eight drake warriors to their ship. D'Shay argued all the way, claiming that the word of the Blue Dragon was obviously worth little more than the sand on the beaches. The Dragon King bristled when he heard this later on, but by then the wolf raiders were out at sea.

"I should have turned him over to you," he commented sharply as he returned to the Gryphon.

The thought had occurred, over and over, to the lionbird, but he had forcibly reminded himself that the Aramites were a minor problem compared to what they possibly faced from the Ice Dragon. "As pleasant as that may be, I have no time for him— and we have no more time for this. I was going to suggest that perhaps you should use this crystal to study the Wastes."

"A useless task, bird. My brother shields his domain, and my power is insufficient to pierce the barrier. . . ."

The Gryphon noted the pause. "What is it?"

The drake lord had closed his eyes. When he opened them again, he smiled. "If you are willing to link yourself to me, our combined strength might be sufficient to break through. I suspect that between us we represent a great degree of power."

It was still difficult for the Gryphon to accept working with this Dragon King, much less linking with him, but the lionbird understood the importance of what his temporary ally was suggesting. If they intended to use the libraries, it would help greatly to have some idea of what it was they were up against. Blue had explained earlier that he believed Ice's plan had something to do with the desolation of the Barren Lands by Nathan Bedlam, but beyond that he did not have a clue. The Ice Dragon had always kept to himself, appearing at councils only when it might be to his advantage.

"What do we do?" The Gryphon's feathers and fur ruffled slightly. He was not looking forward to this.

The Dragon King was already standing on the other side of the crystal. The combined illumination of the crystal and the walls made the drake resemble something risen from the dead—a shadow person. "I realize that this is distasteful for you. I care for it even less. Perhaps if I tell you that I was just informed that raging blizzards have struck my northern borders, you will be more willing. Perhaps if I also tell you that something follows the cold and snow, something numbering in the thousands, apparently, you will see the need for haste even more. Drakes are dead—and so are members of other races, including the humans you care so much about."

"I wasn't planning to back down," the Gryphon responded coldly. "Whether or not I like the thought has nothing to do with what I feel is my duty. Enough nonsense. What do you want me to do first?"

"Stand across from me on the other side of the crystal."

The Gryphon obeyed. Blue raised his arms, his hands opened with the palms pointed away from himself. "Take my hands and stand as I do."

When they were both in position, the drake closed his eyes. The chamber became deathly silent save for the water lapping against the rock. The Gryphon felt nothing and wondered if perhaps the Blue Dragon had failed.

Then, a shock went through him. Everything stood on end. He closed his eyes tightly and tried to suppress the pain. There had been tales of people struck by lightning who had lived to tell of it. Trying to explain what it felt like to have such raw, elemental power coursing through your body for even a brief instant was impossible. Now, the Gryphon understood why.

He felt the flow of his own power as it was drawn from him through his hands. It did not flow into the Dragon King, as he had expected, but instead seemed to gather, like a cloud, around the crystal. He noticed then, even though his eyes were still closed, that the same thing was happening to the drake. The Blue Dragon was creating a field of power around the crystal, building it up to a level he believed would be sufficient to cut through the Ice Dragon's barrier.

As the field grew, the Gryphon felt great warmth. He dared to open his eyes and suddenly found himself staring in awe at the crackling glow about the crystal. The pain was gone now, only a sense of exhaustion remained. The lionbird knew that it would be very soon; neither he nor the drake lord could long withstand such a draining before one of them collapsed.

"Now!" the Dragon King shouted. The Gryphon was not sure whether his companion was speaking to him or not, but he allowed the drake to keep control of the situation rather than take the chance of disrupting everything.

The field began to shrink—no, the Gryphon corrected himself, it was not shrinking. Rather, it was entering the crystal, feeding it.

He looked up to see that the Blue Dragon was now gazing at the center of the crystal with great anticipation. He followed that gaze but saw nothing but milky white within the gem. His shoulders slumped a little. They had failed.

"Do not give in to defeat!"

Even as the Dragon King shouted those words, the Gryphon saw the milky-white substance thin until something else became vaguely discernible. It did not seem to be shaped like anything either of them recognized, but considering how poor an image it was, that meant little.

The Blue Dragon tightened his concentration, hissing in response to the challenge facing him. This was the best he had done; he refused to give in now. He had to know, if only for himself.

Despite that, the Gryphon felt the Dragon King wavering

slightly. The strain was greater on the drake, for he was both originator and focus of this spell. The lionbird clamped his beak shut and consciously added even more of his strength to the flow of power.

The drake lord's eyes gleamed as he realized what his ally was doing. Skillfully, he manipulated the power, using the new flow to cut through his brother's spell as a knife cuts bread.

The veil was pierced. In one instant it fell away, revealing . . . a thing of monstrous size with claws as large as either of them! The Blue Dragon briefly lost control and the image began to dissipate. With a hiss, the drake pushed back the gathering mists and strengthened the connection.

It was cold, they knew, horribly, terribly cold. The cold seemed to be both a part of the creature and to be moving parallel with it. As it moved through the countryside, the few trees became first frost-covered, then brittle as the chill increased. The thing tore up four or five with one blow and both watchers shivered as they saw the trees first wither, then solidify. The abomination threw them aside, ice-hard corpses. Behind it, they came to realize, was a trail of death. Whatever had lived there before was now like the trees, be it plant or animal.

Even as the first moved away, another came up from behind and to the right of it. It was larger than the first and no less eager. Try as he might the Gryphon could discern no mouth on the thing, and for eyes there seemed to be two little black dots, perhaps, but no more. This was no natural creature. This was the creation of the Ice Dragon. Living death. Monsters that sucked all life from what they touched. The Gryphon recalled what little he knew about the devastation of the Barren Lands. Something about it struck a sinister, similar note, but he could not say what.   .

"They cover the landsssscape!" the Dragon King whispered in open horror. He was correct, and the Gryphon bristled. They were everywhere, these creatures, and if the landmarks around them were any indication, they were already well into the northern areas of the Blue Dragon's kingdom and still heading south.

South to the rest of the Dragonrealms.

He had trouble concentrating after that and felt the drake lord waver as well. If the strain was telling on him, how badly did the Dragon King feel? He watched as the image faded away, to be replaced by the milky white once more. They had lost the image for good.

With a gasp the Blue Dragon released his hands, and both of them were collapsing to the floor of the chamber.

"My . . . my apologies, Lord Gryphon. I'm afraid my concentration wavered too much." The drake was gasping for breath. The Gryphon felt little better himself.

"Understandable . . . drake lord."

They both sat there, sprawled on opposite sides of the crystal, which had returned to the same dim glow it had had originally. Neither of them wanted to speak of the terror they had just observed, as if that would make it go away.

"It would seem we are too late already. Those things move well beyond the borders of the Wastes. They will be near the northern edge of the Tyber Mountains before long. If any more of them turn east, they will enter the central regions of my domain in three to four days and join up with the others. I must ready my defenses." The Blue Dragon struggled to his feet.

The Gryphon followed suit. "What can you do? What sort of defense can you prepare?"

"I have legions. . . ."

The lionbird shook his head. "You've felt the hunger; I know it. You know what those things are doing. Your legions would barely whet their appetites."

"I have spells!"

"How long before you tire? They flow like a river, drake lord. There must be thousands of them. The Ice Dragon has had time to prepare—or don't you think him capable of planning ahead?"

The Blue Dragon hesitated, then nodded his head slowly. "As you say. Ice is devious. He will have planned for measures such as I would use. The libraries are still our best hope. I will prepare a blink hole."

"That could be dangerous."

Blink hole. The tunnel through the Void, some called it. A blink hole was a passage beyond, which one could use to transport large objects to another destination in only a few minutes, regardless of distance in the real world. The Gryphon recalled the misty paths and wondered if they were related in some way.

"Azran knew how to control them and some of his secrets are

now mine." Noting the expression on his associate's face, the drake explained. "Did you think that I would leave such a treasure trove as his citadel alone? It was abandoned, Gryphon, by those who by rights could have claimed it." It was obvious that the Dragon King knew that his "guest" was responsible for the blow that had actually slit Azran open, though Cabe had fought the bulk of the battle.

"You really can create a stable blink hole?"

"It is easier than you think. With it, we can move back and forth from your domain and mine."

"Can we be assured that no one will enter without our knowing?" He did not voice the thought that a tunnel to his palace would be a perfect way for the Blue Dragon to invade Penacles. The Gryphon shook his head. Old suspicions died hard, although . . .

"I can take care of my end. You will have to deal with where we exit." The Dragon King smiled, revealing all of his teeth. "Don't you trust me?"

"Barely."

"Give me time to rest—and decide where you want the exit to be. Be as precise as possible, because it is from your mind that I will draw the image."

The Gryphon nodded. The Blue Dragon bowed and departed, leaving him alone once more. It chafed him to be forced to wait; his instincts were those of a hunter and waiting only increased his frustrations. He was not certain that the magical libraries of Penacles, which when they did reveal answers tended to be obscure at best, would be of any assistance, nor was he totally secure with working with a foe such as this.

There was nothing else he could do. Until they returned to Penacles, things were more or less up to the Blue Dragon. He settled down to relax, expecting a long, boring wait, and fell asleep only moments later, the spell having drawn more from him than he had imagined.

The sound of marching feet woke the Gryphon. There was no way of telling exactly how long he had been asleep, save that the water level in the back of the chamber had lowered slightly. Tides in an underwater cavern? Not knowing anything about the sea—

and not especially wanting to—he dropped the thought. There were, after all, more important things to settle.

He rose to his feet just as the Blue Dragon entered, the latter accompanied by two other drakes, possibly the guards who had confronted the Gryphon earlier. It was always difficult to tell one from another as far as he was concerned.

"Have you kept yourself occupied, lionbird?" By the Dragon King's tone, he knew exactly what the Gryphon had been up to.

"What time is it? I lose track in these underground chambers. I look forward to seeing the countryside of Penacles once again."

"Charred as it is?" The drake lord smirked. While much of the land controlled by the Gryphon remained as it always had, most of the countryside to the east of his city still suffered the effects of the siege by the Black Dragon. That was by no means the only area, but it was most definitely the worst. It was doubtful that the land would recover for several years at least.

The Gryphon's claws extended involuntarily. "Don't test the limits of our truce too often, reptile! You'll find my claws as sharp as yours!"

"Temper, my lord, temper! Merely a little humor in these dark times!" The Blue Dragon sobered. "Dark, indeed. While we— I—slept, the creatures of my brother have chosen to divide themselves into two main packs, each pack taking one side of the Tyber Mountains, thereby, ironically, giving Talak a brief reprieve."

"They can dig. Why go around the mountains?"

"Think, lord Gryphon! There's very little in the Tybers that they desire. In the time it would take them to find something satisfying—if they can truly be satisfied—they could be well beyond the Hell Plains in the east and the lands of the hill dwarves to the west! Irillian would already be theirs."

The Gryphon sheathed his claws. "They are remarkably capable for such brutish creatures. Surely they cannot reason that well."

"They cannot. I'm sure of that. Which means that they are controlled completely by brother Ice. They move like his left and right hands. One wonders if they truly have any will at all."

"Feeding a hunger . . ."

The Dragon King looked at him keenly. "You've thought of something?"

"Only something that should have been obvious to us. We've felt the hunger, the driving force that keeps those things moving. Big as they are, their hunger should have been sated by now. No creature eats that much. It isn't efficient. Why would Ice bother with such a creature? Surely, he could devise something more to his benefit? It is the constant hunger that is the key!"

"You are suggesting that the lord of the Northern Wastes is feeding off of the abominations, are you not?" the drake to Dragon King's right blurted out. It was the first time either of the two had spoken. The Gryphon realized that these were not guards; these were Blue's dukes, most likely his own hatchlings.

"He is suggesting that, Zzzeras, and it is a suggestion to be taken to heart, yes?" the Dragon King snapped. The duke nodded quickly and quieted, though his stance seemed to be that of a child sulking.

"For what purpose, Gryphon?"

"I would say to keep the spell going, though I may be wrong."

The Blue Dragon hissed. "Whatever the case, it would be wise if we departed soon."

He snapped his fingers and the other two drakes stood back. Zzzeras seemed to hesitate briefly, then thought better of it. The Dragon King raised his hands and began an intricate pattern. The Gryphon watched in total fascination, the scholar in him once more taking control.

As the drake lord completed the pattern, what could only be described as a rip in reality appeared. The Blue Dragon nodded to himself and then began a second pattern. As he formed the pattern, the rip grew, becoming circular as it did, until it was taller and wider than a man—or drake warrior, in this case.

The Dragon King turned back to his ally. "I hope you don't mind, but I had Zzzeras draw the memory of your personal chambers from your mind while you slept. Rest assured, he sought nothing else. He knows better than to disobey, and I need your trust. It is possible to ascertain what I have said."

The Gryphon made no reply, not trusting himself to keep to civil words. He was tired of being used, tired of the invasions into his mind. Had it not been for the madness being perpetrated by the Ice Dragon . . . "Let's get on with it."

"Kylin." At the Dragon King's summons, the other drake

stepped forward. "This gate is to remain open for as long as necessary. While I am away, I expect you to keep things running smoothly, yes?"

"Milord."

"Zzzeras, you will assist us here. We'll need the crystal and those items over there," Blue pointed to various items that he had gathered together at some point previous to the Gryphon's appearance. This revealed the confidence with which the Dragon King had plotted his course of action.

"I will have one of the servitors take it through."

"No, I want you to do it. The fewer who know what we do, the fewer with the capability to interfere. Perhaps, though, I will take this." He removed the crystal from its base. "Lord Gryphon, I must ask you to lead the way. If someone should somehow be in or near your chambers . . . or if my planning is faulty and we arrive elsewhere in your city, they will not take kindly to the intrusion of a drake."

"As you wish."

"Kylin, you are dismissed. Zzzeras, follow us."

The Blue Dragon reached over to a shelf and pulled a small case from it. He handed this to the Gryphon with a warning to be careful. He did not bother to explain why, but the lionbird took his word.

Zzzeras stood ready, his fingers tapping on the former resting place of the crystal. He seemed very impatient. The Gryphon doubted he liked playing servitor. Like many drakes, this one was arrogant and self-centered. He wondered whether Zzzeras had been born with the proper markings on his egg. Hopefully not. This one would make an impatient, dangerous Dragon King.

"Lord Gryphon?" The master of Irillian was waiting by the blink hole, the crystal nestled in his right arm.

His thoughts once more turning back to the misty paths utilized by the Draka, the Gryphon stepped forward. He felt a slight tug as he moved through the blink hole.

The world evaporated, to be replaced by a vast field of nothing. A great white nothing. Directly below his feet, he saw what resembled a path—only there was nothing below *that*, either. His mane bristled. Behind him, he heard the Blue Dragon and then . . .

. . . the path vanished beneath his feet and he was floating with nowhere to go.

XIV

The citadel of Azran was an ominous sight. It stretched high. There were turrets that jutted here and there for no practical reason that any of the trio could think of, save that this had perhaps once been a domicile of the Seekers. Cabe shuddered to think that the avians had once been so widespread. He wondered if any still remained in the ruins. It might have been a mistake to stop here.

"Fresh horse tracks," Haiden suddenly commented.

Cabe looked down. The only things he saw were more bones. It seemed impossible to avoid them completely. Granted, there were marks that might have been made by hooves, but at the same time it was impossible for him to differentiate them from tracks left by the countless scavengers who had picked this bounty clean after the battle. "How can you be certain?"

The elf looked at him solemnly. "It is one of those things my people can tell." He broke into a grin. "Actually, some of the horses left rather obvious reminders behind and our mounts have chosen to step on the reminders."

Cabe sniffed and realized Haiden was correct. He had assumed the odor was merely something left over from the carnage. "But how—"

"I've worked with horses long enough to tell the difference—and no wild herd would bother to be out here. If you want further proof, we passed some garbage that someone left behind."

"If you're not careful, Haiden," Gwen interjected. "you're going to give away all the secrets of your people."

"Small loss. Too many of my people think too highly of themselves."

132

The longer he rode with them, the more human the elf seemed to grow. Haiden had explained that one of his duties had been to act as liaison with the city of Zuu, which lay near the southwest portion of the Dagora Forest. Cabe recalled a warrior he had met, Blane, the prince-commander of the horsemen from Zuu, who had died in the fighting within the walls of Penacles. Blane, a large, burly fighter, had died the way he wanted to and had taken the sadist Kyrg with him. There was a monument to Blane and his men in Penacles now.

"Are we going inside?" Gwen asked in general, though both she and Haiden looked at Cabe for an answer.

This was the sanctum of his father, the castle in which Cabe himself had been held prisoner for a short time. The only memories he had of this place were evil ones . . . yet, there might be something here to help them. Azran had been one of the most powerful necromancers—the undead creatures that had kidnapped Cabe from Penacles were proof of that. With the entire Plane of the Dead from which to draw knowledge, it was possible that they would find a solution here.

The citadel was also a nightmare Cabe felt he had to face if he was ever to have Azran's shadow lifted from his soul.

"We go inside."

Gwen especially was not pleased with the answer, but she nodded. Haiden's smile had diminished to a mere memory.

"You don't have to go in," Cabe suggested.

She shook her head, sending a luxurious wave of red hair flying. "No, I think it might be a good idea after all."

"Has anyone bothered to think that someone else might be inside?" Haiden asked.

Cabe turned to him. "You're the elf; you tell me."

Haiden grimaced and their mood lifted a little. One of the first things that Cabe had done on their way to the citadel was to seek out possible inhabitants. One did not go into the former home of a mad sorcerer without some precaution. That he had thought of that before the others had made him a bit proud. Despite all the knowledge he could draw from his grandfather's memories, he was still somewhat of a novice when it came to actual experience.

The elf moved to obey, but Cabe shook his head and informed

them that it was indeed an empty building. Even as he said that, however, a slight hesitation caught him. He hoped he would not be proven wrong.

They entered the gate and the first real evidence that someone was using this as a base of operations became evident, for the stables were clean and there was fresh hay and water for the horses.

"Now we know where those riders came from, anyway." Gwen muttered. Having entered the grounds had subdued her.

"We'll only stay the night, Gwen. If we cannot find anything of use by then, it's either gone or somewhere we won't find it. Besides, we've run these horses into the ground these past few days. Unless they get some rest now, they're likely to die before we reach the Northern Wastes."

They dismounted and Haiden took the mages' horses. The elf was more than happy to be in the stables for now; it was the most mundane place in the citadel. Gwen and Cabe, hand in hand, took their belongings and walked across the yard to the massive iron doors which marked the entrance to the actual building itself.

"I wish we could have taken another path," the enchantress muttered. "One that would have avoided this *place*."

"This is the quickest and safest region and I forgot this would be here. I'm not that happy with entering a place that was home to Azran and built, as far as I know, by the Seekers." Cabe stared at the iron doors again.

If this was truly a Seeker relic, he started to wonder, why bother with doors and such? Why not make it more of an aerie? Had the Seekers in fact taken over a relic of some earlier race? Where did the list of dominant races begin? When were the lands that were now called the Dragonrealms first inhabited and by whom—or what?

So many questions. Nathan, he knew, would have told him that it was a sorcerer's duty to continually ask such questions, even if it proved impossible to answer them in his lifetime. Not a satisfying way to look at things, Cabe thought.

The doors were not locked; there was no real reason for them to be. As far as most were concerned, Azran's home had been stripped of everything useful. It was said that the Blue Dragon had been the first to stake claim, though others mentioned the Storm Dragon, Talak, and even the Crystal Dragon, though that last one seemed unlikely considering the reclusive nature of that drake lord and the great distance between the Hell Plains and the Legar Peninsula, which jutted out on the southwestern corner of the continent.

As they wandered through the abandoned building, their respective fears diminished. There was nothing here but dust and cobwebs now. The marauders had left a few things behind, but it was obvious that this was not a permanent camp. They would not have left it unguarded, otherwise.

Decay had set in. After standing for so many ages, the citadel was now without preserving spells. Azran had drained those away at some point for his own use, most likely during the slaughter of the Red Dragon's horde.

Cabe glanced at a stairway leading down. He turned to Gwen, who was inspecting a few tattered tomes that had been left behind. Judging by her expression, which might just as easily have had to do with the tremendous amounts of dust, they had been left behind for good reason.

"I'm going to have a look down here. I shouldn't be long. It looks like a storeroom."

"Do you want me to come with you?"

He shook his head. "Wait for Haiden. When I come back up, we'll eat. I'm sure that whatever sort of room is down there has been cleaned out."

As he descended, he tried to identify what he saw with what little he knew about the citadel. For the most part, he had remained in one room. Only briefly had he seen the outside. As far as he knew, he had never been down this way.

As he suspected, it was a storage area of some sort and one that had been picked clean. Even shelves were missing, though the brackets remained. Still, he felt that there might be something here. . . . Cabe ran his hands along the walls, thinking to himself that if there was indeed a secret panel, someone would have discovered it by now.

He touched the far wall, the obvious choice, but felt nothing. However, touching the wall on the right side made him tingle. It was an odd sensation, almost as if the wall was trying to identify him and was having some difficulty.

Cabe concentrated, seeking out the point of origin. It was not hard to do, but somehow he suspected now that others would have had a rougher time. He reached with his mind and forced his will on it.

The wall was no longer before him. He fell face-first into a room from which a terrible stench rose. It was as if all the dead outside were still rotting. Cabe quickly covered his nose and looked up.

There was a pool, but water certainly was not what filled it. A brackish liquid of some sort, with a greenish ooze overlaying it. It bubbled and belched. Cabe rose to his feet, his nose still covered, and turned back the way he had come. There was a blank wall behind him.

Uneasily, he returned his attention back to the pit. Azran would not have hidden it if it were not something important. He remembered his own thoughts about his father's dealings with the dead. This room would certainly qualify as ideal for that.

The bubbling was slowly growing more intense, he realized, as if something were coming to the surface. Cabe had no desire to see what that something was. He tried to relocate the spot that had allowed him access to this godforsaken room, but it was nowhere to be found. Evidently, that was not the way to leave.

The pool was frothing now and Cabe noticed that the stench was becoming even more nauseating. He was almost ready to throw up.

The—a description escaped Cabe for the moment—rose out of the muck and ooze.

"Who do you seek?" it rasped. The voice kept changing, as if there were more than one speaker attempting to take charge.

Cabe tried to avoid looking at the odd collection of limbs, eyes, mouths, and indescribable appendages as he gasped out a response. "No—no one! It's a mis—mistake!"

"The summons was clear—though whether it was you or another is not." There was just the slightest hint of puzzlement in the—its—voice(s).

Several thoughts flashed through Cabe's mind, including, of course, Azran, who . . .

"I will bring him forth."

Bring him forth? Cabe forgot about the stench, forgot about the horrible appearance of the other, and shouted, "No! Not that one! That's not the one I want!"

Azran! He had come that close to facing the specter of his father! Great caution was called for here, Cabe realized. If he was not careful, he might next summon the Brown Dragon or—he quickly squelched the last thought. He did *not* want to speak to the Brown Dragon!

Another idea occurred to him. "Bring me Nathan Bedlam!"

The—*guardian* was the most reasonable title Cabe could give it—hesitated. "That proves . . . impossible for the moment." It was silent for several seconds, then: "There is one who hears you, who wishes to speak to you."

"Not Azran!"

"No. He calls himself . . . Tyr."

Tyr! One of the Dragon Masters! One of the two undead forced to kidnap Cabe for Azran! "Yes! That's the one!"

The guardian sank slowly into the muck. It vanished and with it went some of the potency of the stench. That did not mean that Cabe was not having trouble breathing.

The pool bubbled again. A head slowly broke free from the ooze. Cabe watched as a tall figure rose above the surface. The remnants of a dark blue robe covered him. Unlike the guardian, he was free of muck.

The skin was wrinkled and dry and overall the man had the appearance of one who had died violently. Tyr had not survived the Turning War and he showed it. Once, he might have been thought of as handsome, but only the memories of that remained.

The eyelids of the unliving mage opened, revealing blank, white, sightless orbs. Yet, Tyr turned his head and looked directly at Cabe. The dead, it seemed, saw things with a different sort of vision.

"Cabe—Nathan. You came as I hoped. When I felt your presence near, I tried to reach out, to draw you here." The macabre figure folded his hands. "I rejoice in seeing you. I rejoice in knowing that Azran has come to us to pay for his misdeeds."

Cabe shifted uncomfortably. He did not want to even think about Azran. Tyr apparently saw this and smiled. It did little to reassure the young sorcerer. Part of Tyr's jaw was loose.

"When the gatekeeper felt your touch upon the wall, it was confused. You were too much like Azran—yet, too little as well. If you had been other than you are, one who is two, it would have recognized you as only a relative or an outsider and forbidden you entrance. But that which Nathan has bequeathed you gave you the key."

"This place," Cabe finally managed to blurt out, "this place is where he summoned you from."

"And forced us into misdeeds. There are penalties for abusing the sleep of the dead, but Azran thought he would live forever. Now, he will suffer for some time before he is given his rest. But that troubles you. Let us instead speak of why you came to this place. The lord of the Northern Wastes has unleashed the Void."

"The Void?"

"Not the actual Void, but something that can only be thought of in those terms. The Void is a place that is the absence of matter. Open a hole to the Void and matter enters. You have seen the place. You have seen the debris that litters it."

Cabe nodded, thinking of an owl creature he had seen. A mage or something from some other world, dead most likely because it had been careless. There had been fragments of other things as well. "I remember."

"The Void can never be filled. The Dragonrealms as a whole would not diminish its hunger by a single iota. So, too, is the hunger that the Ice Dragon now contains within himself."

"Within himself?"

Tyr nodded, shaking loose a bit of flesh from the right side of his face. It struck the murky liquid below with a dull splash and sank quickly beneath the surface. Cabe paled.

"There must be a focal point, a place for the power to gather. You know that. Nathan knew that."

Nathan had been the focal point for that spell. Yet . . .

As if anticipating Cabe's thoughts, Tyr added, "Soon there will come a time when the Ice Dragon will be able to release himself from the spell. Then, he will control it completely and no one will be able to turn it back. It is only while he himself relies on the spell that he is vulnerable—I think. My mind is not what it was. For all I know he may be unstoppable now—but no, that can't be right. . . ."

Tyr was losing substance, both fading and deteriorating. Cabe started to reach out, but thought better of it. He did not want to chance falling into the pool. There was no telling whether he would be able to climb out again. It was not yet his time to cross over to the Plane of the Dead—at least, he hoped not. Besides, Tyr seemed unconcerned with the loss of his physical body. Being dead, it might not hurt him. Perhaps this form was only one he had recreated to speak to Cabe.

The dead sorcerer shook himself from his stupor. "This is all unimportant. The reason that I wanted to speak to you concerns you alone, Bedlam." Tyr was transparent, and much of his flesh had already fallen from his body. Cabe could barely keep from looking at the skeletal figure, but he knew that the Dragon Master would not have sought him out if it was not important. "I shouldn't warn you, but when I knew that you were here, perhaps because I hoped you would come, I knew that I must defy the rules. . . ."

"Rules?" Cabe watched Tyr fade away, then reappear, little more than a smoky blur. "Tyr, what rules? What do you mean?"

"They've done this, the guardians. I . . . should have known better. They wanted me to speak to you of other things, albeit important things, until my time was gone from here. . . . A pity you do not have the knowledge of the dead that cursed Azran had; I could walk the earth and tell you in my leisure. . . ."

Tyr faded away again.

"Tyr!" Cabe stared down at the pool. It bubbled obscenely. The odor became very noticeable again.

"Wait!"

The very force of the voice made the young mage stumble back against the wall. With an effort obviously taxing for one of the dead, Tyr brought himself back to full corporeal existence. It would be a momentary thing, Cabe knew. The strain was probably as painful as anything a living creature could feel, if not worse.

"Damn their games! Damn their melodramatic ways! Damn all petty gods or those who think themselves gods! Bedlam!" Tyr's eyes were burning into Cabe's mind. "Your destiny lies in the Northern Wastes, but . . . if you go there, you will almost surely at last die! I—"

Tyr vanished; this time for good, Cabe knew. The pool bubbled, but nothing more. Even the horrid guardian did not reappear.

He was going to die.

He was going to die and the dead Dragon Master had tried to warn him, tried to prevent him from going on . . . but no! He had said that Cabe's destiny lay in the Northern Wastes! Did that mean that they were going to fail? No! Tyr had said nothing of the sort!

I'm going to die, Cabe repeated to himself.

Cabe.

He felt his own name in his mind. His first thought was that Tyr had found the strength to reach out to him again.

Cabe. This time, his name was followed by a low chuckle. He knew then that it was not Tyr.

Somehow, his groping hands found whatever it was that would allow him to exit this chamber. He fell forward even as the low chuckle began again. Only when he was completely through the wall did it seal and, with that action, cut off the mocking voice.

He recognized that voice, and thanked the heavens and the earth that he had not had time to think upon its owner for any length of time. Had he still been in that chamber, he might have died right there—unless something worse could have occurred.

Cabe stumbled up the stairs, where he fell into the arms of a startled Gwen. She held him tight, only comprehending his shock and not understanding what had caused it. Haiden was nearby, but he kept his peace.

He was going to die in the Wastes. That must have been why the voice had chuckled. He knew that voice, knew it for Azran. Azran was mocking him.

Azran had told him, only with Cabe's own name and that laugh, that he was expecting him soon.

At last, Toma thought to himself. *At last I have found the exit to this blasted labyrinth of a tunnel!*

While he did appreciate the aid the Seeker had given him, he cursed it for making him crawl through a maze of ice for who knew how long. His hands were numb; most of his front side was numb from crawling along without rest. Toma had not dared rest. There was no telling when the Ice Dragon might decide it was time to check on him. Even now, there might be scores of the unliving ice servants searching for him along the outskirts of the mountain range. There might even be a number of them crawling through the tunnel system like a multitude of rats. How could the Ice Dragon not possibly suspect such a complex system of tunnels within his own citadel? Was this merely a trap? A game for the Dragon King's entertainment?

Toma longed for the time when he would regain his own sorcerous powers. Then, he would be ready for a fight. Then, he would crush the Ice Dragon once and for all.

He closed his eyes and hissed quietly. His mind was addled. He had to escape first. All his boasts would be for nought if he perished in the Wastes. It was cold out there, far colder than it had been since his arrival. It had something to do with the mad plan of his ''host.'' There would be a winter like this everywhere, apparently. No domain would be untouched.

He shivered, the tatters of his cloak no more protecting him from the onslaught of the cold than if he had not been wearing a cloak at all. He continued to try to wrap it around himself out of reflex action. A part of his mind told him that he was slowly losing touch with reality, but the other part went on with life, such as it was. After all, there was now the Wastes to conquer.

It took some maneuvering to keep himself from falling headfirst from the hole into the ice and snow below. He wondered vaguely how the Seekers did it. It probably helped that they could fly; they did not face the risk of falling to their deaths. Headfirst was probably normal. They would need to go that way in order to gain the wind currents and fly.

How long before the Ice Dragon was on his trail? At the moment, he no longer saw this as a game played by the Dragon King. Ice had no desire for games such as this.

With the greatest of difficulty, he made it down to a ledge some three-fourths of the way to the bottom. He was honestly amazed that his hands had any sort of grip left at all. Turning around, Toma gazed at the great expanse of the Northern Wastes. It had changed since last he had seen it. No longer was it a flat, dead land. The ice, snow, and earth had all been churned up, as if great worms had dug their way up to the surface after a heavy rain. He hissed an oath that would have shocked even the Ice Dragon. Now, the going would be even worse. He would have to climb and climb and climb.

The image of great worms digging was not far from the truth, it suddenly occurred to him. He had seen how one of his captor's monstrosities had risen from beneath the earth. This was merely a case of more than one.

Many more than one.

Toma scanned the horizon as far as he could see in every direction. Not one area of the Wastes had been left unscathed by the digging creatures—and the drake could see the landscape for miles away. There had to have been thousands.

He had to cross this alone and without his magic.

Toma shivered. Not for the first time since his arrival here and not, certainly not, from the cold.

XV

"The blink hole! Someone hasss disssrupted my ssspell!"

Both the Blue Dragon and the Gryphon floated helplessly in the nothingness of the Void. The drake lord spent the first few moments cursing those who had placed him in this predicament—whoever that might be. The Dragon King had not gotten that far in his cursing yet, though it sounded suspiciously as if he had a notion.

The Gryphon was trying to be more practical. This was his first true visit to the Void; he had glimpsed it more than once, but had been fortunate never to have needed to travel through it more than briefly. He would have been happier if he had never had a reason to. Nevertheless, he was not going to let the Void overwhelm his emotions.

The two were slowly drifting from one another and, since the Gryphon had no real working knowledge of the blink hole, he determined that it was very much to his benefit to stay near the drake.

Magic, it seemed, was unaffected for the most part. Utilizing the bare minimum of raw power, the lionbird pushed himself toward his companion, whose curses were quieting down. At first, the Gryphon assumed he would come to a gradual halt, as would have been natural under the laws of his normal plane of existence, but in fact he lost no momentum whatsoever and very quickly was heading into a collision. Before he had time to react, the Blue Dragon was boosting himself to the side, one clawed hand out to grab hold of the Gryphon. More experienced, the drake caught him and brought both of them to a spinning halt.

"A dangerousss maneuver, Lord Gryphon," Blue commented. "You should have waited. I wasss not about to lose you."

"At the time, it was hard to say what you planned to do at all."

"Forgive my outburst, but I have alwaysss prided myself on thinking things through. It never occurred to me that there might be those among my clans who would so actively betray me like this. They must feel very confident to make such a move."

Revolt by drakes against their own ruler? The Gryphon knew of lesser kings who had revolted against the Emperor Dragon, but that was a completely different scale. Clans never overthrew their clan leaders—did they?

Blue was laughing mirthlessly. "You know less about our race than you think. In some ways we are as violent, as unstable a race as the humans. We are also pragmatic, though. Long-term revolts against our own kind are not common. When it is known that a leader has been overthrown, the clans do not continue to fight among themselves. They accept that new duke or even king as their proper one. After all, with few exceptions, the antagonists are both of royal markings. No one will accept the rule of an unmarked drake—not even if that drake is Toma or Zzzeras."

"It was Zzzeras, then?"

The Dragon King did not reply, already considering their options. "Blink holes always leave residual traces. I've never had to try to find one from within, but there's always a first time."

"What about the crystal?" The Gryphon suggested. "It served us well in your chambers."

The drake lord showed him an empty hand. "I fear that the crystal is now merely one more artifact floating in the Void. I relinquished my hold when the path vanished and I have no idea in which direction it was hurtled. Trying to find it will take away precious time. I cannot say how long the traces will remain noticeable."

Since his work required the use of both hands, The Blue Dragon made his companion take hold of his belt from the backside. He also gave the Gryphon a warning; there was a slight chance that they might face some sort of danger here in the Void. Not everything was dead and even the unliving objects might prove hazardous, as some of the larger ones might be floating at speeds several hundred times faster than what the Gryphon had been moving earlier. Impact against a soaring, hill-sized chunk of earth would easily shatter their skeletons and leave no more trace of either of them than two messy spots.

The Gryphon got the point.

It was difficult going at first. The drake's gestures kept moving both figures this way and that, making concentration almost impossible. The Dragon King was finally forced to gesture very slowly, making him look more like a dancer. The Gryphon refrained from commenting on this to his companion, knowing all too well the unpredictable humor of the drakes.

"Damn!" Blue hissed at one point. "I can barely feel it! We are running out of time!"

Frustrated, the Gryphon spoke out. "Let me try!"

"You don't know the spell!"

"You can show me, can't you?" When he saw that the drake was reluctant, he added, "Preserve your secrets all you like, then. It'll give you something to think about while we spend the rest of all time floating about like leaves in a pond!"

The other hissed, then agreed. "You have a point, my friend. Very well, see if you can locate it. It's much like trying to tap into a source of power."

The Gryphon nodded and then closed his eyes as he concentrated. For some time he felt nothing, and his confidence began to slip. All he felt was the blank nothingless of this undimension.

It was like having another Void within him. It was almost too much.

When he was on the verge of giving up, he caught hold of something tenuous. The Blue Dragon had said it would be like tapping into the powers. That was the way this felt. His mind traced it back a little. This was indeed the blink hole; there were still mental after-images of the hole itself.

"I have it!"

The drake lord hissed again, but this time there was a note of triumph in the sound. "Open your eyes, then. I'll have to do this physically rather than possibly make you break your hold on it."

Releasing himself as slowly and carefully as possible—in order to minimize drift—the master of Irillian began to repeat the spell. The Gryphon watched, matching the movements as precisely as he could. The two were beginning to float apart, but he tried to ignore that fact. All that was important was for him to complete the spell.

There was suddenly resistance from the other plane, as if someone definitely did not want them coming back. That was nearly the case, for, involved with this new problem, the lionbird almost missed a movement. He was able to correct himself barely in time.

"Someone . . . someone's fight . . . fighting me!"

"Ignore them! They cannot stop you at this late point. They can only hope to slow you down or make you miscast!"

The Blue Dragon revealed the last part of the spell.

The Gryphon completed it.

They were standing on the path again. The drake wasted no time. "Hurry! Back the way we came!"

In the next instant they were leaping through the blink hole and back into the mortal plane. The Dragon King came down in a pile, striking the floor hard. The Gryphon, attempting to jump over him, struck one of the walls with his shoulder. He fell to ground, groaning as every bone and muscle in that side of his body shouted out in pain.

Through watering eyes, he saw two other drakes. One was even now slumping to the floor, a savage blow from the other having ripped out his throat. The victor looked at the injured lionbird and there was bloodlust in the burning eyes. Then the drake turned and gazed at Blue, who was rising to his feet. The other drake sank to one knee.

"Milord! I thank the Dragon of the Depths that you have made it back!"

"Kylin." The drake lord looked down at his duke, then at the corpse.

"Zzzeras." He whispered.

"Milord." Kylin dared to stand. The bloodlust had vanished the moment he knew his monarch had been looking directly at him. "I returned here to have a last-minute word with him, only to discover him standing here laughing, claiming that he would now be ruler. He was certain of his success and certain that I would bow to him once I realized you were gone. I did not."

"Zzzeras hoped to rule, unmarked as he was?" the Blue Dragon asked, his voice low and even a bit sad.

"We knew his ambitions, milord. Before the chaos that tore your council apart, he often met with Toma."

"I remember. It seems that wherever he goes, Toma spreads madness. Had he not been protected by the emperor, I would have challenged him—as dangerous as that could have been." The drake lord looked down on the corpse. "A pity. I wish truly that it had not come to this."

Kylin was reaching out a supporting hand when the Blue Dragon, claws extended, caught him by the throat, ripping the entire area out with that one blow far more cleanly than Kylin had done to Zzzeras.

The other drake did not even have time to look puzzled before he fell to the floor, to join his counterpart.

Blue turned his attention to the Gryphon, who was rising slowly, eyes glued on the Dragon King. "As I said, lionbird, you know less about my race than you think."

"You . . . you killed him. Ripped out his throat like a madman—for serving you loyally?" It was incredible. Unbelievable.

The drake shook his head. "I killed him for betraying me . . . and for murdering Zzzeras, whose greatest fault was playing the dupe. It was Kylin who sought to abandon us in the Void."

"Kylin?"

"Does that surprise you?" Blue shook his head. His voice was tinged with disgust. "Zzzeras did not have the skill to cut us off. Kylin did not know that Zzzeras also only dealt with Toma on my orders. Toma was always one to be watched. Poor Kylin. He never realized that I used the crystal to spy on him. To spy on all of them. How else does one remain ruler in troubled times?''

In the short time since his first meeting with the Blue Dragon, the Gryphon had learned much about drake society—more than he would have wanted to know. He could not say that it differed greatly from the human society that he, in all honesty, had to consider himself a part of. It did not give him any satisfaction to know that the drakes were no better.

''He must have thought this the chance of a lifetime. I played the fool perfectly, imagining that his delusions of power were only that. I didn't think he would actually do something like this.''

The Blue Dragon shrugged. ''Enough of this! I would say that the guards Kylin sent elsewhere should return in a matter of moments. In the meantime, we have new things to consider, most important of which is the loss of the crystal. I had hoped that, if we discovered something, it might prove of use for focusing our power.''

At the moment, the only thing on the Gryphon's mind was to leave this domain and never return, but he knew that such a move would solve nothing, and the Ice Dragon was not a threat to be dismissed.

''Our greatest concern, drake lord, is the libraries themselves, not your crystal. We can worry about possibilities later on, but the first thing we need to do is discover what avenues we may take. There may be nothing in the libraries, or there may be some reference so obscure that we won't find it in time. It may be possible that we have to confront the Ice Dragon face-to-face, though I cannot fathom what we might do then. One thing I do intend to do is to contact Cabe Bedlam and your counterpart who rules the Dagora Forest.''

The Blue Dragon glowered, and the hiss that escaped from his frowning mouth held no love for the last suggestion. Blue cared little for his turncoat brother and even less for anyone of the surname Bedlam. From his point of view it might make sense, but the Gryphon was having none of that now.

He pointed a taloned finger at the drake lord. ''Hear me on this. This is a time when enemies will have to embrace, much as you and I have had to do—at your suggestion. Whether that enemy bears the name Bedlam, it is nothing compared to the danger we presently face. I would have dealt with Azran himself if it meant saving the Dragonrealms from the frosty lord of the Wastes. Do I make myself clear?''

"Clear. Perfectly so," the Dragon King admitted. "If I may, we shall depart as soon as I have rectified this situation." With one hand, he indicated the two still forms.

"I have no qualms about that."

"It will not take long. When things have been settled, I will open a new blink hole . . . unless you wish to try."

The Gryphon shook his head. "I have no desire to revisit the Void for any length of time, and that is what will probably happen if I attempt that spell. My concern was less with memorizing it than getting us back."

"Then, I shall construct the hole. We should have no interruptions this time." As the Blue Dragon finished speaking, several drake warriors and servitors came running in. One of them apologized profusely for having been duped by Kylin, and offered his life. The Dragon King did not take him up on the offer.

An eye on the proceedings, the Gryphon's mind returned to the libraries. He was certain that something concerning what they faced was located in the libraries; as far as he knew, *everything* was in the libraries. The question was, whether they would find the answer and understand it before it was too late.

The more important question was: would there be a solution at all? Was this one case where the Seekers or whoever had designed the spell had not had time to create a counterspell?

The Gryphon pictured himself wading in volume after volume in search of a ghost that might be standing right before him. He wondered whether the builders of the libraries had considered this when they had built it. Had they designed the structure just so? Was it intentionally confusing or was there a pattern that neither he nor his predecessor, the Purple Dragon, had discovered?

In frustration, the lionbird began to silently curse the madmen who had built the libraries. He stopped up short, though, considering then the sudden notion that those mysterious builders were watching him even now and that to curse them would only be inviting new complications when he began his search.

"I am about to open a new hole," commented the Dragon King. Somehow he had walked directly up to the Gryphon without the latter's noticing him. "All will be under control this time."

The Gryphon's mane ruffled in uneasiness. A more idiotic statement he had never heard.

Gwen looked at Haiden and shook her head. "He still won't tell me what it was he came across down there."

They were in the main hall of Azran's citadel. A small fire was burning itself in the fireplace and a meal had been left half prepared on a table that the elf had dusted off. They had given up searching the building after Cabe had come screaming through the wall. Gwen had searched for some sort of passage, but even her abilities could detect nothing behind the stone blocks. Yet, she knew Cabe had come from somewhere. There had to at least be some trace of a dimensional gate or a blink hole. There was not; at least, none that she could find. It did not surprise her. This had been the home of Azran, and she already knew too well how devious he had been. For a moment, she even thought she heard him laughing at them in that mocking tone of his.

Cabe had calmed, almost so much that both his companions worried that much more. He seemed almost indifferent at times, though that could change any moment. It was almost as if he were of two minds—which he was in a way, but not the way Gwen thought him now. On the one hand, he seemed to accept everything they planned as inevitable. On the other hand, he hesitated when it came to actually doing anything that would further their efforts.

Haiden walked over to the stairway and peered down. "Maybe I can discover something."

"Don't bother," Cabe finally muttered. "Only Azran and I have the ability—and I shouldn't. If you do manage to break through the barrier, I wouldn't doubt that my father left a few surprises before he departed for the last time."

The elf turned back to him, frustrated. "Then why don't you tell us what is in there—and where 'it' is, for Rheena's sake?"

Cabe stood and seemed to shake himself out of his stupor. "It wouldn't matter. We can forget about searching any further. There's nothing here that would be of assistance to us. We leave as early as possible in the morning. I want us at the edge of the Northern Wastes by the next day—which will mean teleporting at some point, I guess.''

The elf whistled and Gwen stared deeply into Cabe's eyes. She did not like what she saw—or rather, did not see—in them. It was as if he was purposefully cutting her off from a part of him, something she had never known him to do so adamantly.

"It will be a terrible strain on the horses. I don't think they'll last into the Wastes, then," Haiden commented.

"Then we'll get fresh ones from your companions up there. At the very worst, we only need one horse.'' He did not have to elaborate on what that meant; if it came down to it, Cabe planned to go on alone.

"Two," corrected Gwen. Cabe did not even try to argue with her—which did not mean he agreed. She knew that the closer they came to their destination, the more she would have to watch him. It was not unlikely that he might try to slip ahead of them. He was beginning to really frighten her now. "If you plan on trying to teleport, you'll need someone to assist you. A spell like that is liable to leave you helpless.''

Haiden sighed. "Very well, lord and lady, if we are to rise early, I had best get our meal taken care of. That way, we can call it an early evening.'' He studied the hall, taking in the shadowy corners, the dust-covered walls, and the grotesque reliefs that lined the walls.

"I could not ask for a more peaceful, pleasant abode," he added dryly.

They spoke little over their meal and even less afterward. Gwen cast a protective spell, as she had so many times before, but Haiden was not satisfied this time. Azran's former home disturbed him. He volunteered himself for watch, assuring them that he would remain alert all night if necessary.

They woke early that morning . . . That is to say, Cabe and Gwen did. Haiden was rolled in a ball on the floor, oblivious to everything. It took several attempts to wake him, which said something about the tales of elves' legendary stamina. Haiden confessed that he had remained awake for most of the night, dropping off an hour or so before dawn. The red in his face did not vanish for the next half hour.

It was noticeably colder, an unusual climatic change for a land aptly titled the Hell Plains. Even here, they could feel and hear the eruptions of minor volcanoes. Gwen was the first one to put the thought into words.

"The Ice Dragon's powers are growing. He can already maintain a steady cold this far south in the Hell Plains. What must Irillian and Talak be like?"

"This is more of a natural cold," Cabe commented almost emotionlessly. "The soul-numbing cold hasn't reached this far yet, at least not with any regularity."

"And how long will it be before that happens?"

Cabe gave them that look that reminded Gwen so much of Nathan. "Far sooner than we can hope."

They were on their way a few minutes later. None of them was displeased with leaving the crumbling citadel of Azran behind. As far as they were all concerned, the sooner the Hell Plains tore the place apart, the better. There was nothing good about the structure, and whatever or whoever had built it no longer mattered; Azran had tainted it with his presence.

With the exception of a handful of times when they were forced to go around unstable ground, they met with no difficulties for the better part of the day. The cool weather remained steady save when they were forced to ride extremely close to some of the more active craters. Only then did the land live up to its name. Despite the fact that there were very fertile areas in this domain, no one could see why anyone, even a drake, would want to live here.

As if in response to that thought, riders materialized on the horizon.

They were not men. No man rode a minor drake unless his life depended on it . . . and even then many would have hesitated.

"Haiden," Cabe whispered. "You mentioned nothing about drake activity."

"That's because there hasn't been any, sorcerer. From this distance, I cannot say what clan they are. Gold's, perhaps, or maybe remnants of Red's."

"We'll find out in a moment," Gwen added. "They seem to be coming in our direction."

The trio readied themselves for the worst. They could not possibly outrun the riders at this point and it was obvious that they had been spotted. The ground behind them was too unstable for a reckless retreat. It would be child's play for the riders to pick them off from behind.

As they neared, it became evident that these were indeed remnants of Red's clans. A whole clan, in fact, for there were dams and young as well as warriors and servitors like Sssarekai.

"Refugees," Cabe muttered.

"Which still won't prevent them from running us down," Haiden added.

Astonishingly, the riders did slow. By the time they were within hailing distance, the drakes had slowed their mounts to a trot. It was probably a difficult task; minor drakes had big appetites and these looked as if they had not been fed properly for the last couple of days. They eyed the horses with growing interest.

"Cabe." Gwen's voice was tinged in uneasiness. "Isn't it said that the Red Dragon died battling Azran?"

He nodded, already having seen the reason for her question.

The crimson dragon warrior raised his hand, bringing a halt to the drakes. His helm was the most intricate Cabe had ever seen, save those worn by the Dragon Kings themselves. That, more than his color, proclaimed what he was.

"Apparently, the previous Red Dragon planned in advance. He had an *heir*."

"A new Dragon King . . ." That was all Haiden could say. The mixture of disgust, hatred, and fear in his voice was enough to jolt even Cabe.

The Red Dragon—for there was no denying him the title of his predecessor—urged his mount slowly forward until he was close enough for Cabe to see the burning eyes.

"An elf. An elf and two humans . . ." The new lord of the Hell Plains studied them closely. "Two human mages, at that."

"Milord—" Haiden's attempt at diplomacy was cut off by a sharp wave of the hand from the drake.

"I have not given you permission to speak, leaf-eater. Besides, it is the humans I wish to speak to."

Cabe urged his own mount forward a little, no small task considering the animal's quite natural urge to be as far away from dragons as possible. He bowed his head and waited for the Dragon King to speak again.

"You do not have the look of murderous raiders about you, but humans are a treacherous lot. I could attack you; I would probably kill you, but possibly at the loss of my own life and that of some of my clan."

The arrogant boasts almost made Cabe smile before he realized that there had to be some truth in them. He was King by birth, or else the others would have never followed him. That meant that he controlled the forces of his predecessor, which made him a formidable opponent indeed. The last Red Dragon had been known for a fierceness that had rivaled his brother Brown.

"I would know, human, to whom I am speaking. You look to be of some importance, despite the fact that you ride with only a dam with hair nigh as red as fire and a worthless tree-dweller."

Haiden made a choking sound, but the drake lord ignored him.

Cabe took a deep breath. Matters had been hanging heavy on him and now this had to be added. He might have tried to lie, but somehow he suspected this new ruler would recognize a lie. "I ride with my wife, Gwendolyn, known as the Lady of the Amber, and Haiden, a worthy guide and scout. My surname is familiar to you, as my first name may be. I am Cabe Bedlam."

The Dragon King hissed loudly, causing much unrest among his followers. For the briefest of times, Cabe thought he saw fear in the drake lord's eyes. He could imagine what it might be like, a new ruler who suddenly finds himself confronted by a name synonymous with the darkest evil as far as his race is concerned.

To his credit, the drake quickly recovered. Sitting as tall as possible, he stared directly into Cabe's eyes. "Have you come, then, to complete the destruction of our clans by both your sire and the soul-stealing death to the north?"

The Ice Dragon's creatures were moving quickly. The horror the already-battered clans of Red had faced must have seemed to them a sign that their extinction was demanded by the powers. Now, just when they might be safe, they faced an older fear—a mage whose name was Bedlam.

Cabe shook his head. "My only desire is to see the Dragon-

realms at peace, with both drake and human coexisting. The death
of your predecessor was due to the madness of one of my kin.''
He decided against pointing out that it was the old Dragon King's
fault as well. ''What I am concerned about is the death from the
north that you just mentioned.''

''And why is that?''

''I hope to put an end to it.''

The drake lord was silent at first; then, a low laugh escaped
him. There was only pity in that laughter, pity for what the Dragon
King thought surely must be a madman.

''Have you seen what comes from the Wastes? Have you seen
the gift of my brother, the lord of the Northern Wastes?'' Evidently, Cabe realized for the first time, all Dragon Kings considered one another brothers once they held their respective
thrones.

''I've seen them. One wandered south long before the others.''

''One?''

Cabe could see the false mouth of the drake smile, revealing
teeth almost human. Actually, he realized that this new Dragon
King looked more human than any of the others.

''One?'' The drake repeated. ''You have not seen horror until
you have seen hundreds—thousands—digging their way through
the soil, reaching out to devour, not our bodies, but the life-force
within us! You have seen nothing!''

Gwen dared to urge her own steed near Cabe's. ''We know
more than you think. We know something of what's going on up
there. We mean you no harm, drake lord. If you have information
of value to us, we would appreciate it. If not, we have no quarrel
with you and would wish nothing else than for both parties to be
on their respective ways.''

The Dragon King listened intently, though his eyes never left
Cabe. ''I have more than you see here, Bedlam. Most of my kin
have gone to Silver's domain. We are the last, the most northern
of the clans and the wall of defense behind which the others were
able to depart. I started out with a group nearly a third again this
size, but those ungodly leeches caught them either one or a few
at a time. My scouts report that they have penetrated even farther
south in Blue's Kingdom, no surprise since there is a much more
bountiful feast awaiting them in Irillian. How do you plan to stop

an unliving wave that devours all life before it? Are you going to pull demons from another dimension? Can you cleanse the Wastes with fire?''

"There is a possibility, but I have to go deep into the Wastes. I have to confront your counterpart himself.''

"Madness!'' The Dragon King shook his head. "I see no reason to hold you from your task, then. It only brings the abominations closer to us and prevents you from fulfilling your deathwish any sooner.''

Cabe had gone pale at the last statement, thinking that perhaps the drake lord knew something, but the latter was only mocking what he felt to be a fool's quest.

The reptilian monarch sobered. He started to turn his mount around in order to rejoin his subjects, then twisted so that he faced Cabe once more. "If there is truly something you can do, I wish you the best. I have no love for your race—and especially your clan—but I have no desire to see the lands under the icy claw of that cursed colddrake who rules the Wastes. Better we all be dead than bow to his rule.''

Cabe bowed his head briefly, with Gwen and Haiden following suit. The Dragon King turned away and returned to his party. At his signal, the group moved to one side, allowing the humans and the elf to pass by. Cabe nodded his gratitude to the drake lord, who suddenly called to him.

"The lair of my most damned brother lies within a mountain range toward the west. Beware. His servants blend with their surroundings—and avoid the elves' paths!''

Haiden stiffened and would have questioned the Dragon King regardless of their mutual dislike, but the drakes were already riding south. He turned quickly to the two humans, seeking some sort of comfort. Cabe could only shake his head; he had no idea how the elves up there might be faring. Gwen pointed out how skilled they were at not being seen.

The last did not encourage the elf. "We are good when we have something to work with. Where will they hide if the trees and earth have been torn asunder?''

Neither of the mages could answer his question with any conviction. Cabe pulled his cloak tighter around himself, noting with some apprehension that it seemed to be getting colder.

Something white as snow and very large rose over the horizon and then vanished before he could see it clearly.

"We have trouble."

"What sort of trouble?" Gwen asked.

He pointed toward the horizon. "The Red Dragon erred when he thought there was more distance between his band and the creatures of the Ice Dragon."

Haiden and Gwen followed the direction his finger pointed. They saw nothing at first, then another white mound materialized momentarily.

"They're heading this way."

XVI

"They're everywhere!"

Cabe nodded, his mood darker and darker by the moment. Tyr had talked about his death in the Wastes and, as far as Cabe was concerned, any place where the Ice Dragon's behemoths roamed could be considered part of that domain.

"Cabe!"

At Gwen's call, he broke partially free from the darkness. "What?"

"We have to try to teleport!"

"Where?" Haiden asked hesitantly. "Those things are all over the horizon." He did not add that there was no doubt now that they must have overrun his fellow elves. No one was willing to bring that up.

"It would have to be in the midst of the Wastes itself. There's a chance that by now they're all beyond the original bounds of the Ice Dragon's domain! We could jump behind their lines!"

Despite himself, Cabe could not help feeling hopeful. It would mean a respite. Nathan would have approved of such a move and, judging by the feeling within him, Nathan did. It was at times like this that the younger Bedlam was grateful for the link he had with his grandfather. Things would have been so much more difficult if he had no one to turn to.

"Can you teleport other objects?" Haiden looked worried. Both mages realized then that one of them would have to carry the elf. There was also the problem of the horses. At such a great distance, the power needed to drag a mount as well as rider would be tremendous. At the very least, neither of the mages would be able to defend themselves very well.

Gwen took a deep breath. "Let me do it, Cabe. It will *have* to be a blink hole. I was never very experienced at those myself, but I think it better if I do it than you. I'll need a few moments. You two will have to keep an eye out—and pray that it works."

She dismounted, gave Cabe the reins of her mount, and chose a spot behind them. Closing her eyes, she began to draw a pattern with her hands. Haiden and Cabe measured the distance between their party and the creatures and saw that they should have some time. Something small materialized in the air before Gwen. Cabe belatedly realized that he *did* have the knowledge with which he could have formed a blink hole himself, but then decided that in his present state of mind it was probably safer for them all that Gwen was casting it. One of his would probably have proven unstable.

"How long does this take?" Haiden whispered.

The ground to the front of their party erupted. It was an eruption of white fur and daggerlike claws as long as Cabe's body. One of the Ice Dragon's abominations, more anxious than the rest, judging by how it had outdistanced the rest of the pack. Gwen shook violently, but she succeeded in continuing her spell. It would only be a few more seconds before they had their escape route— if the monster would give them that long.

Haiden's maddened steed turned in circles as he tried to regain control. Cabe put a hand on the head of his own mount and that of Gwen and cast a false illusion in their minds. As far as the horses were concerned now, everything was peaceful. They readily would have stood where they were, even up to the point when the digger would have leeched the life from each of them. Cabe, however, had no intention of letting things get that far.

It was almost reflex action. The gleaming bow was before him in that same instant, the shaft, which glowed like a piece of the sun itself, ready. He only had to look at the target; the bow did the rest. With a precision that would have been physically impossible for an inexperienced bowman such as Cabe, the shaft sought its target's most vulnerable spot. Cabe watched the arrow disappear into the thick fur. He had a momentary fear that there was no vulnerable spot.

The digger had one great clawed appendage high in the air when suddenly the creature's entire frame shuddered. It moved forward a bit more, as if trying to deny that anything was amiss. Then it began to tip to one side, seemingly unsure in which direction to turn. It did not stop tipping, however, and in seconds it was down on its side.

Lifeless.

Haiden finally succeeded in calming his horse. He turned to gaze at the hulking corpse and shook his head. "I have heard tales of the sun-spawned bow that some mages can form, but never did I think to see a Dragon Master actually use it. One shot."

Cabe watched the bow vanish. He hoped there would not be need of it again for some time. "That was only one creature. If we're attacked by several, the bow won't be able to save us. I don't know if I could do it again, either. It seems to come when it wants to."

"It's done!"

They both twisted around. Gwen looked proudly at the blink hole, then, with a bit of an uncertain stagger, returned to her horse. When she had remounted, with a little help from the other two, the trio wasted no time in riding through the gate. Cabe wondered briefly if the Ice Dragon would notice the loss of one of his vampiric monstrosities and whether he would realize what had killed it. If so, they might arrive in the Wastes to find an army of the creatures waiting for them. Or something worse.

What they emerged into was a terrible, horrible cold. Haiden called it an obscene cold, and neither of the mages argued. It tore not only at their physical bodies but at their minds and souls as well. This was the ultimate goal of the Ice Dragon; this was what all the domains would be like if the lord of the Northern Wastes was not stopped. Nothing would remain but a lifeless, chill landscape where even the mountains and hills would eventually be worn down by the rough winds.

They had planned in part for this moment, and each of the trio now pulled out furs. These they wrapped tightly around their bodies. The furs protected them fairly adequately from the physical cold, but there was little they could do about the other. The horses shivered. Physical cold they could understand; the soul-numbing cold was something new and frightening. It was only training and trust that kept them from trying to turn back.

Cabe took some time to cast a small spell about them. It lessened the wind and warmed up their immediate environment a little. He would have preferred to avoid casting such a spell so near to the Ice Dragon's citadel, but Gwen was in need of help. Her initial enthusiasm over the success of the blink hole had given way to exhausted depression. If they were forced to fight in the next hour, she would be of little use. The blink hole had been a chancy thing; Gwen had never been to the Northern Wastes. The extra effort needed to ensure their safety had drained her.

It was as she had suggested. The Wastes were riddled with the burrowing trails of the monstrosities, but there appeared to be no more of them. The thought that there might be a second wave was not spoken out loud, though each of them knew that the others had thought of it as well. Such thoughts had a nasty way of coming true if one was not careful.

Far ahead, Haiden could barely make out a jagged range of mountains. For all practical purposes, they were on the Ice Dragon's front step. It was not unlikely that the Dragon King had servants other than the nearly mindless leviathans moving south, and that meant that each step closer increased the chance of discovery. In no way could they relax their guard now.

Haiden whispered something in a language vaguely familiar in Cabe's memories. "What is that?"

"A death call. Mine or the Ice Dragon's. If that's what it takes, I'm prepared to give it."

Cabe shuddered, reminded again of his own future. He dared

not dwell on it much, fearing now that he would bring Gwen and the elf with him. "I hope that won't be necessary."

The elf shrugged. "There are worse ways of dying. I could become trapped in a cell with a dozen sprites—those things you insist on calling wood elves—and die of insanity."

Haiden broke into a slight smile a moment later. Cabe was amazed at his companion's ability to joke even now and it raised his own spirits a little. Gwen smiled but said nothing; even conversation was too tiring for the moment.

The stark emptiness of the landscape overwhelmed them for the first hour, then merely became yet another obstacle in what was becoming an endless list. The cold continued to gnaw at both body and soul and the horses began to stumble. Even increasing the potency of the spell around them did little good. It was, they knew, because they were moving ever nearer to the caverns of the Ice Dragon. They also knew that, with each waking hour, the drake lord was growing stronger. Soon, it would be doubtful if anything could overcome him.

A mist was developing, further hampering their progress. The mountains loomed more like indistinct specters than actual peaks. The ground, torn asunder by the marauding behemoths, was proving treacherous. The mist was low, forcing them to ride carefully. Often, they found that they had arrived at some gully or unstable hill formed by the creatures; that meant turning back or seeking another route. Once, the earth began to give way beneath Cabe's steed, but he was able to back the animal up before the last of his support crumbled and fell into a new ravine some two or three hundred feet deep. No one wanted to hazard a guess as to the actual size of a beast that could bore such a vast tunnel. Their pace picked up for some time after that.

Something began to nag Cabe on the edge of his consciousness. It was as if Nathan were taking an active part, watching for something that Cabe did not understand. It comforted him until he realized that to draw that which had been his grandfather from his own being must surely be a threat of the direst proportions. If he was to die in the Wastes, Cabe was at least hoping for a swift, painless death. Not the sort of thing he suspected his guardian was watching for.

There was a tickle in his mind and at first he believed the dire threat was upon them. Then, Cabe came to understand that it was his own innate senses—the difference between one and the other was debatable, but he was not inclined to contemplate it here and now—and that he was feeling the touch of another mind. Not one of his companions, either.

Very near, he decided. *Just—next to me?*

Swift and silent, the attacker pulled Cabe from the saddle. He had a glimpse of reptilian features and then was locked in a life-or-death struggle. His mind, dulled by constant exposure to the Ice Dragon's numbing spell, could not ready a proper defense. He was forced to go hand against hand with his adversary.

"Bedlammmm!" the drake hissed. His voice was chillingly familiar and the young mage decided then that his death was fast approaching.

This was Toma.

On reflex, his hand went up in a basic defensive spell. The drake should have seen it, should have reacted, but all he did was laugh and attempt to throttle the human. Cabe's spell was only half complete when another form joined the battle, wrapping strong arms around the drake.

Toma lost his grip and began cursing wildly. Cabe surprised himself; instead of continuing the spell, he formed a fist and lashed out at the drake. Every bone in his hand vibrated and the pain was probably worse for him than for Toma, but he succeeded in driving the air from the warrior's lungs. Haiden assisted with a great bear hug. The drake fell to his knees and a simple spell bound him so that even at full strength he would have a long, tedious time escaping. Time they would not give him.

When they felt it safe, they turned him over. Toma's eyes blazed and his sharp, tearing teeth were quite visible. He was suffering from exposure and moved in a slightly drunken fashion. The assault had taken the last of his energy reserves. It was obvious that he had been out in the Wastes for days.

"Toma." Cabe sought the drake's attention. Toma's eyes kept wandering to the horses and it was very evident that he was not thinking about them as riding animals.

The reptilian warlord turned to gaze steadily at the speaker.

When his mind acknowledged that it was Cabe, Toma's eyes narrowed and he spit, not an easy feat for one with a long, forked tongue.

"Bedlam."

"You've obviously been through a lot. Cooperate and we'll treat you fairly."

"What are you saying?" Gwen, partially recovered, stood ready to slay the drake. She had not forgotten the days she had been his prisoner. Toma had chosen to torture her each time she spoke back or attempted escape.

Cabe understood her—a part of him wanted to see Toma die slowly for everything he had done—but this was a time when, distasteful as it was, there were priorities. The warlord who had been the driving force behind the massacre of Mito Pica had to be wandering the Wastes for good reason. That reason could only have to do with the Ice Dragon.

"Well?"

"Cabe . . ." Even Haiden was protesting. Cabe quieted both of them with a look. Before him was the drake responsible for the death of the man who had been the only father he knew, the half-elf Hadeen. Having an elf with him did not make his present decision any more pleasant. Yet, the Ice Dragon was a far greater threat, for his success meant the destruction of everything and everyone and a land where only the clans of the Waste would rule—if even they survived.

A semblance of sanity returned to Toma. "You've bound me. With sorcery that should not work. What a fool am I! I could have struck you all down from a distance!"

That was doubtful, considering the drake's present health, but Cabe said nothing about it. "Did you come from the Ice Dragon's citadel?"

Toma closed his eyes briefly, as if there were memories he did not want to bring up, and then nodded slowly. The three exchanged looks of consternation. If this was what contact with the lord of the Northern Wastes had done to as powerful and deadly a nemesis as Toma, then what could they expect?

"He's mad." Toma added quietly. "You probably think this is some conquest, some master plan to make all the lands become one—his own."

"It's not?" Gwen had to force the words out. She knew already that she was not going to like whatever answer their prisoner was about to give them.

"No. We've all been fools, humans. I came to him for aid for my parent, my emperor."

Cabe remembered. Toma had been a prisoner of Azran, and the dragon emperor had been reduced, by Cabe himself, to a near-mindless child. Both drakes had been missing when he and the Gryphon had succeeded in destroying Azran. Now, he knew where they had headed.

Toma continued, the story spilling out now. Difficult as it was to read his features, there seemed to be great relief; for days he had sought to tell someone. "He offered me a place to stay while he sought a cure. The Ice Dragon has always been the most traditional of the Dragon Kings, even if he is more concerned with our ruling race as a whole and may despise the emperor. If the emperor is in danger, he would be the first to step forward to offer aid—so I thought."

Bloodred eyes began studying the horses once more. Cabe quietly signaled Haiden to bring something from the packs. While the elf hurried, Cabe urged the prisoner on.

His eyes switching to Haiden, Toma said, "I waited . . . and waited. Always there was something that prevented him from aiding me. Then, he began talking about his grand plans, always only a little at a time. As with you, I saw a plan of conquest and worried that I had made a fatal mistake; I had delivered the one stepping stone he needed. My parent. He placed a handful of his warriors near me—to assist me, he said—but in actuality to watch me. I wondered then why these were the only members of his clan that I ever really had contact with."

Haiden returned with some near-frozen meat. He was set to at least warm it when, shedding his dignity, Toma lunged forward in a desperate attempt to pull it to him with his teeth. Disgusted, the elf tore off a chunk and held it gingerly before the prisoner, suspecting with each passing second that Toma would take his hand with it. When the piece had been devoured—Gwen had turned away—Cabe blocked an attempt by Haiden to feed Toma further.

"You've more to say. Then, we'll feed you." Cabe did not

like what he had become, but he justified it by telling himself that much of it was really the drake lord's fault.

Toma nodded. "Agreed. I will cut to the meat of it, so to speak, so that I can satisfy a bit of my hunger even as I satisfy your curiosity."

"This is it, then. Those four and a few others were all that remained of Ice's clans. The rest had been sacrificed—no—the rest had sacrificed themselves to his grand experiment."

Cabe shuddered. "His own clans fed the source from which he draws his power, the power that he uses to turn the lands into one great Waste."

"Something like that. There is a thing . . . much like those creatures out there, but horribly more so. It draws from them and he, in turn, draws from it. He calls it his queen. Dragon of the Depths! The mad lord intends to turn the entire land into one Waste, yes, but not so he can rule! There will be no one, not even the Ice Dragon. In the end, he will unleash the full force remaining within him. The backlash will kill that monstrosity that is so much a part of him and that in turn will kill those other things, they being only parts of the whole. By then, though, the upstart vermin, you humans, will be dead—as will every drake, elf, dwarf, Seeker, and whatever else is a part of the Dragonrealm."

There was more the drake intended to say, but exhaustion had made him pause for breath. Cabe stood up and looked at the others. "This is far worse than memory indicated. Whatever Nathan discovered, it was only a minute portion of what the Ice Dragon has. I thought I understood, but—I was wrong." Briefly, he was the Cabe who had never known life other than as a huntsman's inept son. "I—I don't know what to do next."

He heard laughter then. Laughter that mocked him; laughter not quite sane. Cabe looked down and stared into the eyes of the smiling Toma.

"In the end, you are as weak as all your kind, Bedlam," the drake said disdainfully. "One wonders how the Ice Dragon could believe you warm-bloods will inherit our kingdom. If we were not so close to death, I would rejoice that the greatest threat of the manlings is a coward and a fool."

Toma shrieked in pain, for Gwen, at the limits of her patience, had decided to give him back some of the agony she had suffered at his hands. Cabe reached out with his mind and canceled her spell. She whirled on him.

"He's said all that he has to say! You know he's too dangerous to leave alive. The Gryphon has ordered him slain on sight. The Dragon Kings will certainly not miss him! None of them want anything to do with this . . . this *pretender*!" She virtually spit out the last word and Toma, recovered from her assault, bared his teeth and hissed. Had it not been for the cold and a lack of food, he might have become a threat. As it was, his brief surge of fury was followed immediately by a collapse. He was barely able to stay conscious. His eyes closed and then opened.

"A truce, Bedlam. I see it now. There is only one way that we might overcome the mad monarch of the Northern Wastes. We —we must work together. I know the caverns. I know where that "bride" of his lies and some of the things he has for servants. I will swear by the Dragon of the Depths if need be!"

Cabe did not look at Gwen, for he knew the response she wanted. Instead, he waited for Haiden to respond. The elf shifted uncomfortably. No matter what answer he gave, he knew that someone here would not be forgiving. Haiden, well versed at reading faces, also knew what Cabe's decision was going to be, regardless. What the sorcerer wanted was for the elf to tell him why that decision was not right.

Haiden shook his head, also refusing to look at the Lady of the Amber. "He's right, lord and lady. And if he swears by the Dragon of the Depths, he will keep his word."

Gwen said nothing, but her face was pale. At last, she acquiesced, albeit very reluctantly. "Make sure he swears first, at least."

They waited. Toma cleared his throat and slowly said, "I swear, as one of the living line of the Dragon of the Depths, he who is sire of us all, that I shall abide by the truce until this threat to all of us is at an end." He stared up at them defiantly. "That is the most I can promise."

It was not much, but Haiden nodded satisfaction. With some hesitation, they removed the drake lord's bonds. Toma stood up slowly, hands before him, and brushed himself off. His legs were shaking and all three of them could see that he lacked even the power to walk for very long, much less attack or shift his shape.

He was also covered with splotches, possible signs of frostbite, though not one of them knew if drakes suffered that problem. Toma eyed the meat in the elf's hand and then glanced at Cabe. The young mage nodded and Toma reached out a hand for the ice-covered food. Haiden gave it to him, being careful not to hold onto the meat any longer than necessary. It was a wise move, for the drake jerked it out of his hand and began gorging himself on it. Cabe sourly reminded him of the dangers of eating too much too fast after starving and then purposefully turned his back on their new ally.

Cabe wandered over to the horses and petted them absently. Gwen joined him a few seconds later.

"I can see something is bothering you. Can't you tell me?"

He sighed, watching vaguely as his breath floated away in a cloud of mist. "There are a lot of things bothering me, Gwen. Most of them I can't even name. A couple I don't want to even mention because I'll really start to think about them." He turned and took her in his arms. "I want you to know . . . I'll always understand if there's a part of you that will always love Nathan. I try to be everything he was; I try to be the pillar of confidence I know everybody is looking for."

"That's not—"

"Shhh. Let me finish. I'm not always those things, but I will promise one thing. Whatever it takes, whatever it costs, I'll make sure that the Ice Dragon fails . . . if only to save you."

"Cabe . . ."

He refused to let her say anything, instead holding her tighter and kissing her. They did not separate until a mocking hiss alerted them to the presence of another. "How . . . warm-blooded. You can say your goodbyes when we confront my dear 'uncle.' Time is, I promise you, running very, very short."

Duke Toma had regained enough strength to walk, but little else. "I regret also that I will be in need of your powers, Bedlam. My own, now that I have them again, are still far less than perfect. I could use, indeed, I need, something to keep me physically warm."

Cabe shook his head. "No more spells. We have to conserve." He pulled a blanket off his horse, hating himself all the while for depriving his mount so that one like Toma could keep warm. Another thought occurred to him.

"Much as I dislike it, I'm going to let you ride, drake. I can walk for a while and then Haiden can take a turn. We'll need you coherent and your powers at some level of usefulness."

Smiling, Toma reached for the reins of Cabe's horse. "My thanks, Bedlam."

As he struggled to mount, some of the human's anger died. The warlord was barely able to climb up, despite his bravado. Again, Cabe found his thoughts turning to the caverns of the Ice Dragon and how little time remained—for the Dragonrealm and for himself.

XVII

How many more days of this?

General Toos ran a hand through his thinning hair as he sat down upon the chair he had ordered his men to place in the audience chamber of the Gryphon's palace. He had the men place it a level below and to the right of the throne, so that any who came would know without a doubt that he was acting on behalf of the Gryphon and was not entertaining thoughts of a coup.

As much as they argued, he could see that with very few exceptions the ministers and various functionaries were relieved to know that it was he who would command them in their ruler's place. They knew the general for what he was, an honest and blunt man who played no favorites, no matter how obvious the bribes might be. Toos understood the nuances of politics, but he had developed such a system of honesty—which he always claimed he had learned from the Gryphon—that even those ministers with the dirtiest pockets generally dealt with him fairly. It was, they had long discovered, to the best of their interests.

A page announced the captain of the guard, a fellow who had served under Toos for nearly seven years. Alyn Freynard was from the hill men of the western coasts. His people were the most secluded of the major human settlements and generally preferred to keep it that way. They proved industrious in their own right, which was why they had never been disturbed by the Iron Dragon, who had ruled that region until his fatal attempt to usurp all power from Gold.

Freynard had been different than most. His father was a trader from Zuu, a tall, burly man, much like the late Prince Blane, who had chosen to stay his winters with one of the local women. Freynard's people tended to be more open-minded about such things, which had caused no end of grief the first time the young mercenary had chanced to bed the unhappy wife of one of Talak's leading merchants. In the years since joining the guardsmen, however, Freynard had become more a younger copy of the general and incidents like Talak were left behind. Unlike Toos, he had eventually taken a wife, something his former countrymen would have looked at in almost as much shock as the merchant had upon finding the tall, sandy-haired man with the clean-looking face in his bed with a supposedly ill bride.

The captain saluted sharply. The sandy color of his hair had begun to give way to speckles of pure white, even though he was several years younger than Toos. His visage remained much the same as those earlier days, still the clean look of a green recruit, but there were a few scars. It was rumored he kept his own wife very contented and several other men's wives very disgruntled because of Talak.

Toos would have trusted him with his life—and had several times.

"What is it you want, Captain?"

Freynard approached the general respectfully. "Sir, I have received reports that two men, perhaps more, from the List have been reported in the city walls."

That caused the general to sit straighter. The List, as it had come to be referred as, was a sheet outlining the known facts concerning several humans and nonhumans that the Gryphon or

Toos felt should be watched out for. Most of them were cutthroats or renegades from some mercenary group. A few others were known traitors who had sought escape from Penacles but who might return. A few, like Azran and Toma, were in a different league altogether. It was because of the List that the Gryphon had had the captain of the guard also trained as a sort of secret law officer.

"Who?"

"The description of one matches the foreigner that our majesty has been so concerned with of late. He has at least one accomplice who matches the description of the other raider who arrived with him in Irillian."

Gripping the arms of the chair so tightly that one cracked, Toos leaned forward. "Let me understand this, Freynard; D'Shay is in Penacles—not Irillian?"

"If the watchers were correct—and I have no reason to doubt these men."

"I see." The general's mind raced. Somehow, for some reason, the wolf raider who had obsessed the Gryphon so much was now in the city—which meant that he had gotten past a very well-trained unit of guardsmen.

"Where were they seen?"

"At the Silver Unicorn." The Silver Unicorn was the most expensive of inns, a vast place that catered to merchants and diplomats. Toos blinked. Odd that D'Shay should pick so vulnerable a spot to hide.

"Has anyone moved to pick them up?"

"No, sir. I ordered my men to continue watching while I sought instructions from you. This seemed a special case, general."

Toos nodded. Freynard was correct. D'Shay was about as special a case as there could be. From what little the Gryphon had told him, the man was very dangerous. Toos had the impression that much of what his lord had told him had come from some buried memory, that the Gryphon knew more, but could not recall anything but impressions.

"Have them continue to watch. Find out if there are only two of them or if we have a nest of vermin developing here. Also find out how they got past the city gates."

"Sir!" The captain saluted and turned to leave.

"Alyn . . ."

"General?"

Toos turned his head, revealing to Freynard the foxlike profile. "If it looks as if D'Shay is slipping away from us, I want him captured or killed. Use your own judgment. A trial is not necessary for this one."

"Yes, sir." The captain departed. Toos knew that Freynard understood. If D'Shay did die, that would be the end of it. The Gryphon's obsession would be no more. He would settle down and rule the city he had freed from the tyranny of the Dragon Kings.

That was the way it should be, Toos decided. Both he and the Gryphon had gone beyond the point where they had personal lives, personal obsessions. Penacles was their duty now.

Nothing else mattered.

The blink hole had opened into his personal chambers.

The Gryphon stepped out, once again very relieved that he was free of the void. He glanced around. It was night. Nothing had been disturbed since his departure save where servants had cleaned up after him. His books were still in place, the iron golems were still guarding the door on this side, and he assumed that meant that there were two more on the outside.

He stepped to one side and and waited for the Blue Dragon to follow. It had proven harder for the drake to correctly locate the new blink hole than he had thought. After several attempts, each followed by several hours of recuperation, he had finally succeeded. It was about time, too, as far as the Gryphon was concerned. Precious time was slipping away.

Still, the days had not been wasted. They were now certain they had every parchment, every artifact from the Blue Dragon's collection that might be of use to them.

The Dragon King, one arm filled with scrolls and whatnot, stepped out. "Well, I—"

Whatever the drake lord was about to say was forgotten, for suddenly two heavy figures reached for him. The scrolls spilled to the floor as the Dragon King sought escape. One attacker failed to reach him, but the other caught hold of one of his legs.

The iron golems were fulfilling their purpose: defending their master from any enemy, including drakes. In his relief to be in his own quarters again, the lionbird had forgotten that an enemy did not have to attack him; he or she merely had to be there. Some portion of his mind had assumed that since the Blue Dragon was acting as his ally, there would be no attack.

Before the situation grew any worse—for he knew that the Dragon King would defend himself and then where would the palace be?—the Gryphon shouted "Stop!"

The iron golems hesitated, but did not halt.

"Gryphon!" Blue shouted. One hand was already going up. If the Gryphon did not hurry, his ally would be unleashing something particularly nasty at any moment.

"I command you! Cease all movement!"

This time, the golems froze. Another command allowed the Dragon King to free his leg. After that, the Gryphon was able to order the unliving creatures back to their normal locations.

"My apologies, drake lord. I had no idea that would happen."

The Blue Dragon studied his leg for broken bones. "Indeed. Remind me never to attack you in your private rooms."

"Or in the hall. Any more commotion, and there would have been twice as many."

"I am impressed. Iron golems are difficult to make. Golems in general are, but iron is one of the most difficult holding cases for the elemental spirit."

"The work in creating one is made up by their efficiency, such as it is," the Gryphon added.

"So I see."

With calculated movements, the drake lord carefully picked up the scrolls. He straightened and looked at the Gryphon expectantly. "It would be best if we went straight to the libraries. Are they far from here?"

The Gryphon could not help smiling a little. At present, the tapestry, which was the only entrance to the libraries, hung on the wall behind the Dragon King. "Not far at all. If you will follow me please."

While the puzzled drake watched, the lionbird walked past him and over to the tapestry.

It was the most perfect combination of needlework and sorcery that the Gryphon had ever seen. Each and every detail of the city was included. Everything was up to date. A small shop was missing from the merchants' district. The Gryphon suspected that he would hear about a fire in a day or two.

The symbol for the libraries, of late an open book in red, was in none of the usual locations. There were always a few surprises, it seemed. He finally located it underneath, of all things, one of the schools he had instituted during his early years as ruler of Penacles. For a city legendary as the seat of knowledge, the general population had been one of the most ignorant in all the realms. The Dragon King who had ruled here had been no fool; it knew that a learned citizenry would be a troublesome citizenry. It was one of the first things the Gryphon had changed and the results had shown. Penacles was not only an oasis of knowledge, but it was the cradle for new thought. More innovations came from the Gryphon's domain than all the others combined, save perhaps Mito Pica before it fell.

He turned toward the Blue Dragon, who was admiring the tapestry but growing impatient. The Gryphon placed a finger on the mark of the libraries. "See how this compares with your blink hole."

His concentration was broken by the sounds of men outside. At least one of them was shouting.

One of the golems suddenly announced, "General Toos demands entrance."

"Demands?" The Gryphon glanced at his companion. He did not think Toos would take kindly to a Dragon King standing in the royal chambers themselves, a Dragon King about to depart for the precious libraries.

"If I may, drake lord, I'd like to suggest that you perhaps step into the next room for a moment. I want to break the news of your presence to my second, but I want to do it calmly."

"As you wish." There was a touch of disdain in the drake's voice. In his own domain, he would have shouted down any protest; either that or he would have killed the protester.

When the Blue Dragon was out of sight, the lionbird said, "Toos alone may enter."

His exact words must have been repeated, for there was some debating. A minute later, the doors opened and the general entered, very anxious and not a little bit angry. Several other figures stood outside, trying to see what was going on. The doors closed in their faces.

Toos bowed. "Your majesty—Gryphon. I am relieved to see you once again."

"Relieved? You looked as if you were about to kill me, Toos. I have to admit that my actions were not entirely my own before my departure, but everything is satisfactory now."

"Not your own?" The ex-mercenary studied him closely. "Who was responsible? D'Shay? I'll—"

The Gryphon shook his head impatiently. He did not want his aide getting worked up. It would not do the introduction of their new ally any good. "It's over with. Speaking of D'Shay, the wolf raiders have departed Irillian. You can sleep easy tonight, old friend. I won't be running off after him for the time being."

He expected the news to satisfy Toos at least a little, but the general only looked even more unhappy. Evidently, the last few days had worn him down. It was probably best to bring out the Dragon King now, before matters worsened.

"You are aware of trouble to the north?" When the human nodded, the Gryphon continued. "The Ice Dragon moves, Toos. He's mad and even his brethren have no use for him any more. It turned out that the true reason for going to Irillian had to do with that."

The Gryphon had always counted on his second for his ability to grasp situations and make the best of them. It was one of those skills which some said were the sorcerous abilities he seemed to lack even though the man was marked by a silver streak in his hair. Toos did not disappoint him.

"Blue sought a pact with you."

"Correct."

The foxlike visage turned grim. "You wouldn't be telling it the way you are unless you were considering accepting it—or you already have."

"I have."

The narrow figure turned and gazed about the room. "Someone reported noise up here and thought they heard your voice. They also thought they heard another voice." Toos swivelled and asked, "If I may be bold, Gryphon, how did you return here? I knew when you left; it's part of my job. The trouble is, I didn't know when you returned. I expect many things from Freynard, but some things I do myself and I should have heard. While I know you have the power to teleport, even you would think twice about teleporting from Irillian. Too much chance of something going awry.''

"I came through a portal. A thing called a blink hole.''

"I see.'' Toos shook his head. "There is nothing I can say that will change the situation, Gryphon. You've made your decision and, as your aide and subject, I will abide by that decision. From the way you talk, I assume you did not come alone. The Dragon King need not hide; it is unbefitting for any being of his stature, enemy or ally.''

Heavy footfalls told the Gryphon that the drake lord had indeed stepped out of the other room. "Well said, human. I approve of loyalty, especially when seasoned with reason. You are to be commended. My spies were not wrong in their judgment of you.''

The last was said with a touch of humor, but all three knew it to be true. As the master of Irillian had profiles on his enemies to the south, so too did the Gryphon have profiles of many of his adversaries. Only a handful, such as the Storm Dragon and, most especially, the Crystal Dragon, were nearly total unknowns. The Gryphon wondered how much more the Blue Dragon really knew about the last two. They were fellow Dragon Kings, true, and there was some contact between Blue and Storm, but that meant little in the long run. The Ice Dragon was an example of how little even the other Kings knew about one of their own brethren.

"Milord.'' Toos bowed.

The Gryphon walked over and put an arm over the general's shoulders. "Toos, you trust me.''

"Yes . . .''

"I'm going to take him with me to the libraries.''

The human tensed. The lionbird's grip on his shoulders tightened before Toos could get out of control.

"You said you would abide by my decision, friend. Hear me now. The Dragon King is a master sorcerer and a historian as well. Those are the two greatest qualities one needs when facing the absurdity of the libraries.''

"Forgive me, milord. It is your decision and, as I said, I will obey.''

The Gryphon would have been more satisfied if the look on his second's face had not been so sullen. He made the best of it, though. "Fine! We will be popping in and out. There's no telling what will happen. I want you to keep an eye out in the north, though. Alert me to everything."

"Yes, milord."

A few of the Gryphon's feathers ruffled, but he said nothing more. He released Toos and returned to the tapestry, the Dragon King close on his heels. As the lord of Penacles placed his finger on the symbol of the libraries, he turned to Toos and added, "Contact Cabe and the Lady Gwen. Tell them I need to speak to them as soon as possible."

The Gryphon and his drake ally became blurry. Toos instinctively blinked, trying to get them back into focus. He knew better, but he did it every time. Gradually, the two dwindled away until the human was alone in the room. He shook his head and departed.

The others were still waiting for him; the news of their monarch's return had everyone in an uproar. Toos patiently raised his hands and waited for the hall to quiet.

"His majesty the Gryphon will not be available for the near future. He is conferring with others on a matter important, not only to Penacles, but to other domains as well. If there should arise any problems of such magnitude that I myself cannot give approval, I will speak to him. That is all."

Everyone wanted to ask more, but the soldier was not having any of it. He barged past the ministers and assorted bureaucrats, his greatest desire to be as far away from the royal chambers as possible.

It was a rare thing for him to not divulge information to his lord. The Gryphon had come to trust him as a brother and Toos felt that he was now betraying that trust. He had not told the Gryphon about D'Shay's sudden presence in the city, a sudden appearance made even more suspicious when it coincided with the lionbird's own return, something even the general had not known until after it had happened. It had also proved impossible to speak of the plague of horrors coming out of the south; already, they were well into the Hell Plains and, more importantly, into Irillian.

Toos knew it was wrong, but he wanted the Dragon King weakened before he spoke out. If the Blue Dragon became desperate, he would be more open to influence by the Gryphon, which meant more influence by Penacles.

He had neared his own chambers when one of Freynard's aides came rushing up. The man was out of breath; he must have searched almost the entire palace, Toos realized. The general gave him time to calm down.

"Sir . . . sir, Captain Freynard sent me to report that the wolf raider and his companion are on the move."

All thoughts of his dealings with the Gryphon were pushed aside. "Clarify."

"Several minutes ago, both figures—they'd been eating—suddenly rose as if something they'd been waiting for had happened. They hurried upstairs, supposedly to their rooms. One of our men went up to investigate and did not return after the allotted time. Captain Freynard himself went up, came down a couple of minutes later, and shouted that they had slipped away. They'd discovered our man and knocked him senseless. The captain ordered some of the others after them and sent me to tell you what happened."

"*Damn!*" The guardsman jumped from the sheer intensity in the general's voice. The ex-mercenary knew it was not fair of him to take out his anger on the guard, but stopping now was impossible. "You return to Captain Freynard and remind him of what I said earlier. He'll know what you mean. Tell him to make sure that those two and any accomplices do not leave this city in one piece! Is that clear?"

"Sir!" It was impossible for the young soldier to stand any more at attention than he was already. Toos took a deep breath and counted to ten. In a calmer voice he said, "That's all, get going."

The guardsman practically left a smoking trail behind him. Toos could not help smiling despite his troubles. He needed sleep now. This day had been far too hectic, especially the last few hours. If he wanted to be sharp, at least a couple hours of rest would be needed. Since the Gryphon's departure, the number of hours he had rested collectively added up to less than the sum total of the digits on both hands. Most of those hours were cat naps.

He hoped tomorrow would bring some sort of peace, but, judging by past experience, he knew that was wishful thinking.

"General, sir!"

Evidently, he was not to get sleep after all. Toos wondered if some god had it in for him. With more bite than he intended, he snapped, "What is it *now*?"

The soldier, who had been on sentry duty and knew nothing of the sort of day Toos had been having, was forced to take some time to regather his suddenly scattered thoughts.

"There . . . there is an . . . an elf waiting without, sir. A messenger from the lord of the Dagora Forest, so he says."

"Does he? What does this messenger want?"

"He says that his words are for the Lord Gryphon and he will not speak them to any other unless by his orders."

"*That* might prove a bit difficult. While the Gryphon has returned to Penacles, he expects to be . . . to be in negotiations for quite some time with one of his counterparts."

"Sir?" The soldier had not understood a thing.

Toos waved the matter aside. "Never mind. Bring him to me. If I can't convince him to tell me what's so important, he'll just have to wait until the Gryphon is available. Go get him, lad."

"Sir!"

As the young guard hurried off, Toos tried to calculate how long it would take him to return with the elfin messenger and whether or not there would be at least enough time for the general to restore a little of his depleted energy reserves.

"Manaya," he muttered, thinking of a particularly volatile wine he drank. Manaya would wake him up—though he would regret it come the next day. He hoped the message from the Green Dragon warranted the elf's attitude. If not, it was possible that the Dragon King would be short one obstinate messenger before very long.

The Seeker adjusted its balance and closed its eyes, the avian's mind searching the thoughts of those within the palace. It was a difficult task; contact worked better for the transmission of alien thoughts. Still, the patterns of the primitives within were easy enough to pick up once it located them. Only staying in contact for any extended period of time might prove a real hazard. More sensitive primitives might detect the intruding presence.

One of the arrogant ones was here, as was the hybrid who ruled here. The Seeker had not yet made up its mind about the hybrid;

its avian qualities did it justice, but it continued to ensnare itself in the workings of the humans. This was something the Seeker mind could not fathom. Lesser races were to be used. They were rewarded if they did well, as one rewards an intelligent animal, but they were to be punished or forgotten if they failed.

Both the arrogant one and the hybrid were gone. They could only be in the libraries. This Seeker had never seen the libraries, only the eldest had ever seen them, but it knew that the libraries were worthy of the respect of even the elders. That meant that things were progressing as they should be. All the Seekers needed was time.

The avian stretched his wings momentarily, secure that its hiding place on the roof would not be suspected by a race that could not fly.

The Seeker allowed itself a moment of satisfaction concerning its appointed task and then readied itself for the night's wait. Beginning the morrow, it knew, things would happen of great interest to all.

XVIII

There were few things capable of truly impressing a Dragon King, but the Libraries of Penacles had most definitely succeeded in doing just that.

Staring down the endless corridors of books, the Blue Dragon had shaken his head and muttered, "Astounding!"

"You've never seen them before?"

"Never. Brother Purple was quite protective of his power. He did not trust us."

The Gryphon squawked. "I wonder why."

After that, it was a case of hit or miss as the two sought out clues. A gnomish librarian—the lionbird was never certain whether there were several or just this one—was waiting to assist them. He seemed undisturbed by the presence of the drake, taking his requests as he would the Gryphon's.

Unlike previous visits, the librarian did not lead them to particular books; instead, he brought them to a table and two chairs, something the monarch of Penacles had never encountered in all his time down here. The presence of these three pieces of mundane furniture bothered him, because they were an indication that this might be a long, involved search. Even before they had made any specific requests, the little man was bringing them an armful of thick, distinguished-looking books.

After going through the first hundred or so and discovering some of the libraries' tricks—such as nonsense verse and unanswerable riddles—the Dragon King threw one of the heavy volumes against the shelves. The Gryphon watched with annoyance.

"This is preposterous! What madness built this place?"

The Gryphon sighed and closed the tome he had been perusing. "From what I gather, even the Purple Dragon, with all the time available to him, never discovered that one fact in here."

Standing, the drake lord began to pace; a scholar though he was, he was also a warlord of his kind. Inactivity, or worse, useless activity, made him nervous. He eyed the Gryphon. "Tell me something that I have grown curious about. I have heard conflicting tales concerning the Purple Dragon's death. Some attribute it to you, some to Nathan Bedlam. Which is the case?"

"Both. Nathan had weakened himself with other activities. A stalemate was the best he could achieve. He needed an opening. By sheer accident, I brought him that opening. I discovered the key to the libraries and, being as possessive as he was, the Purple Dragon turned his attention to me. He underestimated me, apparently, because he left himself open for too long. Nathan was able to summon a Sunlancer bow. The action left him depleted, regretfully, and your fellow drake turned back in time to prevent a killing shot. I struck, adding yet another wound. He knew then that he was dying, and he meant to take all of Penacles, including his precious libraries, with him to wherever it is Dragon Kings go. Only Nathan's quick thinking prevented that. The force he contained destroyed both of them. . . ."

"Leaving you the spoils . . . ."

The Gryphon glared at his temporary ally. "Someone had to help these people. Apparently, some people decided they preferred a living hero to a dead one, which is why many of them think I alone was responsible. There are those with the opposite view. As far as I'm concerned, the glory can all go to Nathan Bedlam."

"Some of my brethren would be interested in this, though I doubt I'll bother to enlighten them. I meant no disrespect, Lord Gryphon. It is as I thought; Purple was arrogant and self-serving to the end. He was missed for his mind, but none of us were sorry he perished."

The gnome was bringing yet more books. The little creature looked aghast when he saw the one tome that the drake had tossed in anger. He retrieved it as soon as his hands were empty. The glare he gave the drake would have done one of the reptiles proud.

"Why do you persist in bringing us these useless volumes?" hissed the Blue Dragon.

The gnome, book in hand and anger seemingly gone, stared at him blandly. "It is my function."

"These books are filled with gibberish!"

The librarian shrugged. "To those without the knowledge— yes. It must be admitted that the specifics you seek are no longer among the contents of the libraries, but the other volumes do contain important refer—"

"Cease!" The Gryphon stood up and turned on the elderly gnome. Even that did not disturb the librarian. "You are saying that we've been wasting our time?"

"No, present lord of Penacles. What you seek can be inferred from the sources I have been bringing you. Specific information no longer exists."

"What happened to it?"

Puzzled, the gnome replied, "You do not recall? A good two dozen volumes were utterly destroyed some months back when you requested information on winds."

Winds . . .

The Gryphon stared at the books lined along the entire wall. The libraries had been invaded—somehow—and, as the gnome had said, several books were destroyed and many others damaged. At the time, the Gryphon had assumed it was the work of either the Black Dragon or Azran, both of whom would have had good reason. How stupid he had been!

The Dragon King had caught the gist of what the gnome was saying. "All of these books have some clue, then. We've just failed to understand. We should take these back to the palace and pass them among your learned men. . . ."

"We cannot. If we try to remove them, the pages will turn blank. Occasionally, some scrap of information will remain, but usually because I've taken the time to really understand it. That seems to be the only way to retain anything. Also, the more potential contained within the information, the less of a probability that we will succeed in remembering it once we've used it once."

"Such twisted thinking is the Seekers' way."

"Neither the Seekers nor the Quel, who succeeded in keeping their civilization at least partially functioning all through the avians' reign and the early years of your kind, had any knowledge of the true functions of these libraries. I can only hazard a guess at what the builders had been like. I know a few rulers have added to the structure, but most of the growth seems to be self-generating—as if the libraries were an entity."

The Blue Dragon looked around uneasily. "Not a pleasant thought, even if it is impossible—I hope." He pointed a gauntleted hand at the gnome. "You! You know nothing of this place's origins?"

In a patient voice which indicated that he had heard this question countless times before and repeated the same answer as many times, the tiny creature said, "I have always served the libraries. I only remember the libraries. I have no interest in anything else save my duties."

The Gryphon nodded. "Undoubtedly. I think, drake lord, that we should retire to the palace. There are duties which I would like to discuss and the time spent down here only serves to increase my appetite."

"A fair suggestion. I've found it difficult to concentrate on the last two volumes."

To the gnome, the lionbird said, "Leave the books we have. When we finish with those, I'll want the other ones we had before."

The librarian acknowledged the command only absently, already hard at work straightening and organizing the books on the table. The Gryphon and his reptilian ally departed.

They materialized in the Gryphon's chambers. The golems did not assault them this time, but one spoke. "General Toos left a message. He wishes to speak to his majesty upon his return."

The Gryphon did not reply at first, amazed to learn, as he glanced toward a window, that it was daylight. "What a coincidence. Did he say where he would be?"

"Message ended." The golem stared blankly ahead.

The Dragon King slowly moved toward them. "I cannot help but admire them. The secret of their manufacture came from the libraries. . . ."

"Yes, and it's well hidden. Trust me."

Turning, the drake revealed a dark smile. "As you should trust me. I was merely wondering what other treasures those books contain—if we could understand them."

"Occasionally, I get a straight answer. Why, I don't know. The whims of the libraries, I suppose."

The last statement made the Dragon King frown. "I would prefer to cease speaking about that structure as if it had a mind of its own. It makes one feel like they are in the gullet of a beast and don't know it."

"As you wish." The doors opened and the Gryphon turned to leave. He paused halfway through the doorway. "If it's all the same to you, Dragon King, I would prefer you with me. As great as the shock will be to some of my people, I would rather have you with me—in case the golems forget you are my ally."

They both knew that the Gryphon did not want to leave the drake alone with the key to the libraries. When this business was past them—providing they were alive—the lionbird would take steps to ensure the safety of the tapestry. For now, however, he lacked the time.

"I understand completely." Blue's tone matched the Gryphon's exactly. Once more, they were rulers vying in the treacherous battle of diplomacy.

The golems outside stirred briefly, but the Gryphon waved a taloned hand and they subsided. No guards were stationed in this hall. That did not mean it was undefended. At the moment, several pairs of eyes watched the progress of the two. The Gryphon knew that word would be spreading to Toos even as they walked. He doubted that they would have to be forced to walk all the way to the general's quarters.

Someone did meet them at the corner, but it was not the Gryphon's second. Rather, it was Captain Freynard and one of his men. They came to attention when they realized it was their king. Both Freynard and the guard, who must have been his own aide, gave the Dragon King a long, steady stare.

The Gryphon cleared his throat. "This Dragon King is allied with us for the moment. I trust, Freynard, that you will be discreet and tell only those who need know."

"Yes—sir."

This was proving easier than he had expected. He nodded approval to the two soldiers. "Have you seen General Toos?"

"Last time I saw him, he was in his chambers, majesty. 'Getting some rest at last,' he said. May I say it is good to see you." Freynard smiled broadly.

"I appreciate that. That'll be all."

Both men saluted, Freynard's companion with evident relief. It must have been difficult to keep calm in the presence of one of the legendary Dragon Kings. Mothers in Penacles used tales of the drake lords to frighten bad children. The lionbird wondered what Blue would think if he knew that. Then again, the master of Irillian probably already assumed such things.

The Gryphon and his companion continued on only a little further before they found themselves confronting Toos. The fox-like man might have been standing there waiting for them. He was in uniform and his breathing was very even for someone who no doubt had been running—unless he really *had* been waiting for them.

"Your majesty."

"You never cease to amaze me, my friend. I understand you wanted to see me."

The ex-mercenary glanced momentarily at the Dragon King. I would have preferred a more private audience, milord."

"Unless it really concerns something our 'comrade' should not hear, you can tell both of us."

"As you wish. In fact, it's probably proper that he hears it as well. A messenger came from the Green Dragon."

"A messenger?" Beside the Gryphon, the Blue Dragon hissed.

"An elf. I . . . There's been trouble . . . bad trouble . . . at the manor, Gryphon." Toos hesitated and then finished, "The three royal hatchlings . . . and the other four . . . uh . . . smart ones . . . are . . . are *gone!*"

"*What??*" The Dragon King took the human by the collar and raised him high. "The emperor'sss get are gone? How? Why?"

"*Put him down!*" The Gryphon did not threaten and his hands were at his sides, but the drake unconsciously obeyed him regardless of that.

"My . . . apologiesss, general. Please. What happened?"

Toos rearranged his shirt and, clearing his throat, he explained. "Marauders. The band from Mito Pica. It took me some time to get the answer out of the messenger; he was only supposed to speak to you."

"Was the Green Dragon at the Manor?" asked the Gryphon.

"He was, which makes him all the more shamed. They were protected by medallions of great power. It hid them from the sight of his eyes in the forest and allowed them to slip through the protective spell surrounding the Manor grounds."

"I do not like thisss," the Dragon King muttered. "for such rabble, they are remarkably well armed."

"Melicard probably supplies them."

"With Seeker magic as well? We have sorely underestimated that human, then. I'll rip his . . ."

The general dared speak out. "There's more. . . . And your kind is partly responsible for Melicard, drake lord. It was Kyrg who drove Melicard's father, Rennek IV, to madness."

The Blue Dragon hissed.

Toos ignored it. "As I was saying, Gryphon. They succeeded in getting in unnoticed, but then everything seemed to go wrong for them. One of the servitor drakes, a Ssarakei, I think the elf said, noticed one of them. The alarm was raised and it became a full-fledged battle."

"Surely, Brother Green and his clans were able to overwhelm them instantly! Either through magic or sheer brute strength . . ."

"The protective spell, *my lord*, apparently prevents shifting of form—and the marauders were again *protected*."

"What happened, then, Toos?" The lionbird hoped that his draconian companion would stay silent until the rest of the story was told.

"It becomes a bit confusing. Some of the marauders got into the Manor. One, who the lord of the Dagora Forest seems to think was one of the leaders, broke into the rooms set aside for the hatchlings. At the same time, the entire area was plunged into what . . . into what the Green Dragon says can only be described as a . . . I admit it sounds foolish, but an explosion of *utter darkness*!"

"Darkness?" This time, it was the Gryphon who interrupted. Darkness?

"A darkness in which the marauders in the Manor stole away with Gold's young!" the Dragon King concluded angrily.

"*That* is the confusion." Toos frowned. "The explosion was an accident. So the hapless instigator claimed—before he passed out again. Lost an arm and part of his face. It won't heal properly, either. Talak's going to have one ugly king if Melicard survives."

The Gryphon could not believe the last. "Melicard? Melicard was *with* them?"

"It was to have been his glorious victory. He wanted to rally his own folk and any others who had suffered under the—under the drakes." When the Blue Dragon said nothing, the old soldier pushed on. "Melicard said that the medallion was suppose to blind his enemies, not everyone."

"And the hatchlings?"

"They found the marauders dead and the female drakes who acted as guardians in a daze. Something had thrown the one marauder who broke in out the window. They were three floors up. He won't tell anything to anyone; he's dead. The young drakes —no one knows what happened to them in the confusion."

"What isss my brother doing to find them?"

"The messenger didn't know. I *did* ask."

The Gryphon nodded approval. "Where is the messenger now?"

"He's waiting your summons in the guards' quarters."

"Have someone get him. I want to question him and see if there might be anything he held back, though I doubt it, knowing your luck." He started to turn, but Toos was still standing there. "Was there something else?"

Toos was embarrassed. The Gryphon finally realized that, though it would have been impossible to tell that from the man's visage alone. The general had an excellent face for betting games.

"Milord, I fear that the wolf raider D'Shay is somewhere in the city."

"What?"

"Impossible!" added the Dragon King.

Toos shook his head sadly. "He was seen in the city several times. I finally had Freynard dispatch some men after him, but he and a companion escaped. No one's sighted him since."

"Freynard mentioned nothing of that when we encountered him a moment ago, but then, it wasn't his place to, I suppose. Why didn't you tell me, Toos?"

"I should think that's obvious, Lord Gryphon," the drake commented.

The lionbird turned from one to the other. Rare though it was, both man and drake were in agreement. "You were afraid I was going to go after him and forget everything else."

His oldest and dearest companion, the only man remaining from his original mercenary army, bowed his head. "I am fully prepared to be dismissed from my post and suffer whatever consequences you deem necessary."

He was being sincere, too, the Gryphon realized. "Don't be absurd, my friend. Anyone who replaced you would be no more efficient and probably a lot less capable than you. If you want to redeem yourself, keep your post and find D'Shay, hard as it is to believe that he is here."

"He must know," the Dragon King remarked. "He must have discovered our alliance."

"Which explains the speed and relative lack of resistance when his people departed *your* city."

"Point taken. It seems we both have been remiss, Gryphon. All the more reason to make haste. A pity we lack my crystal; it would have proven useful in our search, not to mention as a means of spying."

"There's . . . Yalak's Egg!"

"I beg your pardon?"

The Gryphon shook his head. "I'll tell you in a few moments. Suffice to say, I think it best we return to my chambers. Toos! I am not trying to demean you in any way, but could I ask that, when you send someone for the messenger, you also have someone bring food to my rooms, food for both of us? Make sure it's prepared and delivered by someone you trust completely, please. Oh, and make sure you have them give us something strong to drink."

"You can be sure of that. Does the— Do you have any preference, my lord?" Toos addressed the Blue Dragon politely, but there was a hint of mockery in his eyes, as if he expected the Dragon King to order raw meat.

"Fish, if you do not mind. Well salted. You need not remove the bones." The Dragon King smiled at him, predatory teeth fully displayed.

The general was not disturbed. He saluted the Gryphon, bowed very quickly to the drake, and went on his way. The lionbird turned and headed back to his chambers, a curious and annoyed Dragon King trailing him.

"We have only just departed from your rooms! Why the haste to return?"

"Yalak's Egg." When the Blue Dragon only looked more confused, the Gryphon asked, "You have heard of Yalak, I hope?"

"A Dragon Master. One of the worst of the scum."

"Yes, I suppose you would have seen them—and myself— that way. Yalak had a knack for visions. He studied the process and, when he believed he had captured the essence of such abilities, he created the Egg, a way for him to bring forth hints of the future, events of the present, and glimpses of the past."

"You have this Yalak's Egg."

"He asked me to watch it for him, not knowing his foresight would fail him and he would be one of many to fall at Azran's hands." They reached the doors, but the Gryphon did not enter immediately. He was glimpsing the past himself. "You should have made him an honorary drake, my 'friend.' Azran did more than any of your kind to bring defeat to the Dragon Masters."

"I would rather have had a human victory than deal with that shark spawn."

"Hmmph." The doors opened and the Gryphon stepped through. He felt a tingle and his mane stood on end. The Dragon King followed him, apparently unaffected by anything.

How odd, the Gryphon thought. He scanned the room, but nothing seemed amiss. The doors closed behind them. He caught sight of the Egg.

"There it— Awk!"

Impossibly strong fingers caught him by the neck. The Gryphon tried a spell, but nothing happened. *The Blue Dragon has betrayed me!* was his first thought. Then, he heard a struggle and saw the drake lord thrown across the room by the other golem. The hapless Dragon King struck the opposing wall with incredible force, cracking the wall itself and falling limply to the floor. A moment later, one golem had the Gryphon's left arm while the first one shifted its grip so that it held his right arm and his mane. It pulled his head back.

Someone stepped into the chamber from the other room. Slow, measured footsteps. More than one being, actually. Even without seeing them, the Gryphon knew who at least one of them would be.

"Things could not have turned out better," D'Shay commented to his unknown companion—most likely the other wolf raider he had been seen with. "We have the Gryphon, the vast libraries of Penacles, and even a soon-to-be-willing ally who will give us the permanent base of operations our dear commanders desired. Quite satisfactory, eh, D'Laque?"

The other raider, D'Laque, replied, "Very much so, Lord D'Shay."

A hand, a human hand, gripped the Gryphon beneath his beak. "Now. Shall we commence with plucking this prize bird?"

The Green Dragon hissed in frustration. He could not tell whether the resistance he felt was due to exhaustion on his part or defiance on the part of the one he was attempting to contact. Certainly, it would not be the first time they had refused to talk to one another. It was even worse now, with the Dragon Kings all at one another's throats.

Blue was nowhere to be found. For some reason, he had departed his kingdom. He was not the type to run, of that Green was certain. There had to be another reason.

To his surprise, somone else had answered his summons. A new Red Dragon, an heir to the one who foolishly believed he could destroy Azran. This new one would be no help to him; the few good lands of the Hell Plains had already been overrun and the remaining clans were fleeing southwest to Silver's domain. The new Dragon King's only words had been that he had come across Cabe, the Lady of the Amber, and an elf on their way north at some point. From what was babbled as Red broke the connection, the three were riding into a huge pack of the soulless creatures from the Wastes.

Silver refused his summons with a sense of pure hatred. Silver saw himself as Gold's successor, and his brother to the south as the darkest of traitors for having made peace with the human mages. Green did not bother to point out the contradictions, such as the fact that the other Dragon King still allowed Talak to remain an open city. He suspected that Silver was still having trouble bringing the domains of Iron and Bronze under his control and now had the horrors of Ice to contend with as well. In the end, the other drake cut contact off as if he had been wielding an ax. The withdrawal made the Green Dragon's head throb.

Storm deigned to speak to him, but only long enough to say he would defend his own realm and that the concerns of Green were Green's alone. The last was said with the typically flashy trait of that King; thunder and lightning punctuated each statement. He, too, left the master of the Dagora Forest with a throbbing head, but more because of the noise than anything else.

That left the Crystal Dragon.

He had avoided contacting this drake. What the Crystal Dragon had been once was certainly nothing compared to what he was now. Now, that Dragon King was a remote, enigmatic figure whose very presence at the Council of Kings always had stirred up uneasiness. Part of that uneasiness, Green had discovered, had been due to the fact that Duke Toma had apparently used the Crystal Dragon's form as his way of spying on his masters. Even still, there had been times when it could only have been the true monarch of the Legar Peninsula, the land that glistened even from the Dagora Forest.

The resistance continued, but he was not about to give in. He suspected that, in his own way, the Crystal Dragon was possibly at least as powerful as Ice was to the north. Legar had been the last bastion of the Quel race; it was rumored that some still existed, though the Green Dragon had taken Cabe's tale of thousands of sleeping creatures as pure fiction from a strained young human mind. There had never been more than a few, but they were savage and crafty fighters, invisible to many senses. The thought of thousands of the sleeping creatures was the thing of drake nightmares.

"What is it?"

The other might have been standing behind him. The Green Dragon jumped, not out of fear, but because his mind had started to drift to other things. He found it difficult at first to formulate a response.

Unlike contact with the others, he could draw no clear image of the other Dragon King. That was by the Crystal Dragon's choice. Nevertheless, it was disconcerting. The only image Green had was of a vaguely reptilian form in the midst of a blinding field of light. One of the crystal caverns. Even the ice caves of the Northern Wastes could not compare to the elegant beauty of the Crystal Dragon's home. They did have one thing in common, though; both were so alien that the lord of the forest knew he would never have any desire to visit them.

"Well?" The voice was deeper than most drakes' and it seemed to shimmer and echo as if part of the crystalline structure itself.

"You know of the doings of our brother to the north."

"Yes."

"Have you seen what he has unleashed on us? What even now makes its way south through the Hell Plains, Irillian's lands, and Silver's domain?"

"I have. I have seen everything."

"I fear that he will soon have Gold's three royal hatchlings as well."

For the first time, the glittering figure stirred. "How?"

"A ploy by the Seekers, we think. Either working with Ice or intending to use the hatchlings in some bid of power with him."

"A dangerous bid."

"I can gain no support, no combined effort from the others. I have turned to you, because you and Ice are the eldest. You two are truly brethren of one hatching, whereas the rest of us are from later ones, some of us by more than a few human generations, and can only call you brother because of our status." It was true. Humans believed all the Dragon Kings to be true brothers, born at the same hatching or from the same progenitors. In truth, the use of the word "brother" was more as an honorary title, an indication of the so-called equality between the kings. The drakes did not discourage those beliefs.

The Crystal Dragon was quiet and, in his mind, Green saw the indistinct figure stare off to one side. At last, the glistening drake said, "I will take your words under consideration. It is possible that I may have to take an active role and, then again, it is possible that I may not. For now, I will continue to observe."

"But—"

Contact was broken. This time, the drake lord knew an emptiness, as if his world would soon cease to exist—a very real possibility, he decided. The Crystal Dragon had taken his last chance for cooperation and left only the crumbs of hope. He might or might not act and even if he did it might be only when his own kingdom was threatened.

The Green Dragon's eyes blazed. Ice was as much the antithesis of his existence as was possible. The master of the Dagora Forest had no intention of giving up his domain without a struggle. His subjects were already prepared, should the abominations come this far. There did remain one other hope, too. The Gryphon.

The lionbird would not deny him. Bedlam and the Lady would not run and hide. They were his true allies, moreso than the other Dragon Kings had ever been. In truth, those three were something he could never have considered among his own kind.

Friends.

And his brethren wondered why their own kingdoms crumble about them. He smiled grimly at their ignorance.

First one landed. Then another. Then four more. They came in groups and they came alone. Regardless of how many arrived at once, the citadel of Azran was soon covered with them.

These were not the only Seekers in the Dragonrealms. They

did, however, represent the opinions of the majority. It was the choice of that majority that had led the Seekers back into the activities of the realms at large. It was because of that majority that the Seekers in general were risking much of what remained of their civilization.

More than a dozen of the avians arrived together, landing in the midst of the open courtyard. They carried seven bundles among them and each bundle wiggled and howled. The leader of this band reached down to a medallion hanging from its chest and concentrated. The bundles quieted.

There was still some debate between the Seekers as to what exact use the contents of the bundles would be put to. A few still wanted to destroy the contents as an example of the power the avians still held. They were quieted down by the cold stare of the leader of the late arrivals. This was too precious a cargo to waste so, his eyes said. The original plan would continue.

The Seekers had no true leader at the moment, their last one dying during the battle for this citadel. This one and others vied for that spot now and, if this plan succeeded, there would be no difficulty guessing who would be chosen. Yet it was a double-edged claw, for failure in such an important project would mean death at the claws of those gathered here.

In a fit of vanity so unlike its kind in general, the Seeker in charge of the newcomers had some of those in its flock unbind one of the bundles. It pointed specifically at the largest one.

Unwrapped, it revealed the eldest of the hatchlings—but not as any of the avians had expected to see it. Calmed by the Seeker artifact, it gazed out at the creatures, more human than drake. The hatchling had not yet learned to form the helm, which the adult males used to cover their incomplete and alien visages. There was little need; while it could not pass for human, it lacked the reptilian horror of the male drakes and the sensuous, inhuman beauty of the females. Given time, the hatchling might succeed where its elder brethren had failed in their shapeshifting.

The young drake reached out with one hand, but the Seeker swatted it. Hurt, the hatchling held itself tight, as if that would make the monsters around it go away.

The Seeker in charge indicated for the drake to be bound once more. When that was done, it picked several other avians from the gathering and indicated that they should join with the original band. No one hesitated.

Satisfied, the leader spread his wings and rose into the air. Two by two, the ones carrying the kidnapped hatchlings followed. When they were all aloft, the others in the band followed.

The remaining Seekers watched until the group was gone from sight. There was no discussion, no comment at all. One by one or in groups, the remaining avians departed for their respective nests. The reckoning was close at claw. It was now the time to wait. Wait either for success or possibly the beginning of the end.

XIX

While the Gryphon had pored over leagues of ancient script, Cabe and his companions had slowly pushed their way over a much longer and equally frustrating track of land that even the hardiest of creatures would have normally shunned. Now, pausing for a moment, they stared at their destination.

The ice-covered mountain began to loom overhead, even though it was still some distance away. It was by far the largest of the chain, a jagged behemoth approaching the height of Kivan Grath, the greatest of the Tyber Mountains.

Toma laughed mockingly. "Don't let appearance make fools of you. The Ice Dragon would like to think that his citadel compares to that of my sire, but, as with the dreams of many, this frosty edifice is more a house of glass—or should I say ice?"

It was certainly imposing enough to Cabe. "What's that suppose to mean?"

"Merely that most of this mad drake's home is nothing more

than ice. The mountain is very small and as much a glacier as it is earth. I know. Stripped of its glorious mantle, the Ice Dragon's citadel would be a tall hill in comparison with the giants of Tyber.''

"Which makes our adversary no less weak," commented Haiden. "I doubt that making disparaging remarks about the cold one's hearth and home are going to defeat him. He does not strike me as a sensitive soul."

Gwen agreed and added, "Doesn't it strike anyone as strange that we've not come across any defenses or even felt the touch of his power—besides that damned chill of his?"

"I have noticed a bit of snow and wind."

"Don't be sarcastic, Haiden. You know what I mean."

Cabe looked around them. White. Cold and white. It was beginning to disgust him. "I daresay that the weather to the south of this is far worse. Remember, the Ice Dragon has no need to cover his own domain completely, only those he wishes to overcome."

"If what you sssay is true, we may be in one of the more attractive ssspots in the Dragonrealm, Bedlam. Ssstill, I could do without this chill that shroudsss me within and without."

The cold was getting to all of them, but the chill within was doing more damage. There were long periods of time where no one wanted to speak nor wanted to be spoken to. There were times when they were surly with no reason, though that was debatable in the case of Toma.

The drake experimented, causing a tiny flame to burst from one hand. "We ssstill have our powers. I have felt the touch of Ice. I would know if he wasss observing usss."

It was the elf who discovered a likely reason. He had been scanning the Wastes from ground to sky, ever cautious, and his persistence was finally paying off.

"Look there!"

At first, it was only an indistinct shape coming from the south. Toma turned to the others. "We should take cover!"

Cabe felt the touch that he knew was more Nathan than him. He shook his head. "There's no reason. They don't care about us. In fact, I get the impression that, if anything, they would approve of our actions."

"They?" Gwen concentrated, then, even as the shape separated into a number of smaller ones, she gasped. "Seekers!"

Toma nodded to himself, remembering how the one had aided him in his escape. The avians *were* plotting something. Perhaps his escape had merely been a delaying tactic while they prepared this. It may have been that they cared little whether he succeeded in crossing the Wastes. Certainly that was within Seeker thought as he knew it.

Now they could see that there were probably at least two dozen of the creatures, more than any of them had seen at one time, save Cabe, who recalled the day when the former Red Dragon had assaulted Azran's citadel, and how the Seekers had risen in a frenzy only partially caused by their forced servitude to the mad mage. The areas near the castle had contained one of their ancient rookeries, their breeding places.

The Ice Dragon had indeed made some dangerous foes.

The avians appeared to be carrying a number of litters with them, though what they contained was beyond the imagination of anyone in the party. The creatures were flying slow, sinking occasionally, and Cabe hazarded a guess that they were forced to make frequent stops. Whatever the avians carried, it must have been valuable.

Nothing impeded their flight. The foursome watched as the Seekers flew past, not even acknowledging their presence with so much as a glance. Cabe knew better, however; he had felt the skilled touch of more than one alien mind. The Seekers knew why they were here and, as he had suspected, they approved. It was their combined opinion, though—and the arrogance of the creatures surprised the young sorcerer—that the humans and their party would not be necessary. Cabe and his group were considered just one more plus. Something else to encourage the Ice Dragon to see their way.

"What's the matter?" Gwen asked. She, too, had felt the touch of Seeker minds, but could not read them so clearly.

"I don't know. Nothing, maybe. I just wish I knew what they were up to."

"We may find out soon enough," Haiden added.

"Why?"

"There are things moving through the Wastes. Heading in our general direction."

They had visions of the huge, digging creatures coming to steal their lives. The elf, seeing their expressions, shook his head. "Not those. These were smaller, manlike. Any more than that, I can't say."

"Drakes?" suggested Cabe.

Toma cut in. "There are no more drakes out here save the lord of this land. No, Bedlam, I think these are his unliving servants, as horrible in their own way as those things moving south."

"We can't afford to wait for them."

"Which means we have to fight them, yesssss." There was anticipation in the drake's voice. A chance to strike back at his former captor.

"If we can avoid it, we will." Cabe glared at the warlord until the latter finally nodded. "Purposely trying to fight them will do us as little good as hiding. We'll waste time!" In the back of his mind, Cabe almost wanted to give in to hiding. Anything to avoid what Tyr had predicted. He wished the dead Dragon Master had not warned him.

They rode cautiously, avoiding as best as possible places where Haiden claimed to have sighted the Ice Dragon's minions. Their minds reached out to seek any hostile presence nearby, but they felt nothing but the continuous scourging of their souls by the spell. It was becoming more and more difficult to get the horses to continue; they were cold within and without and frightened by their surroundings.

Another hour passed. The icy home of the monarch of the Wastes grew impossibly taller. Mostly ice, yes, but it was unnerving in a way that the towering Kivan Grath was not; it was cold with death, that was the only way to put it. Kivan Grath, home of the dragon emperor, had an overwhelming dignity, despite the fearsome awe most felt. Here were only the dead. The Northern Wastes were as much responsible for their fatalistic attitudes as the decay of their power.

Cabe shook off some of his melancholy. He began to wonder which would get them first, the induced weariness of life or their shadowy watchers.

Time passed, the mountains stood just before them, and they

still were not attacked. Toma, presently walking, tested his powers by melting a hole into a snowdrift.

"This is sssome game. The Ice Dragon would not let us come ssso close otherwise."

"Maybe he just has his mind on other matters," suggested Haiden.

"The Ice Dragon is far more capable than that. Besides, his servants watch our every move."

Cabe looked around. "I'm beginning to wonder about that."

Gwen understood. "The Seekers?"

"The confidence I felt was strong. Very strong. I don't think those creatures would put all their hopes into one attempt."

"You're suggesting that those things watching us belong to the birds?" Toma shook his head. "This close to the lair of Ice himself?"

"Why would the Ice Dragon leave us be? Why not take us before we come too close and possibly risk all?"

"I told you . . . The damper spell!"

"You have your powers. I've been . . . prepared." He felt this was one aspect of the protection from Nathan. "Nothing."

"The Seekers must be inside by now," Haiden commented. "Perhaps they are responsible after all."

"Unless we have an ally we don't know about," added Gwen quietly.

At that moment, two ice-covered creatures stepped miraculously through the mountainside. Toma jumped back and Cabe and Gwen both began casting spells. Haiden's longbow was out and ready.

They were the unliving servants of the Ice Dragon. The party studied them with revulsion, for their nature was quite apparent. Within each were the stiff forms of some hapless being. One was human, that much Cabe could tell. The other might have been an elf or a half-elf, but the distinction was pointless. Both of these unfortunates had died and now their corpses gave these monstrous forms existence. Clear, icy fingers moved. Blind eyes saw.

The servants did not attack. They did not even look in the direction of the party. Instead, they each moved to one side of the hidden gateway and stood there, completely at attention, but entirely unconcerned with the nearness of the enemies of their master.

Cabe turned to Toma and whispered, "Do you understand what is going on?"

"Either we are like vermin being led to the trap by a piece of cheese or, asss you mentioned, we have an ally of incredible strength. Could it . . . No, not possible."

"What?"

"He doesss not interfere."

"Who?"

Gwen came up behind them. "Wouldn't it be better to talk about this when it's a bit safer? There's no telling how long this will go on!"

"She is correct," Duke Toma said reluctantly.

"What about the horses?"

"We leave them. What else can we do?"

The animals will be removed.

Cabe blinked. "What was that?"

The others looked at him curiously.

They cannot hear. They are not necessary. Follow my Words if you wish to defeat the lord of the Northern Wastes.

Gwen, worried, put a hand on his shoulder. "What's wrong?"

Do not waste my time. Tell them nothing. The less that know the safer.

He shook his head. "Nothing. Let's go."

They walked past the oblivious ice creatures as quickly and carefully as possible. Gwen closed her eyes briefly as she passed next to one and Cabe quickened his own pace. When they were through, he turned back to see if the servants had noticed anything. What *he* noticed was that the horses were indeed gone. Even at their fastest pace, there was no possible way they could have disappeared yet. There was a chance that one of the others had cast a spell, but when?

Ice entertains himself with the Avians. They believe their prizes will tempt him from his madness. I have my doubts. It keeps him from noticing certain things, though.

Who are you? Cabe thought.

There was no answer. This was not Nathan, he knew that immediately from the sense of foreboding that enveloped him, a feeling in no way related to the Ice Dragon's spell. Nathan had spoken to him before, in his own mind, but his grandfather's spirit had always emitted a . . . humanity . . . that this intruder did not.

Toma, as the only one who had ever been in here, led the way. From the glares he gave the halls, the others knew that, had he his own way, the firedrake would have seen the icy portion of this citadel reduced to a lake.

"This is preposterous!" Toma hissed quietly. "There is no possible way he could not be aware of us!"

"Perhaps," was all Cabe dared to say. Gwen stared at him briefly, understanding, it seemed, much more than the drake.

"This place is so dead," whispered Haiden. To an elf, such a place as this, where only the darker aspects of nature existed, was an abomination as horrible as the creatures the Ice Dragon had let loose on the rest of the realm.

The comment made Cabe come up short. The words of Tyr had thankfully slipped his mind for the past few minutes, but the elf had brought them back to the fore. Almost, he turned back.

Of what point would that be?

He did not answer the voice's question and knew that the entity expected no answer. Both knew that Cabe had no real intention of turning back.

They walked for what seemed a mile of twisting tunnels. Toma assured them that they were on the correct path. The voice within Cabe's mind did not add anything.

Three figures suddenly crossed their path from an adjoining corridor. Toma froze and the others followed suit. Two of the unliving servants were leading someone by the arms and he followed obediently like a newborn pup.

Gold, the dragon emperor. His mind still suffered the emptiness caused by his struggle with a desperate Cabe so many months ago. The young warlock stared at the once-omnipotent drake lord with some pity. Better a clean death . . .

"No!"

Before anyone else could react, Toma was racing around the corner, hands outstretched in preparation of some spell. This time, even with someone shielding them, the group could not go unnoticed. The two horrors turned with amazing speed and grace for such bulky, awkward-looking creations. One raised a previously unseen staff about two feet long.

Toma did not give him a chance to use it. The firedrake stretched his left hand forward and a carefully aimed streak of flame enveloped only that creature. The staff exploded, sending the Gold Dragon and the other unliving servant backwards. Toma's hapless adversary literally melted, until all that remained was the blackened corpse from within.

A fool! This one would rule us!

That was all the voice said to Cabe. He felt the connection between himself and the entity vanish, as if that other had decided this small band was of no further use to it. Cabe could not blame it for thinking that way.

Gold whimpered and the other servant rose to fight. Toma pointed at it, but before he could do anything, the creature cracked into several pieces and collapsed. The drake turned and found Gwen matching his gaze.

"You've probably brought death to us all now, Duke Toma!"

"Bah!" The reptilian warlord stalked over to his fallen parent. Close, his demeanor made a complete turnaround. Cabe and the others watched in amazement as Toma gently tried to help his sire up from the ground, his voice soothing the frightened piece of wreckage that had once ruled all the Dragonrealm.

Once Toma looked up at Cabe, and the sorcerer knew there and then that the drake had not forgotten who had turned the Gold Dragon into this. It had been a distasteful maneuver, and Cabe had used it only when nothing else could save him. He was not even sure he could do it again.

"Don't struggle!" Toma hissed at the other drake.

The floor beneath his feet seemed to melt. He sank a couple of inches.

Gwen pointed at the floor of the corridor. "The ice! It's moving!"

Ice had already spread up the duke's legs. Toma put out a hand, seeking to melt it before it spread any higher. Nothing happened. "Gone! Again!"

Ice was encroaching on the warlord's knees. He tried to pull his legs free and failed. Cabe tried to go over to him in order to assist, but found his own feet frozen into the floor . . . and . . . Was it his imagination? Were there icy fingers grasping his legs?

Gwen and Haiden cried out also. Cabe recalled a simple spell that should have torn the ice from his feet and legs. Nothing happened.

"I knew it!" Toma cried. "A trap all along!"

Had circumstances been more peaceful, Cabe would have corrected him. They had been abandoned and with reason. Their guardian—and Cabe knew that he, she, or it had been with them since long before they had entered the Wastes—had given up on them. All because of Toma.

The Gold Dragon was already encased and only one of Toma's arms was free. Cabe could no longer turn to Gwen, for the ice was already past his waist. Both his wife and the elf were silent now. Dead or soon to be dead, he thought.

Tyr had not spoken the entire truth. It was not Cabe alone who would die. Because he had not known any better, Gwen would die, a victim once more of a glistening prison, this time permanently.

Fools.

That was the last thing Cabe heard. The ice rose and covered his head with alarming speed. Cut off from the air, he blacked out.

Air. Precious, wonderful air.

Light. Light burning his eyes, burning away the comforting darkness.

He dared open his eyes.

The nightmares of childhood sprang to life.

Cabe was hanging on a wall in a vast, ice-covered chamber. His feet and hands were frozen into that wall—if they still existed. He could not feel them. From the moan next to him, he knew that Gwen was there also. He wondered if the same was true for Toma and Haiden. Turning his head was impossible, for he wore a brace of ice there as well. All he could do was stare at the one he had sought all this time, only to fail in the end. Stare at the triumphant lord of the Northern Wastes.

The Ice Dragon lay across a gaping hole on what Toma had said were the remains of a temple. Somehow, he was even more overwhelming than the drake's vivid description had made him sound. He was of gargantuan proportions, but so emaciated it was like facing a gigantic corpse. That might have been an apt description, for when the Ice Dragon noted that Cabe was awake, the ice-blue eyes ensnared his own. Cabe recalled the eyes of the demonic entity Darkhorse; those eyes, too, had been icy blue in color, but Darkhorse had conveyed a touch of life despite his nature while here there was nothing but the emptiness of something worse than mere death.

"Bedlam. The last of the clan. The last of the cursed. The last of the Dragon Masters."

The Ice Dragon rose and spread his wings, creating a frost that covered his prisoners. Somewhere Toma cursed, but not too loudly.

Cabe heard a squawk from somewhere to the Dragon King's left. The great leviathan turned his attention there. The Seekers, Cabe thought. They were still negotiating with the Ice Dragon.

The huge drake lord inhaled sharply and the room grew steadily colder. Was it his intention to freeze them to death?

"At last, all things have come together. It is fitting that the last of the Bedlams be here, along with the Lady of the Amber, and the misfit who would rule the dragons as *Emperor*. The Seekers and an elf, representing pasts that will never repeat themselves. And the emperor's hatchlings, they who would have been kings if not for the human plague."

It was impossible to say what was more horrifying, the absolute finality of the Dragon King's words or the total lack of any emotion save perhaps a cold fanaticism.

Again, there was a squawk. This time, the demand for attention was something even Cabe could understand.

The Ice Dragon swung his head toward Cabe and, with false politeness, said, "You will forgive me, but apparently this must be attended to now."

None of them, save perhaps those who hung at Cabe's extreme right, could see what was happening. They could only watch as the huge form of the dragon shifted so that he could face the Seekers. The Ice Dragon gave his avian visitors the barest of smiles, not something pretty on the massive visage of such a creature.

"I have put up with you this long because I wished to see what it is you plotted. I see now. Artifacts to dull my senses and weaken my power, hatchlings to bribe me with, spies within my very walls, and unseen mages in my citadel. An interesting bag of tricks and, in any other circumstance, an effective bag of tricks. But ''—the Ice Dragon rose, overwhelming all else with the sheer magnitude of his size—'' you have miscalculated. There can be no future for the hatchlings, not with the sea of vermin that now covers the Dragonrealm. The day of the drakes is over. The day of the Seekers has been over for far longer, and I will emphasize that by pointing out the decay within your minds. Your trinkets are still useful when dealing with my brethren or the disease known as Man, but, as all your vast powers eventually do, they have failed you in the end.''

The Ice Dragon inhaled again and Cabe was struck by the image of someone drinking in pure power itself. The Dragon King literally grew, though he seemed to become more gaunt at the same time.

''I have no need to waste any more time on you.''

A flash struck the Dragon King. It did nothing, apparently, but make him laugh humorlessly at such a weak effort. Thick black smoke rose about his massive paws, seemed to ensnare him much the way the ice had ensnared Cabe and his companions. The Ice Dragon seemed to watch the deadly smoke with mild curiosity. When it had risen to cover the lower half of his body, he shifted ever so slightly.

The smoke *shattered*. Pieces fell all about the leviathan.

Cabe felt fear. Not his own, but the emanations of creatures shocked that their supposed superiority had just been tested and found lacking.

The Ice Dragon smiled broadly, revealing frost-covered fangs at least as long as Cabe's arms. As with the laugh, it was false. ''*That* was your last chance. Now, I will be done with you.''

The walls shook, banging the prisoners against them again and again. Vast chunks of ice fell from the ceiling. There were squawks and shrieks recognizable as Seeker noises. They rose to a deafening high that coincided with the worst of the tremors and then died, the voices cutting off one by one until there was silence.

All this in less than a minute.

The massive head of the Ice Dragon turned to one of his unliving servants. ''You know what to do with them. Take my emperor's young to their sire, so that they may enjoy a moment together.

"Senile birds." His attention focused on Cabe again.

"Irillian is nearly half overrun already. The Hell Plains will be gone in another day. Foolish Silver's domain is already enshrouded in ice, and my children move on both him and the arrogant human city of Talak. Within two days, the packs will converge on the lands of Penacles and the Dagora Forest. Soon, the Final Winter will cover the Dragonrealm. Soon, it will be cleansed of the human disease. There will be no successor to the drake race. We will be the last and the greatest of all the civilizations birthed here. When my children reach the southern shores, my duty to the memory of our forebears will be completed."

He eyed Cabe closely. "But before I can rest at all, before I can join my clans in the last sleep, I will see the last of the Bedlams become the pivotal nail in the coffin of his people. I will make your power mine—and with it, irreversibly draw forth the life-force, the heat . . . everything . . . from the human race. From the Dragonrealm itself."

"There will be nothing; nothing but an emptiness—within and without."

As the Ice Dragon ranted, so, too, did the wolf raider D'Shay.

"Let him see us!"

The command was not to the Gryphon's golem, though in the end it was that creature that obeyed. When the iron grip had relaxed, he looked bitterly at his captors.

D'Shay he recognized. The handsome, bearded face—similar in its foxlike aspect to that of Toos—tinged with a cruel arrogance worthy of a Dragon King. D'Shay was clad in the now-familiar ebony armor, the wolfhelm on his head and the long, flowing cloak that the Gryphon immediately knew was for more than wear. Briefly, he recalled the two-handed sword that the wolf raider had pulled from nowhere.

The other Aramite was slightly shorter than D'Shay but no less dangerous-looking. At the moment, he seemed to be concentrating on a gleaming fragment of something that the lionbird realized was what was controlling the iron golems. Strong magic, then, and one he was totally unfamiliar with.

D'Shay smiled, looking more like the predator that served as the crest of his helm. After their initial encounter, the Gryphon had wondered whether the raiders might be like the Dragon Kings—that is, shapeshifters. He now knew that that was incorrect and that the Aramites were human, but that did not mean they could be defined in the same way as the humans of the Dragon-realm. Not at all.

He realized he knew even more about them than he had thought and that they, in turn, knew far, far more about him than he had hoped.

"The last of the old, the last of the tainted. With your death, the fools at Sirvak Dragoth will surely give in and accept the inevitable. The Dream Lands will become a memory. The Ravager's will will extend over all!"

The Gryphon could keep quiet no longer. "*What* are you talking about?"

Near him, the other Aramite momentarily lost his composure, causing the iron golems to loosen their grips a little. The raider quickly regained control, but the lionbird found he could move and breathe a bit easier. He caught a glimpse of the Blue Dragon. The drake was still unconscious, having been taken totally by surprise by a magic both he and the Gryphon had apparently underestimated by a vast margin.

"You don't know?" The look on D'Shay's visage was almost amusing, until his eyes narrowed and he smiled. "You don't remember! D'Laque! He does not remember the Dream Lands, Sirvak Dragoth, probably not even the guardianship!"

With great difficulty, the Gryphon prevented himself from showing too much emotion. With each mention of some bit of his past, it was as if a door was being opened. He did not yet understand the minute glimpses of memory, but, given time, it would come to him. Time he probably did not have.

"This will certainly be a tale to tell, eh? All those years of wondering, all those years of watching. Only a few of us are left from so long ago, bird, but we remember well. I remember well. And all for nothing! You were building yourself a kingdom over here and didn't even have a thought to spare for the lands of your birth! Ha! What a grand jest!"

Another door opened and the master of Penacles was suddenly filled with such a loathing for the aristocratic raider that it shocked him. D'Shay's words had released something, some horrible memory of sadistic brutality, murder, from one who had been trusted.

The words were blurted out before he knew what he was saying. "You'll pay for all the friends you betrayed, D'Shay!"

All humor drained from the Aramite's face. "So! You *do* remember a few things, misfit! Perhaps, you would have even if we had never met again! All the more reason to put an end to you—but slowly. Only one thing prevents us from ending this and that is the secret entrance to the libraries. We have discerned that it must be in your chambers somewhere, but so far we've drawn a blank."

The Gryphon merely glared.

"No answer? I suppose we could question the Dragon King. He really has nothing to lose—except his life. Still, even despite this incident, it may be possible that we can deal with him. After all, the balance of power seems to have shifted now. We have control of matters now."

At that point, a powerful, bitter cold swept the room. The raider D'Laque nearly dropped his talisman and D'Shay went pale. The Gryphon writhed as the chill tore at his insides. This was by far the worst he had felt.

Gradually, this new wave of cold lessened. It did not dissipate completely, however, and the Aramites were forced to pull their cloaks about them. Frost enshrouded those portions of the room nearest to the windows.

"I will be glad to return to our homeland, misfit, not only to bring back your head, but to escape this miserable cold. I do not look forward to your winters."

It appeared that neither of the Aramites knew the true cause of the cold, and the Gryphon doubted that they would believe him. Time, he felt, was running out for more than just him. With the cold reaching this far south with such intensity, the Ice Dragon's creatures could not be far behind. Irillian was probably under siege. He did not even want to think what might be happening to the farmlands to the north. Toos had already reported refugees coming south by the hundreds. That might swell to the thousands, providing they survived that long.

"You have just this one chance, bird. I can promise to make your death swift and relatively painless if you tell us how to gain entrance to the libraries. Well?"

One of the golems holding him suddenly stiffened and spoke. D'Shay was backing away, expecting a trick. Instead, all the creature said was, "The food requested by the Lord Gryphon is here. The manservant requests entrance."

"What?" It took a few seconds for the message to sink in. When it had, the Aramites laughed in relief. D'Shay smiled and replied, "Tell the manservant to leave the food and depart. The Lord Gryphon will retrieve it later."

The golem was silent, but there was a sense of the message having been delivered nonetheless.

"Well, so much for that."

"The manservant still requests entrance," the iron golem uttered.

The two wolf raiders exchanged glances.

"A ploy?" suggested D'Laque.

D'Shay nodded and turned back to the golem. "Describe who is out there."

There was evident communication between the golem who spoke and those outside. "One human of later decades, low mass, average height. Facial—"

"Enough!" D'Shay studied the Gryphon. "Remarkable products of alchemy, misfit, but there is a great deal of room for improvement. Your servants also show excessive tendencies, it seems. Watch him, D'Laque. I shall deal with our overzealous friend."

The other Aramite looked worried. "Wouldn't it be better to just keep ordering him away until he left?"

"Possibly, but he may alert others about this turn of events. Better to take care of him and keep him quiet until we are away."

"As you say."

D'Shay stood to one side of the doors. He pulled out a long, wicked dagger as deathly black as his armor. The Gryphon struggled in vain. Without speaking, D'Laque had evidently ordered the golems to silence him, for one of them reached up and held his beak tight. This meant that one leg was free, but the lionbird would have welcomed any suggestion right then, for he could think of nothing to do with it. The Aramite with the artifact was too far away to kick, and striking the golems would only hurt him, probably break his foot at that.

Glancing back at the imprisoned Gryphon, D'Shay whispered, "Let him in."

D'Laque looked about in confusion, but apparently he did not have to command anyone, for the doors began to swing inward.

D'Shay lunged forward, but found himself impacting against a solid, blue-gray arm. With a gasp, he tried to shout something. He did not have time. The Aramite was thrown backwards with inhuman force and the knife flew from his grasp. D'Shay struck a wall much the way the Blue Dragon had and slumped to the floor. Unlike the Dragon King, he groaned loudly.

The two golems from outside stalked in, behind them what appeared to be the manservant. There were voices in the hallway and the sound of several armored figures rushing toward the open doorway.

Mouth wide open, D'Laque held up the glowing artifact in his hands and stared at the golems holding the Gryphon prisoner. One released the lionbird's arm and turned toward the newcomers. The other one tightened its grip on the Gryphon and prepared to twist his head off. Against such an opponent, the lord of Penacles stood as much chance as a newborn chick did of defeating a hungry, adult minor drake.

A familiar voice barked out a word in a language only three others in the room recognized. The golem stiffened, but did not release its prey. The creature that D'Laque had turned against the others also froze. The wolf raider gaped and reached into his cloak. He was too late. One of the remaining golems was already across the room and reaching for him. The Aramite succeeded in ducking the massive arms, but he stumbled against the wall and lost hold of the item he had used to control the golems. It hit the floor with a clatter and rolled away.

D'Laque reached for it. An iron foot applying several hundred pounds of pressure stepped on both the artifact and the raider's hand. The black-clad figure howled loudly, stared at the red mess that had been his hand, and collapsed on the floor, writhing and moaning in agony.

"My apologies, my lord, for taking such a chance."

The manservant stood before him, grinning. He ordered the golem to resume normal functions. As if horrified by what it had done, the iron creature released its prisoner and stepped back several feet. The Gryphon began rubbing the sore points on his body—sore points which constituted *most* of his body—and then patted his rescuer on the shoulders.

"Damn, it was you, Toos! I was beginning to wonder just how many people had free access to my quarters and command of my bodyguards!"

The general grinned, looking some twenty years younger. Escapades like this had been part of the original reason he had become so valuable to the Gryphon in the early days. "It was your own precautions that helped us succeed."

"True, but there are very few people I would trust with the one command word capable of overriding all previous orders of my metal friends here. Only one, in fact."

Long ago, when the first of the iron golems had been created, the Gryphon had contemplated the possibility, however rare, that someone might turn his creations against him. He had, therefore, added a fail-safe. A word—a name, he believed—from some language that floated in the back of his mind. A language he knew was as much a part of his past as D'Shay was. Unless one searched deeply into the essence that was the iron golems, the code system was safe. It required a great deal of skill and time, the latter of which the raider D'Laque had lacked. Spells within spells, ploys within ploys. Years as a mercenary had taught the Gryphon that.

Guards were assisting the still-stunned Dragon King to his feet. A physician was checking on D'Laque, who was now deathly still. Other guards were chaining D'Shay's wrists behind him. The Gryphon's nemesis had still not recovered completely from the swing of the golem's arm and his subsequent crash into the wall. The lionbird turned his attention back to Toos. The urge to smile was too much for him, and a beak could not possibly convey the feeling. He shifted facial appearance, becoming, for the moment, the handsome, hawk-faced man that only a few had ever glimpsed. The smile spread freely across his visage.

"Well, worker of miracles, explain to me how you came out of the blue—if you'll pardon the choice of colors—and rescued us in the proverbial nick of time! One could have not staged a better rehearsal."

Toos shrugged modestly. "Again, it was you who gave me the clue. I was off duty. It is Captain Freynard's responsibility to take charge when that occurs. When you said that you and he had met in the hall, it took me a few moments to realize that he should have been nowhere near here, especially with the hunt for D'Shay on. Admittedly, I reacted by expecting the worst and assumed there might be trouble in your very chambers."

"Your 'infallible' talent for making the right decisions again. You still claim you have little sorcerous power?" The Gryphon chuckled, his face slowly reverting to that of the astonishing creature he was named for.

The ex-mercenary, long used to the facial alteration, gave him an innocent look. "If I have so much power, milord, it is as much a mystery to me as it is to anyone else. I will admit, though, that it does come in handy."

"To be sure. So you countermanded the golems outside and—" He paused as the physician who had been examining D'Laque walked up to him and waited patiently. "Yes?"

"Your Majesty, I apologize profusely but there is nothing I can do for the wounded one. He is dead."

"Dead?"

The physician was a veteran of many a conflict and his expertise was beyond questioning. He nodded morosely. "The hand was cared for almost immediately and was not, at least directly, the cause of death. It seems he suffered some massive shock or withdrawal unrelated to it."

"That thing in his hands."

"Lord?"

"Nothing. Pity. He might have told us much. Now we'll have

to rely on D'Shay for that." D'Laque, the Gryphon thought to himself, had died because his artifact—why did the name Ravager's Tooth come to mind?—had been crushed. There was a link between one such as he and the object.

Another door in his mind had opened.

Someone alerted him to the fact that the Blue Dragon was recovering. The Gryphon excused himself from Toos and the physician and joined the drake, who was apparently well enough to chase those assisting him away. He looked up at the lord of Penacles.

"Are those egg-eaters gutted? If not, I want D'Shay so that I can skin him alive!"

The Dragon King was definitely recovered. The Gryphon shook his head. "The other one is dead, but D'Shay is my prisoner. It was my palace and my life he was after."

The drake tried to rise. "How did you turn the tide? I was struck down by one of your supposedly loyal metal men."

"General Toos acted in his own indomitable way." He was not about to tell a Dragon King about the one word that would override whatever command the golem was following. He did, though, tell the drake that his second had taken control of the two outside before they could react and, since the golems only contact one another when they have to relay information or questions, informed the creatures of what they had to say. The golems within, limited in their thought patterns, would not suspect. Toos knew that the Aramites might suspect a trick, but not one that included retaking control of two rampaging creatures easily capable of tearing them apart. The arrogance of the wolf raiders had done them in.

"There are too many 'if's' in that plan."

The Gryphon's face had reverted to avian, but he seemed to radiate a smile of some sort. "Not where General Toos is concerned. I've found his instincts to be more or less infallible since I've known him."

"You are not telling me sssomething."

"Our truce still exists, if you're worried about that."

The Blue Dragon shook his helmed head. His eyes then focused on D'Shay, who had, in the time the Gryphon had taken to talk to the others, fully recovered. He was struggling with his bonds —quite unsuccessfully. Four guards stood near, two holding the prisoner, and Toos was already attempting to question the dark-clad figure. Judging by the look on the ex-mercenary's face, he was not making any progress.

The Gryphon made his way to the prisoner, the Blue Dragon right behind him. D'Shay's eyes left Toos and impaled the lion-bird. There were anger, frustration, and some emotion the Gryphon could not identify but which made him uneasy. He was not at all satisfied that the wolf raider was completely harmless now.

"I hope you searched him thoroughly, Toos. Last time, he pulled a two-handed sword from nowhere." It was debatable whether D'Shay was a sorcerer or not. That was the only time the Gryphon recalled him doing anything truly magical, but his recent memories of the wolf raiders, the Aramites, would not have filled even a page in a book. Two face-to-face encounters. He wished dearly he could remember what part D'Shay had played in his past and why he knew the man for one who had betrayed friends.

"The misfit." The aristocratic marauder smiled coldly. "You always seem to have a knack for survival."

Toos was bristling. "I was attempting to find out what had happened to Captain Freynard and the other man."

"They never left the inn, did they, D'Shay? At least, not by conventional means."

D'Shay said nothing, but his eyes darted from the Gryphon back to Toos and back again. The general was red; Freynard, the lord of Penacles knew, had been almost like a son to his comrade. Both had assumed it would be the captain who succeeded the general, if he retired. Now, that would never be.

The soldier's eyes darkened and the look he gave the raider was one that had unnerved more than one prisoner, so much that confessions often spilled out. D'Shay acknowledged it as one might acknowledge a light spring rain. Toos slowly pulled a knife from his belt.

"This is my responsibility now, majesty. My men will take the prisoner to a cell where he can be interrogated thoroughly. I'll also have that other piece of refuse disposed of while we're at it." He nodded toward the still figure of the other ebony-armored figure.

This caught D'Shay's attention. "D'Laque is dead?"

He might very well have been asking what the time was, but

the Gryphon caught a brief flicker of emotion that the Aramite was unable to conceal immediately. It was not fear—never fear from D'Shay, he suddenly remembered—but bitter anger. The man D'Laque had been an important piece in whatever game he was playing.

Toos, however, misunderstood. "Your friend with the rock is dead and his trinket is in a few thousand pieces. Let that be a warning."

The aristocratic raider shook his head. "Poor D'Laque! He warned me of the folly of doing this, but I convinced him otherwise. Keepers aren't supposed to be so near the action, but they dislike that. Certainly, Senior Keeper D'Rak disobeys his own rules. Ah, D'Laque. He trusted me—I have a reputation, you know." D'Shay had been smiling coldly and the chill in that smile was nearly as numbing as the Ice Dragon's spell. "Another thing you will pay for eventually, misfit. You can depend on it."

General Toos made sure that each of the guards had the black-clad figure in a tight grip. "You won't have anything to do with that, friend. We're going to lock you away somewhere that even the rats refuse to visit. Then, we'll pry a few answers out of you."

D'Shay continued to smile. The Gryphon was tempted to slap the smile off his face, but he knew the Aramite would have taken satisfaction in that. "We have much to talk about, D'Shay. I remember more and more and, with your help, I'll remember everything before long. Then, maybe I'll see to your masters."

"I see."

The prisoner scanned the room briefly, his eyes taking in everything, especially the tapestry. The Gryphon braced himself for some escape attempt, but D'Shay merely smiled in self-annoyance. "A lesson to be learned. I should have been more careful. I underestimated you, misfit, but I've learned from that as well. Perhaps . . ."

Still smiling, D'Shay suddenly broke into spasms. He coughed and some blood dripped from his mouth.

"No!" Someone shouted, and the lord of Penacles realized belatedly that *he* had. This was *not* from some injury his prisoner had sustained! He knew what D'Shay was doing, knew that his nemesis was seeking an escape of a sort from which there was no return.

The Gryphon took hold of the shaking figure even as Toos turned and summoned the physician. The wolf raider's teeth were clamped tight against each other and his lips had curled back somehow, giving him a truly feral look as he continued to smile in open mockery of his captors' efforts. The eyes stared through the lionbird.

With horror and anxiety, the Gryphon knew that he was losing the only source of information he had concerning his own past. D'Shay was snatching a victory even in defeat.

"Damn you, carrion!" he squawked angrily. "You can't do this! Not now!"

The physician joined them, but by then it was too late. With one final jerk and a sigh that hinted at satisfaction, the wolf raider slumped like a marionette deprived of its strings. Not trusting the Aramite, the Gryphon had the guards secure his shoulders and legs while the physician inspected him.

After a thorough examination, the man rose. "I have no doubts whatsoever that this man is dead. I believe he's ruptured something. I'll know more given time to cut him open."

Staring down at the corpse, which somehow still retained its former tenant's arrogance, Toos shook his head. "With your majesty's permission, I would like to burn this rot immediately. It would help us both rest easier, I think."

The lionbird nodded. He was no necromancer; he could not raise the dead and he suspected that, even then, D'Shay would have found some way to cheat him. Besides, as Toos had said, he would be able to relax only if he knew that D'Shay was truly gone. "Do it, Toos, then scatter the ashes somewhere where they won't poison the animals."

Guards were already removing the other body. The Gryphon caught the Dragon King watching, with something in his demeanor that approached satisfaction.

"Not what I was hoping for, but a satisfying conclusion, nonetheless. The Aramite can have his little victory. I would rather be alive and fighting."

The Gryphon snorted. The Blue Dragon might be satisfied, but this turn would always leave a bitter taste in the lionbird's maw. "We might have to enjoy that little victory—or have you forgotten we still have another battle on our hands?"

"I had not, but it is still pleasant to watch one's defeated foes being dragged lifelessly away."

"Revel in that, then." The Gryphon picked up Yalak's Egg, which had been resting comfortably on a shelf all this time. He studied the crystalline artifact briefly, forcing D'Shay to the back of his mind, and then added, "And let us hope that it keeps you happy even if we fail, because we won't have anything else to think about except how long it will be before the Ice Dragon's abominations come looking for us."

The Seekers in the aeries about the Hell Plains knew the moment their emissaries had failed. The ones who represented those and the aeries scattered about the continent argued with one another in the decaying citadel of Azran. Not a sound issued forth from any of the Seekers, save for the occasional involuntary squawk. They spoke in the language of their minds, the only true way each could profess its opinion.

As set as they were in their ways, they could not conceive of yet more danger to them. When the first rumble occurred and the entire structure shook, many of the avians froze, not understanding in the least. Only when the first heavy pieces of the citadel began to fall on them did they finally react. The Seekers rose into the air as quickly as possible, but for many it was already too late. The first of many great diggers rose through the courtyard, grasping a number of confused and dazed avians before they could fly above its reach.

The Seekers had played their hand and it had proven insufficient. Now, the Ice Dragon was revealing to them the utter lack of concern he felt about their once-great power. They, like all his foes, were as nothing. It had meant delaying the process of the Final Winter to urge his creatures to concentrate on the avians, but the lord of the Northern Wastes was not concerned. His enemies were nothing now. This interruption would not last long. A few minutes, maybe more. Nothing could halt the nightmarish tide.

Some of his children, the things that were extensions of his being, would die. The Seekers, being what they were, would not take the destruction of their lives complacently. Yet there were so many of the beasts, and each one required the efforts of several of the bird-people.

Even to the arrogant Seekers, it was obvious what the outcome would be.

In the caverns, to the confusion of his prisoners, the Ice Dragon laughed.

With each passing moment he continued to grow taller, and more gaunt. A veritable skeleton sheathed in parchment. The Spell of the Final Winter, as the Ice Dragon had come to call it, surged toward the point where it would be impossible to reverse.

Absently noticing the puzzled, cautious look on Cabe's face, the leviathan grinned as only a dragon can grin. The young warlock stared back defiantly. He no longer knew how long he and the others had hung here. The Ice Dragon appeared to be waiting for that proper moment to dispose of his "guests." Evidently, it was his desire to assure that his power, when needed, would be at its peak.

"The avians are in total chaos. The last obstacle is crushed. Destiny merely waits now."

This new show of emotion was so foreign to the demeanor of the Dragon King that it shook them all. That he could take pleasure in something showed how close to total success he was.

"Brother Ice."

The voice seemed to echo all about the caverns. There was an odd quality to it, as if the very ice about them were the source.

"Brother Ice."

The Dragon King's head shot up and ice-blue eyes flared coldly. "How is it you come unwanted into my chambers, Brother?"

"Is not part of your domain mine? Do not your caverns glisten with lesser reflections of my power?"

"What is it you want?" There was menace in the Ice Dragon's voice, showing once more that he had not become completely unemotional.

"This must stop."

"I offered you a place in this once, and you refused."

Toma started to say something, but Gwen quieted him.

"Ritual suicide serves no purpose," the voice replied.

"This does!" The Ice Dragon was warming to his cause. "There will never be a successor to our kind! We are the pinnacle, the epitome of power! To let the human vermin rule these lands would be to shame the glory that was! Better there be nothing!"

"I cannot condone this."

"What will you do?" The frost-coated dragon gazed around, as if trying to place the other in some certain location.

"I will do nothing. Your own actions will condemn you."

All of them waited for more, but the walls were silent. Toma finally whispered, "We are dead. Even the Crystal Dragon will not stand against him."

"That didn't sound like surrender," Gwen retorted, but the tone of her voice indicated that she, too, had given up hope.

Cabe would have spoken then, but an intruder familiar to his mind returned in force. He felt also the overwhelming presence of that part of him which had been Nathan Bedlam, as if it still sought to protect him against some dire fate—which he apparently was going to suffer regardless of that protection.

Bedlam. I believe you to be less of a fool.

He did not know what to make of the statement or why the other had returned.

The secrets brother Ice uses; they came from two sources. One is destroyed. The other is you.

I *know*, Cabe thought to the other. He wondered if this was the Crystal Dragon. Could the conversation before have been a ploy? He felt annoyance from the being in his mind, as if this was not the time to wonder about such insignificant things. The mage could not argue with that logic.

I am no longer strong enough to aid you directly, but, if you

*agree, I will borrow from you the very same secrets that Ice stole.
I lack the tools to take them by force, as he did. I need your
agreement. There are those that can still aid you, but they run
short on time.*

There was an anxiousness that Cabe had not detected before
and he suspected that his mysterious ally was hardpressed by other
matters—matters, no doubt, whose tremendous forms were
dwarfed only by their appetites.

"Do it," Cabe muttered.

In Penacles, the Gryphon and the Blue Dragon, immersed in
the books of the libraries, stiffened as Yalak's Egg began to cloud
up and vibrate.

"Is that . . . normal?" The drake lord, having suffered more
than one assault in the past few days, now looked at every odd
occurence as a possible threat. The Gryphon could not really blame
him, for he was feeling the same way.

"No, it's not." The lord of Penacles gingerly lifted the crystal.
When nothing out of the ordinary occurred, he studied the Egg.

The cloud gave way briefly to the image of an abyss. Things
seemed to be drawn to the abyss. More and more until then, as
if nothing would satisfy it, the abyss began to warp and twist.
The Gryphon realized that it was swallowing itself. He watched
until the abyss was no more.

*The hunger grows and will ever grow until it must devour itself.
The life feeds it, but the life kills it. The source is the beginning,
but it is also the end.*

The Gryphon blinked. "What was that?"

"I felt nothing," the Dragon King replied in puzzlement. "I
heard nothing. I saw only mist in that crystal of yours."

"Does this sound at all familiar to you?" The lionbird repeated
the phrases and then described the scene that Yalak's Egg had
revealed.

"Sounds like something one of these cursed tomes would say,"
Blue commented.

"Sounds like . . . It probably is!" The Gryphon whirled around.

"Yes, lord?" The gnome was already standing there, a massive
book in his arms.

The Gryphon eyed the tome critically. "Is that what I was about to request?"

"I overheard you as you spoke to that one." His nose was pointed toward the Dragon King.

"And you wanted to save me some time."

"Yes, milord."

"You knew exactly what to look for."

"Those phrases are in this book. Similar phrases may be found in some of the other volumes."

The Gryphon carefully studied the tiny librarian. "*We* have to have a talk if we survive this."

"If you think it will do any better than the last nine, present lord, I will be happy to tell you what I can."

The lionbird grimaced. He *had* spoken to the gnome before. So far, he had not gained a thing from the talks. Still, there was always hope. *If* they survived the Ice Dragon's assault.

"Of what use *are* these libraries?" muttered the Dragon King in response to the librarian's answer. The Gryphon did not have time to respond. He had already taken the book from the gnome's hands and was thumbing through what seemed an endless number of blank pages.

"There's nothing here but—" He held his breath. The phrases that had been revealed to him were at the top of the right-hand page. Below them . . .

Ignoring the gasps from the elderly librarian, he tore off one of the blank sheets and used it to keep his place. Slamming the book shut, he jumped to his feet. His eyes focused on the Egg.

The Blue Dragon was already on his feet. "What is it? What did it say?"

Yalak's Egg nestled in his arms, the Gryphon murmured, "It said we may already be too late. I can only hope. . . ."

"What is he waiting for?" Gwen whispered. "Why isn't he doing anything?"

Cabe twisted his neck so that he was able to see her. Beautiful as ever, even after the trek to the Wastes and their subsequent capture by the Ice Dragon. It was a silly notion, but it made him smile briefly. Then he remembered her question, and the answer came to him instantly. He was surprised that he had not seen it before.

"He's waiting for the Twins to align themselves."

He saw that she understood. The two moons, Hestia and Styx, when aligned, created a period when access to power was far, far easier. "You mentioned that the Brown Dragon did the same thing. An increase in the sensitivity of the powers."

"It'll give him the push he needs. The Ice Dragon is still in great danger from his own spell. He would be a fool not to know that."

Gwen closed her eyes. Knowing that they had no access to their own power, Cabe watched her in puzzlement. She was concentrating, he could see that, but, without power, what did she plan to do?

Several seconds passed. The Ice Dragon ignored them, seemingly preparing himself for the grand moment to come. His unliving servants, with their gruesome interior forms, seemed oblivious to the enchantress's actions. If they understood anything, they probably knew that she had no magic to work.

At last, exhausted, she sighed and opened her eyes. There was a look of disgust on her face. Disgust at her own failure. "I'm sorry, Cabe. I didn't realize how difficult it would be."

"Difficult?"

"I was seeking out some kind of life, some creature that might be able to aid us."

"Without sorcery—"

She cut him off with a shake of her head. Assuring herself first that the Ice Dragon was still concerned with his own needs, she continued. "I have some rapport with nature that goes beyond mere magic. That was why the Green Dragon allowed me to enter Dagora Forest when I was younger. I thought it might work here, but I—there's nothing out there, Cabe! Nothing! Everything has either been killed or has fled!"

"The hour is near." The voice of the Ice Dragon suddenly echoed through the chamber. The leviathan turned toward them. "The hour of glory. The hour of the Final Winter."

"Does he have to go on like that?" muttered Haiden.

"No one will be able to stand against me. The Twins are almost in position. When the alignment begins its first phase, your time will be at an end." The icy blue of his eyes had given away to the dead white they had seen before. Soon, Cabe realized, the eyes would stay that dead white. It was all the result of the spell.

Tiny ice storms danced around the form of the Dragon King as he began to study the prisoners before him. His eyes focused on one after another until they finally fixed on Gwen. "I think . . . Yesss, I think *you* will be first."

Cabe struggled uselessly. "No!"

"Yesss. I understsand your kind well, I think. Let the last of the Bedlams watch his dam be the first to give her life. It isss . . . appropriate."

One of the servants straightened. "Hestia is in position."

"Excellent. Take the Bedlam's female."

Two of the creatures lumbered forward. Cabe screamed silently for his supposed ally.

I hear you. I cannot promise much. Ice's abominations are within my domain. Prepare yourself. If his control drops, your power may return. Shield yourself if you wish to maintain control of it. I cannot guarantee much more than that.

The voice had departed. Cabe held his breath and watched anxiously. The creatures were slow, but Gwen had only a couple of minutes of life left at best.

One of the unliving servants reached toward the icy manacle that held Gwen's left hand. The dead creature within seemed to stare at her. The enchantress, to her credit, tried her best not to look frightened.

There was a crack like thunder and the servant was reduced to flying bits of ice that somehow avoided the prisoners, instead blowing into the visage of the Ice Dragon. He snarled, more out of annoyance than pain.

"Do not interfere!"

There was another crack and this time Cabe knew that it was indeed thunder. Thunder and lightning. A bolt struck the floor of the chamber, charring the spot and creating a fissure in the ground a good ten yards long. One of the ice creatures stumbled and fell in. There was no sound of it hitting bottom.

He had been wrong, the young mage realized. His ally had not been the Crystal Dragon, but another Dragon King entirely—

Storm, master of the marshy lands in and around Wenslis. Storm, as much a master of the elements as the frost-covered behemoth before them.

Lightning bolts ripped through the caverns, striking the Ice Dragon's minions with deadly accuracy. They seemed, however, unable to strike the drake himself. Bolt after bolt struck around the huge white dragon, sometimes missing by no more than a few feet. Pieces of the cavern flew about in fantastic whirlwinds that seemed to snap at the dragon. Oddly, through the entire assault, the lord of the Northern Wastes only looked . . . irritated.

Still, his control had slipped, if only a little. Cabe felt the tugging of power, but it vanished almost instantly.

I . . . am . . . buying time. There are others. They are almost ready.

They? Cabe did not know who "they" were, but he did know that the Storm Dragon was tiring. The bolts were coming with less and less frequency and the Dragon King's aim, if it could still be called that, was now so erratic at times that the prisoners were in danger of being roasted.

What was worse, though, was that the Ice Dragon was striking back at his counterpart. The four could not see the results of his counterattack, save that the lightning bolts dwindled until only a few succeeded in striking anywhere. A miniature snowstorm overwhelmed the lightning and thunder, seeming to devour it.

"Traitor," the Ice Dragon was saying to empty space. "You would rather the manlings rule. Well, then, suffer with them."

In Cabe's mind, he felt rather than heard the scream of the Storm Dragon. Then, the master of Wenslis spoke to him in a voice wracked with pain.

Another . . . mo . . . moment. Prepare! I cannot . . .

They were blinded as one more grand assault was unleashed on the Ice Dragon. Bolt after bolt of lightning struck the floor around the leviathan. Gaping fissures opened everywhere and water flowed from half-melted walls. The entire mountain shivered as the heat generated by the lightning storm weakened ice that had rested here for longer than even the Dragon Kings had existed. The Ice Dragon's footing slipped time and again. A great block of snow and ice fell not twenty feet from Cabe. Once, a lucky strike slipped past the lord of the Wastes.

It is up to . . . to them—and you.

The cavern was filled with smoke and steam. The Ice Dragon was breathing hard, and it was evident that the final attack had cost him more than he would admit. Cabe knew that many of the Dragon King's hungry abominations had died—had been burned out—by the excessive amount of energy the huge drake had been forced to draw from them. Not enough, though. Cabe could feel it. The Ice Dragon still had more than sufficient strength to see his dreams through.

It was unlikely that the Storm Dragon was dead, but Cabe knew that there would be no more assistance from him. His own kingdom was under attack and he himself was undoubtedly severely injured from the other dragon's reprisal.

Who was left?

Who were "they"?

Better yet, *where* were they? If there was anyone left to fight the Ice Dragon, Cabe estimated that they had only a few more minutes before any further assault would be pointless.

The lord of the Northern Wastes returned his attention to his prisoners. "A minor delay, at best. Come to me now, Lady of the Amber."

With no servants to perform his will, the Ice Dragon was forced to utilize his own power. The wall where Gwen hung twisted and re-formed, more like something alive than mere ice. Still holding her prisoner, the ice became an appendage. A hand of sorts, controlled in the same manner that the floors of the corridor where they had been captured had been, carried her forward to the waiting Dragon King. She struggled, but uselessly.

"Lady of the Amber," the drake lord was saying. "You who stood beside the foulest of the Dragon Masters and now stand with his heir and incarnation. You represent the rise of the manlings almost as much as the Bedlams. Your sacrifice will truly be symbolic, as well as useful. You are strong, and your lifeforce will contribute greatly to the spell."

This was it—and Cabe had no power to save her! Without thinking, he shouted, "You're a fool, Lord Ice! You don't realize the mistakes you are making!"

The gigantic head turned toward him, no hint of amusement or annoyance visible now. He was too close to victory. "What say you, *last* of the Bedlams? I have made no mistakes worth worrying over.''

"Haven't you?'' The words came from Cabe out of their own volition. He listened in amazement at himself.

"Amuse me, spawn of a mortal demon. Tell me.''

Cabe smiled, though the smile was not his doing. He was disturbed, because he could not even hazard a guess as to where Nathan—it had to be Nathan's presence making use of him—was leading things.

"Something similar to this was used to create the Barren Lands.''

"I know that.'' The Ice Dragon was looking at him closely, as if wondering whom exactly he was speaking with.

"It was to be a complete and final destruction by the Dragon Masters.''

Gwen was staring at him, realizing who was actually talking.

"Yet, the Brown Dragon brought the Barren Lands to life, though it cost him his own life and that of all but a handful of his already nearly extinct clans.''

"What are you driving at?'' hissed the dragon. He had gone from complete indifference to slowly growing anger and confusion.

"Do you think that your spell will be so final? Do you really think that the *winter* you plan to spread across the lands will hold forever?''

"It will. The knowledge came from the books in the libraries of Penacles and even from your own mind. I know *everything*, Bedlam!''

"And you think the latter went unnoticed. You think that everything you learned from this mind was the truth or was not distorted in any way.''

There is a cold so intense that it burns. The Ice Dragon's eyes burned with such a cold. Cabe shivered involuntarily, feeling just a touch of that cold. He had thought *the spell* agonizing!

"I know you now for certain!'' the Dragon King roared with sudden rage. "The Grand Deceiver! The Dragon Master himself! I'd heard the tales, but not believed the extremity of them!''

"Then you know that what I say can be true.''

Within his own mind, Cabe worried that the Ice Dragon would

see through what had to be a bluff. Wasn't it? That which was Nathan, which had, after Azran's death, seemed to have melded with Cabe forever, now controlled him. Was it truly possible that Nathan had been prepared for this?

"I think you lie," the Dragon King muttered, but his confidence had slipped. He glanced at the captive Gwen and then at the pit beneath him.

The cadaverous dragon hesitated. His guard dropped for only a second.

Cabe tried to cry out as he felt himself yanked from reality. The cavernous citadel of the Ice Dragon appeared to pull away from him, shrinking and shrinking until it was . . . *gone*. He floated in nothing. It did not even resemble the Void. He was just . . . elsewhere.

The decision is yours, a part of his mind seemed to say. It was impossible to say whether the thought was his own or that of his grandfather.

He did not hesitate. Gwen was back there. If nothing else, he had made a promise to her. If it meant his own death, as the unliving Tyr had predicted, then so be it.

"Yes."

Without further thought, he was thrust back into reality. This time, he *did* scream.

XXII

In the Dagora Forest, the Green Dragon prepared. While his lands were far south compared to the Hell Plains or even Wenslis, the first forerunners of the unholy packs let loose by the Ice Dragon had already made their way into his domain. Overenthusiastic, the drake thought sourly. They had been destroyed, but the cost was far more than he would have liked. He could only imagine the suffering to the north. From his eyes around the Dragonrealm and from those who had sought refuge in his forest, he knew that many fields and forests were withering and hundreds of animals and people—drake, human, whatever—had perished from exposure, hunger, or, worst of all, the voracious hunger of the Ice Dragon's children.

New attempts to contact his brethren and plead for cooperation had achieved little. Storm did not acknowledge him, though the Green Dragon was now of the opinion that his brother to the northeast was planning steps of his own—providing he was still alive. Silver's domain was under assault; that one had no time to speak with him, though it was hastily hinted that any aid would not be rejected. Lochivar's master was silent, as was the enigmatic lord of the Legar Peninsula. How the Crystal Dragon could still remain indifferent puzzled Green. Then again, the Crystal Dragon had always puzzled him. As for the Black Dragon, he apparently seemed to think that if he hid in his domain and did nothing, the Ice Dragon would leave him be. Hardly.

Penacles, however, proved to be an even greater enigma than his fellow Dragon Kings.

He had discovered the Blue Dragon's presence there and the temporary alliance forged with the Gryphon. That in itself was still amazing, but now they were in the midst of something that the lionbird would only say was as much a danger as it was their only hope. Even word that a band of Seekers had, at one point, been sighted ferrying several large bundles toward the north had not bought more than a few seconds of the lionbird's time. The young of the drake emperor were of little import at a time when the entire realm might cease to be. Muttering under his breath, the lord of the Dagora Forest had felt the Gryphon break the connection with such finality, he knew it would be useless to seek further enlightenment.

And somewhere in the Northern Wastes, in the lair of his mad counterpart, the hatchlings which might have given his race a future alongside that of humanity were now probably moments from death themselves. At the claws of one of their own.

He stalked the perimeters of the central chamber of his citadel, helpless to do anything but fight off the abominations and pray that either the Bedlam whelp or the Gryphon could succeed. Placing his future—his very life—in the hands of such was unnerving, even though he had done something akin to that when he had made his original pact with the Gryphon.

As the true abodes of many of the Dragon Kings reflected their respective natures, the Green Dragon's citadel was the bonding of nature with civilization on a scale even more grand in its own way than the Manor. A vast King of oaks, larger and older than any other tree in the forest, had been shaped by the Seekers—at least, he assumed it was the Seekers—so that there were rooms and hallways, some of the former quite immense, throughout the plant even though the oak itself was strong and healthy. If the Green Dragon harbored any superstitions, it was that his domain would crumble the day the tree died. Not surprisingly, one of his predecessors had made daily care of the oak top priority. It still was.

"Lord Green!" A voice rasped.

The Dragon King froze.

A tiny dot before him seemed to unfold continuously, quickly gaining a humanoid form that focused into the very human form of Cabe Bedlam. Drake guards, alerted by the unfamiliar voice, came rushing in, one leading a pair of half-grown minor drakes. The Dragon King waved them away.

Cabe's face was pale and he was panting. He paused briefly in amazement at what he had just done and then remembered why he was here. Ignoring protocol, he gripped the Green Dragon by the arms and asked hurriedly, "My lord! You've amassed a great treasury of artifacts from the Seekers, the Quels, and other civilizations, haven't you?"

"I have." There was a tremendous build-up of energy within the human and it was such that the drake lord had every intention of treating him with nothing but respect.

"I must see it! Do I have your permission?"

"Yes, I—"

"Teleport us there! I . . . I have a balance I must be careful to maintain!"

Stunned as much by the demanding tone as the very idea of being given orders by any human, the Dragon King still only hesitated for a second. This was, after all, a Bedlam. One who should even now be in the Northern Wastes. If Cabe was *here* . . .

He wasted no more time on words. They were gone before either of them could take another breath.

"It isn't working," the Gryphon muttered. "We're too late!"

"Hestia has only just entered the first portion of her phase. Both moons have to be in position, Lord Gryphon. It cannot be too late!" The Dragon King sounded as weary as the lionbird felt. They had given it their all and the only results had been a drain on both of them. As far as they could tell, the Ice Dragon had probably not even felt their assault.

"Something is missing . . . ."

The drake hissed. "Obvious! What, though?"

They were sitting on the floor of the Gryphon's chambers, Yalak's Egg between them. The Egg glowed with energy; it was the only thing that had thus far benefited from the spell. The Gryphon could not help thinking that it was waiting for them to do something else—but what?

There were many passages in the book that hinted at other possibilities. Had he missed one? The Gryphon was reaching for the book when a hiss of indrawn breath from his draconian ally made him turn back.

Cabe's *face* peered out at them from within the crystal. This was not a vision of things to come; he was actually looking at them. His eyes lingered questioningly on the Blue Dragon, then fixed on his friend.

"Gryphon, have you followed the passages in the book?"

The two in the chamber glanced at one another before the lord of Penacles replied, "Yes, how did you—"

Cabe smiled, but it was a tired, worn smile. "I guessed, actually. I've also been in contact with a few of your . . . associate's . . . counterparts."

"*Have* you?" There was restrained curiosity and even a mild bit of instinctive distrust eminating from the master of Irillian by the Sea. Cabe ignored the Dragon King.

"You've failed. Don't ask how I know that; I do. You've misunderstood one section, I think, because you really didn't understand it. Don't worry. I know what to do. I just need you two to continue on with it. As long as you have the will, the power. Don't stop until exhaustion makes you collapse. It's the only way."

Even as he spoke, Cabe was beginning to fade. The Gryphon called out to him. "Cabe! What are you going to do?"

There was some hesitation and then, in an almost wistful tone, Cabe's now wraithlike voice answered, "What the Brown Dragon tried to do to me once—more or less."

Yalak's Egg was once more a foggy, glowing shell.

"What did the Bedlam whelp mean when he spoke of Brown? Brown died at that human's hand in the Barren Lands!"

The Gryphon was brooding. He had a good inkling of what Cabe meant. Absently, he answered the Dragon King. "The Brown Dragon took Cabe into the Barren Lands; it was he who brought Cabe's powers to the fore. He . . ." There could be no mistake. Cabe's captor had had only one thing in mind that night, a night when the Twins were high in the sky. In just about the same locations they would be shortly. In mere minutes. "He intended to sacrifice the boy's life to twist the curse around."

At last, the Blue Dragon understood. "Until now, I had trouble believing a human capable of such an act."

"Then let's make it work. For him." The lionbird shifted back into position. "We only have to give our strength. Cabe Bedlam intends on giving his life."

The Ice Dragon's rage at Cabe's escape—due to his own overconfidence—was as short as it was terrible. The walls of the chamber, already weakened by the assault of the Storm Dragon, began to crumble more. The ceiling creaked and threatened to collapse. Snowstorms burst into life about the form of the chill monarch. Gwen, closest to the dragon, turned away as best she could, her body already half-buried by the magically created snow.

Toma felt the grip on his right hand loosen as ice clattered to the floor. He made no sign, however; the Ice Dragon had regained control, and none of his remaining prisoners could utilize their skills. It was not even possible for Toma to shift to his natural form.

"Bedlam!" The name, spit out in a burst of frosty smoke, marked the end of the Dragon King's tirade. The cold, lifeless mask returned once more. "No matter. Even if the last of the Bedlams is nothing but a cowardly hatchling, I still have his dam."

His gaze turned to Gwen, still caught in the grip of the ice. To her credit, she stared back.

"You show more teeth than your mate, little one. Your power, your spirit, will increase my strength greatly. If there are no *further* interruptions, we shall begin again."

The gaunt leviathan rose on all fours and moved to the side of the pit. The thing within that pit stirred, and Gwen had a glimpse of something at least as large as the Dragon King himself. Her defiance gave way to uncertainty and, regardless of her attempts to hold it back, fear.

There were hisses and shrieks from the dragon's far left. The hatchlings had gotten loose from their guards and were now swarming around the indifferent figure of the Gold Dragon. They seemed to be trying to urge him to some action. Their hisses were of anger and fear, not for themselves, it soon became evident, but for the Lady. Belatedly, Gwen realized that they must have felt her call before. There was nothing they could do to help, however.

A grunt of annoyance escaped the master of the icy Wastes. "Perhaps, since they are so tainted by interaction with humans, I should give them to my queen now. It will wash the shame away so much quicker."

"No!" Gwen shouted. "At least let them live! They're your own kind! Your emperor's young!"

"And humanity's future puppet rulers. I think not. I think they will join you shortly. Better they give their lives for the glory of our race than ever bow and call warm-blooded vermin 'master.' "

Gwen was carried toward the pit by the icy pseudopod. With each foot closer the despair generated by the Dragon King's spell grew even more oppressive, until she could do nothing to fight it any longer.

And then . . .

And then, the despair was gone. The fear was gone. The cold was retreating. The storms swirling around the cavern dwindled

away before a summer warmth and the entire chamber was illu-
minated as it had never been.

And there was Cabe Bedlam, arms outstretched, a small object
in his left hand, looking all the world like his grandfather. The
Ice Dragon's monstrous queen moved uneasily, suddenly cut
off from its feeding, cut off from that other link that kept it
acquiescent. A link that now spread its massive, frost-encrusted
wings wide and glared with eyes filled with death at the tiny
human.

"What have you done?"

The Ice Dragon seemed to fill the chamber. Both magnificent
and terrible, he rose above all else. Far longer than any of his
brethren. Parchmentlike skin that barely covered his bones. An
anger so great that it lent the dragon a calmness nearly as chilling
as his lifeless, emotionless attitude of late. The light, the heat,
began to fade. New storms blew into existence.

"Bedlam."

"I warned you that you did not know everything, Dragon King.
I did not lie."

"There was nothing that I missed. Nothing."

Cabe shrugged. A part of him was as indifferent as the rest of
him was frightened, but he had no choice. Things had to be played
out this way. Even if in the end it meant his doom. "As it pleases
you. The truth is evident enough."

Fooled once before, the Ice Dragon increased his dampening
spell. His other prisoners remained shackled, harmless, but Cabe
still glowed with the fury of his own power. Disbelief began to
gnaw its way into the dragon's iron-hard heart. He needed more
strength.

The thing in the pit protested. He ignored its annoyance and
drew forth that power, unwittingly causing the deaths of countless
of his creatures, his extensions, by literally starving them as he
took what energy they had and made it his own. He glowed now,
but it was a bitter, lifeless glow that made him appear as some
huge harbinger of death—which perhaps he was.

Still the Bedlam whelp did nothing but wait.

A mocking laugh escaped from the throat of the Dragon King,
a coarse sound that shook the fragile ceiling further. The ice about

Cabe suddenly took form, took a false life of its own and twisted about him like a giant claw. Cabe looked about, saw his danger, and rose into the air. He only barely succeeded in dodging a second hand of ice coming from above. Free of both, he turned the powers to his own command and brought the two hands together so sharply that they shattered in one massive clap. Tiny fragments flew with great precision at the Dragon King.

"A wasted effort," Cabe remarked casually, hoping that the Ice Dragon did not know how close that attack had really come to achieving the drake lord's goal.

Cabe was now closer to the Ice Dragon, closer to the pit. He could feel the unseen assault of the Dragon King, the constant battering at the shield that protected the young mage's tenuous connection to his powers. The energy drain, Cabe knew, must be massive. The lord of the Northern Wastes was seeking to maintain the spell of the Final Winter, prevent his other captives from regaining their own powers, control his remaining creatures' actions—all while still assaulting the human before him with both invisible and quite visible threats. There was also to be taken into account the massive level of energy that the Storm Dragon had caused him to utilize. If the latter had not also been fighting a battle on more than one front . . .

"Ifs" did not matter. Results were what mattered. Results that needed to manifest themselves when the moons were at last in position. Hestia was already there. Styx still needed a few minutes. Minutes Cabe was not sure he had.

What would the master of this snowbound domain fear? Heat, of course. But heat alone would not be sufficient, unless . . .

Nathan, he thought, *if you know what to do . . .*

"What isss—" the Ice Dragon began. The entire mountain was shaking again. Steam rose from the largest of the crevices. The temperature of the chamber grew noticeably. A thick, red-hot substance began to spew from the cracks in the earth.

The dragon hissed. Molten earth rose steadily, urged from the depths of the world by Cabe/Nathan. Fear eminated from the abomination. Heat was deadly to it, would bring pain to its children.

The Ice Dragon flapped his mighty wings, inhaled sharply, and blew on the encroaching lava. With horror, Cabe and his companions watched the molten earth cool and freeze in a matter of seconds. Enhanced by the drake lord's power, the cold seemed to spread down into the crevices. The cavern became even colder than before. Cabe shivered momentarily and knew that the others, who lacked any magic, must be suffering terribly.

A wave of chilling frost suddenly enveloped Cabe while he still floated in the air. Perhaps at one time it would have been enough to stop the human, but days and days of enduring the inner chill of the Dragon King's soul-numbing spell had inured him to this at least enough for him to counter it with more heat of his own. Even as the Ice Dragon again pulled back from the warmth it despised so much, Cabe prayed that it would not realize what a price he himself was paying. Unlike the dragon, he had nothing to call upon but his own reserves and what little he dared to steal from the drake's abominations—and in that last lay his hopes for victory.

Great chunks of ice came clattering down as the dragon stumbled against one of the chamber walls. This was taking a toll on him as well. How much longer before the leviathan's control over something slipped? The breaking point had to come soon! If not, then Cabe had seriously overestimated his own chances.

While the two fought a war of wills, Gwen found herself aswarm with worried, fearful hatchlings seeking to pull her away. Only the eldest seemed to understand that it required more than tugging at her clothing and hair—the latter action one she quickly reprimanded them on—and began to scratch at the ice that gripped her. His claws, however, were pathetic excuses; he had not yet learned to shift completely from one form to the other and still wore a shape that was three-fourths human and one-fourth drake. His claws were little longer than those of a person and not very much sharper. He hissed and uttered something that he could only have learned from one of the manservants back home.

The Lady looked up as a shadow covered her. Almost she let out a gasp that would have surely caught the attention of the Ice Dragon. Standing near her was the dragon emperor himself, red eyes vacant of any true thought, only here because he had been led by the hatchlings. Yet she could still feel power coursing through him; the Ice Dragon had not bothered or would not bother with his own lord. As she had inadvertently done with the hatchlings, Gwen began to seek out what remained of the mind of the King of Kings and soothe it.

All over the lands, the sudden and inexplicable deaths of so many of the ever-hungry diggers brought hope to those under siege. The Storm Dragon actually began to beat back the still impressive hordes and, in the domains of the dragons Blue and Silver, defenses began to hold. All knew that it was not through their doing, that some miracle had been wrought. They also knew that there were more than enough of the monstrosities remaining to overwhelm them once they tired more—and, at the present rate, that would not be long.

The thing within the gaping hole was active now, its hunger greater than ever. The Ice Dragon continued to draw from it, and was now forced to turn some of that power drawn against the very source lest he lose control.

Hestia waited high in the sky, also hungry. Her brother, Styx, was only now coming into his proper position. Both moons had risen in the sky early, as was their custom in this time of the year, but to those who waited, it seemed as if the second would never reach his destination. Cabe could see neither of the two moons, but he felt their pull, felt their collective hunger even as he felt the growing hunger of the Dragon King's "queen."

And then, the sign he was waiting for revealed itself. The sign that the Ice Dragon was faltering.

Toma burst free of his bonds, his power returning to him in a rush. Long green tendrils rose from the wall behind him as he pointed toward his "uncle." His eyes burned with vengeance. The tendrils gathered and shot toward the huge, pale drake. The Ice Dragon had finally reached his limitations. He could not hold everything together.

He was not, however, by any means defeated. A wave of intense cold buffeted Toma even before he was more than an arm's length from the wall. With a crackling sound, the hapless drake was tossed against the ice. He was not unconscious, but any advantage he had had was now long gone. The tendrils withered and died in an instant, no trace remaining.

"You cannot stand against me!" the Ice Dragon was shouting

almost calmly. "I have seen my duty and I know it just! The reign of the drakes will be the last such of these lands even if I must sacrifice myself now!" He turned back toward the last of the Bedlams.

Time! The Twins were in position!

Cabe glanced briefly at the object he had held in his hand all this time. The crimson blade with its beaklike point was not quite suited for his human grip, having been designed by the Seekers. Still, it was the proper tool, the one that Nathan had chosen not to use in the Barren Lands, thereby condemning it to its deathly state until the Brown Dragon's mad attempt to sacrifice Cabe. Nathan refused to make such a sacrifice. That he had been able to stem the tide had proven sufficient—then. The spell was too far advanced for that now. Now, only the sacrifice of his own life could reverse what the Ice Dragon had done. It was such a sacrifice that the Brown Dragon had attempted and it was Cabe who would have been the victim.

With a final whisper to Gwen, even though he knew she could not hear him, he clumsily thrust the blade through his own heart.

Back in Penacles Yalak's Egg shuddered, and the energy gathered within was sucked out by a force so strong that it brought both the Gryphon and the Blue Dragon to the point of total collapse. They fell back from the crystal simultaneously, both, in those brief remaining seconds of consciousness, wondering if they would wake.

A storm of overwhelming proportions whipped across Penacles, throwing objects and even a few inhabitants about like so many leaves in a wind. It was a storm that covered nearly all the Dragonrealm save the Legar Peninsula. It was a storm that raged in magnificent fury—for no more than half a minute.

When it suddenly ceased to be and everything had settled to the ground, those that could opened their eyes in order to see what, if anything, remained of the world.

It was gone.

The Ice Dragon understood that, but the realization was so overwhelming that all the leviathan could do to acknowledge it was to blink. The Final Winter had been reversed. He knew that it would require a sacrifice of such potential that only a master sorcerer's existence would satisfy the requirements. It was a sacrifice that he himself had been about to undertake—but someone had beaten him to it and, by doing so, had twisted his spell so that nothing he did could undo it. He had spent everything on the creating, building, and maintaining of the spell; there was no way he could begin again.

The creatures were cut off from him, but not from that which was the true source. Without his control, without the Dragon King to act as a focus, she was becoming wild, drawing the life-force from her children—his children—so that they died by the dozens, by the hundreds, until soon, so very soon, they would all be dead. She did not even know that she did it, actually believing, as far as her mind could comprehend, that she was working to save them.

Worse yet, the damage they had done would eventually repair itself, even as the Barren Lands had when the Brown Dragon had become the victim of his own folly. Not even the Wastes would be exempt. They would still remain, but the cold would dwindle. Life would push farther north than it had in millennia.

He had failed. His massive head turned this way and that in a mad frenzy—until his eyes at last found the slumped figure at the far end of the chamber.

"Bedlam."

The figure did not stir. If the human had done his work properly, the dragon knew, then this was only a lifeless shell—which did not mean that the Dragon King would not tear it apart nonetheless.

"Cabe!"

His spell sundered, the Ice Dragon's captives were freeing themselves. The behemoth forgot the still figure, realizing now that he still had a chance to avenge himself on living, fragile creatures, most especially the mate of the Bedlam whelp.

"Damn you, dragon lord!" The enchantress rose into the air. Below her, the hatchlings crowded around the Gold Dragon, who stared vacantly in the general direction of his frosty counterpart. Toma was rising at last and, seeing that Cabe was down and Gwen was preparing to take on the Ice Dragon, turned his attention to his sire. There was a time to fight and a time to flee, and with his father unable to defend himself Toma realized that his best choice was to depart in haste. Once he had the emperor safely hidden again, he could return to settle things with the survivors.

A fist backed with elven strength struck him hard across the back of his neck. The drake stumbled forward and fell to his knees. From behind him, he heard the voice of Haiden.

"Since you consider your alliance with the Bedlams at an end, drake, I see no reason not to count you as another foe—one worse than the Ice Dragon at that."

Toma turned so that his helmed visage faced the elf. Haiden turned pale but held his ground.

"You should stay hidden in the background, tree-eater," the firedrake hissed. Toma waved his hand and Haiden found himself completely surrounded by a bubble of some soft substance. He punched it, but it held. What magic he had did little more than create a temporary aura as it burned itself out on the bubble.

The firedrake watched as the elf dulled his knife on the inner surface of the sphere. He laughed and turned to find his father.

The knife.

The knife which Nathan had known would be in the Green Dragon's collection of Seeker artifacts, for, after the creation of the Barren Lands, he himself had planted it where the drake lord would find it. Without the knowledge of its use, it was merely one more odd piece. As those who studied them knew, the avians formulated no spell without having already conceived a counterspell. The knife was the focus of that counterspell, and to utilize anything else was to invite the same sort of disastrous side effects that had resulted in the carnivorous plantlife with a taste for the flesh and blood of the Brown Dragon's clans and no others.

Nathan could not bring himself to destroy the blade. Not because he had believed that someone like the Ice Dragon would resurrect the spell, but rather because he was, in the end, a lover of history. A fortunate flaw in the end.

Cabe had understood all of this. Cabe had understood everything, thanks to Nathan, including the fact that he would have to die to save the Dragonrealm.

Then, why was he still *alive*?

Anyone glancing at him might have differed with his opinion. He was haggard, at least thirty years older in appearance, and, at the moment, as weak as a newborn puppy. Yet he *was* alive.

But he had succeeded! How?

How?

The Seeker blade lay on the floor before him, not one drop of blood on it. Slowly, he put a hand to his chest, not actually wanting to feel the gaping wound, but still attracted to it in much the same way many people are fascinated by death itself. It *had* to be there.

Nothing. No wound, no blood, not even a rip in his shirt—but something had been torn from him nonetheless.

Only then did he realize that things were far from over. The ground shook, throwing him down again, and he turned over to see Gwen desperately battling the Ice Dragon, who, though worn, was still a Dragon King.

More than a dozen bright blue rings circled the behemoth. They seemed to be trying to loop themselves over him, but something held them back. One by one, the dragon *breathed* on them. As he did, the ring he chose would pale and fade away. Gwen was running out of rings and her face was almost as pale as the snow.

Cabe rose, picked up the knife, and stumbled toward the pit, which the lord of the Northern Wastes had abandoned in his quest for vengeance. It was really not that far a walk, he thought absently, although there were portions of the short trek he would not even remember making when he was finally at his destination.

One of the Ice Dragon's few remaining servants staggered into the chamber and Cabe, still weak, prepared to defend himself with the knife as best he could. The creature, however, made it only a few steps further before it began to crumble before his very eyes. Cabe felt another presence, and realized then that the thing within the hole was still trying to feed the hunger within it, a hunger which the Dragon King no longer controlled and which was even now searching about for new food.

Somehow, he found the strength to deflect the searching mind. The horror below was desperate now, taking even the energy which animated the Ice King's servants, foul as that probably was to it.

It was that desperation that Cabe hoped for—for there was one obvious source it had yet to draw upon.

Gathering himself up, Cabe turned toward the Ice Dragon and shouted, "Dragon King! Lord of the Northern Wastes! Have you forgotten me, then? Are you so frightened of the name Bedlam?"

"Bedlam." The behemoth said his name quietly, calmly, but his reaction was anything but that. As the last of the rings ceased to be, the Ice Dragon whirled, forgetting a desperate Gwen. "Bedlam? Will you *never* cease to annoy me?"

The gigantic, gaunt dragon lumbered toward him, frosty smoke issuing from his nostrils in great, constant puffs. To the Dragon King, Cabe must have looked like the dead come to life—and only barely, at that. Certainly no threat, but a chance at last to make the sorcerer suffer for the blight he represented in the drake lord's mind.

It was not until he neared the pit that the Ice Dragon realized there was another hunger possibly stronger than his own. Cabe stumbled back as the dragon shook his head in disbelief and confidently sought to regain control. That confidence turned to uncertainty and then frustration. The ice-white leviathan began to twist as he sought in vain to overwhelm that other mind, a mind with a desire he understood all too well.

"Nooo!" The Ice Dragon hissed angrily. "Not yet! Not until the Bedlam whelp is mine! Not until the vermin are cleansed from the Dragonrealm!"

The dragon began to flail about. His tail was nearly as long as the chamber was tall, which meant that when it swung to and fro, there was little place to hide. Gwen succeeded in dodging the massive appendage, but Cabe could not tell whether any of the others had been as lucky. The fiery-tressed enchantress came to rest not far from him and chanced the tremors that the Dragon King was creating. She tumbled into his arms, both shocked by his appearance and thrilled by his survival. Great spears of ice embedded themselves in the walls as the lord of this frozen land struck out blindly. Both mages were forced to duck.

"Cabe . . ."

His legs and arms were losing sensitivity. "Help me to somewhere safer."

"The Ice Dragon . . ."

". . . will take care of things for us, I hope." He pointed in the direction of the massive drake.

The Dragon King was only half the size he had been earlier and he moved with a stiffness that reminded Cabe of the unliving servants. As his strength faded, the dragon's gaze fell on a figure walking aimlessly in the midst of all the rubble. The Gold Dragon. Clinging near him were the hatchlings, who innocently believed that their sire would protect them from anything. The eyes of the behemoth narrowed.

"No!" Battered, Toma rose from rubble that had once made up a good portion of the ceiling. Haiden, inadvertantly protected by the bubble, could only watch. . . .

"My emperor." The Ice Dragon's voice was haggard. "My lord. I am failing you, failing the glory of our kind."

As if drawing strength from the other drake's presence, the lord of the Wastes straightened to the limit of his much-diminished height and added, "But your hatchlings will never lick the boots of human masters. Never."

Cabe felt the sudden rush of energy from the mad Dragon King as the latter, briefly surrounded once more by his pale aura, roared, "Feed one last time, my queen!"

A full-fledged snowstorm overwhelmed them. It was the Final Winter contained in the one chamber. Gwen cast a spell, shielding herself and Cabe. Jagged knives of ice shattered against it. The crevices widened further and she had to grab Cabe as the icy floor beneath him tumbled away. They heard a strangling cry from Toma, then nothing. Of Haiden, the Gold Dragon, the hatchlings—even the Ice Dragon—they knew nothing. The storm raged for what seemed like hours, though they knew that, in reality, it was only a few brief minutes. But those brief minutes seemed more terrible than the days spent riding north, constantly buffered by the Dragon King's spell.

And then . . . it faded to nothing.

XXIII

Cabe was the first to understand what the silence meant. He could not believe it any more than he could believe he was still alive after Tyr's words and his own sacrifice—although he had a frightening suspicion that he now understood the true meaning of the ghostly Dragon Master's warning.

"Gwen." He put a hand on her shoulder. Her eyes flew open. She had not been unconscious, but the effort of protecting the two of them had been so great that she had been forced to tune out the real world. Her eyes stared uncomprehendingly for several seconds, then focused on her husband.

"We're alive?"

"Yes." Something—many things, actually—had changed. Without even being able to see yet, Cabe knew that the thing in the pit was dead. Somehow Cabe had the feeling that it had, in the end, fed upon itself. He would never know for sure. At the very least, it saved them the trouble of dealing with it. As for its master . . .

Cabe felt some of his strength returning. He dared to create a ball of light, knowing that the Ice Dragon was no more threat, but fearful that he might be in error. He commanded the light to flitter to what remained of the ceiling of the chamber and turned his gaze toward the platform and, in particular, the pit.

"Rheena preserves us!" Gwen whispered from his side.

Cabe could only nod, both fascinated and revolted by the spectacle.

The Ice Dragon stood there, wings outstretched, in his full glory. He had not had time even to fall before every bit of life, energy, heat—whatever it was the creatures truly had extracted—had been drawn from him. Like the victims of his "children," he stood a lifeless, rockhard corpse.

Now, Cabe thought idly, *now he truly is an ice dragon.*

That was so. The remnants of the Dragon King's last assault had left him covered with a second skin of pure frost. In the light of Cabe's spell, he glistened. A monument to what once was. A monument to obsession.

A monument to madness and wholescale death, Cabe concluded bitterly.

"The others . . ." Gwen rose. "Where are the hatchlings and Haiden? Where's Toma?"

Toma? Cabe scanned the wreckage of the chamber. The storm had broken loose countless chunks of ice and rock from both the ceiling and the walls. The fissures created by the Storm Dragon's earlier attacks had widened even more and then been filled by falling fragments from above.

There was no sign of anybody.

A hapless, reptilian hiss rose from near the center of the chamber. Gwen hurried down. Cabe followed, sure that, considering how aged he felt, his bones would crack from the slightest fall.

Tyr was right and wrong, he thought to himself. *I did die . . . yet . . . I didn't.* Nathan—what had once been Nathan—had realized the truth long before. Small wonder his grandfather's personality had begun to emerge, had begun to exert itself once more.

Cabe's powers still remained, but his memories—Nathan's memories—were little more than half-seen shadows now. When Tyr had said there would be a death, he had meant Nathan. Cabe was alone in his mind now, and would always be. Nathan had understood what his former comrade had meant, understood the tangled web the lords of the Other had spread, and that was why Nathan had encouraged the sacrifice.

He had known that it was not his grandson who was going to be sacrificed, but his own essence. He was long past his time and Cabe no longer needed his . . . essence . . . to survive.

It had been so different when his grandfather had supposedly merged with him after the death of Azran. He was gone, yet still a comforting presence. No more. Nathan Bedlam had relinquished his power and his hold on life for both Cabe's and the Dragon-realm's sake. He knew that his grandson was no longer the sickly child or the totally ignorant young boy.

There was no more reason for Nathan to stay.

His musings—for that was all he knew they could truly be called—were interrupted by Gwen's summons.

The hatchlings were safe, but only by a miracle almost as unusual as Cabe's. In the end, through either reflex action or some long-buried memory, the Gold Dragon, King of Kings, had protected his young from the raging storm. Death had taken him while he was still more humanoid than dragon, but his growing form had created a barrier, a shield for the hatchlings. Whether he had been trying to protect himself or them was anyone's guess. They were unharmed, albeit confused and, like Cabe, more than a little dazed.

That left only two.

"Haiden?" Cabe turned to where he had last seen the elf and Toma. "Haiden?"

"I'm not coming back in there unless you promise me it's finally finished."

"There's nothing to be worried about."

Both Gwen and Cabe turned to the corridor which led to and from the master chamber. Disheveled, shivering, his clothes in tatters, and his face an odd blue color for an elf, Haiden stepped gingerly back in the room.

"Well?"

Cabe pointed at the Ice Dragon. Haiden's eyes widened and he whistled. "And his . . . 'queen'?"

"No more."

"I wish I could say the same for Duke Toma."

Anger washed over Gwen's face. "Again? He's run off again? Will we never be free of him?"

Haiden grimaced. "I have to thank him, really. It was because of him that I survived. He trapped me in a sphere of some kind, one meant to imprison me, but one that ended up saving my life by protecting me from the brunt of that last . . . madness. It finally collapsed near the end, which is why I look like this." The elf indicated his battered appearance. "It's not *quite* as terrible as it looks, though I am feeling a bit cool." He sobered. "I saw him duck out of the chamber when the fury broke loose. My first reaction after I was free was to chase him, knowing what he might do if he escaped. I regret to say he knows these chambers better than me.''

''He also has his powers back,'' Cabe reminded him. ''He would have killed you easily. You're lucky he didn't kill you before.''

''There is that.''

''What now?'' Gwen asked. She had herded the young drakes into an almost manageable group.

''We put an end to this,'' a voice that seemed to echo from everywhere suddenly said. The devastated chamber lit up with a brilliance that burned out Cabe's own humble spell.

The Bedlams and the elf formed a triangle around the hatchlings. Neither the mages nor Haiden could find the source of the voice. Cabe was the one to finally recognize it.

''You . . . You're the Crystal Dragon.''

''I am.''

In that instant, wherever there was a reflection, there was a glistening image of an indistinct dragon shape. It was beautiful, terrible, and enigmatic all at once—and somewhat like seeing the world through the multifaceted eyes of an insect. They could not help blinking wildly at first. Here was a sense of power so totally different from any Cabe had encountered. Greater in its own way than that of the Ice Dragon.

Were they to fight this menace as well?

An amused chuckle reverberated through the chamber, loosening yet more chunks of ice. ''I am no menace to you. I have merely come to add the final touch to the end of my brother's insanity.''

The reflections seemed to contemplate the towering form of the Ice Dragon. At last the voice said, ''I warned him about his folly. I warned him that he would do little more than bring drake and human closer together, if only temporarily. He refused to let me shatter his illusions. Well, now I shall do more than that. It is only fitting and what he certainly deserved.''

The brilliant light increased. Hatchlings hissed and the two humans and the elf were forced to shade their eyes. The gleaming form of the late master of the Northern Wastes quivered as if life were returning to him once more. A kaleidoscope of color whirled about the chamber. Cabe briefly looked down at his hand and watched it change from green to blue to red and so on. Gwen's hair turned black, orange, violet. . . . It was not merely a change of color, either; he could feel the distinct power represented by each as it washed over them. This was what the Ice Dragon only pretended to be. He had been an imperfect replica of *this* Dragon King.

The living rainbow began to gather about the huge, icy form. The Ice Dragon vibrated more violently, bits of snow and frost falling in showers from his body. Just when it seemed that the motions of the leviathan's corpse would bring down what remained of the cavern, the Ice Dragon *stopped* quivering.

Cabe and Gwen realized what was happening and fell to the ground, the latter forcing the hatchlings down with her. Haiden was already on his stomach, no fool he, not when Dragon King magic was running amok.

The Ice Dragon *shattered*.

A sea of fragments flew in all directions, but those that neared the tiny, huddled group in the center of the chamber melted into a fine mist.

When the last pieces had fallen to the ground, the voice of the Crystal Dragon, somewhat less poised than before, whispered, "*Now* it is ended. You need not have feared for yourselves; I was watching over you."

The humans, their elven companion, and even the hatchlings gazed around in newfound respect—respect that grew to awe when the Crystal Dragon added, "Soon, the Seekers will come to claim their home of ancient. There has been enough strife and I have things of greater interest to do. As you are understandably torn by your ordeal, I shall allow you to conserve your strength. You will have enough to do after I send you home."

Which he then did, with no more than a nod.

The next few days passed quickly. There was so much to do. They were not as bad as the weeks that had followed the siege of Penacles, but they were days that Cabe would have enjoyed doing without.

One major problem solved itself. Once the Ice Dragon's spell had been reversed, the countless corpses of his abominations began to decay at an alarming rate. They did not even leave time for scavengers to take their fill, though it was said only the worst scavengers even bothered to sniff the remains. No one and nothing wanted anything to do with the late Dragon King's creatures.

What to do with Melicard was a situation that took three days to discuss. In the end, the crippled sovereign was returned to his city in the hopes that his people would take the cue and make peace. His marauders were scattered all over the countryside. Whether they would continue their fanatical slaughter of drakes was questionable; their ranks were depleted and they no longer had the Seekers or Melicard to provide them with supplies and protective devices. Besides, most people were, at the moment, more interested in rebuilding their own lives than aiding some mad cause.

The Gryphon talked with the others about some sort of expedition to the continent on the other side of the Eastern Seas, but nothing definite was planned. He had mentioned it once before, after his first encounter with D'Shay in the domain of the Black Dragon. Toos, who had just gone through one session as "temporary" ruler and now saw the possible nightmare of another, longer period, protested the idea.

"Dammit, bird, I'm too old to do this on a regular basis." The general's eyes flared, but there was a hint of humor in his voice.

"Old? Toos, you con artist, you've more sorcery than you either think or pretend to think. You've lived longer than most men and you still have the reflexes you had in your prime. You once claimed your line was long-lived, had elven blood, but you've pushed past the point of reality. If anyone who knows your past is still fooled, it must be you alone. Only powerful sorcery can keep anyone with human blood alive and fit for so long. You have special abilities, my friend, so subtle that we tend not to notice unless we force ourselves. I think your powers would keep you fit and running this city for several decades to come—if the need arose, of course. You might even consider marrying and fathering a few young." He raised a hand as the ex-mercenary turned red. "Don't protest; I've seen some of the ladies of the court eye you, *old man*." The

Gryphon laughed, an odd-looking sight, considering his avian visage. "Don't worry so! I haven't said I was actually going!"

The general mumbled something that no one could hear and everyone decided was better left a mystery. The lord of Penacles nodded imperceptibly. He had lightened what had otherwise been a fairly dreary mood on the part of his companions. After what they had been through and accomplished, they deserved better. He formed a human face and sipped some wine a servant had brought them. Cabe was the only one who truly worried him now. He watched as Gwen took her husband's hands. The two had hardly even gotten a chance to become used to their lives together. The Gryphon hoped and prayed that things would finally calm down a bit.

Hoped, but did not expect. Expectations in the Dragonrealm had a way of turning inside out before long.

He took another sip of wine.

Cabe and Gwen eventually stepped away from the others. The Gryphon was speaking to the Green Dragon about the possibility of extending the truce with his counterpart in Irillian. Haiden, invited with the Bedlams, was talking to General Toos about places the two of them had seen during their lengthy lifetimes. They were both men of the land and had more in common than Cabe would have thought possible.

When they were far enough away, Gwen finally pulled him to one side and asked, "What's wrong, Cabe?"

His face was pale, drawn. "He's gone, Gwen. This time, there's nothing left of Nathan. I'm entirely alone. The power is there, but it's me now. Whatever he was—soul, essence, my own imagination—he gave that so I would live. It's hard to be alone, though, after becoming so used to having another presence *always* there."

The Lady of the Amber said nothing, instead choosing to put her reply into a long and lingering kiss. Cabe knew what she was saying and his misery slowly faded.

"You'll never be alone, Cabe. Not as long as I can help it."

He felt a twinge of guilt that his sorrow for his grandfather was dissipating so quickly, but, knowing Nathan as he had, he doubted the elder Bedlam would have minded a bit. Possibly, he would even have reprimanded his grandson for moaning and groaning when there was a beautiful woman waiting who also happened to love Cabe dearly. He should be taking her in his arms and returning that love.

Cabe smiled slightly and did just that. Perhaps, he thought just before he allowed the present moment to carry him away, Nathan Bedlam was *not* completely gone after all.

A breeze danced briefly about them, but it was warm and they did not even notice it, caught up as they were in more important matters.

Fantasy Books by Richard Knaak

SCIENCE FICTION

☐ ## ICE DRAGON
(E20-942, $3.95, USA) ($4.95, Canada)

Volume II in Questar's *Dragonrealm* series—
a tale of dragons, intrigue, and magic from the
New York Times bestselling author of
Dragonlance Heroes, The Legend of Huma.

☐ ## FIREDRAKE
(E20-940, $3.95, USA) ($4.95, Canada)

Richard Knaak takes readers to the
Dragonrealm: an explosive new world of
dragons, intrigue and magic.

 **Warner Books P.O. Box 690
New York, NY 10019**

Please send me the books I have checked. I enclose a check or money
order (not cash), plus 95¢ per order and 95¢ per copy to cover postage
and handling.* (Allow 4-6 weeks for delivery.)

___Please send me your free mail order catalog. (If ordering only the
catalog, include a large self-addressed, stamped envelope.)

Name_____

Address_____

City_____ State _____ Zip _____
*New York and California residents add applicable sales tax.

420

Fantasy Books from

SCIENCE FICTION

419